A NOTE ON

Rosemary Goring was born in Dunbar, and took
St Andrews University, winning a prize for Scottish His.
year. She began a career in publishing in the role of in-house .
Chambers Biographical Dictionary and has since edited and writ...
many reference books.

She was Literary Editor of *Scotland on Sunday* for several years
before taking up the position of Literary Editor and columnist at the
Herald and *Sunday Herald*. In 2007 her book *Scotland the Autobiography:
2,000 Years of Scottish History by Those Who Saw It Happen* was published
by Viking to great acclaim. *Dacre's War* is the sequel to Rosemary's
first novel *After Flodden*.

DACRE'S WAR

ROSEMARY GORING

Polygon

For Marie

First published in Great Britain in 2015.
This paperback edition published in 2016 by
Polygon, an imprint of Birlinn Ltd
West Newington House
10 Newington Road
Edinburgh
EH9 1QS

www.polygonbooks.co.uk

ISBN: 978 1 84697 341 3

British Library Cataloguing-in-Publication Data
A catalogue record for this book is available on request
from the British Library.

Characters

THE SCOTTISH COURT

John Stewart, Duke of Albany, cousin of James IV and Regent of
    Scotland

Margaret Tudor, the dowager queen, widow of James IV

James V, only surviving son of James IV and Margaret Tudor

Archibald Douglas, Earl of Angus, Margaret Tudor's second
    husband

James Hamilton, Earl of Arran, one of Margaret Tudor's strongest
    allies, enemy of her husband

Alexander Montgomerie, Earl of Eglinton, privy councillor and
    guardian of the infant king James

John Stewart, Earl of Lennox, a staunch defender of James

William Herries, Lord Herries of Terregles, son of Andrew who
    died at Flodden

David Forsyth, cousin of Archibald Douglas

THE ENGLISH COURT

Henry VIII, King of England and brother of Margaret, Dowager
    Queen of Scotland

Thomas Wolsey, Cardinal, Archbishop of York and Lord
    Chancellor, one of Henry's closest advisers

Thomas Howard, Earl of Surrey, soldier; son of Thomas Howard,
    veteran of the battle of Flodden, second earl of Surrey, and now
    Duke of Norfolk (Surrey takes his father's title on Norfolk's death
    in May 1524)

Sir William Eure, Vice Warden of the English marches

THE CROZIERS

Adam Crozier, head of the clan
Louise Brenier, his wife
Tom Crozier, his younger brother
Old Crozier, Adam and Tom's grandfather
Hob, head stableboy and groom
Benoit Brenier, Louise's carpenter brother
Ella Aylewood, Benoit's wife
Wat the Wanderer, Adam's cousin and henchman
Murdo Montgomery, Adam's cousin and henchman
Samuel Jardine, clan chief, and ally of the Croziers
Mitchell Bell, head of local clan, and ally
Father Walsh, the village priest
Oliver Barton, sailor, and cousin of Louise
The wolf, the family dog, born of the late vixen

THE DACRES AND THEIR HOUSEHOLD AND ASSOCIATES

Thomas, Baron Dacre, Warden General of the English marches
Bess, his late wife Elizabeth Greystoke
Blackbird, Dacre's butler and personal attendant
Sir Christopher Dacre, his brother
Sir Philip Dacre, his brother
Joan Dacre, his youngest daughter
Mabel, his married eldest daughter
Anne, his married middle daughter
Mary, Joan's maid and companion
Ethan Elliot, thief and reiver
Edward Elliot, his son
Sly Armstrong, outlaw leader of the Liddesdale Armstrongs
Black Ned, Sly's cousin, leader of the Tynedale Armstrongs

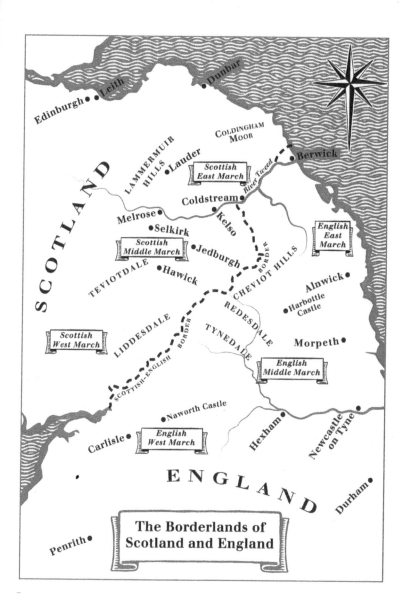

The Borderlands of Scotland and England

Epigraph

For me, the ransom of my bold attempt
Shall be this cold corpse on the earth's cold face

Richard III, Act V, Scene 3

10 September 1513, the day after the battle of Flodden

He picked his way over the hillside beneath a fog of heavy rain. The turf was strewn with sodden flags and toppled guns, abandoned swords and quivers. His boots slipped on mud made oily with blood, but the soldier who had brought him the news moved swiftly, as if untroubled by the scene. Dacre, after little sleep, and even less to eat, felt his stomach slop. He gripped his staff, and trudged on. Overnight the battlefield had been partially cleared, hundreds of corpses carried off on drays to await the lime pit and dead horses dragged to the valley top, where their stookie limbs prodded the sky, pyres of flesh awaiting the flame. Only at the foot of the slopes, where bodies were half buried in glaur, was the carnage untouched. The river washed on around them, turning a hand or shuddering a leg, as if the owner had been merely asleep and now was roused at last.

'He's over here,' said the soldier, calling the baron's attention to a hollow near the top of the hill, where they were heading. Some distance behind him, cloaked in rain, Dacre moved at the speed of one reluctant to reach his destination. When he did, gulls were mewling high overhead, a sound he would ever after think of as a lament for the sorry figure they circled.

The king's body had been turned upwards, though beneath the black crust of a face savaged by sword and arrow and axe few would have recognised him. His chain mail coat was torn, and around his shoulders the mantle bearing his coat of arms lay in shreds, its lion slain. His helmet was trodden into the earth by his side, where his standard bearer lay, the boy fallen upon the Scottish flag, now stained with his dying.

The baron barely noticed him, looking only at James. Crouching by the side of his old enemy he wrenched an arrow out of his neck and hurled it aside. For a moment, mist clouded his vision. He rubbed his face, and the king came back into sight. Dacre lifted an ungloved hand, almost severed from its wrist, and saw the marks where night-time scavengers had removed the rings. He laid it down, as one would a sleeping child's.

Raising the metal tunic, he found the proof he needed. The Warden General of the English marches, whose soldiers had helped bring about the Scots' defeat, lowered his head in sorrow. There could be no doubt. The king's iron belt was locked around his waist, chafing purple on clay-coloured skin. Dacre counted the links, and found one for every year since the death of James's father, in whose memory he wore it.

With a long sigh, he got to his feet. 'This is him, James IV, King of Scotland no longer. You've done well to find him. Had he gone missing, rumours would have kept him alive for years.'

He straightened, and put a hand to the small of his back as he stared into the downpour. Beyond the rain lay the sea. He could smell it. So could the gulls, and as if reminded of where they belonged they gave a last call and flew off.

Later, Dacre marched back to the village, ahead of the pall-bearers. 'Get back!' he shouted, as a crowd gathered, jostling for a glimpse of the stricken king. 'It's only another body, like the thousands ye have already seen. Are ye no sick of the sight by now?' He raised his staff to clear the way, but he understood why they peered. How often would they see a king brought lower than they?

Dacre shouldered past them. James had been his enemy, but also a friend, a man who could be trusted. The same could not be said of his own king. Brushing rain out of his eyes, the Warden General thanked the saints that Henry never ventured this far north. Should he ever show any interest in the borderlands, it would bode as ill for Dacre as for the Scots.

Part One

1523

Foul Deeds Will Rise Again

CHAPTER ONE

March 1523

From the crown of a grizzled oak, a buzzard blinked as three men rode out of the woods and onto the empty hills. Hunched as a tax collector counting his coins, the bird did not shift from its perch but kept the riders in its sights as they moved steadily across the valley. Only when they had reached the farthermost peak did the glint of helmets and swords disappear, leaving the moorland quiet in their wake. Watchful still, the buzzard scraped its beak and refolded its wings. These men had passed this way often before. They would no doubt soon return.

The threesome rode abreast, bridles chattering. Their dark garb brightened only by steel, they did not speak but cantered over turf and moss, scattering white cattle and goats as they moved west. Adam Crozier's horse was a short head in front, setting the pace and finding the path. The borderer's eyes were fixed on the track, and none would have guessed that his thoughts were not of the assignation that lay ahead, but of the past that raced to meet him at every bend of river and curve of hill.

He had trodden this land since he was a child, and would have known it blindfold: bridlepaths overgrown with wild garlic; river pools where moorhens paddled between soft-scented water lilies or scuttled, chittering, onto the bank; and everywhere the dry, warm scent of beech, hazel and oak, under whose canopy a boy could make a hideaway from branches and bracken as comfortable as anything a stonemason could devise.

Teviotdale was Crozier's domain, the sweetest nut in the border-lands. A cradle of gentle hills and loamy plains, a sparrow's flight from the English border, it was well hidden from the eye of the authorities in Edinburgh. Here, in his youth, crops had grown lush under a fitful sun, and animals had grazed, fearing nothing but the wolf. To look at the hillsides and pastures now, where grain barns were as fortified as castles, and livestock were herded each night into byres only a cannon could breach, such a time seemed as distant as the myths bards sang of when they plucked their lyres on feast days.

The riders slowed as the hillside turned to ash, and their horses picked their way over grasslands charred by flame. The borderer's face tightened. His mare skirted the wooden stumps of a hamlet whose cottages had been fired to dust. Barely twenty miles from Crozier's Keep, he reflected, and the countryside was fast becoming wasteland, so often was it scathed by the gangs who roamed these parts. Soon there would be nothing left for them to steal or destroy. Even then it was unlikely the dalesfolk would be left in peace.

That he and his men were on their way to meet Ethan Elliot, one of the most audacious thieves and ruthless killers this side of Carlisle, made the desolation even more bitter. In his time, Elliot had ravaged the middle march as if it were enemy land and not that of his neighbours. In the Crozier household his name was spoken rarely, and then in whispers, for fear of invoking the evil spirits that none doubted the man harboured or had at his command. For few knew better than they what he was capable of.

In these parts it was commonly believed that it was Elliot who had murdered Crozier's father, when Adam was still a boy. There was no proof, but few doubted it was true. Had he not been so intent these past few years in restoring his family's fortunes, he might have taken revenge, but the condition of his lands, his people, and of the country itself after Flodden, left little room for such an indulgence. Until he reclaimed the honour of his family name – lost long before that fateful battle – and with it their rightful place as leaders of the middle march, he had no spare thought for the man so reviled that they called him the Leper of Liddesdale. If he did not carry the disease himself, he spread a pestilence wherever he went that was almost as disfiguring.

Glad to put the fired earth behind them, the three quickened their pace. Tom Crozier brushed alongside his brother's horse as they negotiated a narrow trail at the head of a gully and indicated the path wending south. 'See, the prints are fresh. They've been here this past day or so, since it last rained. I reckon they're lying in wait ahead of us.'

'Who, Dacre's men?' asked their companion. Wat the Wanderer's skill with the crossbow he carried on his back made more powerful men pause before risking his wrath. 'Unlikely. This season, the Deadwater Marshes would swamp them. If the Warden General is headed into the dale, it'll be by a higher route than the causeway, and we'd have heard of it.'

Tom did not look convinced. 'I don't trust Elliot,' he said. 'It wouldn't surprise me if we're riding into an ambush. And who better for him to summon to finish us off than his paymaster, who can get here in a day by this route, and scarper in half that time?' His eyes gleamed at the prospect.

Crozier gathered the reins in one hand. 'Could be you're right,' was all he said, urging his horse up the slope.

There was a poor crop of honesty when Ethan Elliot was born. In its place was a cunning so deep that as he grew from boy to man it appeared to ooze from his pores, slicking his hair, dampening his palms, and giving him an oily sheen that matched his slippery eye. Crozier had never met him – by the time he found his father's corpse, the murderer and his cronies were gone. Yet when, a week earlier, Elliot's youngest son had arrived at Crozier's Keep bearing a message, the borderer had looked into the boy's defiant face and fancied he found reflected in it a glimmer of the man who had brought his family to its knees.

Edward Elliot had knocked at the gates with a club, leaving his companions at the edge of the woods with their horses. A sentry had stripped him of cudgel, sword, dagger and knife, and left him to await his master in the guardroom. Uneasy in the enemy's camp, black forelock drooping over one eye, he wrung his greasy woollen cap in his hands under the stare of the watchmen who were waiting their turn on the walls.

His father had told him to expect little more than a farmer's house, but it was clear the old man had not seen the place in years. As he approached, thick outer walls towered over him until he felt like an ant at the foot of a tree. Once through the main gates, an inner wall guarded the keep, whose ramparts and stonework were so immaculately kept one would have thought them newly built, had not the stories of the keep's long history, and Crozier's battles, carried through all the borders. When finally the clan chief and his brother entered the guardroom, the young man's face revealed a temper as overstrung as a new harp. He had been left idle all morning, but the thought of his father's anger if he did not deliver his message had kept him there.

With a look, Crozier sent the guards out, then closed the door and leaned against it. He was not a tall man, but he filled the room. Edward Elliot was ashamed of the tightness of his throat, the prickle of heat in his hands. 'I am sent to you by my father, Ethan Elliot,' he said loudly. 'He requests a meeting with you. He says it is urgent. He must speak to you, and will accept whatever time and place you like, so long as it is soon.' He felt more foolish yet as the words fell onto silence.

Crozier looked at Tom, and back at Edward, who swallowed hard. In that space, all three heard it. There was a long pause. 'Is that so?' the borderer said at last. He took a step towards Edward, who forced himself not to move. 'You are too young to remember, lad, but your father's last visit to this place made him, and now you, the least welcome guests we have ever had.'

Edward raised his eyes to meet Crozier's. His heartbeat quickened, but for his father he would face down any threat, and not merely for fear of his rage. 'He said you would not believe me, nor trust him, and he asked me to give you a pledge of his honour.' He placed a small gold ring in Crozier's hand. 'If ye take a good look, you'll see his and my mother's initials, and the date of their betrothal. It is her wedding band, and since Ma's death it is his most precious possession.'

Crozier handed it back without a glance. 'I need no pledge, lad. Your father's word is worthless. Yet I am curious to know what he has to tell me.' He looked up at the arched bricks above their heads, as if searching for an answer. Tom licked his lips, a gesture of anticipation, not fear, and Crozier was pleased. Both of them thought alike.

'Very well,' he said, looking at Edward, 'you can go back to Ethan

Elliot and tell him that I and my men will meet him a week from today, on Blinkbonny Hill on the Overstone Pass. We shall find him at noon, but he must come with none other than you, nor try to trick or deceive us, or he shall dig his own grave on that hill.' He opened the door, and a sentry appeared to lead the young man back to the gates.

Edward was cantering home with his cousins, breathing deep with relief to be free of the keep, before he realised he had dropped his cap in the guardroom. By then, it was on the sentry's brazier, sizzling with sweat yet barely singed, as if even the flames were reluctant to touch anything that belonged to an Elliot.

A crescent of elms topped Blinkbonny Hill, stark against the sky. Crows circled overhead, but they were the only creatures abroad, their cawing the solitary sound. Concealed behind a thicket of scrub overlooking the hill, Crozier and his companions waited.

The sun had not quite reached its peak when there was a crackling of undergrowth from across the valley as riders approached through the woods. When two horses came into sight, crossing the stream that meandered around the foot of the hill, Crozier leaned forward on his mare's neck.

Ethan Elliot rode ahead of his son, his girth swaying in the saddle. A once swaggering figure, with a bull's neck and barrel chest, now Elliot's head drooped as if he knew the fight was over. Crozier frowned. This was not what he had expected. Had he been summoned to hear a confession and clear an old man's conscience before he met his maker?

Plodding up the hill, the Elliots took their place under the elms, where they sat so still they might have been carved from wood. Time passed, and the sun rose higher, as Crozier waited to see if the robber had been followed, or if his henchmen were already in hiding, encircling the hill and its players.

In years past, no man would have ridden to meet Ethan Elliot without first bidding his loved ones a long goodbye. Even Elliot's allies knew better than to turn their backs in his presence. The man had a temper like a rabid dog, they said, docile one minute, savage the next.

His corner of Liddesdale, already famed for its outlaws, had become so feared that the common tracks across his lands were overgrown with weeds, few daring to pass that way in case they crossed his path.

But some could not avoid him, no matter how hard they tried. From his fortress-like castle Elliot's hands hovered over the region, casting shadows across the sweetest harvests and fattest cattle, swooping to pluck the best for himself. Retreating to gloat over his spoils, he would for a spell be sated. There were weeks of quiet while he wined and wenched, gambled and squandered, and grew another chin. Then, when his cellars and coffers and larder had dwindled, he'd go back on the prowl, he and a hundred men, whose hoofbeats and yowling filled the border nights with dread.

Only a leader with greater courage and more men could bring him to heel. One such was Sly Armstrong, whose band of thugs was almost as feared as Elliot's, and five times the number. Nobody who valued their skin would say no to Sly and his brothers, and from time to time Elliot did their bidding. But more commanding yet was Thomas Dacre, Warden General and lord of the marches. Dacre was the only man on earth – and beyond it – who scared Elliot. Though the thief had no scruples, he was not without brains.

When it seemed to Crozier that Elliot had come alone, he, Tom and Wat made for the hill. Dismounting at its foot, they led their horses up the slope. There was no sound but the horses' breath, and the slither of leaves as they advanced towards the watchful figures ahead.

As they drew close Edward Elliot got off his horse, but Ethan stayed in the saddle, swaddled in furs. It galled Crozier not to meet him eye to eye, but when he saw the pallid sheen on the old thief's face, the tremor in his hands, he knew he was looking at a dead man.

For a moment, nobody spoke. Ethan's eyes were red-rimmed and weeping, but they held no hint of remorse. 'Aye, lad,' he said, in a voice still flavoured by his reiver's roar. 'Well might ye stare at me like that. I've done ye no favours, I know. And if you'd been in the room that night alongside your da, I'd have slit your throat as well. I'm no here tae make amends, if that's what you're thinking. God forbid!'

There was a movement at Crozier's side as Tom started forward, drawing his sword. He did not have time to loosen it before his brother's hand pinned his arm to his side. 'Stay back,' Adam said. 'Leave him to me.'

He reached the robber's horse, and put a hand on its bridle. He looked into his enemy's eyes. 'Tell me what was so urgent that we had to meet, and have done with it.'

Elliot laughed, loosening a rusty nail in his throat. 'Man of few words, eh? Unlike your father.' He raised a hand to ward off Crozier's rising irritation. 'Aye, aye, I'm coming to it. Show some respect to your elders, boy. Were Nat alive he'd be a dribbling husk, just like me. Time reaches us all, son, though we all think we can outrun it.' He wiped his rheumy tears. 'As ye have no doubt guessed, I'm not long for this world. I have spent sleepless nights these last few months, thinking over the past. There's been a lot of memories to keep me company. I've had a fine, full life.' He looked at his son, and his expression hardened.

'One thing aye irked me, though. It was said I had killed your father, and so I did. Clean and fast, as always. Believe me, lad, he suffered less in that last minute than I do now each hour of the day. I'll burn for what I did to him, no doubt, and for worse sins too. But I wanted you to know it was not my doing. Or at least' – he coughed and dragged his hand over his mouth – 'not mine alone.'

'Baron Dacre?' asked Crozier quietly.

Elliot nodded. 'The very same.' He reached under his jerkin and pulled out a folded paper. 'In case ye dinnae believe me.'

Crozier took the yellowed message. It was short, and creased with age. Ink splattered the page, showing the writer's haste. *Despatch our mutual foe*, it said, *and your reward will come far sooner than in heaven*. Signed with Dacre's vigorous sprawl, it was dated the day before Nat Crozier's death.

A hush fell over the wood. Crozier's pulse was steady, his heart-beat slow, yet he seemed to be viewing the scene, and himself in it, from somewhere high above. His voice sounded far off and foreign when he asked, 'Can you tell me why? What had my father done to Dacre that he deserved . . . ?' He swallowed, remembering the scene after Elliot and his men had left, his father bled white like a butchered pig, his mother crazed with terror.

Elliot looked down at his hands, but said nothing. His son stared at him, as if willing the hanging head to rise, but the figure in furs could have been made of straw for all the life it showed. Tom and Wat exchanged looks, but Crozier did not move.

Just as it seemed the thief had run out of words and this audience was over, he drew a rattling breath that lifted his chest like a sail catching the wind. He stared at the borderer, a glint of his arrogant younger self reflected in his eyes. 'Dacre needs no reason. There's some men he admires, and others he hates. But nobody threatens Dacre, or not for long. He owns this land from sea to sea, on his side of the border, and on ours too. He can crush anyone he likes, howsoever he likes, and the king far off in London town won't lift a finger.'

He coughed, and stared at Crozier. 'So long as the baron is in charge, the east march, the west march, and the middle march are his private playground, and we, my lad, are nothing more than his toy soldiers. Your father offended him, I know not how, and he simply wanted him dead. I don't understand it myself. It's not as if Nat was a rival . . .'

He broke off, exhausted, and clutched one hand over the other, to steady their shake. His mouth was slack and wet. Edward stepped forward and stood by his father's side, a reminder that the old man might be helpless, but he was not alone.

Crozier shook his head. 'My father was an insolent man,' he said, 'and he often defied the baron, but there were many as bad who crossed him and swindled him, yet lived to die of old age. You are either afraid to tell me the truth, or Dacre did not trust you with it.' He stared into Elliot's sagging face. 'And who,' he added softly, 'could blame him for that?'

Elliot shrugged. 'What do I care? He paid me well enough.'

'But as Dacre said, my father was your enemy too. What was your grudge, to risk killing him in his bed like that?'

'No, laddie,' said Elliot, his face lighting up with a malice that had never failed to come running when called. 'I had no beef against your da. I only played along with Dacre's dislike, so's to secure the job. Tell the truth, I liked Nat. We were two of a kind. If he hadn't grown lazy and slow, more keen on mischief than money, it could be my bones lying under the trees and your old man sitting here, richer than the regent king, and a life of pure pleasure ahint him.'

He leaned forward, his mouth working. 'But just for the record, since I've come all the way here this morning to set things straight, he was also a poxy wee man, your da, a troublemaker, and a braggart. He was as big a thief as I ever was, but not as smart. When he was buried, it wasn't just Dacre was glad he had been despatched. The whole dale rejoiced, though mibbe not all they wenches carrying his bairns.'

A smile was spreading across his face when Crozier drew his sword. At the rasp of steel, wood pigeons rose from the trees with a clapping clatter and flapped over their heads. Elliot's horse shied, wrenching the bridle out of the borderer's hand, and with a grunt the thief slid from the saddle, landing upon the woodland floor with the sound of a rock hitting water. Edward started forward, then checked himself. His father sprawled, his hat cast aside, his bald head blotched yellow and black like a sycamore leaf in winter. He peered up at Crozier, whose sword was pressed at his neck.

'You miserable piece of filth,' Adam said, so quiet in his rage that none but the Elliots could hear. 'You kill my father, destroy our family, just to keep in with the warden. You're as despicable as Dacre himself. You sicken me.' The blade found a chink in the furs and probed deeper.

'Go on, lad, you do it,' wheezed Elliot, pulling his shirt aside to bare his throat. 'I dare ye. Show you're better than your old man. If there was one thing he couldnae do, it was finish the kill. He got others to do his dirty work for him. Gutless, was Nat.'

The sky narrowed, the day darkened, and Crozier was about to slide the blade home when he caught the look on Elliot's face. His smiling bravado was not well-disguised fear, but secret relief. His body was tense, but not terrified. He was waiting for his end, and eager for it. This was what he had come here for.

Crozier glanced up, and saw Ethan's surly son, head turned away. What boy would not have leapt to his father's defence? But Edward

21

was following orders, and finding it as hard as any would to watch his father threatened.

The borderer's head cleared. He took a deep breath, and sheathed his sword. 'Get up,' he said. Like a wounded bear, the mound of furs stirred as, slowly and shakily, Elliot got onto his knees. Edward helped him to his feet, and he leaned against his boy. He was trembling, all expression wiped from his face.

'Go back home, old man,' said Crozier wearily. 'I won't be your executioner, whatever you'd come here hoping.' Taking the reins from Wat, he got into the saddle, and wheeled his horse close to father and son. He looked down at Elliot, into his bloodshot eyes. 'Maybe you'll find another who'll be happy to murder you – a man of your own sort, no doubt.' His mare kicked up leaves as he rode out of the wood, their flutter mocking Elliot's palsy as he stood, shaking and helpless.

The buzzard was at his post when he heard the riders return. They were moving fast, approaching the wood from across the night-time hills. As they passed in darkness under his sentinel tree, his yellow eyes blinked.

A day's ride away in the west, the clouds parted and a half-moon lit the scene. A black shape dangled from the bough of a tree, knotted reins around its neck. Some distance from the swaying boots, the unbridled horse cropped the grass and, several miles beyond, the hanged man's son was galloping home at his father's command, believing him not far behind.

The borderer was close to home when Ethan Elliot died, but it was quickly rumoured, then accepted as fact, that he had murdered the old man as the first of his acts of revenge.

CHAPTER TWO

Whitsuntide Sunday, May 1523

The forest lay in darkness as midnight approached, but all was not quiet. Over the tops of the firs and oaks came the sound of music. The valley was for a moment hushed, foxes freezing, owls fluttering onto perches, deer lifting their heads from their hollows. In place of their cries could be heard the strains of a dance, pipes and fiddle sweet as a linnet, drumbeats quick as a boar on the charge.

A pinprick of light flickered at the head of the valley. In the courtyard of Crozier's Keep a bonfire was crackling, sparks flying brighter than the stars overhead. The ramparts were lit by torches, pitch flames casting a molten glow that did nothing to melt the gloom of the clifftop where the keep clung, dizzying as an eyrie.

By day, here in the heartland of Teviotdale, golden eagles would circle as if spinning invisible threads around the keep's turrets. The forest and ravine had been their home first, and their image was stamped on the Crozier crest, an eagle facing the sun. With his cold grey eyes and beak-like nose, Adam Crozier had, if not the look of the bird, then something of its manner. Few could hold his stare, which seemed to see to their marrow.

This night he was seated on a dais in the keep's great hall, his wife Louise at his side. Gathered around them, goblets in hand, was a posse of chieftains, heads of the dale's lesser clans. Their finery outshone that of their leader, as did their conversation, but there was no doubt in anyone's mind that Crozier was lord, of this domain at least.

In place of his usual drab riding gear the borderer wore a silver-buckled cloak. Dressed in green, as was his wife, it was as if the pair had grown out of the woodlands around them, one in winter ivy, the other in springtime leaves. On Crozier's wrist a hooded kestrel perched, bell tinkling as its head swivelled, watching their guests. Louise's hair was netted in gold, and pinned by a circlet of blossom. She was laughing at the sight of her brother cavorting in a jig, a beer cask bobbing in a lade. Crozier bent closer to catch her words. He did not smile, but it was obvious to any who watched that when his wife spoke, he listened. The men standing near them smiled indulgently, but two glanced at each other and, as if they too were in a dance, peeled away and left the stage, making towards the trestle tables at the end of the hall where ale and wine were being served. Around them was a seething mill, the music setting feet stomping and loosening throaty yells. Arms were raised aloft like fire tongs, and clansmen whirled their women, or those they hoped would soon be theirs, around the rush-strewn floor.

The Whitsuntide feast at Crozier's Keep was famed across the dale. It had begun as a small event, years ago, at Louise's suggestion: a day when the villagers from the valley could forget their work and quarrels, and kick up their heels to the play of skirling pipes. The smell of roasted boar would waft over the forest from early morning, and by noon the path to the keep was churned into mud by villagers enticed up the trail by the mouthwatering scent.

These were anxious years, in the aftermath of Flodden, when Scotland trembled at the thought of what fresh disaster might be coming its way. People were right to be afraid. Almost before the battlefield had been cleared of bodies and bones, Teviotdale and the Merse were ravaged by a series of raids, the border left smoking as Henry VIII of England took a boyish glee in deepening his enemy's despair. Like a child who wearies at last of tormenting a tethered dog whose whimpers have begun to bore him, the king eventually turned his army elsewhere. In time the borderlands grew to fear others more than Henry, kept in a state of perpetual unrest by the assaults and thieving of other clans from both sides of the border.

Nearly ten years earlier, when Louise Brenier, daughter of a sea merchant from Leith, married Adam Crozier, the keep had been unkempt, the clan ragged, and her husband exhausted, maintaining order, filling their barns against the long winter, and warding off the threat of raiders. Seeing him harried by clansmen from neighbouring lands who had more reason to be their allies, Louise suggested he repair the friendships his hot-headed father had broken. It had taken only that for Crozier to realise what he had to do. 'You are a clever woman, and many other things besides,' he said, kissing her before saddling up and riding out to turn their lives around.

'They say my father was a pirate,' she replied. 'I get my cunning from him.'

In the early months of his venture, he did not take his brother with him. Tom was too quick-tongued, his temper unpredictable, and Crozier feared a cross word or thoughtless insult would jeopardise the fragile new bonds he was forging. But where old Ned had been short-sighted and petulant, Tom soon proved he was sharper. Not only did he applaud his brother's tactics, he began to mimic them, turning his youthful fighting foes from nearby hamlets into a loyal band of guardsmen who looked to him for orders.

In the quiet of their chamber, Crozier admitted to Louise that he had misjudged him. 'He has a way about him that makes men like him. Trust soon follows, drunk though they usually are by that stage.' He sighed, and his wife looked at him thoughtfully.

'But you, my love, do not need to be liked. Better, perhaps, that you are not.' She rubbed his hands, as if to soften her words. 'At times like these, you must instil fear in your enemies and courage in your allies. Friendship can follow later, when our troubles have passed.'

'But will they ever? That's what I want to know.' Crozier closed his eyes as if to keep at bay the question that rose before him every hour, its answer all too plain.

It did not take long to persuade his father's old friends that an alliance was in their best interests. Samuel Jardine was first to pledge himself to Crozier's band. 'I aye liked your faither, Adam, thistly though he was. It has grieved me to be at odds with your family. This is a bright day for all of us,' and he gripped Crozier's hand so tight, his thumb ring left a weal.

This bald, bearded giant brought with him the clans of the eastern dale, among them the foul-mouthed, stout-hearted Bells, the Scotts with their flying axes, and the Taylors, whose laburnum-tipped arrows made them as fearsome in the saddle as the Scotts were on foot. Between them they created a cordon protecting the middle march, a steel army whose size might not equal that of the Elliots or the Armstrongs, but whose mettle was a match for any.

Yet even this dauntless force was not sufficient to keep them safe, as Crozier soon realised. Too often his soldiers were taken unawares, good men lost to dawn raids and ambush. So he began to organise a more robust defence, not just of Crozier's Keep but of all his allies' lands. A web of far-flung lookout towers was built, and a roster of watchmen drawn from village and dale, whose reward was generous but dismissal swift should they daydream, malinger, or doze.

In time, Crozier's Guard became renowned. Young fighting men were soon eager to join its ranks, but had to bide their time. Few of the Guard willingly relinquished their positions, and most of those who left did so with an arrow through the eye or a blade under the ear, and a wooden cross on a hill where their widow or mother would go to weep.

They went to their posts carrying border broadswords, Leadhills bugles, and cudgels made from Teviot ash. Above light mail vests and black leather jerkins, their steel bonnets were stamped with the Crozier crest. No eagle scanned the horizon by day or peered into the night more gimlet-eyed than these eager soldiers, whose name was to become legend.

Though the villagers were always invited, the Whitsuntide feast was now held in the guards' honour, they and their families piped into the hall at the start of the banquet and seated at tables as if they were lords. A ceaseless procession of plates brought them fish and fowl and boar and beef, and they ate till their bellies were bodhráns. Meanwhile, out in the cheerless dark, the Crozier kin kept watch in their place, grumbling at their banishment but grudgingly in awe of the hardy men who endured such tedium, and danger. Their relief was always ill hidden when, four shifts later, the sore-headed Guard resumed its post.

Nearly tripped by a dancer's flying boot, Samuel Jardine refilled his mug and stood back from the fray, Mitchell Bell at his elbow. Froth settled on his moustache before he lipped it off, and sank another deep draught. For a moment the pair watched the spinning reel, and their leader, sitting as if enthroned as he looked down upon his people.

'There's something he's no telling us,' said Bell at last.

'Aye,' Jardine replied.

'They say he hanged auld Ethan Elliot,' Bell added, 'then gralloched him like a stag.'

'And who could blame him? If it had been my faither he'd murdered in cold blood, I'd hae done it years ago.'

They were not the first to speak of it that night. Word of Ethan Elliot's death was being whispered in every corner of the high, gaunt hall, but none dared ask the lord of the middle march if his hand had been behind it. Those who would not have had the stomach for such a job were secretly pleased they were on Crozier's side, such a man being needed in this turbulent land; those who would have snapped Elliot's neck long before his confession saw in Crozier a man they were glad to do business with: less squeamish, and perhaps less fair-minded, than they had always presumed.

'It's no Elliot that's on his mind,' Jardine continued. He fingered his shirt sleeve, eyes narrowing at the sight of their leader's hand on Louise's waist. Bell followed his glance.

'I take yer meaning,' he said, snickering.

Jardine frowned. 'Naw, it's no that either. Nor could ye blame the man; she's no a bad-looking wee thing, after all.' He stared at the rafters, which were wreathed in smoke. 'There's something else afoot, and it's making me nervous. Him an' all, by the look of it.'

As they charged their mugs, fatigue and drink began to claim them, conversation thickening, along with their thoughts. Jardine was mid-sentence when a hand pressed on his shoulder. There was a fluttering and the tinkle of a bell at his side, and he found himself held by the glassy eye of Crozier's kestrel.

'You've a bleary look, the pair you,' said the borderer, with the hint of a smile. He slapped Bell's back. 'Been enjoying yourself, I hope. Goodwife Bell is lost in the throng, dancing her boots to ribbons.'

Bell focused, with difficulty, and raised his mug in his spouse's direction. 'It's the only chance she ever gets, me being on watch most nights.'

The men nodded agreement, and stood companionably, thinking of the dale that spread out from the keep, already emerging out of the melting dark into the fresh summer's day. As they talked, they were joined by leaders from their fellow clans, and in the abundance of rich cloaks and jewelled caps the party took on a regal air, as if Crozier's Keep were a court.

A trumpet set the hall quivering, and the bird on Crozier's wrist flapped, as if to escape, though it did not leave his arm. He beckoned the men to follow. In the gloom of a side chamber, so low Jardine stooped in fear of cracking his head, Crozier pushed the door shut, and leaned back on the table, releasing his hawk to find a perch on the walls.

'You'll be aware, my friends,' he said slowly, 'that trouble is on the way.'

Jardine inclined his head, waiting for more. 'In what shape?' asked Bell, whose beery head had suddenly cleared, and with it his yellowed eyes.

Crozier looked round the room. 'Lord Dacre has been given orders to destroy the border towns, and he's picking them off like shies at the fair.'

'So the war begins at last,' muttered Sandy Scott, not without relish.

Their leader nodded. 'We must double our guard and prepare our defences, and gather again when we're less soused to plan how we will respond.'

'Where did ye hear this news?' asked Jardine.

'Murdo's scouts. They say villages are already burning down Yetholm way. But Henry of England wants more than that. He wants the border this side of the Tweed razed to ashes, and our spirits crushed.' He looked at them, and the room grew cold. 'He's coming for the abbeys. Then, no doubt, for us.' At Crozier's tone, the kestrel peeped, ready to fly at his command. 'Here, then,' he said more gently, proffering his arm, and while the men began to talk he stroked the hawk's feathers, as if calming his own alarm as well as hers.

The men had talked for an hour when the music slowed and the dancers could be heard staggering off the floor.

'It's almost day,' said Crozier. 'I must see the Guard off. We shall gather again, and soon.' He left abruptly, setting the door swinging on its hinges, and Jardine and Bell looked at each other.

'So ye were right after all,' said Bell.

His companion grunted. 'Seems so, though it gies me no joy. Couldnae be much worse, what's heading our way.'

Bell tightened his belt, beneath which dinner was already a memory. 'A last drink for our journey home? To put cheer into our souls?' The others moved quickly at the thought of ale, but Jardine was less nimble. 'A swift one, aye,' he said, his thoughts turning first to bed, and then the need to recruit new men, and buy more arms, before the week was out.

While they drank, the throng in the great hall dispersed, hounds and wenches following their men up the stairs, and into the sobering night. There was the clatter of horses and mules, and servants' boots, as the keep emptied, the crowd spilling out over the cobbles, their voices wakening the birds.

By the keep's gates Crozier stood, with Louise at his side. He pressed a pouch of giltsilver into the hand of each guard as he passed, a gesture of gratitude and respect that would last longer, and be of more use, than their aching heads.

CHAPTER THREE

27 September 1523

At the bugler's cry, Harbottle Castle came alive. Soldiers dropped their dice and raced to the gates, stable boys crammed the remains of their evening meal into their mouths before scurrying to their stalls, and sentries streamed from the barracks to crowd the walls. With the groan of a ship about to break up in a storm, the drawbridge was lowered.

Far above them, Francis Blackbird watched from the ramparts as his master returned. He knew at once that something was wrong. The baron was not at the head of his men but out on the wing, riding as if the army he was bringing home were invisible, and he alone was cantering through the early autumn evening off the hillside and into the greensward fringed by trees where Harbottle stood, a haven in the heart of rebel territory.

On the walls, the guards' helmets glinted as if they'd been struck with a flint. The flashing steel was echoed in their gimlet stare. By day, nobody could approach without being seen. Allies were anxious as they drew close, fearing they would be taken for foes; enemies were rarely able to reach the gates before they were chased off by arrows or shot.

The baron's men swept into the castle, steam rising from their horses as if it were the depths of winter and not a golden warm day. Wild-eyed and raucous, they were in good spirits after a week of fighting, but his lordship was wrapped in brooding silence, his mood visible even from Blackbird's lofty lookout as he flung his reins at a groom, and strode up the ramp and into the castle without a word.

His butler feared a difficult night lay ahead. While the army birled around the courtyard as if at a dance, unsaddling their horses and shouldering packs heavy as the dead, Blackbird hurried down the turnpike stair to the baron's private quarters. By the time his master reached the top floor, a fire was burning in the grate, a sprinkling of herbs sweetening the dank fortress air, and fresh hose and shirt lay on the bed, awaiting their weary owner.

Thomas, Baron Dacre was the most powerful man in the north of England. Warden General of the English marches, and Keeper of Carlisle, he was not as rich as his king, but he had so many debts he could call in, so many allies to answer his summons, that he could whistle up a fortune at a day's notice, far faster than Henry could dream of. Nor would his income be recorded by the treasury. No whisper of the gold and silver, the grain and cattle and plate that passed into Dacre's hands from the countrymen around him ever reached the Chancellor. The only evidence lay in Dacre's widening waist, and a smile so full of teeth, it made some think of a wolf.

The north was Dacre's bailiwick, but his heart lay in the west. The middle and eastern marches were too troublesome for comfort. Though he had been in charge of them for many years, he was considered an impostor, an enemy, and the post irked him like a hair shirt. As a young man he would have relished the challenge. Now, in late middle age, the baron was weary. More and more he longed to retreat to the west march, and Naworth, the castle he called home.

Dacre's spurs scraped on stone as he approached his chamber, his tread heavy with more than fatigue. Busying himself, Blackbird knelt before an oaken chest, tidying underclothes and shirts. He wiped his face blank. The baron hated any display of sympathy.

A man more comfortable in the saddle than in a chair, who patrolled the borders in all weathers as if there were assassins behind every tree, Dacre was an uneasy presence indoors. Blackbird had seen veteran soldiers flinch and reach for their daggers as the warden flung himself from dinner table to fireside, more like a man about to begin a charge than one in search of a drink. His vigour and enthusiasms were better suited to the outdoors than to the confinement of bedchamber and hall, and quite how he carried out his dalliances with elegant wives and widows bemused his servant. Surely he left in his wake a tell-tale trail of broken trinkets and paintings knocked askew? Whatever appeal he held, neither grace nor patience was part of it. Blackbird's own affairs, by contrast, reflected a lifetime's study in manners, his conquests planned and executed as cunningly as Dacre's military campaigns, though not always with equal success.

The Warden General stooped to enter the room, which in his presence shrank to half its size. He grunted at Blackbird and unstrapped his sword and belt, dropping them onto the settle by the fire. His man helped him out of his jerkin, and the smell of sweat filled the room. Blackbird raised an eyebrow, and the Warden General stripped off his wet shirt, and threw it after his sword. Boots followed shortly.

His face was smeared with filth, his thinning grey hair greased and unkempt. Blackbird poured water into a pitcher and stood by, a cloth over his arm, while Dacre plunged his head deep, then rose, shaking water from his eyes and hair as if he were a hound fresh out of the river.

Towelling himself, the baron sat half dressed on the bed. Flesh spilled over his belt, but beneath the buttery flab was a chest made of muscle. His shoulders would not have disgraced a blacksmith, nor his hamlike arms. He did not speak, but Blackbird sensed an easing of the atmosphere, and allowed himself to fill it.

'I hear the venture was a great success,' he said in a reedy voice bred on the Cumberland moors. 'They say there is a string of pack-horses still to arrive, laden with goods from the ransacked abbey.' He cast a glance at his master from beneath grizzled eyebrows, but the Warden General's expression did not change. His eyes were fixed on a middle distance where something was happening that neither he, nor his servant, liked the look of.

'My lord,' continued Blackbird, with a self-deprecating cough, 'is it true that Jedburgh burns, and the Scots have been brought back to heel?'

'Aye,' replied the warden at last. He began to pull on his shirt. 'It burns all right.' Blackbird heard a muttered rider, but not the words. 'As do I. As do I.'

Heaving himself off the bed, Dacre looked around the chamber as if only now recognising where he was. 'There'll be dinner tonight for my lieutenants. Surrey and Eure will also be joining us. My brothers too. They will sleep in these rooms, not in the barracks. Have the truckles made up.'

'Goodwife Cooper has dinner in hand, my lord, and I shall help wait at table. The beds are already prepared.'

'Good,' replied Dacre, as if his mind were elsewhere. 'Is Joan still here? She hasn't skipped off to Morpeth with her sister?'

'No, my lord, she was too keen to see you return. She will be waiting for you downstairs. I told her to let you disrobe first, but she's been asking when you'll be back since break of day.'

A glimmer of warmth crossed the baron's face. 'Good,' he repeated.

At dinner, none but Blackbird would have guessed his master's state of mind. Harbottle's hall was cheerless, as spartan as if the warden's smallest and shabbiest castle were nothing more than a garrison. From its lack of decoration you might have thought Dacre rarely visited, but in recent years he had spent much time here, keeping an eye on the eastern march. Even Morpeth, his best-appointed castle, some miles south, drew him rarely. These days his married daughters and their young sister slept there more often than he, enjoying the rich Flemish hangings, the fine carved beds, and fires so well tempered they sent their smoke up the chimney. There was nothing to keep a woman in Harbottle, not even a kitchen. Finding a cook out here who could organise hot dinners that were not reduced to charcoal and still retained a blush of heat was almost as hard as keeping the gangs of these parts in check. Had any of his men known what Dacre paid Goodwife Cooper for her services, there would have been revolt.

There were days when Harbottle's oozing damp and vindictive draughts made Dacre sigh, yet he returned to it, each time, with a lifting of his heart. The bleak and threatening hills it faced, the moors that lapped its stone, were a reminder of his duty, and why he was here. The eastern march and its middle neighbour were a battlefield, and the conflict was constant. Placed as he was here, within a half-day's ride of the Scottish border, surrounded by Northumbrian highlanders as treacherous as the Scots, the enemy could appear in any guise: cattleman, child, serving wench or lord. Trouble was always near, as if the heart of this country beat only when stoked with rage or revenge. Chill and comfortless it might be, but Harbottle cautioned him against growing careless, or feeling safe. In his world, those were the gravest dangers a man could face.

As he joined his guests in the hall, at a table piled with meats and pies, a hearth of flames filling one wall and his hunting hawks perched overhead, beadily awaiting the scraps that would be thrown their way, Harbottle, he thought, was welcoming enough.

'My lords,' he said, with as broad a smile as if he had not seen them for weeks, 'please, take your places. We must eat.' Surrey, Eure and Dacre's brothers Christopher and Philip rose from their benches by the fire, goblets in hand. The baron filled a cup to the brim and raised it. 'A toast, I think, after our labours.' There was a murmur of approval as they held their glasses aloft. 'To Jedburgh,' said Dacre. 'Long may it smoulder.'

'And all Scotland with it!' roared Christopher, already flushed with wine. A laugh ran around the room as drinks were drained, and in the corner a hesitant lute was plucked, the castle's bugler pressed into service as a minstrel though he could play barely three tunes, and those only before he'd touched a drink.

The evening sank low and late in conversation. Blackbird cleared the platters, brought more ale and wine from the cellars, and made a space for himself on the bench beside them. No one questioned his right to a place at Dacre's table. The baron's oldest retainer, a miller's son taken into service in Naworth as a boy, he had become more family than servant. His official title was butler, but his duties and responsibilities were far wider than that. Butler, manservant, steward and confidant, he was the most influential of Dacre's men, and the most feared. His loyalty to Dacre was absolute, a devotion that none could explain or diminish. It was said Blackbird's love of his master was what kept him unmarried – how else to explain the single habits of a man whose lust for wenches meant no good-looking skivvy was safe unless her door was barred at night?

Over the years, Dacre had ignored Blackbird's nocturnal prowling. Occasional difficulties were easily resolved, although eventually there was a limit to the toll of bastards the baron was prepared to find homes for. Placing his own was taxing enough. After his butler had fathered one too many, a severe scolding brought a brief spell of chastity. When contrition wore off, Blackbird took greater care, and chose his wenches more for their meekness than for their looks. At the first hint that they might cause a scandal, he was confident he could quell them with a word, or a slap, or a visit to the healer and her scouring herbs.

This evening's conversation was the sort Blackbird most enjoyed. He never rode on campaigns with his master, seeing his function as keeper of the home fires, a role Dacre's long-dead wife had never performed, at least not to his standards. Now, he would learn what had happened in the time Dacre had been gone.

He knew better than to ask questions, nor was there any need. Dacre's companions were happy to revisit their exploits. So excitable was their chatter, it might only have been Blackbird who noticed how quiet the baron kept, and how much he drank.

'Who'd have thought they would put up such a fight?' said Thomas Howard. A favourite of Henry VIII, he had been elevated to the earldom of Surrey when his elderly father was created Duke of Norfolk after trouncing the Scots at Flodden ten years earlier. It was a victory won with his son's help, and the memory of that appalling battlefield might explain why, despite his still black hair, the middle-aged Surrey was haggard as an old man. It was hard to picture him leading a charge and lopping off heads, but it was said his sword was lethal. He would never match his father's military brilliance or political brain, but he was a worthy foe, and a most useful ally. Dacre might be Warden General of the English marches, but whenever the king wanted his authority stamped on the Scots he sent Surrey north, as he had his father. Like a nurse to oversee a wayward child, thought Dacre, staring into the oily depths of his rich red wine.

'They've been half starved this past summer,' continued the earl. 'Armstrong and his men told us they had made sure of that. Yet they fought like lions.' Surrey's eyes narrowed, and he leaned across the table towards Dacre. 'Can we trust Sly Armstrong, d'you think? Has he been playing a double game with us?'

Dacre's booming northern voice rose to the rafters like a reproof to Surrey's sleekit southern accent. 'Armstrong wouldnae dare cross me. If he said he burned the corn, and all the barns in Teviotdale, he did it sure enough. Where these border rats get their strength from, I couldn't say. For all I know, they eat their own middens, or mibbe their own bairns. Nothing would surprise me. But they fair near did for us this time, and I'll never forget it.'

'It's us they won't forget, not for a long time,' said Christopher, unbuttoning his woollen waistcoat as the fire reached him, and stretching out his legs under the table. He cupped his goblet in a hand bound in a rusted rag. A large, dishevelled man, with a farmer's ruddy complexion, he was more like Dacre in appearance than the whip-thin Philip, though all three shared a manner, and a cast of mind, that showed they came from the same litter.

He caught his brother's eye. 'Ye gods, Tam, I've never seen a blaze like it. Two days later and the abbey was still sizzling. And there's hardly a hovel left in the town. The place is nothing now but ash.' He frowned. 'The screams of the folks as they roasted would've touched the hardest heart. I had to remind myself not to run back and save them. Christopher, I said, they are all infidels. There's not a Christian among them. Even the monks held the devil in their hearts.'

William Eure, Dacre's deputy, nodded. 'Should have s-s-seen them, running around, pressing their crosses to their lips, as if their Antichrist would be able to save them. Pitiful, it was. Getting rid of them, I've s-s-saved a place for myself in heaven.'

From the far end of the table, Philip spoke. 'Our work in the borders is like the good Lord's crusades in the holy land, except that out here the trophies are worthless.' He sniffed, wiping his nose on his linen sleeve. It was one of his lesser drips, a late summer sniffle rather than the ripe winter snorts that, better than a bell round his neck, told the world he was approaching long before he came into sight.

Christopher nodded: 'It's a crusade, all right, but the Moors are half as savage.'

Surrey leaned forward. 'Gentlemen, apart from their misbegotten beliefs, I hear the Mohammedans are educated and civilised men.

Those are not words that could ever be used in these parts – of either Scots or English.'

Dacre shifted in his chair. These were his people the earl and his brothers were talking about. Enemies or not, he was one of them. He eyed his companions with dislike and knocked back his wine.

Night blackened the arrow-slits above their heads, and in the quickening draught tar shadows danced. The tallow flares flickered and darkened and it seemed, for a moment, as if he were once more in the woods by Jedburgh, that the spirits he had met there had followed him back to Harbottle. He shivered. He had seen many terrible things in his time, but nothing so alarming as what he had witnessed in those woods. That was a private message, for his eyes only, though why he could not fathom.

The creatures had appeared with the suddenness of a nightmare. He and his lieutenants had stretched out for a few hours' sleep before the morning's assault. They were an hour's ride from Jedburgh, a douce little abbey town, which Henry had commanded the Warden General to destroy. The king's patience had run out, and he did not want peace in the north. The time for that was past, he said. Overriding Dacre's protests, he insisted the Scots be harried, hounded, and killed.

The month before, he had ordered Kelso, Jedburgh's border twin, to be destroyed. It was an easy conquest and Dacre had fulfilled his instructions to the letter. Within hours of their siege, the abbey and its tower had lain desolate, reduced to cinders. Now that the Scots were at a disadvantage, Henry wanted Jedburgh, Teviotdale's jewel, to be ground to dust, and this time its people with it.

Dacre read the king's orders with distaste. He believed Henry was wrong to punish the Scots in this way. Vulnerable as they were under a regent who was rarely in the country, now was the time to settle a truce, on advantageous terms. Henry, however, did not agree. His venom for the north seemed unquenchable. Quelling his doubts, the baron marshalled his troops and summoned each of the king's lieges along the border, with all the mounted men they could muster.

The riders were eager for the task. As the fighting season gathered pace, so, Dacre observed, did their hunger. It was as if their swords and knives had an appetite of their own. He had seen smallholders and bakers and cattle drovers who at home were kind to their dogs and their women become so fierce in the fight, none would have recognised them. When a sword was in their hand and prey in their sights, it was as if their senses had been smothered and something else had taken control. Once the blade was back in its sheath, they seemed scarcely to remember the way they had behaved. How else to explain their tenderness when they returned to their children and wives?

But perhaps they were all like that. They had to be. He made no excuses, because what they did, and how they lived, was the only life Dacre knew or wanted. Yet in the days after Jedburgh, he found himself wondering if the fiendish horror he had seen was a call to his conscience, a reminder of all the unforgivable things he had done in a long and heartless career.

His bedroll had been farthest from the camp fire, and where he lay the forest gloom was barely touched by its light. Since he was a boy he had hated the dark, and he closed his eyes to keep it at bay. Soon his companions had settled, breathing deep, and he too was almost asleep when he heard a rustle of leaves, as when a boot treads softly upon them. He opened his eyes.

Pines and larches marched row by row into the darkness, like an army in retreat. Where they melted into black, he saw a pale shape lurking behind a tree trunk that, when he peered harder, became a face. Another appeared from behind a neighbouring tree, and another, until he could make out six sets of eyes, all looking in his direction. He sat up with a grunt, shaking his head, hoping he was confused by the murk. When he looked again, the faces had gone. Only then did he feel the pounding of his heart behind his ribs.

He chided himself for his childish alarm, and lying back down pulled the blanket up to his chin. Turning his back to the woods, he settled to sleep, but barely had his breathing steadied when a crawling sensation ran over his scalp. Looking over his shoulder at the woods, he almost cried aloud. The faces had reached the trees nearest him. Their black eyes flashed, and tongues flicked lizard-like from scarlet, fleshy lips.

Dacre leapt out of his bedroll, shortsword in hand. 'How dare ye . . .' he growled, swiping the air as he advanced upon them. Silently, the figures darted out of reach. Fingers beckoned from behind the trees, unearthly pale and tapered, leading him onwards into the dark. As his tormentors crept deeper into the woods, moving from pine to pine in a mockery of hide-and-seek, he saw that their hind legs were crooked, as if they preferred to walk on all fours. It was then that he noticed the nubs of bone on their close-cropped heads, the cloven hooves where feet should have been. As the significance of this sank in, the last of the six turned to face him. Its owner put his hands on his hips. From his untied britches rose a cock the size of a cudgel. The devil leered at the baron and began to tug the monstrous appendage. As dizziness overcame him, Dacre heard a cackling laugh. He dropped to his knees, the night swimming around his head.

A hand was on his shoulder. 'Brother,' said Christopher, 'what's wrong?'

Dacre looked up, wild-eyed. 'Can ye no see them?' he cried. 'Devils, a pack of them, sent to pursue me.'

Christopher followed his gaze, but as Dacre too could see the woods were empty. 'You've been dreaming, Tam,' he said, helping the baron to his feet. 'How much did ye drink at dinner?'

Dacre spluttered. 'Don't take me for a fool. I wasn't asleep, and I am not drunk. God help us, I've seen the devil's own men. They were meant to scare the life out of me, so they were.' Shakily, he picked up his sword, and sheathed it.

'Come over here,' said Christopher, taking his arm, 'and sleep near the fire. I will keep guard for a watch, and Armstrong after me. It's not long till dawn. By light, no one will dare approach.'

Subdued as a sleepwalker woken from his trance, Dacre allowed himself to be coaxed back to bed. This uncommon meekness worried his brother more than the talk of devils. Too perturbed to feel drowsy, he kept a keen look-out until the first cockerel crowed.

Christopher's consternation had faded in the days after Jedburgh, but in the flaring light of Harbottle's torches, Dacre glanced over his shoulder more than once. As the wine took him in its grip, he trembled. The devils had boded ill, and their promise had been quickly fulfilled. Unsettled by his night visitors, the next day the baron had driven his men to attack without mercy. It was as well they did. Jedburgh had put up a fight worthy of a king's army, refusing to be cowed. As his troops swept down on the town, four thousand and more of them whooping and yelling, brandishing swords and clubs, they were met by a cannonade that sent their ranks tumbling one over the other like breakers reaching a beach.

A bitter fight followed. The townsfolk manned their walls and the abbey with a courage that Dacre could only admire. Women as well as men fought them off. Children launched nursery missiles – stones and bricks, old apples and tumshies – and screamed in delight when these found their mark. More than a few English raiders were toppled off their horses as the young catapulters broke their noses or blackened their eyes.

By dusk, Dacre doubted they would breach the town's defences that day. Calling his lieutenants, he ordered them to slacken their assault. Given false hope, he said, Jedburgh might relax its guard sufficiently for them to slip through it.

And so it proved. As the Warden General's men retreated, as if to remuster, the Jedburgh defenders put down their weapons. In their relief, they did not notice a line of raiders slithering over the abbey walls, slitting the throats of the abbot and his brothers, and breaking into the church. Not until the first oiled rags had been hurled and flames were blazing behind its windows did they realise their mistake. In fury, they surged towards the abbey, but by then it was too late. Dacre's men had gained entry. A net had been thrown over the town's head, and it remained only to drag it tight.

Street by street, as the sky darkened, the raiders pressed back the townsfolk, fighting hand to hand and setting alight every house and cottage and hut in their path. After an hour, almost as many English bodies littered the town as those of Jeburgh's people, but where Dacre could afford to lose hundreds, the town could not.

By nightfall the place was destroyed. The screams of the dying had ceased, the air was gritted with smoke, and the only sounds, as Dacre departed, were falling timbers, and the whistling whine of fire as it licked from one turfed roof to the next. The crimson glow of the abbey lit a scene of desolation, and brightened his way better than a torch as he galloped after his men.

Their encampment was safe on a hillside some miles out of town, yet it was here that the baron's fears came to pass. Anxious in case his night-time visitors returned, he lay beside his brothers, staring through the canopy of trees at the stars. The sky shimmered with lights so serene and comforting one would have thought that all was at peace with the world below. A barn owl swooped overhead, a pale blur against the oaks, and was heard hooting throatily from nearby. Lulled by the owl's crooning, the baron's eyes closed. He had fallen into a profound sleep when the woods around him came alive.

There was a crackling and snapping of breaking branches, a wild rustling of undergrowth disturbed, and a pounding of earth so thunderous it was as if the trees had uprooted themselves and begun to march. Dacre and his men rose sluggishly, slow to make sense of what was happening. Only when they heard the cry 'The horses are out!' from lower down the hill did they understand.

The loosing had been brutal. Hooded figures had pulled up the palisade posts, cut the ropes, and got between the horses. The beasts had shifted uneasily and begun to trot out of their compound, skirting the bodies of the murdered guards. More had followed, but not fast enough, and the robbers had lost patience and started to yell. Whips were cracked, flanks were lashed, and the horses were terrified into flight. Stamping upon each other in the rush to escape, they surged out of the corral, biting and kicking all within reach in their bewilderment and fear.

By the time the camp awoke, the palisade was emptying fast. The ground trembled under panicked hooves, the terror so great it could be smelled. As the stampede gathered pace and men began struggling out of their bivouacs and reaching for weapons, their shouts were lost beneath the roaring of the animals' flight, their passing as violent as if they were warhorses on the charge.

All this was heard in the camp, yet nobody could see what was happening. Blundering through the forest, Dacre and his men reached the palisade and looked in dismay at the empty, trampled grass. Those beasts that had managed to escape the round-up careered through the trees, a danger to the men and to themselves. Some were later caught, others were lost for ever. These were the lucky ones.

Farther up the hill, the horses were driven on by the thieves, who shrieked and wailed like banshees. 'After them!' cried Dacre, and the swiftest of his men were soon in pursuit, following the path the beasts had beaten, leaving behind the scent of broken pines and sweat. The chase had barely begun when it became clear what was happening. This was no robbery. It was far uglier than that.

The galloping hoofbeats were far ahead of the baron's soldiers, growing fainter as the distance between them increased, when a new noise cut through the night. Beyond the forest, across the hill, came high-pitched, helpless screams. They came not from one horse, or ten, but from wave upon wave, until it seemed as if every one had emptied its lungs in horror as it plunged to its death. Dacre's heart clenched. His horses were being chased over the cliffs.

When at last he came on the scene, the marauders were long gone. So too were the horses. The grass was churned to mud, and the darkness felt alive, the commotion the hilltop had witnessed too recent for the air to have settled. But now it was quiet, horribly so, save for the groans that reached them from the valley where the animals lay.

Flints were struck, lights glimmered, and Dacre's lieutenants were at his side. 'We will send a party down there,' Christopher began, panting from the chase, but Dacre turned away, his back to the cliff.

'No,' he said, so tired he could barely speak. 'There is nothing we can do.' An ache gripped his chest, and he lowered his head, waiting for it to pass. He put out a hand, and Christopher's arm was there. 'No,' he repeated, 'let us return to camp. This has been an evil night. Going down there will only make it worse.'

Behind them their men paced, too disturbed to leave, trying to ignore the sickening noises from below. As they gathered, they cursed and swore and cried, undone by this heartless act. Soldiers who had killed without qualm now felt unsure about what lay out there in the dark. Who would do such a thing, and why?

When daylight broke, the night's work took shape. A thousand and more of the army's steeds lay at the foot of the precipice. The first beasts to fall had pitched headlong into the valley, embedding themselves in a lather of earth. Seeing the danger, those close behind them had tried to veer away, but crowded by the horses upon their tails they were forced onwards until all had spilled over the edge, a waterfall of flesh.

Now they lay on broken backs, stiff as tables upturned in a brawl. Some were spread-eagled, as loose under the skin as if their bones were liquid. Most were dead, but some still kicked, life ebbing cruelly slow. Already men were moving between them, cutting throats for mercy.

Waking armies are as noisy as a gallows fair, but that morning the hillside was subdued. A cook clattered a pan, and felt the rebuke in the men's averted eyes. Few were hungry, yet all tried to eat, for who knew what the day would bring. But many meals were lost when they looked over the cliff top.

CHAPTER FOUR

As the baron recalled the sight, his throat tightened. He spoke slowly, Burgundy words lying thick on his tongue. 'We may have taken the town, but the story doesn't end there.'

'Don't be forgetting your prisoner,' said Philip.

Dacre thought of the disdainful laird captured on his way home as they rampaged over his lands and set his castle alight. His wife had been distraught to see him carried off. Touching it was, to witness her concern. But his men had left her with troubles of her own to deal with, and he doubted she'd have much time to worry about her husband over the next few days.

'Aye, it's good we've got him in our cells. He'll be useful.' Dacre paused, trying to grasp the disappearing thread of his thoughts. 'But this business is not finished,' he said, pulling a jug of wine towards him. 'Not by a long way.'

'What business?' asked Surrey, his voice clipped as an abstainer's, his goblet half full and his eyes clear.

'The horses.' Dacre's mouth twisted as if the word had scalded him.

Blackbird leaned forward. Reports of the carnage had arrived ahead of the baron. He'd heard nothing like it before. It held a menace new even for these plagued lands.

William Eure shook his head. 'Truly vile. I've never seen anything so vicious.'

'A petty revenge,' said Surrey, 'and we should have been prepared for it. The fault lies with us. Our night watch was woefully lax. How it happened that they could be run through and die without putting up a fight astounds me.'

'This was no mere revenge,' said Dacre, staring at the table as if talking to himself. 'Why kill the horses, when they could have kept them for themselves? That I would not have minded so much. But this, this . . .' He raised a hand as if in disbelief, his golden rings burning in the firelight.

Christopher slapped a hand on the table. 'Tam is right,' he said. 'It was not a reprisal, but a threat. Not the tail end of the Jedburgh affair, but the start of something different.'

A murmur ran round the table.

'Who would dare . . .' Blackbird began.

Eure looked grave. 'Only those very sure of their ground. The brazenness of it. The risks they ran . . .'

'It was clever,' conceded Surrey. He narrowed his eyes, as if trying to retrieve the mood of that night. 'And I've a suspicion you may well be right.'

Dacre nodded. 'We aye knew there'd be revenge some day for razing the abbeys. Yet it seems trouble is here sooner than we'd expected, sooner than we'd any need to fear. This was too well planned, too cold-blooded to be the work of Jedburgh town.'

'You think our raid had nothing to do with it?' asked Philip.

'Either that, or the raid merely stoked a fire that was already burning.'

'A few names have been suggested,' said Eure, hesitant as always. All eyes turned to him. 'It could just be gossip; we were so busy rounding up new horses for the men I didn't pay much attention. But the archers had their s-s-suspicions.'

'Tattling town criers,' said Surrey. 'Nervous as nuns.'

'Maybe,' said Eure. 'But the names they gave were plausible enough. One was the Ridleys, who have been needling us for months. Then there was the Croziers, a pestilent family from S-S-Selkirk way. The clan chief has been getting above himself in recent years, growing more pernicious. Could be that they were behind the attack.'

'Who else?' barked Surrey.

'The Fenwicks, from around Coldstream. They are thick with the Percys, who do not care for you, my lord, a fact you already know. It seems they might also still be smarting after we torched their castle and carried off their stock last month.'

Blackbird looked thoughtful. 'So many possibilities . . .'

Eure nodded again. 'And nigh impossible to prove. That's why I didn't pay attention.'

There was a movement from Dacre's chair. The company watched as the baron sat up in his seat, straighter and broader. It was as if he was inflating before them, strength and vigour returning him to full size and power.

'I'd see all of them swing, without a scrap of proof,' he said, running a purpled tongue over his lips. 'The Ridleys are dangerous, but unguarded and rash. It will be a simple matter to find out if they were involved. Even if not, I have a mind to see their leader shackled, for the good of the marches. The Fenwicks are more problematic. I cannot be seen to persecute the Percy clan without solid evidence. Get me that, though, and I will see them choke on the rope. And then there are the Croziers. I doubt that pox-ridden clan would have the mettle to trick us like that; for all the airs of their chief they are little more than savages. Nonetheless, whether we find them guilty of this crime or not, one day Crozier and his men will end on the gallows where they belong.'

He stroked his beard. 'But I will know who was behind this. And soon.' He turned to Philip, whose gaze sharpened, knowing his orders were coming. 'We need spies, brother, for each of their camps, people they'll never suspect.'

Philip murmured agreement. 'I will think on who could do this,' he began, but his brother raised a finger.

'Already I have thoughts on where they might be found. We shall talk tomorrow. But for now, let us drink to our enemy, that he stays deaf and blind to our approach, until the noose is slipped over his neck.'

Blackbird left the hall, returning with a fresh flagon of wine. 'To revenge!' cried Dacre, when their goblets were filled. The table drank as one, and Christopher watched his brother's brightening face. This was the old Tam he knew so well. Nothing cheered him better than settling a score.

Long after midnight, Dacre sat alone in the hall. His lieutenants were asleep upstairs, and even Blackbird had been dismissed. The baron wanted to be on his own. He sat beside the fire, its cooling embers his only light. The castle gathered around him like an old and favourite shawl, and as he stared into the rosy ashes he smiled. An enemy he was able to fight held no terrors for him. Devils he could not handle; border curs he could.

There was a shuffle from the edge of the hall, a glimmer of white in the shadows. Dacre tensed, but the figure moved swiftly towards him, sheltering a rushlight in its hands, and he relaxed.

His daughter, pale and light-footed as a moth in her night-wrap, placed her lamp in the hearth and joined him on the bench. She leaned her head on his shoulder. The smell of wine rose from him as if from an open bottle, and she clicked her tongue. 'You have been emptying the flagon, father. You should drink less.'

'So ye tell me,' he said, 'yet it's done me no harm thus far. You, however, should be in bed.'

'I've missed you,' she said. 'With Anne gone, and Mary too ill with the ague to play a hand of cards, let alone see to my clothes and tidy my room, it's been dull, dull, dull. All I've done is sew and draw, and do my lessons for Father Whitmore, who smells like a gutter. Blackbird would not even let me ride out on my own. He says it's not safe. So I had to have a guard wherever I went. Can you imagine?'

She kicked her slippered feet, more like a petulant child than a woman almost of an age to marry. 'I cannot wait to return to Naworth. How can you bear it out here? Don't you miss home?'

Her tone was that of her mother, her complaint an echo of Bess's nettling refrain. The baron banished the thought of his tormenting, much-missed spouse, and patted his daughter's knee. 'I know, Joanie, it's tedious for a girl out here. But Blackbird was right. This is a dangerous place. That's why I'm here. It has to be kept in order, and there's no one but me to do it, though God knows I'd rather not.'

'You've written to the king, as you said you would?'

'Aye, and much good it did me.'

They contemplated the grate in silence. When a slither of ash sent up a wisp of smoke, Joan lifted her head.

'When can we go home, Father?'

'Any time you wish. I'll send my best guards back with you tomorrow, if you like. I cannot keep ye here. But it may be months before I can return.'

'But Naworth is almost as miserable without you as Harbottle,' she whined. 'Everywhere goes quiet when you leave.'

'I could do with a little peace myself, that's for sure.'

His daughter looked at him. She had never seen her father so tired, and she put her arm through his, as if to infuse him with some of her high spirits. Together they stared into the fire. Her face was a youthful mirror, its Roman nose and wide-spaced eyes a more delicate reflection of the baron's good looks. But where he was broad and strapping, she, though sturdy, was small.

Dacre had an affection for this girl that sometimes caught him by surprise. The youngest surviving child of his marriage, Joan had been a sickly infant. Her twin sister was buried within days of their birth, and he had wondered then, and since, if Bess's burrowing canker had poisoned those in her womb. At mass and private prayer, he never forgot to thank God and all the saints that Joan had outgrown her puling years and was now as healthy a sixteen-year-old as one could ask for. He tried not to think of the two little boys who had followed her twin into the grave in the years after. Better remind himself instead of his robust adult children, whose boisterous offspring assured the family's future.

One day, no doubt, Joan too would give him grandchildren. He wondered what sort of man he should find for her to marry. Unlike her mother and her sisters Mabel and Anne, she would never be a beauty. Happier out hawking than dancing a gavotte, she might complain about Harbottle, but she was at home in the wilds like no other gentlewoman he'd ever met. He suspected, of course, that she followed her father's entourage precisely so she need not behave like a lady. Loose-girdled and unpainted, she went her own way. At her age, her sisters had spent their days knotting flowers in their hair, tightening their bodices, and colouring whenever his officers spoke to them. Joan laughed at his soldiers' crude jokes, but she had not yet blushed.

Dacre was aware he had indulged her. Had Bess been alive, she would have schooled Joan strictly. The time was coming, he knew, when he would have to place her in the care of her sisters, to be prepared for court, and marriage. Already Mabel was urging him to send her to Bolton, where she would turn her into a wise and comely wife-to-be. One day, he promised, one day.

For the moment, he liked her company too much to pack her off. Since Bess's death, her chatter had been a comfort. He sighed. It was a sign of getting old that a daughter meant so much. Though not a fanciful man, he imagined that returning home to find her absent would be like entering a wintry hall where the fire had died. Best perhaps if he married again first.

Joan hugged her wrap close. 'I'll stay a few weeks longer,' she said. Slipping off the bench to retrieve her rushlight, she looked down at the baron, whose face was the colour of curds. 'The birds will soon be waking, Father. We should get some sleep.' Dacre nodded. Shuffling in her wake as if his bones had softened, he followed her out of the hall and allowed her to lead him upstairs. At his door he briefly placed a hand on her head, and in the gloom he sensed rather than saw her smile.

The next morning Dacre's head buzzed like a hive. He rose at his usual early hour, but those who knew him well had found tasks that kept them beyond his call. Joan was nowhere to be seen; nor were his brothers, who, Blackbird told him, had ridden out shortly after daybreak.

'Bring me paper, man,' barked the baron, cutting short his butler's ruminations on where Christopher and Philip might have gone, when they could be expected to return, and what he could provide for their dinner when they did.

Only when seated at the table in his room did Dacre's mind begin to clear. He dipped his pen in ink, stared for inspiration at a butterfly fluttering up to the rafters, mistaking them for the boughs of a tree, and began to write.

CHAPTER FIVE

Linlithgow, 30 September 1523

A hundred miles north of Harbottle Castle, beneath a spreading elm in the garden of Linlithgow Palace, Margaret, dowager queen of Scotland, looked at the letter the courier had given her. The writing was familiar, the furious, spiky scrawl matching the impatient hand behind it. Green sunlight danced on the parchment, and the tree swayed as if craning to see what it contained. It was many months since Margaret had heard from the baron. Her spirits rose. No matter how impersonal or brisk his business, his messages were always a welcome reminder of the times they had shared.

The courier waited as she untied the ribbon and broke the baron's cockleshell seal. She scanned it fast, for bad news, then more slowly. Her eyes widened in interest.

The courier coughed. 'Yes, boy, you will have your answer,' she said, reading as she spoke. 'See your horse is settled, and our kitchen will feed you. You can return to Harbottle tomorrow, with my reply.'

A child in green doublet and yellow hose reached her side, tugging her arm to see what the letter contained. She sighed. James was nearly twelve, but the chances of his being able to decipher Dacre's hand were slim. The boy hated his books. He could barely read Scots, let alone Latin or French. 'Is he a dunderheid?' she had asked his tutor some weeks earlier. Gavin Dunbar had scraped a bow and smiled, as if a full set of white teeth could impress her.

'Absolutely not, my lady. He is as sonsy a lad as I've met for many years – like his dear departed father in that regard. But . . .' The teeth disappeared behind a prim mouth, and his glance brushed hers before settling on the horizon.

'Well?' she asked.

'I believe him to be lazy, my lady. And easily distracted. The men of this court sometimes lead him astray.'

She had turned, sweeping up her skirts and brushing past him in a slither of silks. 'He must learn the ways of the world, Master Dunbar,' she replied. 'The King of Scotland cannot be an innocent.'

Dunbar bowed after her retreating figure, his hat dusting the flagstones. 'But nor should he be a complete ignoramus,' he muttered.

'Let me see, Mama!' cried James, lifting the letter from his mother's hand.

'Careful you do not tear it,' she said, solely from a habit of scolding. Jamie might be slow at his studies, but he was not careless. Even at this young age he would spend an hour arranging the lace at his neck to his taste, or picking invisible dog hairs from his velvet cloak.

'What does he mean, "setting foxes to catch a wolf"?' he asked.

Margaret plucked the letter from him. 'I will explain later.' She looked around to see who had heard, but her maids were fondling the spaniels, her courtiers were deep in conversation, and the guards' ears were hidden beneath their helmets.

She summoned the nearest of her courtiers. 'Send to Edinburgh for the castle gaoler,' she said. 'Bring him to me at once.' The man bowed and set off at a run, no simple matter in pointed shoes. When the dowager queen spoke in that tone, haste mattered more than dignity.

For the rest of the day, Margaret was aloof. Though she saw him only rarely she dismissed her son, complaining that his voice was giving her a headache. Only her maidservants were allowed at her side, and they too were chided if they fidgeted or laughed. Stretched out on cushions and blankets beneath the elm, she stared into the leaves above as they rustled, dusty and dry in the early autumn sun. Her querulous expression softened as she replayed the scenes of happier times, twisting the bracelets on her arms and making them chime, like the hands of a clock going backward.

She remembered the baron helping to broker her marriage to James IV, arriving at Richmond Palace with a party of Scottish lords with whom he laughed and joked as if they were his dearest friends and not an enemy centuries old. He and her father, Henry VII of

England, had been closeted with them all afternoon, trays of ale and biscuits sent in every hour to sustain their negotiations.

When they emerged, her father had nodded at her but not spoken, leading the Scots to the hall where dinner awaited. Only later that night, when his guests had gone to their rooms and she was in bed, did he tell her that her nuptials were arranged. 'You are the best hope this country has of making a binding peace with Scotland,' he had said, dropping a kiss on her forehead in a rare mood of approbation. 'I believe James is a good man. I am sure you will be happy.' She watched his departing back, the light from his candle dimming as he crossed the room. Her spirits faded likewise. She would be a wife before she reached thirteen.

The next morning she had stood at her open window as Dacre and their other visitors gathered for the journey north. The baron was at the head of the group, sword in belt and crossbow on back. His stallion pranced, and he held it on a tight rein, but it was plain that he too was eager to be on the road. When eventually the horses wheeled, he looked up at Margaret's window and raised a hand in salute. She watched, twisting the ruby on her forefinger. With a man like that she might be willing to head into the unknown, she thought, turning back to the room, and wondering whether she would feel the same about the Scottish king.

Some months later she arrived in Edinburgh, clutching Dacre's arm as if she were blindfold. Only an hour earlier that arm had been around her waist as she was overcome by dizziness. Over the past few days she had been growing more and more faint-hearted. Her first sight of the north, at Dacre's castle in Morpeth, had left her homesick, the rich hangings and paintings a reminder of Richmond and everything she might never see again. As her retinue drew near the border, plodding through terrain that grew starker with each village, she had to blink back tears. Here she was, leaving her home and family for an uncouth place and a religious husband who, from the miniature she had seen of him, had an alarmingly introspective air and none of the baron's brawn.

'Courage,' Dacre had whispered as he helped her onto her horse outside an inn on the outskirts of Edinburgh. The cheer she'd taken from his embrace did more to sustain her than the tumbler of hot spiced wine James's servant proffered when they reached Holyrood House. The palace was a shimmer of forbidding grey, hidden beneath a rain so relentless her cloak trailed water up its uncarpeted stairs. She ought to have guessed then that the marriage would be soaked in tears.

In the years that followed, Baron Dacre was a frequent guest at the king's table, as diplomat, dinner companion, and sparring partner at dice. Neither in manner nor look did he suggest he felt more for James's young queen than the respect and honour she was owed, yet Margaret was certain this was a man on whom she could rely for support, and possibly more.

The elm shivered in the late afternoon breeze, and her maids draped themselves in shawls. Margaret picked up the letter and, turning on her side, reread its criss-crossed page.

> Let me not bore you with an account of what you owe me, or I you. In a friendship such as ours, there is no abacus of debt. Yet it must be plainly acknowledged that my obligation is greater than yours. Even so, I feel confident I can make another claim on your good nature. If I tell you that aiding me in this matter will ultimately be to your advantage as well as mine, perhaps that might secure your answer. Although with one so generous as your highness, no sweetener is required, I feel sure, when appealing to your better nature.

Margaret rolled onto her back, the letter pressed to her bodice. Save for passing him information lately that had prevented the regent Albany from marching his army into England, she had done little to earn his gratitude. On her side, the tally of what she owed was as long as a bishop's homily. The slate had begun when Dacre found her dead husband on the battlefield. Without his word that he had seen James's corpse, she might have believed the rumours that the king had survived and gone into hiding. Enduring the weeks after his death had been hard enough. She did not like to think what condition she would have been in had she hoped, in vain, for his return.

In the long months after Flodden, Dacre had proved a friend. Margaret had been appointed regent, but many in the council, and beyond, wanted her gone. It was not just that she was a woman, though for most that was reason enough. Their misgivings lay in the letters that passed between her and her brother Henry VIII, a busy correspondence that saw her named the Tattler. She did not care. Without James at her side, Scotland was an alarming place for a widow with young princes in her care. Henry's support and advice were a comfort. And Dacre, no doubt seeing the advantage in being the counsellor of his sovereign's sister, became her staunchest ally. She never doubted that he acted from motives of self-interest, but then so did she.

Only once did their friendship falter. Less than a year after Flodden, she had secretly married her lover, Archibald Douglas, Earl of Angus. A few weeks before, she had hinted to Dacre that Angus and she were close. His lips had thinned, and he had taken her by the elbow beyond earshot of the rest of the room. 'Bed him if ye must, milady, and no one will blame you for your needs. But marry him and you will seal your own ill fortune, and that of your country. Angus is a fool, as witless as he is pretty. He cannot make any woman happy.' He caught her raised eyebrow. 'Leastwise, ma'am, not for longer than an hour at a time.'

Nevertheless she married the earl, and swiftly regretted it. Angus's ardour dimmed before the year was out, his honeyed words growing more tart. Where once he had been content to lounge at her side, listening to her chatter while he toyed with her fingers, now he could think of nothing but who would run the country.

It was little wonder. Their marriage not only ended Margaret's regency, as they had feared, but brought Scotland under the control of her late husband's cousin John Stewart, Duke of Albany. That Albany's father had tried to usurp James III from the throne and been banished for life, and his associates executed, was conveniently forgotten, but Margaret had her suspicions of him from the start. As the years passed, he proved a presence unlike any she had encountered before. A handsome, haughty courtier, whose Scottish roots lay hidden beneath a veneer of Gallic charm, the scent of the French court was so overpowering whenever he walked into a room that he must surely have marinated himself in cologne overnight.

That a man of such elegance could be so dangerous had never surprised her. Nobody was a greater threat to his ambitions that she. But others also wanted her gone. As resentment grew among a cabal of ill-wishers, led by the Earl of Arran who sought the throne for himself, she began to fear for her life. On a night she did not now like to recall, she had been obliged to ride for the borders, seeking Dacre's protection. That was nine years ago, when a daughter was kicking in the womb, ready to make her arrival. More like bandits than royalty, Margaret and her servants had fled through the night to Harbottle, escaping before Albany and his gaolers knew she had crept out of Linlithgow Palace. Leaving her boys behind, she had taken the hill roads to safety.

It was the last she saw of her younger son. Even now, the fear that little Alexander might have thought she had abandoned him tormented her. From Harbottle, and then Morpeth Castle, where Dacre insisted she retire for comfort, she had written to her boys each week, sending gifts of candied fruits and toys. She told them about their new little sister, Meg who, she promised, would be the perfect playmate for Alexander.

Young Margaret was a strapping child who'd given her mother no worries except with her temper. But at the memory of her green-eyed boy, dying without her at his side to hold his hand, her throat tightened. James IV had not been a perfect husband, but she missed his laughter, his persuasive professions of undying love. He was obliged to say so many Hail Marys to atone for his constant straying, she marvelled he found time to attend council. Yet cruel as his infidelities were, she had learned to ignore what she did not, or ought not, observe. When he was taken from her, the unborn Alexander – her husband's parting gift – promised in some measure to make up for his loss. But within two years the adorable boy, like his father, was also gone.

Margaret tossed the letter onto the grass and closed her eyes, but even from a distance her maids saw the tears washing her powdered cheeks clean.

The following day, the castle gaoler was ushered into the dowager queen's apartment. His hair had been whipped into a tangled cloud, and his face was hot from his unaccustomed ride. The smell of straw and beer and well-worn hose entered the room with him and Margaret reached for a pomander, breathing deep before cupping it in her lap, as if she might require it urgently at any moment. The gaoler flushed and sweat pooled under his wilted ruff, deepening the scent that he exuded.

The dowager queen did not offer him a chair. Though the furniture in this room was carved from wood, the palace's silks and brocades kept for her private quarters, she could not have this begrimed man soiling her seats. Instead, she inclined her head in unsmiling welcome, and waved Dacre's letter at him.

'Keep your distance, my good man, and tell me what prisoners you have in your keep.'

'All ae them, yer majesty?' the gaoler asked. 'The castle holds a hunerd and mair.'

Margaret thought for a moment. 'Very well. Those who are not yet old, and are able-bodied.'

Rocking back on his heels, the gaoler lifted his eyes to the painted ceiling, coughed into his fist, and began to describe his charges. As he intoned his list a parade of ne'er-do-wells entered the small, stylish room, uninvited guests who made the dowager queen shiver. No wonder this man smelled so bad, keeping such company.

It seemed the castle's dungeons were brimful with killers and thieves. The hangman and executioner were kept so busy, there was a long queue for their services. Among them, she learned, there was a cut-throat who murdered scullery maids once they'd given him the key to the larder; a wet nurse who had smothered one too many of the infants in her care; a robber who bound and gagged his victims and threw them onto their own hearth fire to roast their way to the next life; and a religious maniac who believed in doing away with the pope, and would have died at the hands of the outraged folk of Leith had the military not taken him into custody for his heresy.

'And then,' the gaoler continued, warming to his task, 'there's a gang of pirates, your majesty, who're for the scaffold next month. As nasty and vicious a pack as ye've ever met. Stealing, murdering, ravishing – there's nothing they haven't turned their hands to. Happy I'd be to twist the rope round their necks mysel. I seen what they done to one poor merchant's family. Bloody beasts, they are. A shame on the good name ae Scotland.'

Margaret leaned forward. 'Tell me more about them,' she said.

CHAPTER SIX

A week or so earlier, a fleet of French ships sailed within view of the Galloway hills late in the afternoon. The day was mild and the water calm, still as a frozen pond. Marbled with the opal greens of an early autumn sea, its colours shifted and changed as currents dragged beneath its skirts. By the time the vessels had glided into the sheltered inlets that brought them far inland, night was close and mist was rising around the prows of these painted men-of-war, the blue and gold of the French court's livery catching the dying light. Weighed down with their cargo of armoured men and horses, the fleet moved slowly, each ship reaching the Gare Loch and finding its harbour as if guided by a celestial hand.

Long before they had dropped anchor, word of their arrival had licked along the Scottish coast by beacon and messenger. As they sailed into the cupped hand of this hill-bound port, the soaring masts and long-haired crew carried an echo of earlier visitors, butter-faced northerners who had once stepped ashore with swords at the ready and torches that turned the thatch of the first hovels they passed into bonfires announcing their presence.

The loch's new arrivals came not from the north but the south. There were blond heads among them, but more were dark, and none had a face of russet or whey. In the first ship, a gaunt, dark-eyed man leaned on the rails to watch as his men coiled chains around the dockside posts and lowered the narrow ramp. He was John Stewart, Duke of Albany, Scotland's temporary, reluctant and often absent ruler. French by birth, manner and allegiance, the regent spoke the language of his father's land with hesitation and distaste, as if each word were a crust that needed softening.

Dressed more for an evening's entertainment than for the gruelling march he planned into the borderlands, he wore a leather tunic over sleeves so puffed they might have been put to work as sails. On his bonnet bobbed a feather any peacock would have envied, and there was a flush high on his cheeks that, in the absence of a chafing breeze, was the only clue he was fathered by a Scot. When angered, which was often, Albany's complexion turned from rose to red and swiftly into a sunset crimson.

Now, however, the regent was in contemplative mood, and he looked out on this lonely harbour and its tipsy wooden houses with resignation. He sucked his teeth, suggesting he was already hungry for home. But for all his faults, Albany was a dutiful man, and he had never yet shirked the obligations his unwelcome regency imposed. Though he had taken on the role with Francis I's blessing – rather, indeed, at his prompting, the French king seeing how useful Scotland might prove if governed by his protégé – it was his ceaseless demands that kept the Duke shackled at Fontainebleau, or in Paris, or in charge of the French army. Slipping from Francis's grasp needed a tongue as oiled as a mackerel and persuasive as a priest, but the exhilaration of being freed from the king's grip was some compensation for the misery of his days at the cold Scottish court, at the head of a fractious, anxious, vulgar people in a country where rain and the north wind were in a constant duel.

Countless times in the past ten years he had sailed to Scotland. When the lords of the council had voted him regent in 1514, he had thought it would be a simple task to keep this diminutive land under control until the infant King James V was old enough to ascend the throne. Scotland, so soon after Flodden, was in a pitiful state, weak and woebegone after its leaders had been butchered, and worried as Henry VIII growled at their gates. All he need do, the regent initially thought, was remind Henry – a sensible man – of the advantages of maintaining good relations with his neighbour.

He had not bargained for Francis's desire to foment trouble with England, nor for James's mother Margaret, who bitterly resented being ousted as regent. Nor had he anticipated the venom of the Douglases, in the person of the Earl of Angus, Margaret's second husband, who believed his claim to power far exceeded the duke's. As the son of a man charged with treason against his brother, the Scottish king, Albany sympathised with Angus's view, though this he never betrayed. Raised among French courtiers and statesmen, where dissembling and deceit were as necessary to survive each day as bread and ale, he had learned young how to act as if entitled to a seat at the king's table, even if there was no coat of arms over the family's door, nor a sou to spare in its purse.

He had never met the cousin into whose shoes he had stepped, but his father had spoken of him until the day he died. Where he left off, Albany's mother took up the story, reciting the old litany of complaints as if they had never been aired before. Yet from what Albany had learned, Alexander was lucky to have lived to beget him. A less generous monarch than James III would have had him hunted down and executed for trying to remove him from the throne, and more than once. Instead, the old duke was banished, under sentence of death should he ever return. Had it not been for an ill-fated joust, where a splinter of spear pierced his helmet and entered his eye, he would have been allowed to grow old and objectionable in the company of his wife and her haughty kin in Auvergne. As it was, he was dead before young John could remember more of him than the roughness of his beard and the sour smell of his gloves, soaked in sweat after a hard day's hunting.

Albany lowered his gaze from the Gare Loch hills to a callus on his thumb, which he began to pick. He scowled, as if this blemish was what most worried him, rather than the ranks of enemies and naysayers he must soon face. There were as many in this country as over the border. Nor did the Scots make simple foes. They changed sides faster than a gambler turns cards.

He winced as he peeled off a sliver of skin. When, to signal an end to their quarrel some years before, the dowager queen had taken his hand, she had looked startled, and examined the rough skin with a frown. 'James's palm was the same,' she said, 'from the way he gripped the reins. He never had a light touch, always clutching as if he feared they'd slip through his fingers.' She looked up and, to his surprise, cupped his hand against her cheek, eyes closed as if she had forgotten whom she was with.

The regent was that day invited into her bedchamber, where for some months he was a frequent visitor. On that first occasion he was eager but wary, mistrusting a woman who until that meeting had appeared to wish him dead; then, when those fears were assuaged, he hoped she would not misconstrue their liaison as anything more than a dalliance. He was soon to realise that Margaret was the one in control, in this and all her relationships. Passionate and abandoned she might at times be, but there was iron in her soul. Mercury too, he guessed, given her shifting moods and grievances. Albany found her quixotic, unfathomable and fascinating – family traits, if one were to believe what they said of her brother, the English king. Their soft conversations, cocooned in her canopied bed, would have beguiled him utterly had he not remembered the other Margaret, the woman he had met on his first arrival at Holyrood Palace, whose eyes had narrowed at the sight of him.

On the day the court gathered to welcome their new ruler, he bowed, and she curtseyed with a sarcastic flourish. Courtiers and council looked on, eyes shifting from one player to the other. The hall took on the air of a cockpit when the crowd is waiting for the spurs to be removed. While the privy councillors appeared cordial – some preening with delight at his appearance – Margaret's head was held high, her netted coif quivering with pearls. At her side was her husband, Archibald Douglas, Earl of Angus. Striking in a tunic of gold and green, his legs were like stalks of ripe wheat. His smile held no warmth, and although the earl would have offered no serious challenge to the duke had they met in combat, the regent was not accustomed to such naked loathing, and his colour rose.

'Your grace,' said Margaret, before Albany could speak, 'you honour us with your presence, come all the way from France, in such style. It is your first visit to this land, I am told. How extraordinary! Yet Scotland looks forward to making your acquaintance.' She turned to face the court, her fury encompassing everyone in the hall. 'As you will appreciate, it is not easy for me to meet my usurper, nor to tolerate the disloyalty of those in this room who unseated me.' Her voice began to rise, and she pressed her hands on her bodice, steadying herself. 'My beloved late husband James designated me regent should he die. That his court saw fit to overturn his wishes and have me stripped of office is not merely a humiliation for me, but dishonour to his name. Those who have played a part in this deed ought never sleep easy again.'

A muttering was heard from among the courtiers, and heels rasped on the flagstones.

'Queen Margaret,' said Albany, appalled to see her wipe away a tear, 'no one meant you any ill-will. Surely one in your position must recognise better than most that my appointment is expedient, not treacherous.' He looked at the Earl of Angus, who stared at a point above the regent's head as if measuring the beam. 'Had you not remarried,' he continued, 'you would have retained the role until young James's accession.'

'So you say,' sniffed Margaret, 'but I have reason to doubt that.' She raised a hand to silence his reply. 'Enough. I am not one to hold a grudge. I leave it to our holy father in heaven to weigh the scales and settle scores in the next life if not in this. Meanwhile, I ought to warn you that you will find this country very different from your homeland. It will take years to learn her ways.'

Her glance took in Albany's fur-lined cloak and Italian boots, the earring tickling his collar, and her words were heavy with contempt. 'And yet I hear you are not planning a long visit. Such a pity. There is so much work for one in your role, it is difficult to understand how it could be done from France. Scotland cannot be governed from afar, you know. When trouble arises here, it spreads fast. That you will very quickly discover.'

Before he could respond she turned and left the hall, her stiff gown swaying like a tolling bell, her husband at her heels. A burst of brittle laughter came from the passageway as the door closed behind them, but whether it was from Margaret or Angus the regent could not tell.

Once she was gone the Scottish court gathered around him, clucking with excitement, and keen to sound him out on more subjects than could be discussed in a year. After an hour, when it was evident even to the clansmen from the western isles that Albany was flagging, an equerry led him to his rooms, where a table was laid with wine and biscuits. 'You will wish to rest, your grace,' said the servant. 'Dinner will commence in the great hall at the hour of four. Until then I will see you are not disturbed.'

Albany grunted and sat heavily on his bed, listening to the man's steps disappear down the stairs, and wondering how much influence the dowager queen still held at court.

It was not to find an answer to this question that he took the young king out of her care, but in so doing he understood his position at last. Margaret had allies, some of them powerful, but even they did not contest his right to remove James from his mother, for the security of the realm.

When she heard of his edict, he later learned, Margaret put a hand to her throat and fainted. On coming to her senses she had a fit of hysterics, which frightened her almost as much as her maidservants. 'Poppet, I beg you, be calm,' implored her husband, chafing her hands, which she snatched away. Propped against the wall of her chambers in Stirling Castle, she looked blindly ahead, as if Angus were not in the room. He crouched by her side, reminding her that the regent would allow her to see her child regularly. In time he might be permitted to stay with her for a night or two. Things could have been worse, he continued: Albany might have carried James off to France. His words finally reached her, for her breathing calmed, she looked him in the eye, and then a slap rang out.

'Get from my sight!' she cried. 'A night or two? What good is that to me? I cannot live without him. No mother could. I will surely die of grief.' Her howls resumed, bringing maids to her side. The earl stared at the flurry of aprons and skirts and caps around his wife, then left the room, pale with rage except where a stinging palm print glowed upon his cheek. No one dared tell the queen that the boy king was waiting downstairs, ready to be escorted off under the regent's guard. That was to be a farewell none would ever forget.

CHAPTER SEVEN

The distressing scene that day merely confirmed what Margaret and the earl had long known: they could not bear each other's presence. The years that followed saw the dowager queen's dislike of her husband turn to hatred while Angus, for his part, realised that his scheme to topple the regent and take his place would have to be achieved not only without her help, but despite her opposition.

As Angus's appetite for power grew, Margaret came to recognise that the regent was not the rival she had presumed, and might even be useful as an ally against her conniving spouse. That the Frenchman had no desire to reshape the court, or carve out a fortune for himself, was soon plain. He made no secret of the fact that he saw his position coming to an end once James was old enough to rule. There was an endearingly businesslike manner about him, and his offer to help her reach a settlement for divorce allayed the last of her doubts. Albany never knew if it was this promise that sparked the queen's lust, but it did not matter. He was grateful for the comfort it brought to his cheerless time in a country he was beginning to detest.

In gaining Margaret's trust, Albany became privy to court gossip, of which there was no end. But as well as scurrilous tales of the country's aristocrats, priests and gentry, she had stories of her own to reveal. As if to underline how temporary an arrangement theirs was, she would tease him with tales of former lovers, unlocking the strongbox beneath her bed and showing him their gifts and tokens of devotion. There were letters too, she boasted, though they were too private to be shared.

Long after, when their romance had all but ended, it was Margaret's response to a letter from her brother Henry that led Albany to suspect the author of those treasured missives. Like the regent, the dowager queen had not been present at Holyrood when the privy council granted a hearing to the English envoys Baron Dacre and the Earl of Surrey. Given safe passage and escort from the border, the pair arrived in Edinburgh in subdued but hopeful mood in the spring of 1523. War had been rumbling since the previous year, but with Albany out of the country, and Margaret in Stirling, Henry's delegates felt their petition would be well received and hostilities soon at an end.

Dacre was well known to the privy councillors, and respected by some, who found in him an echo of the old English king and a more courteous age. There were nods around the table as he rose to deliver the contents of the document he held in his hand. Surrey elicited no such friendly looks.

'Your lords, for the purposes of speed I shall take the liberty of paraphrasing,' said Dacre, with a half-smile, looking around the room like a dominie about to deliver a lesson. 'The earl and I are here to put before you a proposal from his royal majesty, Henry VIII. We hope that you will give it careful thought, for there are those at his court who would prefer a less amicable arrangement.'

Ignoring the muttering that arose, he cleared his throat. 'It is Henry's dearest wish that the Scottish court promise that one day, in the fullness of time, it shall agree to the marriage of King James V to his daughter Mary – and here I quote: "for the keeping of gentle relations between our kingdoms, that harmony matched by the felicity and joy a contented marital union of likeminded parties always brings".'

Dacre allowed the sanctimonious words to settle over the low-beamed chamber. 'He further adds that the strife that afflicts our countries would thereby come to an end, and our energies be put to better use at home and on the continent, where both nations will earn glory, and territory, as yet unthought of.' He placed the parchment on the table, smoothing it flat. 'That, gentlemen, is the essence of his majesty's proposal. There remains only one other element, which it is painful for me to divulge in this company, some of whom I believe are bound in more than ordinary allegiance to the Duke of Albany.'

A murmur ran round the table, and quickly died.

'My lords, Henry makes this offer on the condition that your regent is deposed, and never returns to this country, with immediate effect on the signing of this agreement. If the privy council agrees to these terms, then Henry will guarantee a sixteen-year truce, and an end to a war which plagues us all.'

Amid a clamour of indignation Surrey rapped the table, and stood. The sullen silence he commanded did not bode well. He spoke briskly. 'It is no secret at our court that the regent is not a man well loved, either by the people or its leaders.'

'Contemptible! Unfair!' cried Alexander Montgomerie, Earl of Eglinton, getting to his feet. The councillors alongside tugged him back onto his stool, urging him to hush.

Surrey pushed the parchment across the table so it could be read by all. 'You would be foolish indeed to disregard this offer. It will not be repeated, nor will you ever be given such an opportunity to solve all your country's problems so simply. At a stroke you could be rid of Albany, and of the fear that Henry's army will march north and finish what he began at Flodden.'

There was an intake of breath across the room. Surrey appeared not to notice, though his and Dacre's hands remained loosely at their sides, within reach of their swords.

'You have astonishing nerve, to bring such a suggestion before us,' said the Earl of Hamilton, soft-voiced with fury.

'We do not intend to insult anyone, and we are sorry if it is construed as such.' Surrey looked at Dacre, who nodded. 'We will leave your presence, and await your decision in the chamber below.'

Eglinton saw them to the door, which he slammed behind them, small consolation for not being allowed to whip them for insolence. Back at the table, he vented his frustration, spittle flying. 'It is an abominable offer, as cynical and calculating as I have yet to hear from that devious English warmonger's lips.'

Arran leaned forward, his broken nose like a scold's finger. 'It is a ruse on Henry's part, and nothing more. The minute the pair are known to be betrothed, England will be safe, knowing Francis's men cannot use us as a back door for invasion. This trumped-up notion is merely a means to defuse the threat from France. If we were to eject Albany on Henry's command, he and the French king would never forgive us. We would have got into bed with our oldest enemy, and lost one of our most powerful friends.'

A growl of agreement drew the council closer, hands slapping the table, and much more in the same vein followed. Only one voice was raised in dissent. It was David Forsyth, the Earl of Angus's cousin, who could think of no better stroke of luck than to see Albany sent packing, without so much as unsheathing a sword.

'We are too hasty,' he protested, 'dismissing the offer out of hand. This war is costing us far more than England. There has not been real peace in the borderlands in our lifetime. Such a deal would bring that misery to an end.'

He raised his voice to shout down his decriers. 'There's more, too, to consider. Hear me out. Albany's visits are too rare, and short. He has never made this his home. All the world knows we are a country without a king, as Henry's offer makes clear. We can take offence if we like, but it does not change the truth, which is that Albany's rule is close to an end, and he knows it as well as we do.'

Downstairs, where they sat hunched before a salt-coal fire, Dacre and Surrey heard argument and scraping stools overhead. The earl shook his head, and began to denounce this vexatious nation, which allowed festering sores to cloud its judgement. What sensible country would not leap at the offer of peace and prosperity? Did their old connection with France really mean more than to have the beast on their border tamed?

Dacre watched a blue flame flower in the grate. 'We will learn their answer soon enough,' was all he said, though his silence did nothing to staunch Surrey's complaints.

The reply came so quickly, they knew at once the offer was dead. Less than an hour later, Eglinton and Hamilton appeared to tell them the council's decision, but before Hamilton spoke Surrey was already pulling on his gauntlets.

'Henry will be disappointed,' he said, when his guess was confirmed. 'It was a deal offered in good faith and deserved more consideration than your councillors gave it. I doubt you appreciate, perhaps, how serious the outcome of this refusal might be.'

Eglinton's face darkened with the effort to restrain himself from putting his hands round the earl's throat. Instead, he threw the door open and called a servant to take the Englishmen to their quarters.

Surrey picked up his cloak and followed Dacre out of the room. As he passed, Hamilton put a hand on his arm. 'You should watch what you say, your grace. Our people do not like being threatened. We may be a small country, and poor, but we are also proud.'

The earl would have spoken, but meeting the expression in the Scot's eye he closed his mouth. Hamilton gave an amicable nod, and as he ushered them along the passage his tone lightened. 'We shall dine together tonight and put this disagreement aside. In the morning I will have the council's written reply ready for you. It may not be what Henry had hoped for, but it will not be the first knock he has had from this quarter.'

'That suits me fine,' Dacre replied, sounding weary. 'It is too long since I spent a night in this palace. It brings memories of the dead king that I had thought forgotten. He was a man of honour, and intellect, and charm. He is a sad loss to this kingdom, a fact you must still be painfully aware of, and never more than now.'

Not waiting for a reply, he called over his shoulder to Eglinton, who had not yet spoken. 'I will be given my old room, I trust? James always had it prepared for me. Our guards can sleep on the floor. I would prefer to keep them close.'

It was some days before Albany, in Paris, was informed by courier of this delegation from Henry's court, and weeks before Montgomerie described it to him in person, his anger almost as hot in recollection as it had been when he first believed himself insulted. When eventually the regent recounted the scene to Margaret, thinking it would amuse her, she stared, as if he had spoken in Persian and she could not understand what she heard. 'What?' she cried, leaping up, and sending her stool toppling. 'Dacre was privy to this plan? I was told Surrey had brought the message. But Dacre?' She laughed in disbelief. 'He thought it possible that I would bind James to the English court, as if he were an ass to be ridden round the fairground? I thought he had a fondness for the boy, indeed I did. He used to say Jamie was almost like a godson. There were times I even felt . . .'

Breaking off, she turned away to gain command of herself, but in that moment her lover began to suspect that the baron and she were better acquainted than was wise, and had been for many years.

It surprised no one that after the Scots' rejection of the marriage treaty, the English king's temper quickened. That summer the war gathered pace, Henry launching a sustained campaign of harrying, provoking and destroying the main Scottish towns and castles on the border. One by one he was picking them off, leaving the region in ruins. There was no mistaking his message. He was ettling for a fight. Goaded into action, Albany had returned to meet him, with five thousand French troops at his side.

The Duke lifted his eyes once more to the empty hills around the loch, and was grateful to have been brought up among men who believed wilderness existed solely for the pleasure of the chase. When the hunting season was over, and the woods were daubed with the blood of deer, bears and boar, Francis and his retinue returned to the sanctuary of city and palace, putting on their softest boots and sumptuous rings with ill-disguised relief. Between then and the next expedition, only plague or pestilence could drive them back out to the countryside, with its bad roads and robbers, its comfortless inns and ill-kempt servants.

No surprise, then, that Scotland was too rough for his taste. Even Edinburgh was little more than a town, hills and woods oppressively close. Nowhere in this land could one feel safe from the threat of sudden attack. Nor, he had learned, could its men be persuaded to fight. Their backbone had crumbled, and they were now as nervous as cats.

He still smarted from his humiliation, a year or more ago, when his army had refused to follow him into England. So enraged he could barely speak, the duke had demanded to know what his officers meant by ignoring his orders, by instructing their men to stand fast and not set a foot over the border. A few heads were bowed in shame, but those who were intimidated by Henry VIII's wrath but not their regent's looked at him straight. 'We know what happens to those who cross the border, and poke the hornet's nest,' said Lennox, an earl before his time, and still unnerved by his father's battlefield death. 'You go ahead, but don't expect us to follow. We've suffered enough at England's hands. It's likely you wouldn't even be in the country when he took his full revenge, but we have nowhere else to go.'

Mortified at being thwarted, and determined it would not happen again, this time the regent had brought his own army. If his horsemen could not encourage the Scottish runts to forget their fright, he had done all he could. There were few more skilled or courageous soldiers than his battle-hardened troops, and Scotland was fortunate to have them on their side. Taking a deep breath and fastening his jerkin, he left the ship's rail. He had little doubt that this time he could lead this benighted country to victory in the English borders, and broker a longed-for truce.

Descending the ramp, the duke made for the nearest tavern. His servants had run ahead, and by the time he reached the door clean straw had been strewn on the earthen floor, a sow shooed from beneath a table, and the alewife's apron turned back to front, to hide the worst of its stains.

None but the duke's entourage was allowed to leave ship. It was too late to begin their march, and for the rest of his men a stifling night below deck lay ahead. While the duke and his courtiers slept fitfully on the tavern's tick-ridden sheets, the soldiers were even more restless. Beneath their cramped quarters, in the bowels of the ships, their horses fretted at the airless dark. Shortly after dawn, when the bulkhead ramps were lowered and the beasts led into the light, they pranced in delight, shaking and tossing their heads to create a flurry of flying manes, wild as a quickening sea.

By early morning, the army was on its way, winding south to the borders. As the monotonous tread of hooves gathered pace, so did the regent's hopes. He lifted his gaze to the brightening day. It would not be long before they reached Jedburgh, where he would make camp.

No town was better placed to set a guard on the border, or launch an attack on Henry's henchmen. He nodded, his serious expression easing. It might be that all his past troubles would conspire to help him. The English Warden General and his men believed the Scots too timid to fight. They would neither expect nor be prepared for the assault the regent was about to unleash upon them. The duke's face grew sombre once more as he dug in his spurs and raced ahead, eager to hasten that encounter.

CHAPTER EIGHT

27 September 1523

In Crozier's private chamber, deep in the night, a dog slept by the pinewood fire. A large, long-limbed beast, his grey coat was thick as a pelt. With his blue eyes and hungry teeth he looked more like one of the wolves that roamed the forest than the offspring of the mistress's mongrel, and Louise often wondered who had sired him. Only in his gentleness was he like the little vixen whom, years after her death, Louise still missed.

Low voices disturbed the dog's sleep, and he covered his eyes with a paw. Near the fireside Louise was helping her husband out of his travel-stained cloak. On Crozier's face was the look of a man who is wiping his mind clear of what he has seen. It was always like this, when he came back. The cold-eyed fighter who returned from his expeditions bloodied and exhausted, was transformed as soon as he saw his wife. While she helped him out of his riding gear, setting aside his swords and knives, his steel helmet and silver horn, he would close his eyes and take a slow breath. At her voice, the uproar in his head quietened. It was for her and his home that he lived like this. Were Louise not here at the day's end, he feared he would ride away from the keep and his people and lose himself forever in the hills. The torments of living on the border were not to his taste. He was a farmer not a soldier, yet that was what he had become.

'I was so afraid,' Louise said quietly, as if to match the hush of the forest that pressed at their windows. 'After what happened at Dryburgh and Melrose and Kelso, it seemed you could not get away unscathed yet again. I had the most terrible dreams.'

'But I am here, and all is well,' Crozier replied, and it was fatigue that made his voice little more than a sigh. They sank, clothed, onto the bed. With an arm around Louise, Crozier watched firelight play on the rafters, but the homely sight made him frown.

'The flames devoured Jedburgh,' he said, 'like it was kindling.' He shook his head, but the images would not fade. 'Dacre's men came for it, just as they did Kelso and all the others. They were well prepared, and offered no mercy. No mercy at all.'

Louise sat up. 'What happened?'

'Best you don't hear all of it. You can guess what it was like. There were archers and swordsmen in the streets, fires lit under every thatch and shack. Children cut down, and old folk speared. Even dogs were thrown onto the flames.' He passed a hand over his eyes. 'We fought them off hard, but in the end they were stronger.'

'What then?' asked Louise, catching the note of a story half finished.

'I killed Dacre's horses.' Crozier's face was harsh. 'We crept up on Dacre's army, and herded their horses over the cliffs. It was cruel, but it had to be done. Dacre is destroying our lands, butchering our people, and he cannot go unpunished. If nothing else, the brute now knows he cannot attack the border and get away with it. He's not just lost a thousand horses, but he has been made to look a fool.'

'Not just cruel, but also dangerous,' Louise replied, thinking of the forces he had unleashed that might soon be heading their way. Too vividly she remembered what had happened when the baron had sent his men to raze the keep and kill them all, shortly after Flodden. That time, Dacre had been too cocksure to take on the task himself. The courage of Crozier and Tom in fighting off the warden's troops had become legend in these parts. The borderer had nearly died in the attempt, and Louise still woke shuddering from nightmares replaying the days when it had seemed he would not live.

'Will he know it was you who did it?' she asked, unable to hide her terror.

Crozier gave a shaky laugh. 'If he thought so, it would be nothing but a guess. It could have been any of us, not just from this march but further afield too. Some who joined us came from as far off as the Firth of Forth and the Clyde. They'd heard what had happened at Kelso, and wanted to drive Dacre back.'

Louise lay with her head on his shoulder. By the hearth, the wolf slept at last. Beyond the shutters an early blackbird called, mistaking the torchlit courtyard and its bustling men for daybreak.

'You could be right,' Crozier conceded. 'Maybe I have provoked him.' Unconsciously he touched his side where the scar from that old fight ran round his belly, a gunpowder fuse that still burned. 'But I will be ready for him.' He gripped her arm, as if to be sure she was listening. 'Lou, the time has come to set things straight between him and me.'

She nodded, understanding, as she always had, the bleak code of the borders. Death was not the worst thing that could happen. Preserving dignity and honour mattered far more. After his encounter with Ethan Elliot the past had caught up with them, as she had always known it would. Now they would have to face it.

In the grainy firelight her husband looked weary. Since war with England had resumed, the keep's men and their allies had been riding far across the border, inflicting as much damage on English villages, crops and cattle as had been done to theirs. But there had been an edge to Crozier's mood these past few months, a hunger for action that these excursions did not explain. At last she understood.

She sighed, and he put his hand over hers. 'I couldn't bear it any longer,' he said, as if it were a confession. 'Dacre's been acting these past twenty years like he was the Lord God Almighty and we nothing more than ants beneath his feet. Thinking how to destroy him keeps me awake at night. I owe it not just to my father, Lou, but to us – you, me, and the clan.' He sighed. 'And it was the last promise I made to Ma. She died easier at the thought.'

Few things had made Mother Crozier joyful in her final years, but the prospect of avenging her husband's murder would have sent her into the next life with her lips curled in a smile. Louise nodded, acknowledging the power of that deathbed vow. The old woman had been thrawn, but she missed her barbed wit and flinty charity more than she mourned her own mother, who had died the same year.

'Then let me help,' she said. 'Since the day you met Ethan Elliot, I have been thinking. There might be another way to take revenge, better than pitting your men against the baron.' She pulled the bearskin over them. 'Rest for a while, and in the morning we will be able think more clearly.' There was no answer. Her husband's breath rose and fell, and he was already asleep. Louise watched daylight arrive, and birdsong with it, until she too eventually slept.

That morning, Crozier's Keep rose from a forest of trees fired red and gold in the rising sun. Lapped by leaves, it stood at the head of a high valley, where all comers could be seen on the treeless hills below. Home to Crozier and Louise, her brother, his wife and their brood, Crozier's grandfather, several cousins and a pack of servants whose tongues were never still, it was more fortress than house. Built for protection not comfort, it was a warren of rooms and passageways whose icy chill turned feet and fingers numb.

Since Crozier's return, long before dawn, the courtyard had been alive, men ordering their gear, stable boys forking fresh hay into each stall. From the stable door, Hob watched Louise and Crozier disappear into the trees, the mistress's quick steps barely keeping pace with her husband's long stride. Their heads were bowed, and they were talking. The young groom frowned. He could see trouble in their gait. Picking up a soft brush, he turned to Crozier's mare, sweeping her flanks until she gleamed like copper. That at least would please the master when he returned.

Seated on a throne of rock close to the waterfall, the couple watched the river's headlong rush, and were calmed. For a moment, the threat that hung over them was forgotten, the ageless beauty of this wild land dampening their fears. When at last they began to talk, their words were almost lost beneath the water's roar, so fierce a torrent its mist thickened the air.

As the morning brightened, Louise laid out her ideas. Crozier listened, and slowly his expression changed. He sat straighter, and began to nod. He glanced sidelong at his wife. Wisps of hair had escaped their golden net and were shivering in the breeze, but there was a steel and resolve in her cat-like face that startled him. When it was clear she was as keen to bring about Dacre's downfall as he, a dark smile lit his face.

He had never doubted her loyalty to the clan, even in the first days of their marriage, when she was new to the borderlands as well as to him. At first, she had been timid when suggesting ways the keep and its affairs could be better run, its men put to the best use. She feared offending her husband, but instead she made him shake his head in wonder that she could solve problems he had not even noticed. 'She's got an auld head on her,' his mother said, warming to her son's wife, to the surprise of all.

From their first months together, Crozier and Louise worked in harness, effortlessly in step. Crozier took few decisions without her approval, and while she rarely disagreed with his ideas, he often sought her advice. Thus, this morning, as she told him her plan to outwit Dacre, he did not dismiss it, as most men would, as being not only dangerous but impossible. Her confidence that this might work gave him a glimmer of faith. As in all belief, doubt played as large a part as certainty, but like all belief, rational or not, one could not live without it.

'You are lord of this land, and leader of all Teviotdale,' she said, staring across the river to the birches that clung to the lip of the ravine. 'You have spent years earning that position, yet each month you ride out like a common reiver to maintain your place, and this land. What does a man like Dacre do? He fights, of course, because he is at heart a thug. But he owes his position not to his sword but to his wits. His success lies with his friends and allies, with those whose support he can get by bribing, buying, or bullying. The man has a honeyed tongue and a weaselly brain, and a conscience that's gagged and bound. All this has brought him more friends and riches than anyone else in the north. Not even the King of England can match the allegiance he commands in these parts.'

Crozier frowned, unsure where this was leading.

'It seems to me,' she continued, 'that you should not place all your assurance in your sword, but try to use your influence instead. If you could gain the confidence of those who can do Dacre far more harm by dropping a word into the king's ear than you could with all your men hammering at his door, then the task would be easier.'

Crozier gave a laugh. 'And how do I do that, reiver that I am?'

Louise plucked a long grass, and began to strip it of seeds. 'You are a man of good breeding, and education. Though you call yourself a farmer, you are one of the most powerful and respected men this side of the border.' She put a hand on his sleeve. 'Dacre has the advantage, with his wealth, and the troops he can summon, and his voice at court, but he has grown complacent and lax. Fat too, I believe. You told me yourself that the gentlemen of the marches hate him, that the Percys loathe his being warden of the east, with authority to make them do his bidding. The Ridleys, the Redpaths, and the Carrs all have grievances, as do many others. And even his friends know he is corrupt.'

She stripped another grass, fingers worrying while her mind raced. 'The men in Dacre's pay are thieves and killers, who raid and rape and burn, right across the border. Yet when they have their day in court, they always walk out free men. When did you last hear of an Armstrong on a gibbet? Or in a gaol for more than a week? The fines imposed on them, when they do reach the dock, are as nothing to the money they have stored up for themselves, in league with Dacre. And it's not just the Armstrongs. Half of the western marches, on both sides of the border, are in his purse.'

Crozier stared at the waterfall. 'If the Scottish court knew the truth of it,' he said, 'they would send their army to crush them all, Scots and English alike. They have no idea of what goes on out here. Nor, most likely, does King Henry.'

Louise nodded. 'You'd think these parts were invisible. Perhaps for that reason, Dacre has been allowed too free a hand. But we can make use of that fact. He's going too far. He's taking liberties, risks, acting as if he's above the law. And we are not alone in having reason to hate him, my love. Many people want Dacre gone. I've heard even the Bishop of Durham is growing suspicious, though knowing how well the baron stands with the king, he says nothing.'

Hesitating, she swept seeds from her skirts. 'What you need to do is risky. But,' she continued, as if to reassure herself, 'not anywhere near as dangerous as tackling him in the open and on your own.'

'Out with it,' Crozier said. 'Tell me what you are thinking.'

Louise paused. Her concern was clear as she held his gaze, before dropping her own. 'It might be too dangerous. And yet the more I have thought on it, the more I have come to believe that audacity is what's required. You need to surprise him. And to do that, you must not act alone. You need to be part of an alliance, of men he would never suspect of trying to do him harm. Gain the ear and the trust of his enemies and the job will be half done. They're too scared to confront him alone. Who would have the courage to speak to the king or his counsellors without knowing they have allies to back them up? A single plaintiff risks not only Henry's rough justice, but Dacre's immediate revenge.'

She gazed across the forest to the mid-morning sky, where a lazy buzzard circled. 'Out here, he can kill whoever he likes. Nobody would ever find the body, let alone the culprit. But if you can bring his naysayers together, if you can make them realise that there is strength and safety in numbers, then you have a chance. The king will be obliged to take heed of what men such as those tell him, when they are all agreed. If he were to ignore them, he knows the north could revolt.'

'So I act as the messenger boy,' Crozier said.

'No. Negotiator and nemesis.' Her reply was so grim, he felt a chill creep up his spine. She knew as well as he that what she was proposing might prove fatal.

'There's only one flaw,' he said slowly. 'Dacre's enemies are also mine.'

'You might think that,' she answered, taking his arm, 'but you would be wrong.'

That evening the hall of Crozier's Keep lay shadowed in smoky light. Crooked candles glowed on the long deal table, the fire leapt high in its hearth, and tallow lamps flickered from their niches in the walls. Cast in pewter gloom, the group around the table looked like the Last Supper redrawn for a cold country: disciples wrapped in badger skins and plaid, the table empty but for a quantity of drink even Christ at Cana could not have conjured.

Crozier sat at the top, kestrel on his wrist, and men on either side. Louise was placed at the foot, though her husband looked to her so often she might have been the head of the clan and he merely her consort. Feeding the hawk a scrap and sending it back to its perch on the wall, Crozier called everyone to attention. Jugs and tumblers were put down, conversations cut off, some of the men glancing at Louise, hoping her face would hold a clue of what was to come.

'Gentlemen, cousins, brothers.' The borderer rapped the table with his dagger's hilt, waiting for the hall to quieten. When all were listening he outlined the plot, while the clan nodded gravely as their interest mounted.

'We need to know which knights on the English border we can persuade to our cause,' he told them. 'Even those who want Dacre dead will be suspicious of a man like me: neither noble nor at the Scottish court, and famous for raiding their countrymen. For those reasons alone, many will be beyond our reach. I'd not even get over the door. Some, most likely, would run straight to the baron, loathe him though they do, to win favour for flushing his enemy, and have us dead within the week.'

'It is delicate,' said Old Crozier, from his seat at his grandson's side. Stooped, dry-boned, his scalp liver-spotted beneath a fog of white hair, he retained most of his wits, though he had already been head of the clan when he met the messenger bringing news of James III's accession, more than sixty years before.

'That is one word,' Adam replied. 'Another would be hazardous. In taking this road, I may bring Dacre down upon us faster than we have bargained for. I ask your assent before I make a move.'

Fists thumped the table. 'Let me get my hauns on the bastard,' said Wat the Wanderer, wetting his beard with a long swig of ale, as if this draught was a promise, sealed with a kiss.

'Ye'll be lucky tae get that close,' said Benoit Brenier, Louise's brother, who had learned the language as a young boy new from France, and was now more Scottish than any in the dale. 'He'd send his lackeys out first to cut down the common ranks, before gracing us wi' his presence. He'll no waste himsel on small beer. He'll haud ontae his self respect and only face the top man, once the coast is clear of the likes of us.'

'Cumberland scum,' growled Murdo Montgomery, Crozier's cousin, setting off a muttering around the table.

'Aye, well, scum these English lords may be,' said Crozier, hushing the noise with a raised hand, as if about to bless the gathering, 'but it's them we need on our side if this plan is to work.' The querulous murmur resumed, but he quashed it with a look.

'You could start with the Lord Ogle,' said a quiet voice. Tom Crozier stared around the table. Even in this subdued light the old knife slash on his cheek was plain, but his lively eye and good-humoured mouth softened the scar. Where Crozier was clipped of speech, Tom was wanton with words. A warmer man than his brother, he had a wild temper, though years of struggle had curbed it. There were many, indeed, unnerved by Adam's cool demeanour and his unerring ear for lies, who preferred to deal with Tom. But as Louise knew well, Tom's bonhomie could be his undoing, and theirs too, if unchecked.

Now he had their attention, Tom raised his voice. 'The Lord Ogle of Bothal is an honest man. True to the king, a fine fighter – he can muster a hundred horsemen – and loyal to the tacks on his boots. But he's no tale-teller. If you had his word on oath condemning Dacre, that would count for something.'

More names followed, from all round the table, knights and gentlemen and farmers who lived within a day or two's ride of the border, and owed the king ten, twenty, two hundred men in times of war: Sir Roger Grey, Sir Edward Ellarcar, Thomas Hebborn, Rauf Ilderton . . .

At the last name, Crozier snorted. 'Ilderton is gone to the bad. Does not pay his debts, has enough mistresses to fill a nunnery, and will promise aught to all to pay for another night's drink. His house is falling to pieces, his stables are almost empty, and his men lie around the village as debauched as their lord.' His eyes glittered. 'A more dangerous, useless ally one could not find on either side of the border.'

His wife had cocked her head and was looking at him, curious as a hen at a flea. 'Yes?' said Crozier.

She tucked her hands into her sleeves. 'Surely so venal a lord might serve our own ends, without even being aware he was being useful?'

'How, precisely?' Tom asked, before Crozier could speak.

'His drinking companions will no doubt hear a thing or two, if the right questions are asked, don't you think?' Louise smiled. 'They'd need a good head for barley, of course.'

Benoit began to smile too, the anticipation of dangerous pleasure spreading across his pockmarked face. 'I'm the man for that,' he said.

A laugh ran round the hall. Benoit's growing girth was a matter of pride. His wife Ella was so often with child, some whispered he was trying to compete. He ignored their jibes, and drank on. Only when his paunch threatened to come between him and his carpenter's table would he cut down on his beer, he told Ella, who would shake her head, pat his belly, and walk off with an infant hitched onto her hip.

Crozier cut across the merriment. 'You will do nothing unless I tell you. The man's a wastrel, with a viper's bite. Our venture will be perilous enough without courting the enemy. Ilderton might be a drunk, but he is wilier, and nastier, than you know. We would have to be desperate to risk delivering ourselves into his hands. And we're not in that position yet.'

The evening unfolded, and with it the clan's ideas. Conversation spiralled, excitement mounted, terrors began to recede. It was agreed that Crozier would make his first overture to the Lord Ogle, fourteen miles over the border in Redesdale, and take Tom with him. Thereafter events would be shaped by circumstance. 'Let's drink to that,' said the borderer, raising his tankard and draining it in a gulp.

By midnight, only Old Crozier and Louise were sober. As she helped him to his room, a hand under his chicken-bone arm, she heard him mumbling. She leaned closer. 'It is dangerous,' he was saying, 'very, very dangerous.' When she left him at his door, he gave her a sweet smile, but already his mind had wandered. Confused though he often was, in his clouded eyes she detected fear. In this at least he was still in his right mind.

CHAPTER NINE

8 October 1523

It was a soft autumn day when Oliver Barton rode out of Edinburgh and made for the Lammermuir hills. Rising from a sea of mist, the sun hung over the firth, golden and sweet. Barton tipped the brim of his hat to shield his pale blue eyes. More used to a ship than a saddle he rode stiffly, his horse prancing at his leaden seat, jibbing at the rough hand on the bit. The sailor responded in kind. Digging in his spurs, he drew a beading of blood on the piebald's belly. By the time they had put the city behind them and were heading south, they understood each other. The next morning, when Barton approached the roadside inn's stable and called for a horse, the animal reared its head, and stamped. An ostler led a bay into the yard, but for the rest of the day the piebald was alert for his rider's return. Only at nightfall, when it was clear he was gone, did he finally grow calm.

Barton rode on into the borders, rarely raising his head. He made his way slowly, though an observer would have guessed from the look in his eye that this was no idle excursion. Every few miles he would pull up his horse and scan the hills, his distaste plain at the prospect of so much dry land still to cross. Yet even that did not quicken his pace, and he had been five nights on the road before he came within sight of Swinburn, which lay at the foot of Crozier's valley.

In late afternoon, woodsmoke swirled around the village roofs, fires freshly stoked for the night-time chill. It was an unkempt place, its cottages and hovels warped with age, their timbers arthritic and cracked. As Barton's horse clipped down the street, a baker was smooring his oven, keeping the embers warm for his midnight doughs. He looked up as the window darkened, but the traveller had almost passed, swaddled in cloak and hat.

In the horse's wake, a goat nosed in the gutter, hens pecking by its side. A herdsman whistled his way down the street, cattle and sheep safely byred, mind empty of anything but the prospect of broth. Shuttering his shopfront, a shoemaker was about to settle down by his fire to stitch a pair of new boots when the rider approached. Barton jerked the reins, and came to a halt. The horse snorted, but neither man spoke. Strangers were not uncommon in the village, but they were not welcome. One such as this, whose face was tight as a miser's fist, was doubly disliked.

Barton's eyes narrowed, and he looked off, beyond Swinburn, to where the forested valley began. 'Crozier's Keep up there?' he asked, inclining his head towards the trees. The shoemaker nodded, and made for his door. 'Don't look so feart,' the sailor said. 'I am his cousin. I mean him no harm.'

'You're no like any Crozier I ever met,' said the shoemaker. 'They'd never be seen on a nag like that.'

Barton gathered the reins. 'Thank'ee all the same.' He touched a mocking finger to his hat, and continued on his way down the street, the gathering dusk closing in behind him.

Hob was first to meet the visitor. Leading a fretful young mare back from the meadow where she had lost a shoe, he reached the woods that circled the keep, and saw Barton ahead of him, a swaying shape on a weary horse whose hollow back and short neck suggested she was a posting inn's cheapest hire.

'Hallo there,' he cried, hurrying to catch up. The traveller turned, but did not stop. Hob jogged to come alongside, his red hood falling back to reveal a narrow face, and such a quantity of fair hair it was as if a bowl of syllabub had been tipped over his head. Tall and slender, the keep's head groom retained some of his boyhood charm, his eyes wide and friendly. But he was no fool, and he mistrusted the man before him. 'Where you headed, man?' he asked.

'Crozier's Keep,' Barton replied, moving a wad of dried beef to the other cheek.

'On what business?'

'That's for Crozier's ears, no yours, lad.' Barton kicked his horse on, and Hob was obliged to fall back. Some minutes later he and the limping mare caught up, Barton having reached the gatehouse and its suspicious guards.

With a backward look at the stranger, who returned his stare with a yawn, Hob led the mare into the keep. The guards were calling for Crozier, leaving Barton to warm his hands at the brazier that lit the gate, its glow his only welcome.

Louise looked at the man who stood before her. He had been stripped of his sword and knife, but she gathered her shawl as if feeling a chill. She forced a smile, but did not offer her hand. Barton bowed, so clumsy a gesture it was obviously rare. He too smiled, but the effect was cheerless.

He brought with him the tang of the German Sea, its open skies and salted winds written on his chapped, chestnut face. Son of one of her father's seafaring cousins, he had the barrel build and square jaw of all the Barton clan. The smell of his oiled cape brought Louise's father into the room, his face alight with merriment, as it so often had been when she was a girl.

She gestured to the servant by the door, who took Barton's cloak and hat. His garb was no grubbier than any traveller's, but when she looked closer she saw a brand of puckered livid skin on his neck, ill concealed by his ponytail. A piece of string bearing a silver crucifix was tucked into his shirt, though his look was not that of a godly man, more one who tempts the fates. As a child she had heard about his branch of the family. They had rarely met, her mother Madame Brenier disapproving of the fisher Bartons, who were poor and, to her mind, rough. For once, her genial husband agreed. Nothing was ever said, but it was understood that their relatives from lower Leith were trouble. Also trouble, but far from poor, were the merchant Bartons, who were hand in glove with the king. They were not just rough but vicious, but for them, with their feathered hats and golden rings, Madame was prepared to open her doors.

As Barton bowed, his ribboned hair curling around his shoulder like a rat's tail, Crozier moved closer to Louise's side. Their eyes did not meet, but they sensed each other's unease.

'Your cousin, ma'am,' said Barton, spreading his hands as if baring his soul for her to examine. 'Auld Jock's youngest. I remember ye well, though from the look on your face, you think you've never seen me afore.'

'I believe you,' said Louise. 'I have so many cousins, it's no surprise I don't recall them all. Please,' she gestured, 'have a seat.' She spoke again to the servant, and shortly a platter of bread and cheese was laid by the fire, with a jug of ale to follow. In the next half hour, from his place on the bench, Barton's eyes strayed often towards the hearth, but he understood what was first required of him. It was as well he had eaten before leaving the tavern that morning.

'What brings you to us?' asked Crozier. 'You're a long way from your usual haunts.'

The sailor gave a sheepish grin. 'If you'd not been so hellish landlocked down here, I might have claimed I'd been shipwrecked. But it'll have to be the truth, ugly though it is.' He rubbed his oilskin knees. 'As you can no doubt see, I've had my run-ins with the law.' He twisted to allow them a better view of the stamp on his neck. 'I'm no proud of that, but it's what happens when you make your living from the high seas, where the rules are nae like those on dry land. Then, last spring, when we sailed back into Leith from Dieppe, my captain's ship was impounded, and all us crew thrown intae gaol. We were accused of thieving from the French, of sinking merchant ships to fill our own. No true, of course, but try telling that tae the judge as he locks you away for ten year. Onyways, there was a pardon of sorts for most of us. We were let out of gaol early, I do not know why. A sudden burst of remorse, perhaps, or mibbe they needed space for real criminals. I couldnae say. All I know is, we got out on one condition: we were never to return to the city, nor set foot again on a ship.'

His eyes were empty of feeling as he spoke. 'In some ways, I wish they'd just hanged me and been done. What life can I have now, without the sea? I'm good for nothing else . . .' He shook his head with a dry laugh. 'Well, almost nothing. But I'm strong. I can use an axe, build a wall, or even plough a field, if I'm shown.'

He fixed Crozier with his stare. 'This comes hard, man, but I'm begging here. Take me in, and you'll no regret it. Work me all day and half the night, and I'll no complain. Just gie me a berth.' Drawing a deep breath, he stared between his boots, and slowly let out a sigh. 'I knew what a kindly man your father was, ma'am, God bless his soul. I could think of nowhere better to go.'

Louise looked at Crozier, who nodded. She rose. 'I will have Hob make a bed for you in the outhouse, with the other men. Please, cousin, eat your fill.' Her skirts swept the floor as she crossed the hall.

Crozier stood staring down at the seated man, his hair so lank it too looked waterproofed. 'You can stay until you are back on your feet,' he said. 'My brother will find work for you. There's more than enough do be done.'

Barton rose, and held out his hand. Crozier gripped it hard. 'Mind this well,' he added. 'I can tell the difference between the wronged and the rotten. Your past is your past, but if you bring it here, you won't last long.'

Hand burning from the borderer's hold, the sailor straightened. 'Aye, aye, cap'n,' he said, his eyes alive at last.

In their chamber, the Croziers lay staring at the blackened beams above their bed. The place was quiet, all asleep but the guards. Down the valley, a dog barked. Night closed in around the keep as the couple doused their rushlights. They drew the bearskin up to their chins, and Crozier put his arm round his wife. Neither was in the mood for sleep. 'What does he want?' Louise said, speaking low. 'Did you believe him? He has the sleekit face of someone who's telling lies, and thinks you're too stupid to know.'

'He's not an honest man, whatever else he is,' Crozier replied. 'I trust him as little as you. Could be he is only fallen on hard times, as he says, but his arrival is curious. It seems remarkable that no sooner have I approached Ogle, Ellarcar, and the rest, than he suddenly appears.'

'They sent him?'

The straw-filled bolster rustled as Crozier shook his head. 'I don't know. Perhaps. It makes no sense, but the man is not here for work, I'd lay money on that.'

'What do we do?' Louise's voice was tight. The sight of Barton had brought back memories of her father's corpse, laid out on the family table, killed as he and his pirate cousins tried to climb aboard a Portuguese merchant ship. It was the first she had known of his other life, and it sickened her now, as it had then. Barton brought that misery back to life. Worse, his arrival promised more of it.

Crozier kissed the top of her head. 'We watch every step he makes. Don't be afraid, you will be quite safe. He knows my eye is on him. But first, my love, we sleep. It is late.'

Louise turned in his arms, and ran a hand down his chest. 'No,' she whispered. 'First this.'

Lord Ogle of Bothal had received Crozier in the entrance hall of his drab Norman castle, making it plain that such a visitor would not be shown farther. At his back stood his armed guard, a burly threesome with the blank faces of men who carry out orders, whatever they be. It was late morning, but the castle was dim. When the high doors closed behind Crozier and Tom, birdsong died along with the light.

'Your message was cryptic, Crozier,' said Ogle, his words like a drumroll under his Northumbrian tongue. 'You said we might work together, to bring peace to these parts. I am interested to know what you meant by that.'

Crozier nodded towards the guards. 'I will speak to you only in private, not before a public gallery.'

Ogle's face hardened. He gave but never received commands. This Scottish chief had no title, was no lord, but acted as if he were born of noble blood.

The silence lengthened, and Crozier drew on his gloves. 'Very well,' he said, preparing to leave. Ogle jerked his head at his men, and they marched off down the passageway with a clatter of steel-capped boots. His lordship, unused to being without his guard, touched a hand to the dagger in his belt.

'We can talk here,' he said, taking a seat on the stone bench that ran the length of the hall. Crozier sat some feet from him, but Tom stood. Three crows on a perch were too many.

'From what I've heard of you and your men, this sort of visit is rare,' said Ogle. 'Usually, they say, you come knocking with your swords drawn, and the head of your latest victim in your hand, as if it were a hanselling gift.'

'I had not imagined you to be a man who would listen to gossip,' said Crozier, with a hint of scorn.

Ogle gave an unconvincing laugh, as if his mind was elsewhere. 'Even so, unsure as you must be of your reception, your coming here is reckless, young man. Scots of your kind are more usually found swinging from Redesdale oaks than in polite conversation with the likes of me.' There was a swagger in his lordship's voice, the sound of a man uncertain of the situation he found himself in. 'But I presume you are well aware of the risks. You must deem them worth it. So explain yourself, and fast.'

Crozier swallowed before trusting himself to speak. When he did, his voice was cold but calm. 'I come about the Warden General, the Baron Dacre. It is well known you and many others have legitimate cause for complaint and redress against him. Yet none of you speaks. None dares raise his voice for fear of what Dacre could do.'

Ogle looked at him, but said nothing.

'It is Dacre who makes much of the trouble along this border,' Crozier continued. 'It is his hidden allies, his private army of thugs, who destroy the people's lands and steal their cattle, passing half the proceeds into his hands. Dacre claims he is a man of justice, but his courts make a mockery of the law. He is as much an enemy to his own people as to us Scots. More so, perhaps, since he's like a raven pretending to be a wren.'

He leaned forward, growing urgent. 'If Dacre was removed, my lord, this dale, and all the others around the border, could flourish once more. All it would take is a band of honest men to persuade your king that the baron is a cheat and a rogue. Even Dacre could not defend himself against the word of Henry's highest-born subjects in the north.'

Ogle's face began to redden, though whether with interest or anger it was difficult to tell.

The borderer pressed on. 'I am offering to find out how many are willing to testify against Dacre. I will tell no one who the others are until I have their written deposition, and permission. It is not a selfless act, as you will have guessed. I have my own reasons to wish Dacre's rule ended, but however glad I will be to see him brought to heel, the benefit for all the country, on your side of the border and on mine, will outweigh any private scores it may also settle.'

Ogle got to his feet, and Crozier with him. 'I called you reckless,' the lord said softly, 'but I should have said unhinged. You are mad, to speak so to a man of my standing. Were even a word of this meeting to get out, Dacre could have my lands impounded, my heirs dispossessed.' His eyes narrowed, and he gave a hiss of contempt. 'You ask me to pit myself against the king's man, for a filthy, grasping, power-hungry chieftain who is not worth a hair on Dacre's head.' He took a step towards Crozier, hands shaking, voice rising. 'Damn your eyes, the pair of you. May the rooks pick them out like winkles when they are sitting on spikes on the border crossing – as I promise you, they will be one day.'

Crozier and Tom backed swiftly towards the doors. 'Guards!' yelled Ogle, bringing his men running into the hall with the sound of drawn swords. Before the advance of bristling steel they made their exit, Ogle's roars following them, as did the stumbling guards. Reaching their horses by the trees, they leapt into the saddle and whipped them down the track.

Three days later, a messenger stood at Crozier's gate. A small, red-haired lad from Redesdale, his fingers trembled as he gave the sweated paper into the gatekeeper's hand. 'He begs a reply,' he said, but so quietly he doubted the guard had heard.

'Wants an answer,' said the keeper, passing note and message to a servant, who delivered both to Crozier, polishing hunting horns in the hall. The seal was unstamped and the letter unsigned, but the borderer knew, before he read it, who it was from.

Even the rats in Redesdale have ears, it read, in a staccato hand, as if the words were also in disguise. *Find one good man willing to put his name to this matter, and I too will join you. I believe you are to be trusted.*

Crozier tucked the letter into his belt. 'Tell the messenger his lordship will be hearing from me before the year is out.'

He went back to his polishing, the row of horns gleaming storm grey and silver under his cloth. The charade in Ogle's castle began to make sense. At the time, the borderer had been confused as well as angry. His lordship had received Crozier's message the day before. Had he wished them not to meet, his guards would have turned him back long before he reached the castle doors. Ogle had thus wanted either to ambush him, or to hear what he had to say. Their escape told its own story. It would have been a simple matter for Ogle to send his men in pursuit, yet there had not been a single man at the castle gate to stop them as they fled.

Crozier's expression was thoughtful. What had at first seemed like dross was now proved to be gold. A faint smile brightened his face. Tonight he was headed for Chillingham, on the border, where the chamberlain of Berwick was to be found. Ellarcar was known to be a loyal but shrewd servant of the crown. Like Ogle, he had a zealot of a son, who might make Crozier's task more difficult. Crozier had been glad the younger Ogle had not been present, though it now seemed likely the mummery he had witnessed had been for the son's sake, a tale to be passed from eavesdropping servants to a young man whose view of the world was more clear-cut and less far-sighted than his father's.

At dusk the borderer set off, in better spirits, Tom at his side. They returned the next morning, grim-faced. Ellarcar's mastiffs had been set upon them before they reached his walls. The next week it was Sir Thomas Grayson who bolted his doors against them, a few days later Malcolm Ridley and old Andrew Wark who refused them entry. Yet some time later messengers arrived from Grayson, and from Ridley. Like Ogle, they told him they would be party to this venture once Crozier found a ringleader.

So began an autumn of furtive excursions, riding deep into enemy country. Protected by nothing but the dark, Crozier was buoyed only by the hope that one night he would find a man brave or fool enough to be the first to put his name to this rebellion.

CHAPTER TEN

October 1523

As darkness fell and the air thickened with woodsmoke, Benoit Brenier led his horse from its stall. Hob looked up from his corner by the brazier, where he sat hunched over a rough-hewn chessboard. His opponent, Wat the Wanderer's youngest boy, was deep in thought, transfixed by the pieces, but Hob raised an eyebrow as the carpenter led his chestnut mare into the yard. 'Be seein ye,' said Benoit. 'When Ella asks, tell her I'll be back in a few days. Business to attend.' Hob nodded, before returning to a game that would keep him and Hewie up until the brazier had burned itself out.

Leading the mare out of the yard, Benoit felt like a child bent on mischief, heart skipping, nerves alive. A day after the name Rauf Ilderton had been raised, Crozier had forbidden anyone to approach him. 'If it must be done, it will be I and I alone who puts their head into that noose,' he had told them. 'But should that day come, times will be desperate indeed.' Benoit planned to save Crozier the trouble and prove that, fat and slow though he might be, he too could play his part in the family feud.

He rode cautiously, with no need for speed. When he was well on the way, he would sleep by the road, and the next day should reach Ilderton's demesne, where he would set to work.

The trees met over his head, darkness smothering him like a heavy blanket. He whistled a song for company, but the sound was weak and wavering, and soon he fell quiet. As the hour advanced, the woods grew louder. Leaves rustled, twigs snapped, and the night was broken by startled cries as owls and foxes went on the hunt.

It was not yet late, but a frost was already beginning to bite. Benoit's hands grew stiff in their gloves, and his breath left a cold mist on his face. The prospect of sleeping on a bed of hard earth grew less and less inviting. He plodded on, down the valley and out onto the hilltop track that led towards the border. Here the air was keen. He tasted winter on the sharp, thin wind, and buried his nose in his kerchief. Kicking the mare into a trot, he was suddenly eager to cover the miles and reach a hollow, off the hills, where he could shelter till dawn.

The next morning, long before light, Benoit staggered to his feet, putting a hand to his horse's neck to help him find his balance. Lying since midnight under a spreading beech, he had shivered, not slept. He took a swig of ale and crammed a bannock into his mouth before giving the mare a nosebag of oats. The pre-dawn darkness held a new note, the stirring of day in a robin's brash reveille, in a blackbird's answering call. The strangled cries of the night had died, and with it the sinister thoughts they fed. Benoit belted his cloak, saddled his horse, and set off once more, whistling as if to join the first chorus of birds. Now, as his limbs returned to life, and the ache in his deeply scored belly began to ease, he felt better for his night in the wild.

He had lived too soft for too long. Crozier's Keep had offered a home he and Ella could never have hoped to find for themselves. He had been an invalid the first year of their marriage, recovering from a fighting wound that had left him close to death, and when he was back on his feet he was fit only for his old job. True, people around here had needed a carpenter more than another man with a sword, and business was brisk from the start, yet even as he built the frames for new houses, and mended hammer beams, stables and wells, still he felt the weakling, the odd one out, the man they did not require. He did not want Crozier's charity; he longed to be one of the clan, as fit for the fray as any. Yet if he offered to ride out with them on their raids, the borderer dismissed the idea as if Benoit were as frail as Old Crozier. Sometimes he caught Louise staring as his children climbed over his knees and under his feet, and he imagined she was wishing he was less a family man and more like her husband, a fighter one had to respect. If he met her eye she would colour and turn away, as if embarrassed at having her thoughts read.

The ride into Ilderton's shire on this brittle, frosted morning did much to raise his spirits. The countryside was stitched with trees, fields lying soft and loamy as risen loaves, a bristle of winter wheat casting shadows of green across the furrows. Benoit breathed deep. If he carried off this venture, Crozier for once would be in his debt. If he did not – but he broke off that thought, refusing to think beyond the next few days.

Herdsmen were already elbowing in at the tavern counter when Benoit reached Ilderton's village. These fieldworkers preferred beer to food, and drank their midday meal as if they had been labouring under a scorching sun and not in a snell wind that fingered their smocks and blew back their snoods, intent on reaching their bones.

Benoit squeezed himself in, ignoring the workers' stares. A mug of beer was slapped before him, awash in its own spill. He gulped the first half, then set the tankard down with a grateful sigh. The tavern keeper, wiping the counter at the end of the bar, watched him from under his fringe. The others had half turned from the stranger and lowered their voices, but Benoit appeared not to care. Staring into his drink, he was heedless of company. His lips moved as if in conversation with an invisible friend, but when the bartender approached he lapsed into silence, swallowing his words along with his beer. The Wheatsheaf was dingy, the beer bland, the earthen floor puddled in slops, but Benoit seemed quite content. 'Another,' he mumbled to the host, and tipped his head back to drink it in one.

A knowing look passed between the herdsmen. 'Soaking yer sorrows, then?' asked a ploughman, his black eyes holding a hint of sympathy.

'Nah,' replied Benoit, slapping down his empty tankard, and a coin with it. 'Jist getting started for the day.' His voice was neither friendly nor cold.

'Passing through?' The ploughman moved closer, and Benoit shrugged.

'Too early to say.'

A silence followed, and Benoit was on the point of leaving when he looked the ox-driver in the eye. 'All depends,' he said, as if the words were being wrung out of him. The peasant waited. 'All depends on his lordship, doesn't it? If he'll honour his pledge.'

The ploughman's eyes widened. 'Whit pledge would that be?' But Benoit shook his head, as if already he had said too much. He was at the door when the driver reached his elbow. 'If ye're looking to find him,' he said quietly, 'he's never at home. This time of day, he's most likely asleep with his hoor. Come back at dusk, and he'll be in here, or yin of the other howffs down the street.'

Benoit put on his hat, and without looking back raised a hand in thanks.

Ilderton clung to the bar counter. His back was to the door, but in this, the meanest tavern in town, he would have been able to smell immediately whoever walked in, had his nose not been buried in his drink.

Benoit took a seat by a window so small it offered no more than a keyhole onto the darkened street. That morning's hostelry was sumptuous by comparison, and he wondered what had brought his lordship's tastes so low. The bench creaked beneath his weight, and the empty barrel that was his table wobbled on the uneven floor. Nodding to the man behind the counter, he ordered a flagon of ale and a pair of dice.

The dice were grimed, but in the firelight he could make out their faces, chipped and black as they were. For the next three hours they were his only entertainment, that and his private wager that the mouse slinking around the walls would make it through the evening without catching the eye of the tomcat by the fire.

Two other drinkers were at the bar, but they paid neither him, nor Ilderton, any heed. Their conversation was slurred, but they appeared to be in the Vice Warden's employ. From time to time Eure's name fell onto the counter as if they had spat.

Ilderton moved from his place only to relieve himself in the pail by the door. While he fumbled with his small clothes, arching his spine backwards like a greenwood bow, Benoit shot him a glance. The man's haunts might be common, but there was an air of ancient breeding in his imposing stature, the high-cut nose and silver hair that flowed over his collar.

On the counter were ranged five flagons. As one was drunk, Ilderton pulled the next towards him. When the barman's boy made to remove an empty jug, Ilderton caught him by the wrist. 'Leave them,' he growled. By the time Eure's men had left, he was on to his third. In the draught from the door, Benoit caught the vinegar tang of young wine. When Ilderton turned at last and spoke to him, the smell grew stronger.

'You're a quiet one,' he said.

Benoit acknowledged this with a curt nod, and rattled the dice in his hand. A minute passed, and another, Ilderton staring unabashed at the newcomer. Benoit kept his head lowered, his eyes only on his throw.

'Nothing you want to say?' mocked his lordship.

Benoit looked at him coldly, and returned to his game.

'Stranger and stranger,' mused Ilderton. 'A wild-looking man rides into the village, smelling of the north, but too good to talk to the likes of us. I mistrust those whose tongues are tied,' he said more sharply. 'Smacks of deceit, or trouble.'

Benoit put down the dice, picked up his hat, and got to his feet. 'I'm here only for a bevvy and a bit of quiet,' he said. 'It's my experience that those who talk of secrets have the most to hide.'

He left, followed by Ilderton's braying laugh and the cry of the cat as it pounced, too late, on a shadow.

After that night, Benoit's visits to Ilderton's shire were irregular. A week after their first encounter, he set out again from the keep, shortly after Crozier and Tom had ridden off into the dusk on one of their petitioning calls. Thereafter his trips over the border matched theirs. It made for a restless existence, and some friction with his wife, but Benoit's eyes grew brighter with every journey.

'Where in God's name have ye been?' Ella had demanded the first time. The smell of hops clung to his cloak and beard, and there was a hint of mischief in his round, coppered face.

'That I cannae tell ye, lass,' he'd replied, planting a kiss on her scolding lips. 'But the nichts were cauld without ye.' He put his hands on her hips and drew her close. 'I dinnae want tae deceive ye, hen, but it's best ye dinnae ken where I'm headed, no for now, at least.'

Ella looked at him gravely. 'Does Louise ken?'

He shook his head. 'Christ, she'd no like it. Not one bit.'

Three of his youngest had by now attached themselves to him, one to each leg and another dangling from his arm. The conversation ended, but in the weeks that followed, as soon as Crozier and Tom had gone, Ella packed her husband's satchel with food and ale, and walked with him to the forest track. She did not care if Louise might not approve when Benoit's secret business was finally revealed. Seeing the change in his mood, the lightness in his step, she welcomed it.

When asked what took him from home, Ella said he was on a commission for a farmer in the next dale. She spoke with an air of resentment, as if she thought he was finding an excuse to be off on his own. Louise frowned, not with suspicion, but with worry at her brother's behaviour. She put a hand on Ella's arm. 'Crozier often needs to get away,' she said. 'The keep can sometimes feel like a cage.' Ella cast her eyes down, ashamed of her lie.

On his second trip Benoit did not find Ilderton. Killing dreary hours in the village howffs, his steps unsteadier with each hostelry, was a waste of money, but not time. Word of his reappearance would soon spread, and that was enough.

Days after that visit, Benoit was back. He was huddled by the fire in a high-beamed tavern when Ilderton walked in. The Crown was clean but cold, all four winds finding their way under the doors and through the rafters, making the log flames dip and dance, the rush lamps plume with smoke. Rubbing his hands, his lordship showed no surprise at seeing him. He entered as if the place was empty and all his own, not packed with villagers fortifying themselves against the lengthening nights with draughts of golden cheer.

Benoit turned his back and stared into the fire, but despite the press of bodies he could sense his lordship's stare. A stool scraped at his side and Ilderton joined him, tumbler and jug in hand. 'So then,' he said, as if picking up a conversation broken off only that morning, 'you think I'm full of secrets?' He poured until the tumbler brimmed. With a tremulous hand he brought it to his lips, ignoring a splash of wine which dripped onto his boots, dark as blood.

When it was drunk, and the tumbler refilled, he continued. 'I've been thinking about you, young man. Your sudden appearance, your mysterious ways. I find it curious. No one here knows you, or your business, yet here you are, always at the tap, as if you're one of us. But we know not a thing about you. People don't like that, you know. It makes them uneasy, like an albino robin, or a two-headed lamb. Perhaps you'd care to enlighten me?'

'I'm a carpenter,' said Benoit, avoiding his eyes.

Ilderton looked at the calloused hands and strong wrists and seemed satisfied with the answer. 'And what brings a carpenter here, so far from home?'

'None of your business,' replied Benoit. 'I did not know I needed your permission to drink here.'

'Oh, but you do. It is a tedious duty, but I find I must keep an eye on everyone who passes through the village. In times like these, enemies are all around.' His tongue flickered over his silver beard, catching a lick of wine. 'You look like an enemy to me, my friend. Smell like one too.' A hand caught Benoit's wrist before he could move. 'Careful, now, how you answer,' he said, so low that his voice disappeared up the chimney. His grip tightened. 'Are you one of Dacre's men?'

Benoit started, unable to hide his surprise. Ilderton smiled. He squeezed until Benoit could feel the thrum of his pulse before releasing him and tipping back the remains of the jug, his beard purpling like a plum.

'Come to spy on me, I suppose,' he said, raising a finger and bringing the girl behind the counter running with a fresh flagon. His tone startled Benoit even more than his words. 'I'm a liability, in his eyes, am I not? He thinks I'm a danger to his well-laid plans. And here you are, his little messenger, sent to report what I'm up to, what state I'm in, what needs to be done about me, eh? Is that it?'

His eyes glazed with drink, his voice harsh as a saw, he was sodden with wine yet his head was clear. It was the drinker's most dangerous hour, the cusp between mellow and murderous, when tempers are tipped, and daggers drawn. Benoit swallowed. He had a knife in his boot, and a smallsword in his belt, but in this confined space, among strangers, he would not have time to pull them before he was cut down. His heart hammered, but his voice was ominous in its calm.

'So I look to you like one of Dacre's lackeys?'

'Every pore on your body sweats his name, boy. My guess is you're one of his outlaw band, the roughnecks from the dark side of the border, who do his dirty work.'

Benoit fastened his eyes on Ilderton. 'You do not speak of him with respect. If I were his spy, that would be the first thing I would tell him. If I was who you think I am, I would caution you to be more careful.'

Ilderton snorted. 'Respect? We're all of us rotten, one way or the other. Dacre's no different. He's bad, same as me. Very, very bad. And that I respect.' He cocked his head. 'You can't trick me. I may be a sot, but I still have my wits. You won't catch me speaking against him.'

He returned to his flagon, and when it was drained another was set down before him. His words began to slow, and he tapped the table with his garnet ring at the end of every sentence. 'You can go back to the baron, lickspittle lad, and tell him he has nothing to fear from me. My affairs are in order. My horsemen are ready at four hours' notice. I have fifty and more, all for Dacre to command. The business with my wife was unfortunate, but I can be trusted. She is now safely in care, and who I choose to bed with is my affair. He is not, I hear, so fussy himself.'

The slump of his shoulders showed time was running out. Benoit leaned forward. 'Your loyalty is impressive. Were Dacre to hear of it, he would be proud, I'm sure.'

Ilderton's eyes narrowed. 'So what game is it you're playing, boy? Is it his enemies you're seeking?' Benoit shook his head, measuring the distance from fireside to door. Three paces, four, and he could make his escape. But for the moment, Ilderton was merely curious.

'You don't have far to look for them, do you?' he said, with a damp chuckle. He wiped his mouth with the back of his hand. Benoit frowned, as if bemused, and Ilderton pulled his stool closer. 'There is one who has grievance enough against him, if that's what interests you. His bastard son, John. Noble mother, but cast off by the world, as was she. Both disgraced, and she died of shame. John's never forgiven him. Dacre has bought him an office in the church, but the boy wants the life of a lord, not a monk. When he is on his knees beneath the holy cross, he prays not for the poor but that his father be brought as low as he, humiliated and disgraced.'

'Where would I find him?' Benoit asked quietly.

'Greystoke,' said Ilderton, more quietly still. 'Dacre's dead wife's land, in the west. Find the boy, and you've found your answer.'

He raised his garnet hand, his face quickening with anger. 'Now be gone,' he said, his voice growing loud. 'Be gone. And do not return. We're none of us traitors here.' The room quietened, the crowd turning, circling around them. In the sudden hush, Benoit drained his tankard, picked up his hat, and with unhurried step made his way to the door. The villagers looked to their lord, sticks and knives at the ready. Ilderton shook his head, his neck bowed as a goaded bull's, and Benoit's passage was cleared. Not until he was on his horse and out of the village did the crawling sweat on his back begin to dry.

CHAPTER ELEVEN

October 1523

The Warden General of the English marches was inspecting his lands. It was a blustery morning, and Dacre was many miles from Harbottle, having ridden out at first light. His intention was to reach the Berwickshire coast, the part of his kingdom where he felt least at ease, a stranger in a hostile land. If day had begun to fade before they could return, he would take shelter with the Percys. Rivals they might be, but manners required the earl to offer the warden a bed, no matter their disagreements. But Dacre hoped it would not be necessary. He liked nothing better than his own palliasse. These days he could find sleep nowhere else.

At his side, in fighting gear, were his brothers Sir Philip and Sir Christopher, and Blackbird too, a rare outing for the butler who, to mark the occasion, had packed a satchel with potted game, newly baked bread, and a flask of strong ale.

The ride was hard, the roads narrow and pocked, the woods misshapen by centuries of salted gales, from which they offered little shelter. Baron Dacre was a fine horseman, but there was a twist to his mouth, a line between his eyes, that told he was in pain. Whenever they came to a halt he rubbed his knees, unaware he was doing so, but needing that warmth to comfort his aching bones.

The hours stretched before them, cool and grey. As the sea grew closer, the sky brightened, the land a mere ribbon of faded green against an expanse of blue that mirrored the flittering waves below. Dacre rode doggedly, eyes fixed on the path. It was unusual for him not to keep watch for signs of danger, but this morning he felt his troubles lay in his own lap, and he kept his head down, the better to brood on them.

He had not yet had any reply to his request to be relieved of his post. Twice he had written, both missives ignored. He expected no answer from the king himself, though it was to Henry he had written, but not to have heard from Wolsey, or even Surrey, was unsettling. It could of course mean they were considering his suggestion, but would that take months? A day's discussion would settle the matter. As he had informed Henry, he would prefer to be discharged entirely from the burden of wardenship, but to oblige the king he would consider continuing as warden of the west march, until such time as someone was appointed in his place. His keepership of Carlisle he would not relinquish.

The court's silence was beginning to grate on his nerves as surely as his knees ground with every step in their swollen sockets. He wondered what was being said about him to Henry; how his reputation stood. Thinking of the sort of lies that were likely being spread, he laughed without joy, the noise carried off by the wind like the leaves that were whipped into a reel under his horse's hooves.

Did he care? Not even a little. Devil take them all. They were prattlers, backstabbers, sycophants and saps who took fright when the king so much as coughed. Such men could say whatever they liked of him; he'd pay them no heed. All he wanted was to be allowed to settle quietly, to retreat to Naworth and live out his life as a country lord, among his fields and his horses, a situation to which he was more than entitled after years of service.

He was too old to be commanding the north, with all its tribes and factions. Had he ever asked for such a thankless task? Ever begged for a post as bloody as the executioner's? A grunt escaped him and he shifted in the saddle, a spike of hot pain skewering his foot. At least the hangman and the hatcheter slept in their own beds each night. They did not fear an army of horsemen storming their hovels, or spiriting away their servants. It did not fall to them to ride out in all weathers and all hours to face down men with faces like gargoyles on a parish church and hearts as twisted. Their pay was regular, too, and more than sufficient for their needs. Whereas he was filling the king's treasury, using his own money to pay for his private army, and rewarded with a pittance, an insultingly abject sum for the privilege of keeping the king's order in barbarian lands. A country, by the by, that Henry had never yet set foot in.

By God, he'd like to see the king feed and equip four thousand horsemen on £433. 6s. 8d a year. That would soon put an end to his majesty's popinjay robes and gold-buckled shoes, his tournaments and banquets which lasted for weeks, and left the court clutching its stomach and bathing its head.

He too could dress and eat like a king, if his purse weren't so stretched. Did they think he liked wearing old leathers and patched up boots? Did he keep ponds packed with eels for the pleasure of watching them snake among the weeds, or huts of hens to feather his hats? They were cheap, God damn it. A household could be fed on them alone for a month; and in the depths of winter, sometimes it was.

The countryside passed unnoticed as Dacre nursed his complaints, the drum of hooves setting the beat for his endless list of woes. Only one thought cheered him. Thank the lord for the Armstrongs. Not many could say that, he knew, but murderers and thieves and damnable Scots though they were, they had proved his salvation. Holed up in Liddesdale, two days' hard ride across the border from Naworth, the clan was like his secret army, one he need never pay. Orders could be issued from Naworth at dawn, and Sly Armstrong would ride out to effect them before nightfall the next day. No task, the baron soon learned, was too savage for their taste, no venture so vicious it slaked their thirst for the kill.

When the law threatened to catch up with Sly or his men, the clan retreated to their stronghold, a wilderness of glens and woods where their grass-roofed houses, hidden in hollows, were reachable only by secret paths. These low dwellings might look isolated, but the next was never more than a whistle's alarm away. The fast streams and rivers that fed the hills were uncrossable without bridges, whose splintered stumps greeted travellers brought to an unwelcome halt; roads were made impassable by cannily felled trees; and many strangers rode into the darkest forests, and were never seen again.

Money was the only language Sly Armstrong understood. Dacre

offered him half the booty from every venture, but if the man occasionally took more than his share the baron did not fret. The bounty the Armstrongs had helped him reap in the past few years more than made up for some leakage. That it was money – cattle, corn, horses or houses – that the exchequer knew nothing of made these rewards sweeter still.

But the Armstrongs' worth lay less in the wealth they gathered than in the terror they spread. All the north quailed at their name. When Dacre sensed there had been too long a spell without fear, when peace was threatening to take hold, he would send them out, east and west, north and south, to remind his own people, and those across the border, that they were powerless before the baron's command.

There were mutterings, of course, and the stirrings of rebellion among the titled and moneyed ranks, but nothing he could not crush, alone, or with the Armstrongs at his call. The thought of his unassailable authority brought the hint of a smile to the Warden General's face, though none of his companions noticed.

The morning had almost passed when there was a cry from Christopher, who rode at their head, and the party pulled up behind him. Dacre looked up, and his breath was almost snatched by the fierceness of the wind, but also the beauty of the scene. They stood on the crest of a hill, so buffeted by the gale that a firm hand was needed to hold their horses in line. Below stretched dunes and white beaches, disappearing in both directions into a milky haze of sea. At the foot of their bluff, beyond reach of the advancing waves, a spearhead of black-faced gulls faced into the wind. High above them, a crow was being tossed around by the elements. It fluttered like a scrap of burnt parchment, wingtips splayed but useless, and who knew where it would land.

'Which direction, Tam?' Christopher shouted against the wind.

Dacre pushed up the brim of his helmet and stared out to sea. Northwards, the coast disappeared beneath marching black cliffs, leading to Berwick, with its foul-mouthed keeper, and a few miles beyond that, the Scots. Southwards, by the sands, lay Alnwick, Alnmouth, and the pernicious Percy tribe. Dacre had no taste for either, but he had to choose.

With a kick he turned his horse south, and made for the shelter of the low coast trail. When at last it was possible to be heard, he gathered his men by a stand of spindly pines. 'A night at Alnwick Castle is our lot. Prepare for the thinnest gruel this side of London Tower.' Philip began to speak, but his brother raised his hand. 'I know, I know. Percy's hell-bent on becoming Warden General, and you're worried he might slit my throat while I sleep.' He spat, and wiped his mouth on his glove. 'Then so be it. I have little love left for this life.' He set off at a canter, leaving them to look at each other in consternation.

'The man needs food,' said Blackbird, spurring his horse on to catch his master and set this lack to rights.

Some time later, the sanded trail grew bright in the noontime sun. Dacre raised his face, this late warmth an unexpected boon. When they stopped to eat, at Blackbird's insistence, the grumbling voice in his mind fell quiet, and he recalled instead a real feast, on the cliffs not far from here, when old Henry had been in the north.

'A fine man, he was,' he told his brothers, scooping grouse pâté from its jar with his finger. 'His son would do better if he had his father's cool head.'

'You did not always think so well of him, as I recall,' said Philip, catching a nosedrip with his cuff.

'Aye, well, I could be a hothead. I was troublesome for him, in my youth.'

Blackbird knew the story well, but seeing his master's mood lighten he encouraged him to repeat it. 'Nothing much has changed, seems to me,' he said, handing round more bread. 'You were hot-blooded at twenty, and still are to this day. Where's the difference?'

Dacre considered the question. 'I know better how to hide my tracks, I reckon. How to keep my mouth shut, and my feuds out of the king's sight. But I wasn't that wise as a boy. Who the hell is, at that age? I was a puffed-up braggart, thanks to Bess. I'd ridden off with her under the king's nose, so I had. A ward of the crown, and still I married her without his consent.' He slapped his good leg at the memory. 'Jesus Christ, when I think of it!' He swigged his ale in belated celebration.

'Best move you ever made,' said Christopher, rubbing his fingers together as a river of imaginary coins slipped through them.

'Aye,' said the baron sharply, 'but not for her money or lands. Or not those alone. She was a good wife to me, don't ever say otherwise. I was not the best husband, but I loved her as well as a man ever could his spouse. And I still do, dust and memory though she is.'

Blackbird passed around greengage pies. 'But what of the old king? If he did not put you in chains for snatching Lady Greystoke, the richest heiress in the north-west, then why would you fall foul of him for an act of common rioting?'

'I will never know,' said Dacre, his wife's image fading for the meantime. 'I thought it nothing more than a skirmish. Sir Christopher Moresby and I arranged the day, set the rules, and rode our armies out to test the other's mettle. I like to think I came off better – Moresby's northern ally, Baron Parkes, lost an eye, I merely broke a toe – but since I spent nine months in the Fleet, and Parkes barely a week before he was released and packed off home to Scotland, few saw it that way.'

Sir Philip coughed, and hawked onto the grass. 'You threatened the realm, that's what you did, you and your magnificent pride. You were like a nine-point stag, going head to head with whatever other big beast wandered onto your land. You never thought what it might mean to Henry's negotiations with the Scots, never for a moment considered that you were putting years of diplomatic sweat at risk by near as dammit killing a Scottish noble.' He laughed. 'You ask me, you were fortunate getting off with a fine and a few months in the cells. Pretty lenient, considering you could have lost your head.'

The baron nodded. 'I can see that now, so I can. But not at the time. It made no sense to me. I rode out of that prison, back to my wife, and spent the next ten years fulminating. Pity is, I never had a chance to tell Henry I came to realise he'd been right. He avoided me from then, and even when I was called to council and was obliged to attend, I never once crossed his path.' He picked flakes of pastry from his cloak, licking them from his fingers. 'Of late I've been wondering if he passed his aversion for me on to his son.'

Blackbird was on his feet, packing up. 'We must be off. There's a long ride afore dinner.' Dacre rose from the grass with a groan, shaking his head, as if ridding himself of needless worries. 'Aye,' he sighed, 'a long ride, and much toadying to endure at the end of it before we get a crumb. Look on it as cheap entertainment, the only sort we'll get this night. At the puritan's table there's no chance of cards or dice.'

Blackbird raised a hopeful eyebrow, and the baron's laugh rumbled in his chest like a deadly cough. 'No, you old goat, nothing like that either. We'll all just have to shiver in our beds.'

Crozier was in the stableyard when Benoit returned. The mare's flanks were soapy with sweat, and the carpenter's face shone from the morning's ride. Crozier held the bridle while Benoit dismounted, and saw the dusting of earth and leaves on his cloak.

'Did you sleep rough?'

Benoit brushed his sleeves. 'No, I rode a' night, thanks to the moon herself. But I should've gone slower, for when she took a stumble, a mile or so back, I fell off.' Hob approached, and Benoit patted the mare's flank as she was led away. 'Poor beast, she's mair wabbit than me.'

'What was your hurry?' Crozier asked, growing curious. 'Could your farmer friend not have put you up for the night?'

Glancing over his shoulder, Benoit lowered his voice, though the stable boys were interested only in mucking out the stalls in time for their midday meal. 'We must speak,' he said.

The borderer's eyes narrowed. 'Come up to my quarters.'

As they made for Crozier's rooms, Benoit tried to marshal his thoughts. The chief would be angry, that he knew, but once he learned of Dacre's resentful son, a bishop to outflank the other pawns on the board, he would surely forgive his disobedience.

He was wrong. When they took their seats in the low-beamed room off Crozier's bedchamber, the borderer's expression was benign. Over the years he had grown fond of his wife's brother, recognising the kindness and loyalty hidden behind that dour, pitted face. But Benoit had done no more than begin his story – 'I've made the acquaintance of yon bastard Rauf Ilderton' – before Crozier was on his feet, stool kicked aside, affection forgotten in his fury that one of his men had defied his command.

The ferocity in his eyes brought Benoit to a stammering halt. Crozier turned ashen as he leaned over him, pounding the table with his fist as if nailing each word into place. 'You fool!' he roared. 'You utter imbecile, you ignorant wretch. Do you have any idea what you have done?'

Benoit swallowed. 'I have information . . .' he began, but Crozier was not listening.

'You might as well have laid a trail of gunpowder straight to our door. D'you think you have not been followed? Did you really believe you could outwit him? Ilderton is a knave and a killer, and he is ferociously intelligent. He'd have worked you out before you'd said a word.'

Benoit stared at his bitten nails. 'He doesnae ken who I am,' he said sullenly.

'No need,' spat Crozier, crossing the room and putting some space between them. The first wave of rage had ebbed, and his hands were shaking. 'He can find you, and us, easy as tracking a wounded stag.'

'But he dropped a name,' Benoit persisted. 'Yin who might lead the charge against Dacre, maybe the very chiel ye've been seeking.'

Crozier ran a hand through his hair. Such an act of defiance demanded punishment, and had any other of the clan stepped out of line, they would have been dealt with harshly. Benoit, however, was different. Were it not for his falling into the hands of a murderous traitor ten years ago, on the night before Flodden, Crozier would never have met Louise. Her search for her missing brother had brought her to the borders, and to him. It was a debt Crozier would always owe this man, contumacious, vexatious, pig-headed as he was.

Taking a long breath, he leaned against the wall. 'Tell me, then,' he said, one hand clasping the other lest it fly free of its own accord and send this ass sprawling.

Benoit told his story quickly, without the colouring or wry asides he had rehearsed on his way home. This version, he felt, sounded somewhat reckless. A northern stranger rides into an Englishman's domain, and corners him. He narrowly escapes with his life, but in possession of the name of a man who might help them solve their problems. Even to his own ears it began to sound like a fairy tale. After his account reached John the Bastard and his desire to be revenged on his father, he faltered and fell quiet.

Crozier stared at him. The carpenter looked weary. The chamber felt suddenly airless, though the shutter rattled in the breeze. Soughing leaves filled the room, and Benoit wished he could put his head on the table, and sleep.

'Ye think I was tricked?' he asked, meeting Crozier's eyes at last.

'All too likely,' said Crozier. 'If not, then we will have been fortunate beyond what we deserve. But for now we must work on the assumption that every hour brings Baron Dacre and his men closer. We have to act, and fast.'

Benoit began to speak, but Adam held up his hand. 'Say nothing more.' He turned his back, and stared out of the window at the withering leaves beyond. 'Fetch Tom to me, and join us. I know you are dog-tired, but whatever else this day holds in store, sleep won't be part of it.'

An hour later the three were on the road, Benoit behind the brothers, his face fixed in shame. He had only one source of consolation: thanks to his riding through the night, they had a chance of reaching Greystoke, and young John's quarters, before any messenger Ilderton might have despatched.

'How drunk was he?' Tom had demanded, when Benoit had again recounted the events of the previous night.

'Cross-eyed but conscious. Capable of summoning a message boy, but mair likely to have just ordered another bottle.'

'If that's so,' said Tom, 'we still might have the advantage, if we leave now. It's two days' ride, or thereabouts. We don't know the terrain, but we've less distance to cover.'

Crozier nodded. 'God willing, we'll intercept the messenger before he reaches Greystoke. Otherwise, we will have to go through with the charade.' Benoit frowned, bemused, and the borderer sighed. 'Don't you see? We must introduce ourselves to John the Bastard, as if we are indeed seeking an alliance, and risk the consequences.'

Tom's face was grave. 'Unless we reach him before Ilderton's man, he'll have time to prepare for us.'

Crozier looked at Benoit. 'This is where you get your chance, brother, to prove yourself a riding man. We need you with us. If the message reaches him, it's you that Dacre's son will be expecting. If this is indeed a trap, then you need to walk into it as if you're every bit as simple-minded and credulous as Ilderton believes.' There was an anxious sheen on Benoit's brow. 'Fret not. We will be with you, or close behind.'

'I will show you whit I can dae,' said Benoit, flushing. There was a mutinous note in his words. 'I'm nae coward.'

'It's not your courage that's in doubt,' was the borderer's cold reply.

The ride was punishing. His morning's elation had turned to misery, and Benoit slumped in the saddle, solid as a sack of meal. He barely saw the woods and hills they covered, his mind playing over his foolishness and vanity in thinking to return home to praise. Ilderton's face swam before his, the eyes filmed with rheum and cunning. Where he had thought he was guddling an unsuspecting fish, had his lordship all the while been reeling him in on a hook? Sweat trickled into Benoit's beard. They were riding fast, but it was mortification that made his cheeks warm, the reins slippery in his grasp.

They crossed the border and wound deep into the Cheviot hills, the pounding of hooves on heathery tracks lost in a rising wind that carried off the sound of their passing. Despite his gloom, Benoit's spirits rose. He had never ridden like this, headlong into the dying day. His horse galloped as if he would never tire, but the carpenter's back and legs ached with the strain of keeping up. The Croziers crouched low over their stallions' necks, men and horses moving as one, as if fused in a blacksmith's forge.

Dusk had turned into night before Crozier called a halt. In the shelter of a hillside of ash and oak, by a tumbling, moss-banked stream, they rubbed their horses down, and allowed them to drink their fill. Leaves crackled under their boots, dry as tinder. In the dark, the sound was unsettling. 'Two hours' rest,' said the borderer, passing around oatcakes and cheese. 'We must be deep into Dacre's lands when

111

daylight comes.' He unstoppered his flask and drank. 'Tom will keep watch,' he added, stretching out beside his horse, and pulling his hat low over his face. His brother laughed, without humour, but Benoit, at some distance from them both, was already asleep, fists clenched over his chest.

The next few miles were ridden with care, a fitful moon lighting their way through lonely grasslands and cleuchs. When dawn arrived, they grew more cautious. From now until nightfall they were dangerously exposed, yet they must ride as if they had nothing to fear. Scots were common enough on this side of the border, but in time of war tensions were high, and even a stranger from an English shire would be quizzed on his business. A tradesman might pass without too much trouble, but Crozier did not fool himself that he and Tom looked like merchants. If they must meet anyone, Benoit would do the talking. One so fat and sluggish would never be taken for a man of arms.

That day they stayed well clear of villages, roads and herdsmen. A drizzling rain settled over the hills, and soon the land was hidden by smirr, the riders but a blur beneath it. It was only after a second night's too brief sleep that they reached habitation. Descending from the hills as light broke, they halted. Penrith's crooked roofs huddled below them, thickening the damp air with woodsmoke. The village of Greystoke lay some miles beyond, and the fastest road was through the town. The riders hesitated. Even at this hour the narrow streets were loud with packmen and horses, setting up stalls and unloading their goods.

'Market day,' said Crozier. 'We are in luck.' He turned to Benoit. 'After you, brother. If anyone troubles us, we are on a reconnaissance for Baron Dacre himself. We are your apprentices.' He pushed Tom's hat back from his face, and removed his own. He gave a grim laugh. 'No need to look bashful. We've got nothing to hide.' With a flick of the reins he set off, his horse tossing its head and picking its way off the hill as daintily as if stepping between tacks.

Penrith closed in around them, its blackened walls matching their fears. Benoit led the way, past butchers humping carcasses onto their stands, and weavers stacking cloths on their trestles like a hand of cards, each bale peeking out from behind its neighbour. After the greens and browns and sere yellows of the hills, the blaze of colour was almost as much a shock to the senses as the merchants' cries and the bellowing of cattle and bleating of sheep as herdsmen whipped them into their pens

Nobody paid them any attention. Benoit's stomach rumbled as the scent of roasting pork filled the morning, and he was wondering if they dare risk buying some food when a child appeared at his elbow and thrust a pair of skinned rabbits under his nose. 'Fresh killed the morn,' he piped, holding out his hand for a coin. Benoit recoiled at the bulging eyes staring out of red-ribboned flesh. 'Ah've whelks and cockles if ye prefer,' said the boy, jogging beside the carpenter, the smell of seaweed rising off the chittering creel on his back.

Benoit shook his head and kicked his horse into a trot, but the press of stallholders and townsfolk brought him up almost at once, his horse rearing in fright at the clash of pans from a pie-maker's booth. Benoit flailed as the reins fell from his hands and he would have toppled had Crozier not pushed alongside and pulled him back into his saddle. The borderer's rough grasp stung more than any rebuke. Mortified that he had drawn attention to them, and sure that at any minute they would be accosted, Benoit felt dizzy. By the time the din had faded, the streets widened, and they had reached a bridge that marked the edge of town, his shirt was soaked.

When Crozier rode abreast and slapped his arm with his hat, he was startled. 'Well done,' the borderer said. 'You behaved the part.' At Benoit's surprise, Crozier's expression softened. 'Come on, now. No border hoodlum would almost fall off their horse like that. Thank the lord you weren't born in the saddle.' He gave a curt laugh, and pressed his hat back on his head. 'You didn't see it, but when the urchin was tugging your sleeve, the guards by the market cross had noticed us. Soon as you slipped sideways, they relaxed. One of them laughed, the fool.'

As they rode across the river plain and up into the woods, Benoit breathed deep for the first time in days. It was as if the vice that had been squeezing his chest had at last been loosened. He pushed his hat off his forehead, and looked around, at the track that wandered through the flame-red forest, and the glimpse of rain-sodden hills ahead.

Within an hour the countryside had changed. Where Penrith was glowering, the hillsides rough and the houses dark, the land around Greystoke was trim as a private park. The fields were tidy, the trees lined up as if planted by hand, and when they reached the village it was like a tapestry, so neatly laid out were the slate-roofed cottages around the green, so pretty the pale-towered church.

The riders dismounted by the river that bordered the village. There were two roads into Greystoke, and there was no knowing which Ilderton's messenger would use. Under guise of watering their horses, they conferred. An old woman peered at them from under her cap as she hustled a flock of geese past with a switch. Tom touched his hat, but she looked away without a word.

'We can't stand here long,' said Tom. 'A place this small, we are far too conspicuous.'

Crozier nodded. 'John the Bastard will live apart from the common priests,' he said. 'As Dacre's son and graced with the pope's blessing, he will have a status more like a lord. The Greystoke manor is where we'll most likely find him, wherever that is. There, or in the church. Once we know which, we can hide up, and set watch.'

As one, the brothers turned to Benoit. At that moment, the bells in the church tower began a querulous toll, calling the village to mass. A straggle of figures crossed the green, hooded and humble as they fingered their beads. 'Me?' asked Benoit, but he need not have asked.

Catching up with the last of the late-comers, he tethered his horse by the lychgate and hurried into the church, crossing himself before taking his place near the doors on a bench worn smooth by centuries of shuffling. The monks gathered in the chancel began to chant, a low, liquid murmur that echoed around the high-beamed church, eddying under the rafters and along the aisles as if making sure all were bathed in song. Heads were bowed as the elderly priest entered and knelt, raising his hands to the altar, his hunched back to the church. Benoit peered from beneath his hat. Two younger priests in white chasubles flanked their superior, narrow and straight as the candles that burned on the walls. They too had their backs to the church. Benoit could not tell their ages, nor their rank. The taller seemed more likely to be Dacre's son, but it was impossible to be sure.

The ceremony began, and Benoit's lips followed the litany. A feeling of peace descended on the church, the gloom of the morning lifted by the words of hope and faith. For a moment he forgot his purpose, his spirit lightened by the comfort of a ritual he had loved since he was a child. The priest's assistant swung the thurible on a short chain, incense swirling like autumn mist, and the priest's voice grew louder. The villagers looked ahead, eyes fixed as if mesmerised, fingers working their rosaries.

There was a shuddering crash, the cracking of oak against stone, as the doors were flung open and the church breached by workaday light as well as the violent presence of the man who had entered. Dropping their beads, the congregation turned to see a glistening figure framed in the doorway. His gaze swept over the three priests who stood unmoving, like pillars of salt. Raising his cudgel, the man advanced down the nave, water running from his cloak. 'Is one of you the Bastard Dacre?' he shouted. The salt heads shook. Brushing his way past the benches of believers, the visitor made for the side chapels, throwing open their doors one by one, each slamming against the old stone wall as if slapping its face. When he found no one on one side of the church, he made for the other. Benoit waited only to be sure all the chapels were empty before slipping out. A horse was tethered to the ring by the doors, lathered with sweat as it pawed the grass. Before the visitor had finished his search, Benoit was on his own horse, and out of sight.

Crozier and Tom were waiting for him by the river. They had neither seen nor heard the messenger, but at Benoit's news they led their horses swiftly up to the village green in time to see Ilderton's man whipping his weary hunter down the road to the south. What they did not see was the cassocked young priest drawing water at the church well. It was Dacre's son, whose day it was for serving the almoners. A minute earlier, and the messenger would have found him. While the village thrummed to the beat of chasing hooves, John the Bastard went about his business, unaware.

The borderers did not have long to stop the messenger reaching the manor. Digging in their spurs, they gave the horses their heads. As they left the village plain and found themselves in thick wooded hillside, they began to close in on their prey.

Not until they were almost upon him did the messenger hear their approach. He looked over his shoulder, and his horse veered sharply as he wrenched the reins in surprise. By now the road was widening between the trees. In another minute they would be at the manor gatehouse, and Dacre's men within shouting reach. With a frantic kick, the messenger tried to outride them on the final stretch, but his horse was exhausted, labouring on the muddied track as if wading through water. Tom drew alongside, Crozier rode ahead, and Ilderton's man was brought to a halt. His mount reared in alarm, jibbing at its bit as the strangers pressed in. With one hand the messenger held it steady, drawing his sword with the other. The trees closed in above them, and there was a sudden hush, no sound but the heaving breath of their horses, and the cry of a solitary rook.

At the prodding of Benoit's sword in the small of his back, the messenger dropped his weapon. His eyes were small, and they narrowed further as he took in his pursuers. Much was conveyed in that look. The man nodded, and spat. 'I nearly made it,' he said. He stared at Benoit, whose sword pointed now at his throat. He gave a snort of laughter. 'Ilderton wouldn't have credited a barrel like you with as much brain. His mistake, but I'm to pay for it.'

He spoke in the hope of being told he was wrong, but no one gave him comfort.

'Tell me,' said Benoit, 'is John the Bastard his father's enemy, as Ilderton said?'

The messenger shook his head. This close to meeting his maker, there was no need to lie. 'Close as ticks the pair of them. Like looking in a glass lake, too; the boy's the image of his father. His pride and joy, by-blow or not. He's still but a lad, but one day he'll do his father proud.'

While the man spoke, Crozier edged his horse closer. When he was within reach, he lunged, Tom grabbed the hunter's bridle, and the messenger was dragged off his horse and onto the track. Before he could scramble to his feet, Crozier was beside him, boot pressed on his chest. The man's eyes met his, cold with contempt, and fearless. 'Just do it,' he said.

Without a word, the borderer thrust the blade home. Ilderton's servant let out a sharp sigh, and turned his cheek to the track, as if it were a pillow. As his heart emptied and his mind with it, his last sense was the smell of damp earth, which he was soon to join.

CHAPTER THIRTEEN

Rauf Ilderton would not be as easy to deal with. The ride from Cumberland to the Northumberland moors was less fevered than the race to Greystoke, but the borderers still moved at a pace. Ilderton would be expecting his messenger with news any day. Too cautious to change horses and leave a trace of their journey, they were now obliged to rest fully each night. While sleep was welcome, the delay chafed at their nerves, and the group grew terse as the days passed. Crozier feared that Ilderton would suspect trouble if his man was not back by the end of the week, and Benoit began to fret, knowing the task that lay ahead of him, and how wily his foe. Tom alone was untroubled, only with difficulty curbing his habit of tuneless whistling in deference to their mood.

'You sure we've got to kill him?' Benoit asked one night as he prodded the fire, juice from the rabbits sizzling on the spit, the mouthwatering smell making his belly growl. A lazy curl of smoke rose above the clearing, trees pressing in on their circle of light, as if to snuff it out.

Crozier stared into the fire and did not answer, his attention held by the flames as if they were showing him a story only he could see.

Benoit rubbed his hands at the blaze. 'I ken he knows we're out to get Dacre,' he said, 'but if he disnae ken who we are, can we no just leave it be? He might have tried to get us murdered, but from everything he said to me the man's no great admirer of the baron either. He'd put the warden's head in a noose as quick as ours.'

At last Crozier looked up. 'The risk's too great,' he said. 'Soon as Ilderton realises his messenger's dead, he'll hound us down. Getting rid of his man meant we have to deal with him too. We have no choice, brother. We can't leave loose ends.'

Tom emerged from the trees, a brace of pigeons dangling from his belt. 'Breakfast,' he said, laying down his bow and joining them by the fire. 'Easy pickings when they're at roost.' A flurry of pale feathers soon lay at his feet, as if a fox had been at work.

Benoit crouched by the fire with a stick, turning the rabbits over the flames. 'I ken how to dae it, then,' he said, in a voice the brothers had not heard before. Cast in crimson from the fitful light, his plump face was harsh. Crozier gestured him to sit.

'Let's hear it.'

The three huddled as if eavesdroppers might lurk in the wilderness beyond. 'Beauty of it is,' said Benoit, 'this way no one'll ever ken he's been kilt.' His plan had been long hatched, and he spoke fast and low. As he outlined his dark idea, his words rose over their heads and disappeared into the night, as if they too were smoke.

It was evening when they reached Ilderton's village. Rain and wind swept the street, and Benoit kept his head bowed as he led his horse to the first of the taverns. The brothers were hidden in a copse on the outskirts, waiting for Benoit's whistle to signal he had found their man. But Ilderton was gone. No barkeeper had seen him that night, nor was his doxy at home. Her companions opened the shutters at Benoit's knock, hanging over the windowsill and peering down at him, the bodices of their scarlet gowns invitingly unribboned. She had not been seen for days, they told him. Would he like to come up and wait?

'Will she be wi' her master?' Benoit asked.

'Where else?' Smiles fading as they sensed a customer escaping their hold, they banged the shutters tight.

Benoit hesitated. Were he to ask the way to Ilderton's castle, his lordship might be given warning of his arrival. Turning back to the main street, he had decided there was no option but to do so when a swineherd appeared, racing after a wandering pig that was rootling in the gutters, oblivious of his cries, but skittering away with a squeal whenever he got within reach.

The lad was hot-faced, his torch no more heated than his cheeks. 'Blasted old sow, she dis this every evenin',' he panted, racing past

Benoit and making another ineffectual grab for the grand dame's hindlegs.

'Haud these,' said Benoit, throwing his reins at him. He tiptoed after the sow who, thinking the herdsman had been defeated, soon stopped to truffle in a dunghill. When Benoit lunged, her unholy screams brought villagers to their windows, shutters thrown back to see what was amiss, but in the dusk little could be seen but a ruckus of man and pig, each as wide as the other.

While Benoit held the beast down, the swineherd slipped a chain around her neck. 'Ye'd be well advised tae keep that on her day and night,' said the carpenter, getting to his feet and brushing the filth off his knees.

'Aye, I will,' said the boy, grinning. 'She'll have bitten through it by the mornin', but I'll get a better yin made. Thank you.' He headed back down the street, the animal trotting at his side, the pair, caught in a bowl of orange torchlight, looking as if they were out for a stroll.

Benoit untethered his horse, and was looking around for someone of whom to ask directions when he saw a figure slipping up the street, keeping close under the eaves. Night was gathering fast, but as the shape passed the lit windows of a tavern he caught a flash of red hem peeping beneath the long black cloak. As he watched, she disappeared along the high road heading east.

Swinging himself into the saddle, he was with the Crozier brothers in half a minute. 'Ilderton's manor, that's where he is,' he said, breathless in his hurry. 'Methinks his hoor's companion has set off to warn him. We'll have to deal wi her.'

They nodded, and wheeled out of the woods onto the road. Some way beyond the village outskirts they caught sight of a shadowy form, hurrying towards the hills. Hearing their approach, the woman began to run. She left the road and plunged into the woods, but Tom was after her, his horse picking its way through the tangled undergrowth with the ease of a good huntsman's mount.

Crozier and Benoit were waiting on the road when he dragged her out of the trees by the arm, his horse following on its own.

'Let go of me,' she yelled, kicking at Tom as he twisted her arms behind her back. Crozier took a rope from his saddlebag, and had tied her hands before she could do more than ask them what they wanted. Her legs were shaking, and a sharp stench of fear filled the air as Tom pushed her against a tree and bound her chest and legs to the trunk.

Crozier stood over her. 'Tell us what we want, and we'll do you no harm.'

She looked at him as if she would spit in his face.

He took a step nearer. 'Who is with Ilderton the night? Are his men at the castle, or just his servants?'

For a moment it seemed she would tell him nothing, but at the sound of Tom's dagger leaving its sheath she spoke. 'He's alone with Beatrice, and a couple more girls from the house.'

Tom pressed the blade against her neck. 'That the truth? Because if we find him surrounded by his men, we'll be back before you've had time to count your blessings, and this time we won't be as friendly.'

Her lips narrowed. 'It's the truth. Why would I risk my neck for any of them? Ilderton's a brute. It was Beatrice I went to warn. You can do what you like with him. It's only my sister I want home safe.'

'How far?' asked Benoit.

'Couple of miles at most. Over the ford, and up the hill.'

The borderers got on their horses. 'You're not leaving me here?' she cried, her voice turning into a wail. 'There's wolves in these woods. And wild boar.'

'There's richer pickings for them than a wee scrawny thing like you,' said Tom.

Crozier looked down at the girl, hesitated, and then dismounted. He unstrapped the blanket roll on the back of his saddle, and draped it over her shoulders. 'Here,' he said. 'You've a cold few hours ahead of you, lass, but that's the worst you'll suffer. Come dawn, there'll be someone passing who can set you free. Your sister, perhaps. We'll not hurt her, I assure you.'

'Bastards!' she shrieked as they set off, and the sound of her gusty weeping followed them down the road.

Ilderton's manor rose out of the dark like a man of war, a squat, square castle from the time of the first Norman king. The smell of smoke warmed the air, but nothing could mask the dankness and decay that oozed from these neglected walls.

No guards were posted at the gates, and no dogs prowled the grounds. Their approach was so easy it was as if a trap had been laid to lure them into the very mouth of Ilderton's lair, and would only be sprung once he had them in his hands. Nerves alive, they were more cautious than if there were lookouts at every turn.

Blacker than the deepening night the walls stared down at them, blank and forbidding. Leaving their horses in the shelter of the trees, they crept up the track. The portcullis was raised, but the great doors in the gateway were bolted and studded with iron. Picking their way past mounds of filth tipped from the ramparts, they made their way round the castle. At the rear, Crozier found a postern gnawed by rats. It was locked, but the first kick made the wood groan, the second produced a splintering, and with a third it fell off its hinges, and they were into a narrow passageway that led to the courtyard.

Lights seeped from a row of narrow shutters on the first floor. But for this, and a meagre brazier in the corner of the yard, the place was in darkness. As the borderers crossed the cobbles past the stables, hooves shuffled at the sound of strangers. Tom poked his head into the stalls and came out with the news that there were three horses, one of them a pony. It seemed the whore had been telling the truth: there was no one here but his lordship and his bedchamber guests.

Swords in hand, they entered the west wing of the castle, and found the stairs.

'Who the hell might you be?' came a throaty voice, and a woman dressed in coarse linen, tied at the waist as if she were a sack of meal, stood in their way. By her cap they guessed she was the cook. She was filling her lungs, her bosom swelling like a pullet's, when Crozier knocked her unconscious with the side of his fist. Cushioned in fat, she collapsed as softly as a spent candle. Benoit and Tom dragged her by the ankles into the kitchens, where they locked her in the larder. A maidservant found sleeping by the fire was gagged and bound before she could scream, and likewise bundled into the press to spend the night with glass-eyed pheasants and caged blackbirds, who flapped frantically at their bars, fearing their time had come.

Upstairs, the passages were lit as if for the eyes of pipistrelles. Rushlight cast a glow so watery it was more like the memory of light than an actual flame, but at the end of the corridor a line of brightness blazed under a door, and as they drew closer they heard laughter, the high-pitched merriment of nervous young women, and the low, commanding tones of their master, breaking now and then into a rumble of sardonic amusement.

A stone flagon fell to the floor, its crash softened by a rug. 'Bring me another,' roared Ilderton, and bare feet scampered across the room. Benoit looked at his companions and nodded. His lordship was already well soused.

He lifted the latch and opened the door an inch, and then another. The scene before him was like a bard's ballad in which evil temptresses bewitch a poor old widower, and rob him of his inheritance. Except these women were nothing but villagers, no better or worse than many. Their flesh was pink in the firelight, but pallid beyond its reach. Young though they were, these were no enchantresses. Their charms worked only for a few years, and already for one time was growing short, rolling in lard as she was.

She was crouched over Ilderton, who lay shirtless, his britches untied, on a bed of ancient furs. His hand caressed her bobbing head as she went at her task, while another girl rubbed warm oil over his chest and the third dangled her breasts over his face until he took a nipple into his mouth and was for the moment silenced.

To judge from the height of the fire, and the untouched flagons on the table, the evening was only just begun. Benoit edged into the room, but a man his size could not pass for a shadow or a draught. The girl with the bowl of oil saw him first, and froze. Before her alarm reached the others, Benoit was at the bedside, his sword glistening in the flames as if it too were oiled.

Ilderton's eyes wavered as he took in his new visitor, unable at first to focus. When the haze of lust and wine had fled, he spat out the breast and sat up, dislodging the fat girl, who gave a petulant moan that swiftly turned into one of terror as she saw the blade pointed towards them.

'Look what the north wind has blown our way,' said Ilderton, his lips stained dark, as if the nipple, not the red wine, had brushed its colour onto him. 'Girls,' he said sharply, as the trio huddled at his side, shaking despite the heat of the fire, 'don't be afraid. I am sure that there is something the three of you can devise that could tempt this sullen Norseman to put down his sword and forget his troubles for a while.' As he spoke, he laced his britches and swung his legs off the bed.

'Naw, naw,' said Benoit. 'Stay right where you are. Yer lassies will be safe enough, but you and I need to have a talk.'

While he spoke, Tom entered the room behind him. He surveyed the scene, unblinking despite a display of wanton nakedness he had not seen since Ma Borthwick in the village had been sent a vision of the Virgin Mary and closed her premises. Wordlessly, he herded the girls through a low door into the chamber beyond, returning only to snatch their capes from a chair by the bed. The latch dropped behind him, and Benoit was alone with the man who had sent him to a sure death.

Befuddled though he was, Ilderton made an effort to hide his alarm. 'Did you manage to find John the Bastard as I suggested?' he enquired.

Benoit pulled up a stool by the fire and sat, sword on his knee. 'Pour a drink, and I will tell you all about it.'

Ilderton raised an eyebrow, but dragged a flagon towards him, splashed a tankard full, and held it out to the borderer.

Benoit shook his head. 'Naw,' he said, 'you drink it. I've a long ride ahead of me still.'

Ilderton took a sip and was about to set it down when Benoit raised his sword. 'Finish it,' he commanded.

As his lordship drained the tankard, his eyes flickered with fear. He was beginning to understand.

'Fill another,' said Benoit, though by now the rules were understood.

As Ilderton emptied the first flagon and began on the next, Benoit told him that his messenger was dead. 'You've the backbone of a worm,' he said, 'sending a man like that to do yer treacherous work, and take the fall when it gangs agley. He died well, that much I will say.'

Dampness was spreading over Ilderton's brow. His shirt clung to him from the oils that greased his chest, but sweat began to run down his temples and under his collar. Soon the chemise was so wet it could have been wrung.

'Fearless,' Benoit continued. 'And loyal. Which is not a word,' he added, 'that anyone could ever use of you.' He stood, and filled another beaker, Ilderton's hand trembling too much to complete its task. He held the tumbler out, but Ilderton shook his head.

'Enough,' he mumbled, his tongue blackened by wine.

'Aye,' said Benoit, 'I'm sure for once you've had yer fill, but I insist, man. So drink up. Ye dinnae usually sicken o the stuff this easy.'

'Your accent has changed in the space of a week,' said Ilderton, knocking back the wine, and pressing the back of his hand to his mouth, perhaps to keep it down. 'Who are you?'

'I felt it wis time to be masel', ken. Since we'll no be meeting again.'

'Who?' repeated Ilderton, his eyes scanning the room, as if seeking a way out of this misery.

'Ye asked me that afore, but I won't be saying. My name disnae matter anyway. And soon,' he added, staring into the flames as Ilderton hiccupped through another tumbler, 'nor will yours.'

Wine was trickling down his lordship's chin when Benoit turned back to look at him. The head of silver hair began to wobble, and it fell forward onto his chest, where he began to sob, the heaving gulps of a helpless man, who knows he is beyond saving.

'Here, let me gie ye a hand,' said Benoit, placing a pillow under his shoulders and pressing his head back. He filled another tankard, and held it to the man's lips, ignoring the bubbling choke as it made its way down.

It was long after midnight when the last pitcher had been emptied. Ilderton lay unconscious, but Benoit had not finished. From his belt he took a flask of spirits, a Teviotdale brew so fierce it was most often used by physicians to stun patients before they went under the saw and knife. Almost as pale as his victim, Benoit tipped the bottle down

Ilderton's throat. He stoppered the flask, took out another, and did the same. And again. Three gills of spirits went down that gullet, and eventually his lordship's breath grew shallow, and slow.

Benoit's mouth was twisted in disgust, though whether at the scene or his part in it was not clear. The room reeked of drink. Toppled flagons littered the floor, and the emptied tumbler was lost beneath the furs. Ilderton sprawled on the bed, abandonment in every limb. His chest barely rose. The carpenter took his wrist and felt the dying flutter of a pulse. Then, with a weak cry, the man sat up, though his eyes were closed, and his limbs like butter.

He began to retch, a fountain of dark liquid spewing onto the bed. Benoit pushed him back, but Ilderton tried to turn on his side as another convulsion racked him. Averting his eyes, Benoit pressed a hand on his chest, keeping him on his back so that the vomit flooded into his lungs. His lordship bucked and kicked, but soon the thrashing, the fish-like gasping, the wet, sloshing rattle, were over. Benoit did not lift his hand until he could be certain there was no heartbeat beneath the sodden shirt. When all was still, he stepped back from the bed, made the sign of the cross, and closed his eyes, as if to blot out the memory of this room, which would be with him for the rest of his days.

Stumbling to the door he called for Crozier, who was keeping watch at the end of the passage. Without a word, Benoit brushed past him and made for the stairs. It was Crozier who found the dead body, and in the room beyond it his sleeping brother, the cloaked women at his side. Shaking him awake, he realised that while Benoit had been putting his soul in mortal danger, so too had Tom.

CHAPTER FOURTEEN

Wherries bobbed on the river beyond the windows of Greenwich Palace, the cries of the ferrymen snatched away by a gusting wind. From the corner of his eye, the cardinal watched his king, while appearing transfixed by the view of sunlight on the Thames. It was a trick he had learned as a boy, taught by his cousin Matt, whose love of catching ferrets Wolsey had shared. The chisel-faced creatures would gnaw their willow bars, eyes screwed tight, and intent only on eating their way out of captivity, or so it seemed. All the time, though, they were watching for an exit, calculating their next move. A moment's inattention by their young gaolers, and a ferret would make a dash for freedom, wriggling out of the basket and slipping through their grubby hands as if it had been greased. Once out, it would never be caught again, leaving only teeth marks and the stink of terror.

Cardinal Wolsey suppressed a sigh. The most powerful churchman in England, as Lord Chancellor he was quite possibly the most important man in the country after the king, yet, unlike the ferrets, he could never escape. Even if he wished to abandon court, Henry would hunt him down. And most days he did not want to leave. This was home, however uncomfortable, and the urge to flee always passed. Today, it would fade as soon as Henry grew calm. But for the present he could only pray the king's rage would pass over his head like a fire-eater's breath. To judge by Henry's complexion, however, it seemed his fury was blazing too brightly for him to avoid a roasting of some sort.

The crimson of the cardinal's robes was mirrored in the king's face, but in other respects too they made a matching pair: square-set, broad-faced, rich food and too much wine swaddling their chests in fat. Wolsey was the elder, but his varicose legs were hidden by his skirts, his gnarled knuckles masked by rings. Nothing about the king was disguised. His hefty calves looked slim as reeds beneath his majestic belly, and the gold brocade jerkin and Italian puffed sleeves gave him the shape of a tailor's dummy.

Wolsey tapped the back of his own hand in rebuke. It did not do to mock his king, even in his most private thoughts. Henry was like a hunting hound, quick to sniff out disaffection. Even now, as the cardinal turned his back on the palace window, he saw suspicion in his eyes.

'Has your confidence, does he then? Vouch for him, will you?' Henry waved a travel-stained letter at the cardinal, speaking so softly that Wolsey was obliged to draw closer. He buried his hands in his cummerbund, to conceal their trembling.

'Dacre is no fool, your majesty. Nor is he a saint. That I readily concede. There are questions over his probity, as we all know, and there is no doubt he worships the gods of expediency before those of the law. But in the northern territories, as forsaken a region as you will find within your kingdom – more so even than the wastelands of Wales – it takes a rough man to keep the peace, and hold the savages in check.'

The king's voice thinned, a single string strung so tight, it could snap at any moment. 'Do not presume to tell us about our own country, your excellency. You speak as if it is a foreign land. Yet we know what happens in every town and hamlet, the sums on each moth-eaten tally of tax, every muster roll and court pipe.' His eyes had narrowed like a lizard's in the sun. 'God almighty may be lord of all things in creation, but in England it is we who see under every stone and blade, into each beating heart.'

Bubbles of froth had gathered at the corner of his mouth, like spume eddying in a rockpool. When the king talked like this, there was no reasoning with him. The cardinal took a deep breath, the pounding of his heart making his throat thicken.

'Quite so, your majesty. And that is why I, and the cathedral monks, and the college of cardinals, here and in our sister lands, pray earnestly every morning and night for your endeavours as king of these isles and upholder of the true faith. We know only too well the burdens of state and soul that you carry on your shoulders. And none, your majesty, is more in awe of your knowledge and wisdom than I.'

Henry stared at his cardinal for a moment, then paced towards the fire. Spreading his legs before its warmth, he rubbed his hands. 'You're a wily old snake, Wolsey. You and me both.' He laughed, a cackle that made his dogs prick up their ears at a sound so rare.

The cardinal bowed.

'Nevertheless,' the king continued, his choler dampened, it seemed, by the flames, 'our doubts about Dacre cannot be dismissed. They are not mere fancies. Come, sit here beside us.'

They settled on the high-backed bench close by the hearth, whose blazing logs made the cardinal's veins itch beneath his robes. Henry stretched his daffodil stockings towards the heat and shook his head. 'Not yet November, and this place cold as a crypt. We dread winter, Wolsey. We would stay abed from the feast of St Nicholas to Easter morn, if we had not so much business to handle. And,' he added, 'a wife who'd complain at doing her duty more than once a week.'

Wolsey examined his fingernails, long since bitten to the quick. 'The Baron Dacre, your majesty, is the best man we have for the job. Warden General is a weighty obligation, and none knows the area, or its troubles, better than he.'

'It is indeed a grave responsibility, and since he importunes us twice to beg, in the most intemperate terms, to be allowed to relinquish it, we are curious to know why you think him still well fitted for it.' He examined the letter, as if it could speak, then crushed it in his fist. 'The man is desperate as a landed carp to be off the hook. And we to see him gone.'

The cardinal opened his mouth to speak, but Henry had taken a draught of air that would last some time.

'Under his command, the north has been all but lost to us. The rebels are dangerously out of control, the highlanders of the middle march are in open revolt, the east threatens insurrection, and the west is a hotbed of thieves and killers who are in thrall to the warden, not to the crown.

'When last did Dacre execute more than a couple of miserable miscreants, and then only for appearance's sake? He cannot maintain the law. Not just cannot, but will not. The criminals are his allies, and the titled are his foes. It is a cockeyed command, Wolsey, everything gone arse over tit, and it makes our head spin just to think of it. Yet here we are, given a heaven-sent chance to set him free and bring fresh order to the north, and you tell us no, leave things as they are.'

The cardinal once more opened his mouth, again to be cut off.

'Just think, man, we could put Surrey in his place. The best soldier of our times. Truest of our courtiers, so straight he cannot walk up a turnpike stair without stubbing his toes.'

'But an ailing man, your majesty, despite his high honours,' said Wolsey, when Henry at last paused to catch his breath.

The king thumped his fist on the bench. 'Dacre is far older, and a great deal more decrepit! He whines about his gout, his bad leg, his rotting teeth. If I'm to believe his last account, he has so many things wrong with him he can barely piss unaided, let alone mount his horse.'

The cardinal said nothing. He tucked his feet under the bench, further from the fire, but he could feel his face growing ruddy as his king's.

That ruby moon was now turned towards him. 'Speak, your excellency, God damn it. What say you to that?' But to the cardinal's relief, Henry's growl was only for show.

'All you say is true, I have no doubt,' he replied. 'Dacre is well advanced in years, yet for my part I trust him better than the earl. Either way, Surrey would not give the post his full attention; he pines for the south, and sunnier climes. Better by far he acts as Dacre's commander in times of crisis only. For the time being, I feel sure it would create more trouble, worse friction, to appoint a new Warden General.' He smoothed his skirts. 'I agree that the baron is high-handed. I do not think he is a criminal, or that he twists justice to his own ends, but there we must differ until there is evidence one way or the other. To judge from his constant complaints about hardship, whatever he makes on the side is far from adequate.'

The king roared, setting his hounds' tails thumping. 'Hardship!

The very idea is preposterous. The man is rolling in wealth. Eighth richest baron in the land, so Brother Beecham tells us. More spare money to throw around than either you or me, that's an undeniable fact.'

'Yet few have his outgoings, your majesty.' The cardinal caught his eye, and raised a hand in acknowledgement. 'Fair enough. I will say no more in his favour. Only this.' He clasped his hands in his lap. 'Keep him in post, your majesty, on the provision that he pays the cost of any further insurrection and rioting under his rule. And that he metes out regular justice to thieves and thugs. Let him know that no fewer than ten executions a month will satisfy us. That way you are assured that he is working as hard as he can in your interests, and I have the comfort of knowing the best man is still a bulwark between us and the mischief of the north.'

Silence fell, the king chewing his lip as he considered the cardinal's plea.

'We will think on it,' he said finally, rising and calling the dogs to heel. 'Now be gone. You have exhausted us.'

A servant, till then standing invisible by the doors, opened them with a flourish. Scraping a backward bow, the cardinal left, the flurry of his red robes finding an answer in the hearth as the palace draughts sought out the flames and set them leaping up the chimney.

The king's seal lay on the parchment like a pat of crimson butter, so large it all but covered the sheet. Blackbird took the letter, and locked it in the baron's linen chest. The missive was thick, four pages or more. It seemed that Henry had much to say, but he would have to wait to be heard, to lie in the dark until the lid was opened.

Dacre had left some days before on a raid against the Redesdale highlanders, intent on crushing a band of outlaws under a leader who dared to challenge his rule and raze his lands. He returned a few days later in great good humour, the chase and fight filling his cheeks with colour, his heart with fresh blood. He brought with him a handful of prisoners to be flung into Harbottle's dungeons, the rest already despatched to Hexham, where they would fetch a decent ransom.

The prospect of easy money cheered him almost as much as the expedition. It would help equip his newest recruits, whose tackle and arms were so old they had likely seen duty at Bosworth Field.

When the Warden General limped into the castle, the smell of steel and sweat arrived with him. Blackbird met him at the entrance, proffering the king's missive on a salver. The baron's barking sallies to his men died, and he halted. The pair stood motionless, despite the mill of servants, dogs and soldiers, their silence swallowed amid the noise. Finally Dacre pulled off his gloves, and picked the letter off the plate.

'So our majesty still lives,' he murmured, breaking the seal and scanning the pages beneath. Blackbird heard him catch his breath, then, without a word, he brushed past him, and made for the stairs to his room.

Dusk had long since fallen when Blackbird found him there, staring into the thin blue night. He did not acknowledge his butler's presence, but Blackbird refused to leave. Setting down a tray of bread and ale by the hearth, he put a lit taper to the fire, and to the rushlight on the walls. Dacre stood rigid at the open window, white-faced in the cold. Drawing the shutters, Blackbird turned him round as if he were a child, and set to unbuckling his swords. When he had stripped off his fighting gear, he helped him into a worsted jacket, and brought out his deerskin boots, regretting their new-polished gleam was lost in the chamber's dim light.

Dacre placed a hand on Blackbird's shoulder as he pulled on the boots. Once dressed, he sat by the fire, and nodded to his man to join him. 'It's the worst of news,' he said roughly. 'The king will not release me. That much I expected. I will reply saying I accede to his wishes, but only until Easter. Christ's blood, Blackbird, I climb these stairs like an old man. I shit blood, and spit teeth out in my sleep. It is unreasonable to keep me in harness any longer, and he well knows it.'

Blackbird eyed him with concern. 'Easter is not far off. It's surely not for a few weeks' extra labour that you are cast into gloom.'

Dacre rubbed his knees. 'No. I am disappointed but not dismayed by that. What alarms me, what shows how evilly the king regards me and my trust, is that he insists I must henceforth pay for any losses the raiders cost our people.'

'What?' Blackbird squawked.

'You heard. Whatever destruction is wrought by the Ridleys or the Charltons, or any other ruffians and traitors, in whatever part of the marches, it is I who must foot the bill.'

He shook his head, disbelieving. Blackbird's eyes widened. 'But that is impossible. It will ruin you!'

'That, it seems, is the king's purpose.'

The butler spread his hands, as if it were his purse that would be emptied. 'The destruction these men cause, it would cost you hundreds every time they appeared before the law.'

'Aye. And there's worse. From now, I am obliged to string up ten men or more every month, to set an example and remind the world whose side I am on.'

Blackbird nodded grimly. 'That, at least, is straightforward. The place is awash with thieves. Ridding the dales of a few of them will be no more painful than emptying your rivers of pike.'

Dacre shrugged with irritation. 'But not all thieves are my enemies, as ye well know. They might be rogues of the first degree, but I need to keep their kin on my side. If to maintain the trust of the king I make these families suffer, I will start losing influence here. Who knows where that could lead.'

Absently, the baron ate the bread, and drained the ale. Some colour returned to his cheeks. Neither man said anything, listening instead to the marsh wind whistling at the window, filling the room with the scent of peat and reeds, a reminder of the wilds beyond.

After a while Blackbird bent to stoke the fire, and spoke with his back to his master. 'The executions must be managed in such a way that your closest allies are protected. Warned too, perhaps. And since you are master of your own courts, that, surely, is easily arranged. As for the edict to pay out to those who seek financial redress for their losses, there is an obvious solution, by my reckoning. One certain and simple way to save your skin.'

Crouched by the grate, the butler stared at the kindling sticks as if he wished they were the king's bones. A gallows smile crossed his face. 'Seems to me, only those without fear would dare come to you for compensation. Their pleas will be heard in your courts. And you and your men will be present at those hearings. I wouldn't much like to face you or, for that matter, your brothers, if I were bringing a claim on your purse.'

'Some would still have the nerve. They breed them tough in these parts.'

'They might try it once, my lord, but an example must be set. And if you, being so busy, are unable to teach the east and middle marches a lesson yourself, I am sure there are those who would willingly do it for you.'

Blackbird fed a fistful of dry leaves into the fire, and at last it began to glow. He stood up, to find Dacre nodding. 'One lesson to teach them all,' the baron said, so softly he might have been speaking to himself, or merely making sure the wind did not carry his words beyond the room and warn any of what was to come.

CHAPTER FIFTEEN

November 1523

The Duke of Albany brushed snow from the brim of his helmet and cursed the northern gods. Behind him rode a dejected line of soldiers, the remains of the four thousand who had set siege to the castle of Wark, on the English border, three days before. Had it not been for the weather, Albany would have taken the prize, of that he was sure. But never had there been a country so often held to ransom by the elements. Just when he and his men were in position to assault the castle walls, the River Tweed began to swell. One minute the water flowed smoothly between its banks; the next it was thickening with waves, backing up and piling in upon each other like a crowd at a dog fight, until the river bed was swamped, and the fields on both sides swimming with dirty brown water and half-drowned rats.

On the Scottish banks they barely had time to pull their artillery to safety, but by then the game was over. Alexander Wedderburn, Albany's dour guide, told him that until the Tweed subsided, it would mean certain death to launch their attack. 'It'll suck youse in like quicksands,' he said. 'There's gey few rivers as crabbit as this. It's seen mair corpses this year alane than the pauper's pit.'

Disgruntled, Albany was preparing to sit out the delay in the comfort of Home Castle, whose cellars were famed on both sides of the border, when word arrived that the Earl of Surrey was fast approaching, with an army as large as his.

So now, on the advice of his timorous Scots lieutenants, he was in retreat, turning tail like a hound that has been whipped and sent to its kennel. Under his ice-crusted helmet, Albany seethed. Had it been possible to peer further than a foot ahead, his men would have seen a face curdled with fury. Gone were the duke's good looks and charm, in their place a glower that threatened any who fell into his sights. His French troops would have fought, but it seemed the Scots had lost their stomach for a fight along with most of their men that long-ago day at Flodden.

Half a week later, when at last the army reached Edinburgh Castle, Albany could barely speak for cold. The final ten miles had passed in a blur of loathing, for the country and its people but most of all for his own idiocy in taking on the regent's role. Cursing like a sailor into his beard, he swore it would take a miracle to keep him in Scotland much longer. When he dismounted by the castle walls he threw the reins to a stableboy, who stood shivering in the sleet, awaiting orders.

Baleful under its powdering of white, Edinburgh Castle rose sheer from its rock above the regent's head. Seagulls wheeled overhead, fluttering against slate-grey clouds. Yet cramped, cold and damp as it was, the castle looked inviting. Compared with the ice-blown borderlands and their frozen keeps, it was almost as enticing as the palace of Fontainebleau. Feeling the north wind's bite, Albany vowed never again to go on campaign this late in the year.

Around him soldiers made their dogged way under the arch and up the castle ramps to their quarters. 'Boy!' called the regent, grabbing the first who passed. 'Have my rooms made ready. Be swift.'

'*Tout de suite, votre grâce,*' replied the young man, with a bow. Sopping red hair flapped beneath his helmet, and a river of sleet ran off his cape as he hurried up the cobbled passageway ahead of the regent, to bark orders for his grace's ease.

Once within the castle doors, Albany stood alone before the great hall fire, sweetening his mood with mead. He downed a tumbler, then made for his room, where he found the fire burning high. A bowl of water sprinkled with lavender steamed on one side of the hearth, and on the other a flagon of hot spiced wine. Dry clothes were spread on a bed whose sheets had been warmed.

The red-haired soldier, who had awaited his arrival, bowed and would have left, but Albany put a grateful hand on his arm. He snatched it away. 'See you change swiftly,' he said, 'lest you catch pneumonia. Here . . .' He poured some wine and pressed it into the boy's hand.

'Drink up, fast. It'll warm your gizzard, and stave off the chill.'

'I am most grateful, your grace,' the boy replied, when he'd drunk.

The duke looked at him. 'Not one of us, are you? Your accent, I'd guess, is from the north.'

'Picardie, your grace. But my family lives now in Paris.'

Albany nodded, and began to strip off his jerkin, the young man's signal to depart. He spoke over his shoulder as the boy left. 'Join me and the high command here for dinner, and we'll hope to bring some cheer at last to this misbegotten day.'

That night Albany's men gathered at his table, the northern youth among them, though he spoke not a word. The duke's lieutenants were almost as quiet, not risking speech while the regent railed against the troops, and his humiliation at their hands.

'I should have threatened them with treason for refusing to fight,' he muttered, staring into his goblet as if he were reading runes.

'Too late, your grace,' said Montgomerie, Earl of Eglinton. 'You gave the order to retreat yourself. We all heard it.'

The logs gave a hiss as hailstones rattled down the chimney, and in the silence that followed mice were heard scuttling across the rafters. The duke's hand tightened on his cup. In the firelight, his colour deepened and the group held their breath. When his rage erupted, the young soldier leapt with fright. With a sweep of his arm the regent cleared the table of cups and hurled his dish at the wall. Uttering a wail of anger he stood, knocking over his chair, and set about his room, kicking his bed, his kist, the boots that stood by the door.

'Wretched country!' he cried, ripping off his woollen cap and throttling it. 'I can do nothing right! Your men won't fight, my men are miserable – and who can blame them, badly fed and frozen to death – and the English will not make peace. What am I to do?'

He pulled at his hair, and only the pain made him desist. Panting, he came to a halt, gripping his bedpost as if he were so weary he could not stand without support. Too tall and furious for a chamber so small, he seemed suddenly to have outgrown it. The men at his table had stood as he raged, but now they righted his chair, recovered their goblets and jugs from the floor and took their seats. Already a servant was scampering at their feet with cloths, and soon a fresh table was laid, though the smell of spilt wine would take days to fade.

Eglinton put out a hand. 'Come, your grace, be seated. It does you no good to fly into such a temper. Cool heads are needed these days. We have had our fill of the other.'

The young soldier, who was still shaking, expected a fresh salvo at this rebuke, but the regent merely nodded and, like a sulky child coaxed back to his toys, returned to the table.

'So what do you advise?' he asked, reaching for the wine. 'Henry ignores my petitions for a truce. It suits him fine to be at war. He knows as well as I that the Scottish army is broken, a useless thing that takes fright at its own shadow. How often must I try to persuade these pathetic creatures to cross into England, always to find myself thwarted on the very point of valour? They dishonour the great name of this nation.' He drained his cup and poured another. 'My stomach is sickened. If they cannot, will not, help themselves then I will leave, and soon. The throne of a country such as this is worthless.'

Young Lord Herries leaned forward, his gaunt face cast in smoky shadow. 'Yet who can blame our men for mistrusting their leaders? They have seen them make unforgivable mistakes, all in the name of glory. Few of your standing can command their faith these days.'

'What of it?' barked the regent. 'It's their duty to obey orders, not to question them.'

'Flodden haunts them still, your grace. You need to understand that. Henry takes heart from that vile victory. But,' he said, running a fingernail along the grain of the table as if testing a seam, 'I know of a way that might put spirit into the Scots, and strike dread into Henry's heart.'

'Why have I not heard of this before?'

'You have never asked,' said Herries mildly. The duke held his gaze, searching for insolence, but found nothing he could name. Unversed in Scottish ways, he had yet, after all these years, to interpret the looks he met at every turn, rightly suspecting that bland innocence hid dissembling and deceit, yet never able to detect or unmask either.

'You need a renegade, your grace,' Herries continued. 'Someone with no ties to the court. Such a man, if he could be turned to our cause and bring his own army, might just possibly encourage them to fight.'

As night closed in on the castle and hailstones battered its walls, Herries outlined his idea. He told the king of the Crozier clan, which had no allegiance to the crown, but was under no one else's thumb. 'Baron Dacre is Crozier's worst enemy, a fact we could play to our advantage. If your grace could persuade Crozier that leading your army into England would bring about the Warden General's ruin, you'd have him in your grasp.'

'Who?' asked the regent, his mind bleary with drink. 'Dacre or Crozier?'

'Both, by God,' said Herries, his face tightening with dislike. 'Thistles under all our skins, each as bad as the other.'

'You seem not to understand it is Henry I want to crush, not his minions.' The regent sounded petulant. With a glance at Herries, Eglinton joined the discussion.

'Your grace, it is Dacre who rules the north. Cut off his head, and Henry too spouts blood. With every drop Dacre loses, the king is weakened. Without the Warden General, the region will fall apart. For all his conceit, not even Surrey can hold it together in one piece. Come that day, we can march in and state our terms, and Henry will be in no position to deny us. You would then have peace, my lord, sooner than you could have hoped.'

The regent played with his cuffs. He gave a wintry smile. 'Just this morning I believed – nay, prayed – I would not see the borders again this side of spring, but it seems I was too hasty. The very thought of making that journey once again chills my bones. But what must be . . .'

He stood and, reaching Herries's place, laid his hands on his shoulders. He leaned heavily for a moment, his face wiped of its smile, his mind of its claret fog. The implication was clear. Responsibility for this venture lay on Herries's slate, as much as on the regent's.

Releasing his grip, he looked round his men. 'I hear no disagreement? So be it. Where, then, do I find this nest of rebels?'

Herries nodded to the young soldier, who left the room and

returned shortly with a folded parchment. It was spread on the table, corners held down by cups. The regent's eyes widened. 'What is this?'

'It is a drawing, your grace,' Herries replied, 'composed by the commander of the horse. He has ridden the borderlands all his life, and this is his image of it. Rough, it's true, but useful. If only we had the same for the rest of the country.'

The commander's drawing was faint, the cheap ink faded, and well-worn creases had created new rivers and tracks, but what it showed was recognisable as the uncharted terrain the regent had just left. Seeing it laid out before him made him blink.

'Here,' said Herries, pointing to the empty lands near the border, marked with nothing but forest and moor. Albany stared at the nameless wild. In his mind he was already there, hostile eyes watching from behind trees, the bodies of lost travellers boiled to a cold broth in the marshland stews. It would not be an easy journey, and it would not be safe. Yet as he surveyed the drawing, the face of this unforgiving domain holding his eye, he felt its pull. Desolate and dangerous as they were, the borderlands were calling. It might be a siren song, but he felt powerless before it.

He straightened. 'We leave tomorrow, then.' He turned to Eglinton. 'Give the order to the captain of the retinue. And you, boy,' nodding at the young soldier, 'will be joining them, to keep my gear in order.'

The early snows had melted, and the valleys were bathed in sun, as if to chasten the regent who had expected storms as well as dragons in so benighted a place. The tracks across the hills were impassable in places, strewn with rocks, or dissolved by rain, but the retinue made good time, spending only three nights on the road. Pennants fluttering in the breeze as they passed through Selkirk, the court's men raised their faces to the sun, the last they might see this year. A straggle of townsfolk stopped to watch them pass, sweeping their hats off or bobbing clumsy curtseys, boots catching their skirts. The regent waved, but his eyes were on the road, not his people.

Some miles later, when Crozier's Keep came into view, they slowed. The young soldier was sent ahead to warn of their arrival, and

Albany allowed time for the clan to prepare. He need not have been so thoughtful. When they approached, his bugler signalling the eminence of their leader, he and his men were shown into a great hall where the fire did no more than smoulder. An evil wisp of smoke escaped the hearth and curled around the legs of the clan chief, who was standing by the fireplace, sword in his belt, dagger in his boot. At his side was his wife, and around the hall the rest of the family sat, stood, or slouched, all shrouded in gloom. There was a flutter above his head, and a hawk flew across the hall, and settled on a beam.

No knee was bowed when the duke was led in, no handshake proffered. The mistress of the house folded her arms over her drab plaid shawl and did not smile. Her dog made as if to sniff out the strangers, but with a click of her tongue the beast was kept in its place. The duke was grateful the animal was given no chance to slaver on his boots.

Crozier asked the regent his business. Inclining his head, the duke suggested they might sit while he explained it, and indicated that refreshment would not go amiss. What was brought from the kitchens confirmed his suspicions that he was in the back of beyond, where nothing had changed since Merlin's day.

Chewing dry bread and herrings whose sousing had barely softened their bones, Albany sipped a ditchwater ale and forced a smile onto his face. 'I need your help,' he began, then paused, as if arrested. Never before in his life had he spoken those words.

Louise was to relive that morning often in the months that followed. At the time she could not be aware it would prove to be the hinge on which her life turned, yet even as the regent and Crozier talked there was a crackle in the air, a sense of unreality that set this day apart. All present knew that whatever the outcome, things were set to change.

At first, Crozier barely spoke. Flint-eyed, he listened as Albany explained his visit. The pair were seated side by side at the head of the long pine table, while the regent's retinue and the Crozier clan stood to attention at their back, each side watching their lord as a hawk does its handler.

Louise alone could read her husband's expression. While the

regent talked, sentences tumbling out in such profusion it seemed he hoped to drown his listeners in words, Crozier's mind was at work. When finally Albany wound up his preamble, his digressions, his clever allusions and witty asides, he came to the point. Would the borderer, he asked, bring his men to battle against Dacre? He would make it worth his while.

The great hall hushed. Old Crozier's fingers trembled as he waited for Adam's reply. Tom's eyes narrowed, though he chewed a feathered grass and seemed indifferent to whatever was being said. Benoit stood as if on guard, legs planted, hands clenched. Only the wolf uttered a sound, whimpering in his sleep by the hearth.

The regent's plea made, he too was at last silent, though his chest rose and fell as he watched his host, trying to anticipate his answer. Crozier's face said nothing, but while the hall waited for him to speak, he was calculating how far this perfumed visitor could be trusted. Not very, was his estimation. Men like Albany were true to none but themselves. Today he was asking Crozier to be his ally, but as soon as their countries were reconciled, Albany and Dacre might sit at the same table playing cards, or share a day's fishing on the Tweed. Nothing men like these did would shock Crozier. One thing only he knew for sure: they hated him and his kind. Nothing but desperation could have brought this man to his gates. The borderer lowered his eyes, to hide a flash of calculation. That being the case, he might find terms that would be to the clan's advantage.

Albany was beginning to wonder if Crozier was slow-witted, or had merely been struck dumb, when finally he leaned forward. 'What you suggest,' he said, 'is impossible. You flatter our clan with your confidence in our powers, but you dangerously underestimate the baron. Dacre cannot be beaten by force. He has thousands of men to call on, not just in the north.' He sat back, staring so intently at the regent that the Frenchman felt his face grow warm. It was as if the borderer was trying to see into his soul.

'So you will not help me, then?' he said, his voice hardening with disappointment.

Crozier shook his head. 'I suggest, instead, that you help me.'

The regent looked astonished. '*I assist you?*'

Crozier's mouth twisted in the semblance of a smile. 'The Croziers will never work for the crown. As you will have been warned, we're loyal to none but ourselves. Your very presence here makes the stones weep, so unwelcome is the court in these parts.'

There was a shifting of boots behind him as Albany's men tensed, reaching for their hilts. Ignoring them, Adam raised a hand. 'Have your men sent out of the hall. Mine too will leave.' At his command, the clan filed out, all but Louise, whom he gestured to sit beside him on the bench. Unnoticed, the wolf stayed by the fire, eyes closed but tail thumping.

It looked as if the regent would object. His retinue were on the point of drawing their swords, fearing an ambush, when he sighed. 'So be it.' Raising his voice, he ordered his soldiers to leave. 'Await me in the courtyard,' he said, shaking his head at Eglinton, who looked as if he would protest. 'This man is well aware of the consequences if he plays foul. I trust him. Clear the room.'

When only Crozier, his wife and Albany were left, the borderer leaned back, stretching his legs as if to straighten his thoughts.

'I believe we can serve each other's purpose. Already I have Lord Dacre in my sights, and plan to bring him down. My men and I have lately seen off one threat, a corrupt old henchman of his who learned what we are doing, but I cannot afford to run another such risk. That one nearly proved our undoing. Even so, I am slowly tightening a net around Dacre. With your help I can have him removed from his position far more swiftly, and see the north rid of its guard dog. That brings you a step closer to putting Henry in his place, and setting your court's affairs on a steady course. A more peaceful Scotland is in all our interests, even those of us out here, whose lives are never quiet.'

The regent's eyes widened with interest, but he remained thirled to the prospect of battle. 'That may be true, but I intend to take the Scots over the border, to destroy Dacre's castles, empty his vaults, and sue Henry for peace – or his throne. That is my way, even if it is not yours.'

Crozier shrugged. 'I wish you success. Yet whatever the outcome, my business with Dacre will still work to your advantage. In the event of peace, his removal will further undermine Henry. Should you fail, which is more likely, his deposing will be invaluable. He is Henry's eyes and ears in the borders. Without him, the king will be blind and deaf.'

Albany waved a glittering hand for him to continue. As plain in his speech as the regent was florid, Crozier described his need for denouncers, a band of ill-wishers who would lay their grievances against Dacre before the king. In doing so, he felt a stirring of hope that the game might at last begin to go his way. In that moment he recognised that, until this day, he had known, but never acknowledged, that his venture was all but doomed.

At Louise's bidding, fresh food and drink was brought by the servants, this time from the kitchen and not the guards' cellar. Crozier nearly laughed to see the regent sip with caution at his golden ale, and then, with relief, down it like a goose swallowing grain, his throat working hard to slake his thirst. Louise said nothing, but watched as if mesmerised by the regent's glister. Beneath her wide-eyed admiration she took his measure, and found nothing she liked.

The conversation continued for an hour, and then another. By the time morning had turned into afternoon, Albany had promised an introduction for Crozier to some of the most powerful names in the English north. 'With my imprimatur, a simple letter will gain you the entry and the outcome you desire.'

Louise left to fetch paper, pen, and candle. 'The first you must approach is Lord Foulberry of Foulberry,' he said when she returned, drawing the paper towards him. Glancing up, he looked for recognition in Crozier's face, but there was none. 'I advise you not to let him know his fame has not reached this far. He is a proud man.'

His eyes fell on Louise, then flickered back to his host. 'Foulberry's lands are on the Solway. He can muster two hundred horsemen, and a small fleet of ships. He has a French wife whose connections are almost as important as his. He is a trusted member of the privy council; she of one of the richest families in the old Norman lands near Cherbourg. Foulberry has long loathed Dacre. I can assure you that, knowing you petition him with my blessing, he will open the door to many who would wish to denounce Dacre, in a way none other in these parts ever could.'

With a practised flourish, he scrawled a note to Foulberry, sprinkled sand upon it, and blew it clean. 'Here,' he said, showing Crozier its contents. Crozier nodded, and the letter was folded in half, and half again.

A candle was lit, hot wax dripped onto the parchment, and the regent's signet ring was pressed deep into the scarlet gout, so red and soft it might have been a courtesan's pout. Brightened by the flame, Albany's skin glowed as if it too were wax. He lowered his voice. 'But there is something more I may be able to do for you.' Louise watched as his pupils turned velvet, and malice hardened his face. 'It is just possible that I could put my hands on letters – the most damaging letters imaginable – that, if read by the king, would condemn Dacre to the Tower.'

'Letters from Dacre?' asked Louise, unable to keep silent. He looked at her, as if in pity.

'I cannot be certain, madame. Indeed, the letters may no longer exist. I have merely heard tell of them.' He examined his lace cuffs, as if already he had said too much. 'But if they can be found, and their owner persuaded to part with them, they could prove useful to our cause. Decidedly so.'

'You know where to find them?' asked Crozier.

'I have a fair idea, but offer no guarantee. It seems more likely they have been destroyed, and yet . . .' The regent spread his hands in apology, and reached for his gauntlets. 'Now that our deal has been struck, I will make it my business to discover if they have survived, and if so, attempt to acquire them. It will not be easy. It may not even be possible. But if – if – I manage this, I will inform you immediately. That will be a happy day, for all of us.'

He smiled as he stood and held out his hand. Crozier grasped it, and as their eyes met, each knew he had made a pact he had never before thought possible, or wise.

Long after the regent's party had left, the letter lay untouched.

Late into the night Crozier, Louise, Tom and Benoit sat round the table talking, seeming always to ignore, yet never for a second forgetting, the square of parchment with its imperious stamp. It brought with it the smell of the court, an unwelcome intrusion from a world they mistrusted and feared. And yet, as Crozier was obliged to admit, it represented his best, perhaps his only hope of seeing Dacre defeated. When eventually they retired to their beds, he stuffed the missive into one of the hunting horns by the fireplace, and plugged it with moss. He did not want it near them while they slept.

CHAPTER SIXTEEN

December 1523

Leaning against the wall by the cellar door, chewing a wad of salt beef, Oliver Barton had watched the regent and Crozier conferring. Elbowed to the back of the group, the sailor had caught only snatches of the conversation before the hall was cleared, but there was no mistaking that by the time the regent's retinue left an alliance of sorts between Albany and Crozier had been agreed, and that Dacre's downfall was the knot that bound them. Before the regent's party had reached the mouth of the valley, the clan had gathered in the great hall. Barton hovered by the fire, cleaning his gutting knife with a pocketful of grass.

Little, however, was said within his hearing. He had been two months at the keep, and nobody liked his presence. Maintaining their distance as if he were a rotting fish, their lack of trust was plain. Even Hob, who had no bad word for anyone, would do no more than nod when the sailor passed. The place beside him at dinner sat empty, the clan preferring to stand as they spooned their broth than brush elbows with him. Thus, that afternoon, when Tom saw him loitering at the edge of the hall, his rope of hair lying like a caul around his neck, he sent him outdoors, to do a shift on the walls.

It made no difference to Barton. Untroubled – he had suffered far worse in his time – he kept his thoughts to himself, and made sure he earned his keep in the fields and on sentry patrol. Unheated and unfriendly as it was, Crozier's Keep was better than gaol and the prospect of the gallows. At night he slept with a clear conscience and a full stomach, and dreamed of better times ahead.

For a man such as Barton, looking beyond tomorrow was a new sensation. As long as he could remember he had lived for the day, not thinking about what the morning would bring. The conditions of his release from Edinburgh's gaol had been simple, yet he chafed at the obligation that now lay upon him. The price for his escape from the noose was too high, the offer of money miserly, and the job itself tedious for one who enjoyed the thrill of the chase on the high seas, as well as its spoils. His plan – perhaps the first of his life – was to follow orders for a few weeks, then disappear from sight. Nobody, not even the all-powerful Lord Dacre himself, would be able to find him once he'd set sail for France, or Ireland, or Spain, or wherever a ship would take him.

Knowing his present situation would not last for long, he remained vigilant. A few days after the regent's visit, when his night watch came to an end, he did not make for his bed, but for the stables instead. Tiptoeing in, he chose a young, sturdy horse, fit for a long ride. Binding its hoofs in sacking, he led it into the yard, a fistful of oats and a drink at the trough keeping it quiet. In the loft above the stalls, Hob slept on, undisturbed.

The keep was not awake, the kitchen fires so newly lit their smoke had not yet reached the sky. Black as an unswept chimney, the morning dark clung to him. Waiting for the new watch to pass beyond the gate tower, he hurried under the arch, and out into the woods. Beyond the walls the valley lay cold and quiet. Drawing his hood low, he climbed into the saddle, and set off down the track.

Afternoon was fading when Harbottle came into sight, the lamps on its ramparts glimmering gold. Kicking his horse into a canter, Barton rode off the hills, and met the gatekeepers with a flurry of earth and an imperious shout.

It was Blackbird who led him into the castle. Walking ahead of the sailor, whose weapons had been left at the gate, he cast no word or smile on him. Distaste curled his lip, and he put a reassuring hand to the knife in his belt, fingering its heavy hilt. At the door of the hall, he showed the visitor in with a bow, closing the doors but standing by them, in case his lordship called.

Seated before the fire, Dacre received Barton alone. The sailor bent his head in greeting, but there was nothing of the serf about his stance. He had the stare of a rogue, a man who recognises no authority, nor bounds. A frown deepened the crease between the baron's eyes. He had dealt with more criminals than a high court judge, and he knew all the shapes they came in. Barton, he guessed, was one of the worst: sly, cruel, and clever. He suppressed a shudder. In his time he had employed many such men. One more could do no harm.

He waved Barton to the settle by the hearth. 'I wouldnae say no to a mouthful of ale,' the sailor said as he spread his legs towards the fire. 'Nor a bite to warm my stomach.'

Gracelessly, the baron poured him a mug. 'Ye can eat all you like when we have talked,' he said, as the sailor gulped down the draught, 'but first I need to know what news you bring me.'

Barton stifled a belch, and held the mug out for more. When that was drained, he slapped the tankard on the floor, and looked the baron in the eye. 'Crozier's your enemy, that's for sure.'

'So much I already knew,' said the baron, standing before him, a tree of a man to this stunted shrub, as if to remind him of the gulf between their stations.

'Ye have many, I am sure,' the sailor agreed. 'All powerful men do. But what I saw this week could mean trouble. On his own, I doubt Crozier could do you much harm, but he had a visitor on Thursday who could hurt ye sair.'

The baron's silence would have unnerved a less confident man, but Barton took his time before continuing, picking a burr from his sleeve, and looking into the flames as if for a reminder of what he had come to tell.

He nodded, though Dacre had not spoken. 'It was the regent, the Duke of Albany. And a right peacock he is too, painted and powdered and dressed like a lass, with lace at his neck and his cuffs.' He snickered. 'I tell ye, it takes some guts to traipse around the borders rigged out like that.'

A click of exasperation from the baron made him look up, and he continued. 'That's no important, of course. But he stayed half a day, in private parlay with Crozier. The only part of the discussion I heard was that Albany wanted him to raise his men against you.'

'What did Crozier say to that?'

'Well, he refused outright.' Barton sounded disappointed. 'Said his family would have no dealings with the crown. After that, everyone was sent out of the hall. But when the Regent left, they spoke amicably to each other. I'd say they had reached terms.'

The baron turned to stare into the fire, fisting a hand in his palm. 'So they have made some agreement.'

'That's my understanding. I don't know what it is, but whatever the pact, it's intended to bring your ruin.'

Dacre placed his hands on the chimneybreast and stared into the flames, fine dust drizzling from under his grip as he sandpapered the stone. The air around the sailor grew cool without the fire's blaze, until at last the baron turned. 'Albany is a weak man, leading a country more puny still.' He laughed. 'He was on the brink of taking Carlisle, and I talked him out of it. There we were, my men lined up behind me, facing his army, so nervy their horses twitched as if they were covered in flies. Most likely I need not have bothered. His men would no doubt have fled before they reached the city walls. But I enjoyed the showdown. It was like a scene from my old jousting days. It amused me.'

Barton eyed him, unsure of this new mood. 'It didnae seem to me that there was anything droll about the regent's plans. It's yer head he wants, stuck on a spike.'

Dacre's face was as cold as he found Barton's. 'I am sure he does. But I find it strange that he has joined forces with Crozier. One is a fleabitten commoner, the other one step from the throne.'

He kneaded his reddened palms. 'The border chief is playing deep. He'll be out of his depth with the old king's cousin. I wonder if either side knows what he's doing.' He was talking more to himself than to Barton. 'But is there anything to fear from Crozier? Was he behind the Jedburgh stampede, or is he an opportunist, latching onto a better man's campaign?' He shook his head. 'Whatever the truth of it, I doubt he, or Albany, will do me much damage. Nobody has yet.'

He raised his head, and stared at an arrow-slit window, from which day had fled. His voice was flat, its bombast gone. 'But I am now warned, and it would be foolish to ignore what you have told me. None of my other spies has brought me anything from the Fenwicks or the Ridleys, though their reports arrive almost daily. For all their news – and yours – I still do not know who drove those horses over the cliffs.' He sighed, and spoke with obvious reluctance. 'Ye have done well to bring me this, and I thank ye.' He dug a hand into his jerkin, pulled out a small purse and dropped it in the sailor's lap. 'As agreed at the outset, you'll be paid well for all your reports. For now, it is best ye remain at the keep. If there are any serious developments, I need to be told.'

Ignoring the unspoken injunction to be gone, Barton sat where he was. Dacre stared at him. When it was plain the informant had more to say, he took a step closer. 'This fee is not enough?'

Barton had not touched the purse, which lay where it had fallen on his stained hose. 'First, the food ye promised me, sir. I've eaten nothing since midnight past.'

'Ye'll be well fed from our kitchen, I assure you. And you can sleep in the barracks, where it's warm.' The baron could not hide his irritation. 'But there's something more?'

Barton nodded. 'However much giltsilver is packed into this thimble it's no enough, when you consider the dangers I face every day.'

'Ye were in worse danger in the castle gaol, my man. Whatever price ye put on your life, you'd still be in my debt, even if this purse was empty.'

Barton's tongue ran over his lips. 'Our arrangement, as I recall the queen making clear at the outset, was for you to offer some reasonable recompense for my efforts. That's all I'm asking. And this poxy wee bag does not seem reasonable to me.'

'Ye think they suspect you?' the baron asked, as if he had not spoken.

'They dinnae trust me, and do not hide the fact. Me being gone overnight is sure to deepen their suspicions.'

'A man like you is used to lying, are ye not?'

'Aye, but there's a hundred of them to one of me. It's no what ye'd call a comfortable situation.'

'More comfortable, surely, than awaiting the hangman's knot. A degrading end that would have been, for one such as you.'

The baron spoke with disdain, but Barton did not flinch. 'I'd have found a way out of the gaol long afore that day. The dowager queen set me free as if I was a slater she'd found in her slipper. Nae doubt she thought I should be eternally grateful she had saved me from the dungeons, and from death. But like the louse I am, I'd have found a crack to squeeze through and make my escape without anyone's help, dinnae ye fear.'

Dacre looked at the set of his mouth, the strength in his wrists, the unlit chill of his eyes, and found he did not doubt it.

He turned and called for Blackbird. The butler entered, and the pair conferred. Blackbird's soft boots hurried out, and in the time it took him to fill another purse no word was spoken in the hall. Untroubled, Barton sat with his hands on his knees, staring at the rafters.

A figure passed the open doors. 'Father?' said Joan, seeing him standing as if frozen in place. She came towards him and he moved to stand between her and his visitor, but Joan stepped aside and saw the sailor, a faint smile on his face as he traced the stains of soot and damp on Harbottle's eaves.

'Be gone, girl, this instant!' hissed the baron, a hand in the small of her back. Distracted, Barton shifted on the settle and caught sight of Joan, her mud-spattered skirts, and the sulky frown beneath her crooked wimple.

'Of course, Father,' she said, bobbing her knee, but Barton was not fooled. This was a girl who did as she wished. Before the baron turned to catch him staring at his daughter, the sailor had fixed his gaze on high once more.

Part Two

1524

If Not To Heaven . . .

CHAPTER SEVENTEEN

February 1524

Winter settled on the borderlands, and the earth grew tight as a drum. At the foot of the frosted hills every path was slick with ice. Rivers froze, caught in twisted plumes as waters leapt over a fall or swirled in a pool, trapped in gargoyle form as if carved by a demented mason. Trees stood sentinel, stiffened with hoar, the slightest wind setting them tinkling as their glaze splintered and fell. A haze shimmered around their tops as living wood breathed beneath its cold skin, warmer air creating a cowl of mist that did not lift from advent to a month after Christmas. Even then, it gave way only when the skies shook out their snows, dragging grey columns that blotted the light and smothered the land.

Adam Crozier roamed the borders in this weather as if it were June. A few days after the regent's visit he, Tom and Benoit had begun their forays in search of allies. With Albany's letter in his hand, the borderer approached the most noble families in the region, a tribe whose voices were as hard and expressions as harsh as the season. By comparison the regent, for all his flounces and flourishes, was not half as grand.

Unflinching in the face of a knife or a sword, Crozier found it harder to breach the fortresses and prejudices of these nobles than to launch into armed combat. He was not the first to discover a habitually still tongue miraculously loosened by nerves, and to hear a voice he barely recognised run away with itself and present a fool to the unloving world.

It was to Sir John Wetherington of Wetherington that he introduced his less austere self, and learned his lesson. The knight, who had the king's ear and could muster a hundred men at six hours' notice, cast a look soaked in contempt at his visitors. Steam rose from the riders' frosted cloaks as they stood before the knight's hearth, creating a fug of horse sweat and leather. The noble kept his guards at his side, hands upon their swords, as Crozier explained his purpose, assuring him of the regent's support for his cause. The guffaw Wetherington unleashed at this message made Crozier's face glow with rage. Yet, sensing he was about to be ejected from the tower house by the guards, rather than teach the man manners at the point of a blade he found himself babbling. He did not need to look over his shoulder to feel Tom and Benoit's surprise as he began to describe the day Albany had visited. The weather, the regent's retinue and the food they had eaten were all laid before the knight, whose eyes widened to hear a border chief describe plain fare and humble beer as if it might sway his opinion.

Perhaps it was the oddity that made the knight relax. That, or Crozier's palpable discomfort. No one with treachery on their minds would dare, surely, enter his gates to pour out a cook's tales. Crozier, finally catching hold of his tongue, stood sweating but quiet. He squirmed at the amusement in the noble's eyes as he bade the borderers sit, and set his guards at ease. Offering ale – a Northumbrian amber whose velvet taste spoke as eloquently of the man's wealth as a missal's worth of words – Wetherington too drank, indicating that now they were able to do business.

That encounter proved fruitful, as well as instructive. When next Crozier approached a noble, he had control of himself. Schooled by his wife in silence in the past week, he was reminded that he could command respect with no more than a look. It was just as well. Richard Foulberry of Foulberry, lord of the lands on the English side of the Solway, was not blessed with patience. Nor was his wife, whose cool gaze would, only a week before, have unnerved the borderer, unused to mingling with the higher estates and suffering their aquiline stares.

Foulberry proved as useful as the regent had promised. Cutting across the borderer's opening speech, he flicked his fingers for the letter Crozier held. Breaking the seal, he read it in a heartbeat and handed it to his wife, who looked from the regent's words to the border chief, fresh interest in her dark eyes.

That day, Crozier allowed himself at last to believe he might bring down his enemy. Over a meal of roasted meats and honeyed fruits, whose rich sauces and spiced flavours were a reminder of Lady Foulberry's French homeland, he, his men and the Foulberrys discussed the liaisons they might make between their houses, and those of the most trusted and powerful of Henry VIII's northern subjects.

'Give me the month,' said Foulberry at the end of dinner, removing the eyeglasses that pinched his nose as he read the list they had composed. 'In that time I will enquire of my closest friend, Marcus Selby of Setonlands near Durham, who has men inside Dacre's camp.'

Lady Foulberry put a hand on her husband's ermine cuff. He covered it with his own, and looked at Crozier. 'Isabella wishes you to understand that you and your men are welcome as our guests whenever you please.' He glanced at her ladyship, who was nodding.

'In this treacherous weather, your work is hard enough,' she said, 'without spending a night on the road. There is nowhere in these parts I would allow my dogs to sleep, let alone a man such as you.' She paused, as if contemplating just what sort of man he was, her eyes travelling over his countryman's garb, his unadorned and roughened hands. 'Should anyone disturb us while you are here,' she continued, in a voice that held barely a note of a foreigner's accent, 'we will say you are my farmer cousin from Normandy. That way you need not speak.'

She smiled and hitched her furs around her neck, though a snowdrift of breast remained exposed.

That first visit had been in December, shortly before Christmas. The men had a punishing ride back to Teviotdale, their horses tiring after a few miles on tracks so hard their shoes rang out like chimes. Jolted with every step, the riders were not much less weary. But while they reached the keep with every bone aching, they were in good spirits. Alerted to their return by the wolf, who was barking fit to waken his ancestors, Louise ran out into the courtyard and caught her husband's hands as he dismounted. He pulled her to him, throwing the reins into Hob's care. 'We make progress,' he whispered into her hair, and kissed her swiftly, before any would see.

In the following days, Louise watched Crozier's lightened mood, pleasure mingled with concern. His evident relief revealed all too plainly that until the regent's visit he had been troubled, and afraid. Now he slept through the night without muttering or leaving their bed to stand by the unshuttered window, staring into the dark until he was as cold as the flagstones beneath his bare feet.

Christmas mass had been celebrated, and Father Walsh sent on his way with a mule laden with enough food to last him till Easter. Louise had pressed him to stay, but since Mother Crozier's death, five years since, the keep held few charms for the priest. Where once he would have spent a week among them, now he returned to the village as soon as his offices had been conducted, preferring his warm house near the church to the Keep's promise of chilblains. Perhaps too he was glad to escape the reminder of the place where he had given Martha the last rites, touching holy oil to eyelids that for several days before they closed forever had neither seen nor recognised him. Lifting her head at this solemn moment, when the family was gathered round Mother Crozier's bed, Louise was the only one to notice that the priest's oil was mixed with his tears.

Three days of eating, sleeping and loitering within the keep followed the mass, by which time Tom was restless. 'We need to get back on the road, brother,' he said, eyeing Crozier with disapproval. Adam sat on the settle by the fire, fondling the wolf's ears and eating the hazelnuts his wife cracked for him from her stool by his knee. In response, Crozier gave a lazy smile.

Ella bustled across the hall, two small children trailing at her heels like ducklings, the others seated at Benoit's feet as he carved a toy from a nub of wood. Nothing had been revealed of what had happened while her husband had been away with the Crozier brothers, yet it was obvious to everyone that he had returned with new confidence, and was treated with greater respect. Whatever had taken place, he had acquitted himself well. That he had told her little did not disturb her, nor did Louise enquire. They did not need, perhaps did not want, to know everything their men did.

Smiling as she passed her husband, Ella tapped Tom lightly on the arm. 'For the lord's sake, give him peace. There's folk who need a bit of time by their own hearth. Ye'll be singing a different tune when you've got a wife of your own.' With a sigh, Tom picked up his cloak and left, seeking the village and whatever excitements it might hold this long, dull day. Louise and Crozier exchanged glances, but no one said a word. He was young still, and they were not his guards.

'What do you do next?' Louise asked Crozier, when the noise of Benoit's children drowned their words once more.

'Stay here a while,' he replied. 'I'm waiting for answers from three houses we've spoken to who say they will lodge complaints with the king: Wetherington, Selby and Ratcliffe. I expect their messengers before the snows begin.'

'And then?'

'Then, but not before, we go back to Lord Foulberry, who has promised to get news of Dacre's plans. He's the richest of the lot, and has most to lose from the baron's thieving ways.' Placing a hand on Louise's, though his eyes did not leave the fire, he lowered his voice. 'It is possible that with Foulberry's help we could trap Dacre and destroy him. I shouldn't look ahead too far, but I have this feeling . . .' He broke off, and looked down at her. 'I think we might win, Lou. For the first time, I sense it.'

Louise's eyes glittered, but she would not cry. Instead, she gripped his hand. This was good news. If Crozier was confident, she would be too. She had never met a man less boastful, or with such a level head. Neither fearful nor a braggart, he had his own measure, by which he gauged the chances of every venture he undertook. Rested after his journey, in the fire's soft glow he looked almost as young as when they first met, his face lean as ever but its harshness mellowed, or at least muted, after so many years of marriage. The wintry grey in his hair and beard matched his eyes, which held a faraway look as he leaned back and stretched out his legs. Smiling, Louise laid her head against his knee, staring with him into the scented pinewood flames.

They were on the cusp of a long and uncertain year but, for the moment, all was well.

On the last day of January the three set out again. Black specks on a hard-bitten land, they moved like flies across a sleeping face and left no trace but a trail of scuffed frost. Barely a soul was abroad. Smoke rising from the edge of a wood would tell of a hovel nearby, and occasionally they caught a flicker of cloak or nodding hood as a cottager gathered wood, or went on the hunt for rabbits. But few animals were abroad. Foxes lay low, birds kept to their trees, and the fields were empty, their sheep, goats and cattle huddled in pens and byres, where they sniffed the air, sensing snow heading their way.

Crozier too knew it was coming. As they crossed the border, close by the coast, the wind shifted, and a breath of warmer salt air allowed him to hope they might make the journey in time. So it proved. Changing horses twice, sharing a bed for warmth in inns untouched by brooms or soap, they reached Lord Foulberry's castle in three days. His black walls offered a cold welcome, their sheer stone broken only by arrow-slits and watchtowers, behind which guards moved on patrol.

Crozier was again struck by the contrast between the castle's forbidding exterior and the comfort within. Once over the drawbridge and through the great doors, it was like entering a fairy tale. Newly cut ivy hung in swags from the walls, and its wood-panelled rooms were draped with tapestries brought, had he known it, at painful cost from Isabella's homeland. Ceilings were painted in such a profusion of colour and imagery, it was as if the ancient myths had come alive before one's eyes. Fresh rushes, strewn with bay leaves, lined the flagstones, and carved settles hugged the walls, or were gathered around the castle's many fires, whose blazes leapt so brightly even the hounds had to retreat. On every shelf, table or cranny silverware and pewter caught the firelight and flashed a reply. From a distant corner came the ticking of a clockwork timepiece from Antwerp, its sound so unfamiliar the visitors believed it came from a caged bird.

For all their awe, the borderers marched in as if they were accustomed to such grandeur. Stern-faced, they followed the guard, who led them to the entrance of the main hall. Servants appeared to take their cloaks, and her ladyship rose from the fireside with her husband to greet them. Ignoring Tom and Benoit, she held out her fingertips to Crozier, who removed his riding gloves to take them, bowing low as he raised them to his lips. Smooth as buttermilk, they were scented with rosewater. Something like a smile softened Isabella's face as she led her guests across the hall.

Beneath a corona of candles that hung from the beams, the Foulberrys' children were playing, wooden swords clacking as the boys pranced around like miniature knights, uttering lusty taunts. Two very young girls sat in a corner near the fire, chattering to their painted dolls, absorbed in their private world. In one of their laps a ginger cat lay curled, like a woodsman's winter cap, but breathing. Crozier's expression lightened at the scene, and he bit back a laugh as the boys lunged at each other, uttering startling obscenities, no doubt learnt in the stables. It was their footwork that appalled him, not their language. Were he their father, he thought, he would be drilling them every morning in the yard.

Foulberry, moving almost at a trot, was oblivious of his ill-taught boys as he led them to his private chamber, off the great hall. The panelling was made from leather squares, stitched together like a quilt, and while the effect was sombre it offered such protection against draughts that the room was warm as a bread oven.

Her ladyship swept in ahead of Foulberry, her periwinkle skirts bringing a splash of colour to the dull chamber. Benoit squeezed in last, conscious of his size in this cramped space, although he was thinning by the week. Tom kept by his side, watching the Foulberrys. He had not liked her ladyship's proffered hand, nor Crozier's chivalrous bow. Nobody was less likely to fawn than his brother, and the act made him suspicious.

Perched on benches, their swords scraping the floor, the borderers gulped the hot wine her ladyship offered, finishing their mugs before Foulberry had done more than wet his lips. 'We have news for you,' said his lordship, nodding to his wife to summon more wine. 'Most interesting news, most unexpected.'

Pausing only while fresh mugs were poured, he continued. 'Selby's informant, at Harbottle Castle, has been a fount of secret tales.' A cold smile crossed his face. 'Not all in Dacre's inner circle are content, it seems. None dares break ranks, because they fear him too much, but from some words dropped in the servants' quarters, the Vice Warden, William Eure, is restless. His loyalty, it would appear, is faltering.'

Isabella Foulberry cleared her throat. 'Ambitious is surely the word you seek, my lord. It is plain he has an eye on Dacre's post.'

'Quite so.' Foulberry looked over his desk at the borderers. 'Her ladyship is most astute. Always has been, since the day she agreed to wed me.' He shot her a teasing glance, but his wife had lowered her eyes, fingers pleating her woollen skirts. Crozier doubted it was shyness that made her hide her thoughts.

Sipping his wine, Foulberry continued. 'Whatever the motives, Eure's disaffection could prove most useful for us. Word is he does not wholly approve of Dacre's methods. A recent raid under Sly Armstrong's command left him sickened, they say.'

'What happened?' asked Crozier.

'I am not entirely clear,' his lordship replied, 'but it would seem that Dacre was making an example of a tenant who had won his case in his court for damages against his lands and stock. Although a highland band of thieves was the guilty party, it was Dacre who was obliged to pay the recompense. Some new edict from the king, I believe. But Dacre did not want to oblige.' He picked a speck of dirt from beneath a fingernail. 'So he set the Armstrongs on the plaintiff and his family. It took place around Ridpath, in upper Redesdale. A nasty business.'

'Scumfishing?' Crozier guessed.

Foulberry nodded. 'The Armstrongs' favourite tactic but not, it would seem, to William Eure's taste. It revolts him.' He pushed his chair further from the table, and spread his hands on his ample stomach. 'Quite how he has held on to that post so long if he is squeamish is a miracle.'

'It is an unspeakably beastly deed,' murmured Isabella. 'One cannot condemn him for his scruples.'

She glanced at Crozier, who was looking severe, though whether at the talk of people slowly cooked alive in their houses, the lit straw around their homes smoking them like eels, or merely at Foulberry's news, was impossible to tell.

There was a pause before Crozier responded. 'If Eure is willing to stand out against Dacre he has a stronger stomach than most.'

'Maybe I malign him; perhaps I am unjust.' Foulberry raised a hand in appeasement. 'It is just that I find it strange a man from that quarter drawing a line at one particular act of barbarity, when he and his associates have committed every cruelty imaginable. His hands, every bit as much as Armstrong's or Dacre's, are soaked in blood.'

Tom leaned forward, his tone abrupt. 'Does the king trust Eure as he does Dacre?'

Foulberry raised his eyebrows, as if a child had spoken, unbidden. 'Why yes, I believe he does,' he replied, sounding a little surprised. 'Possibly he places more faith in him now than in the baron, as rumours fly about Dacre's affairs.'

Crozier looked at Tom and Benoit, and the three nodded in private agreement. The borderer turned back to Foulberry. 'We couldn't hope for better than to turn Eure to our cause, and have him lay before the king all the charges we gather against Dacre. For his deputy to lead the attack would surely seal his fate. But for me to approach Eure while all this is pure speculation and guesswork . . .' He broke off, shaking his head. 'Should we be wrong, and Eure still loyal, that would condemn me and my kin to the scaffold.'

Tom spoke again: 'Forgive us, my lord, but we have only your word that Eure might be persuaded to become our ally. We need more than that before we can act.'

'But of course.' Foulberry was unperturbed by the borderers' suspicion. He looked at his wife, who inclined her head at their guests.

'We understand your caution,' she said. 'After all, a month ago we were enemies too, or believed we were.' She stroked her fox fur, her hand sweeping back and back again so that its glass eyes caught the light as if it were awakening. As the rhythmic gesture continued, without pause, Benoit began to feel queasy. He looked away.

'What we propose,' said Foulberry, 'is that we invite Eure to visit.'

Crozier began to speak, but his lordship anticipated him. 'No, sir, have no fear. You would not be present. Not at that encounter, at least.' His voice softened. 'As you can understand, it is almost as dangerous for us to show our hand as for you. We must tread with extreme caution. A wrong step will bring Dacre's troops down on our heads, which would next be seen on Henry's block. No, no, gentlemen, we too must be careful.'

'Most careful,' echoed Isabella, continuing to caress the fox, whose head had slipped off her shoulder, to reveal the low cut of her gown.

Beyond the chamber's narrow window, daylight already seemed to be fading, though the afternoon was young. The fire crackled, and the wine and warmth were making Benoit's eyelids droop. 'There is much else to discuss,' said Crozier tersely, misliking the torpor that had crept into the room. Catching his meaning, Isabella rose, gathering her stole about her.

'I will have a good dinner prepared while you and my lord confer. After that, you must spend the night. You need to leave at first light and make good headway before the weather closes in.'

Tom put out a hand and tried to catch his brother's sleeve, but Crozier had risen and stepped beyond his reach. He bowed to Isabella. 'That's most generous of you, ma'am. We would be grateful to accept.' Benoit's stomach gave a rumble of approval as Isabella picked up her skirts and left. Tom's face darkened, to match the winter sky.

While the smell of roasting fowl and kettled fish escaped from the kitchen, the men drank and talked. Crozier reported the knights and farmers who had now agreed to put their names to any just indictment of the Warden General, knowing Foulberry was at the helm. There were presently seven, including Foulberry, all from ancient families whom Henry would respect: Lord Ogle, Ellarcar the chamberlain, Thomas Grayson and Malcolm Ridley, each of whom had also promised the aid of others they knew would support this cause, and Wetherington and Ratcliffe. All were respectable, and none coveted Dacre's position. Yet, as they deliberated the merits of these allies, there was not one of them who was unaware that seven was few against the forces Dacre could muster. A man of his guile might swat away any charges they laid against him, and convince the king that his accusers, and not he, were the traitors.

'We must hope that Henry is already tiring of him,' said Foulberry, unbuttoning his woollen waistcoat and pushing his chair an inch farther from the glowing logs.

'This is too risky a business to leave to hope,' said Crozier. 'We must lay before the king sufficient evidence to be sure that even if he is besotted with Dacre, and loves him as if he were his wife, he would have no choice but to act. The burden of proof lies with us, and I intend to make sure we throw everything there is at Dacre so that even he, snake that he is, cannot slither out of trouble this time.' Frowning at the fire, he lapsed into silence.

The summons to dinner brought these gloomy deliberations to an end. A rich meal awaited them in the great hall, so many dishes laid before them that the evening was well advanced before the board was cleared and a final tumbler of sack placed before each man. Foulberry ate as if leading a charge, but his wife did no more than pick at her plate. It was no wonder she was so slender, thought Tom, who spoke little and drank less. More than once he saw her ladyship look down the table at his brother as if hoping for a glance, but Crozier was busy with his spoon, or engaged with his lordship, and appeared unaware of her presence.

By the time they made for their bedchambers, each in a room of his own, snow had begun to fall. Benoit put a hand out of the window, the night's touch welcome after the heat of the hall. Leaving the shutters pinned back he got into bed, fully dressed, his sword at his side. All three did the same. Tom and Benoit were soon asleep, but Crozier lay awake, staring into the dark and listening to the wind gusting around the castle, uncomfortably conscious of the dangers they ran under this roof and in this country.

At first light the three gathered in Crozier's room and looked out upon a veiled, hidden land. Beyond the window fields of white lay beneath a chain mail curtain of falling snow that smothered the country in silence. The men said nothing, but a line between Crozier's eyes spoke for them all.

Lady Foulberry met them in the great hall, holding a candle that flickered over the gold in her brocade nightgown, a garment that for once was tied to the neck. Uncapped, her hair fell in a dark plait over her shoulder. 'How bad is it?' she asked.

'The snow's too heavy to travel,' said Tom. 'Until it stops we can't be sure how deep it lies, but it would be madness to set out in this. Already the wind is rising. It'll soon be a blizzard.'

Isabella looked grave, her eyes not leaving Crozier's face, though he said nothing.

'I will go to the stables,' said Benoit, to break the silence, 'make sure the horses are fine.'

'No need,' said Crozier, putting out a hand to restrain him. 'They will be well looked after, never you fear.' He turned back to Isabella, and cleared his throat. 'It would appear we will be your guests for more than a night, my lady. I hope that is not too inconvenient. Be assured, we'll leave as soon as possible.'

She smiled as if he had spoken nonsense. 'It will be not the slightest trouble. Given the service you offer this family, his lordship and I consider you and your men as close as kin. It will be a pleasure to have your company.'

From the hall behind her came the sound of small feet, and her ladyship's sons appeared at her side. They were already clutching their wooden swords, ready for the fray. A smile broke out across Crozier's face and he looked at the older boy, who had pointed his blade at the borderer's heart.

'If we are to be here for a time, let's make good use of it,' he said, pulling out his dagger, and with a flick of his wrist he sent the child's sword flying into the air. He caught it high above the boy's head. 'At the very least, lad, I can teach you how to fight.' Sheathing his knife, he handed him the sword. With a sulky look the boy took it and hid it behind his back. Only when he saw his mother's smile did his pout disappear, and he let out a laugh. 'On guard!' he cried, and advanced on Crozier, sword pointed this time at his gizzard.

CHAPTER EIGHTEEN

The borderers were Lord Foulberry's guests for twelve never-ending nights. When the blizzards had passed, and the snows ceased, all paths were blocked. A bitter cold set in, and held its breath. Trees snapped like twigs under the weight of snow, crashing unseen in the depths of the forest and setting off a pattering of snow from the shaken boughs around them. Birds fell lifeless out of the sky, ducks were trapped in glazen ponds, and in the meanest hovels peasants went to sleep never to waken again.

Out on the castle walls, Foulberry's guards stamped their feet and held their hands to the brazier, but still a few got frostbite. Archers came back empty-handed from the hunt, the river's fish were safe beneath a frozen lid, and no boats dared brave the sea under skies so forbidding. The smokehouse and the cellar's stores of salted beef were plundered, and a permanent watch was put on the castle well, to stir it free of ice.

Each day Crozier opened his shutters, praying for a thaw that would allow them to be gone. The morning he woke to a slither of slush off the roof his heart lifted, but it was several more days before it was safe to leave. Those hours dragged, nerves fraying, and tempers with them. Though Adam was polite to his hosts, with Tom and Benoit he was curt.

When eventually they set off, the way was treacherous still. Benoit's horse sprained a fetlock, with many trudging miles to cover before it could be stabled at a hostler's inn and allowed to rest. By the time the three reached the keep, the brothers were tired and taciturn, Crozier brooding on the fact that the best part of a month had been lost to the snows. Who knew what Dacre had been plotting while they were fretting before Foulberry's fires?

Louise feared that Crozier had brought the winter home with him. The confident man who had ridden off had not returned. In his place was a husband whose thoughts were far away. Harsh in look and all but silent, he was distant and unheeding.

In the days that followed Tom too was quiet, his face set as if hardened by the cold. Only Benoit was himself, describing to all who would listen the sumptuous castle where they had stayed. Louise's eyes widened as he painted a picture of elegance, display and comfort unheard of except at court.

When he and Ella were alone, he handed his wife a packet wrapped in linen and tied with a ribbon of bayleaves. 'What's this?' she asked, finding a small wooden box filled with scented wax.

'Her ladyship's own recipe,' said Benoit. Ella ran a finger over the wax, releasing the scent of primroses. 'She has her own distillery,' he went on, 'this poky wee room in the cellars, where she makes perfumed waters and salves. She gied me this for you.' With a wide smile Ella rubbed the wax onto her lips, making them glisten, though no more brightly than her husband's eyes at the sight of her pleasure.

Crozier brought Louise no such gift. Isabella had offered him a vial of rosewater for her, but he had shaken his head. 'She would not appreciate it, my lady,' he said. 'She is a country girl, very different from you.'

Tom had looked up, startled at the roughness of his tone. Unconcerned, Isabella crossed the hall in a swirl of skirts, and gave it instead to Tom, 'for the love of your life, young man. I doubt there's a woman in these lands who would not enjoy its scent. Even my scullery maids wear it. It makes life for everyone a great deal more pleasant.'

Delighted with her present, Ella showed Louise the primrose balm. Louise held the little box, smooth as a chestnut and scented like the first days of summer. Touching a finger to her wind-chapped lips, she refused Ella's offer of using it herself. 'But I will learn to make my own,' she said, sounding a little grim.

That night, as she and Crozier undressed for bed, she mentioned Ella's gift. Lady Foulberry, she said, was clearly a clever woman. Ella had shown her the wax, and Benoit had spoken of her ladyship's powders and perfumes and oils. 'Did she not offer anything to you?' she asked, hurrying to get beneath the blankets and furs.

'Aye,' said Crozier, 'she did. But I didn't think you'd want it.'

Snuffing the rushlights, he joined her under the covers. In the dark Louise reached for his hand, but he was turned from her, his back as cold as his voice. Wrapping her arms around herself, she asked, 'What is she like, this Lady Foulberry?'

Crozier sighed, then turned, heavily, to face her. 'She is beautiful,' he said, 'in a foreign sort of way. Far younger than her husband, and every inch the lady. She smells like a pitcher of flowers, paints her lips purple and dusts her cheeks white. She covers herself in furs, and wears gowns beneath that would shock a priest and delight most men.'

Louise spoke almost in a whisper. 'And you – did she delight you?'

'No,' said Crozier, his breath warm on her face as he ran his fingers through her hair, the way one comforts a child, 'she did not. Now, can we sleep?'

Tucked in his arm, Louise heard him sink into sleep but it was hours before she joined him. The image of Isabella Foulberry swam before her. It would not have worried her had Crozier not refused the gift, but why would he do that, if all was innocent between them?

The next day, as she picked her way across the icy yard to the brewhouse, she caught Tom glancing her way. 'What?' she asked. Tom shook his head and would have passed, but she grabbed his sleeve and pulled him inside the brewery, where they would be alone.

'Is something wrong?' she asked, her voice as low as the vaulted roof. 'You and Crozier have come home in the strangest of moods. Did anything happen while you were away?' When Tom looked uncomfortable, she added, 'Is it about him and that woman?'

'What woman?' he asked, so unconvincingly that Louise felt dizzy, as if her fears had been confirmed.

She put a hand on the wall to steady herself. 'Does he . . . Did they . . .?'

Tom shrugged, suddenly angry. 'I don't know if anything happened between them, but this I can tell you: I do not understand what game my brother is playing.' At Louise's stricken look, he continued, 'The woman has little breeding, for all her airs. She could not keep her eyes off Crozier and he, he . . .' Tom glared at the roof as he picked his words. 'He did not seem to dislike her attentions. Leastwise, he did nothing to keep her at a distance. And he played with her children as if they were his own.'

'Her children?' Louise put a hand to her mouth, as if this were the worst news of all. 'Played with them . . .?'

'The most part of each morning, he taught the boys how to fence. They clung to his side when we left. But he promised them he'd be back.'

'What did her husband make of this?'

'Lord Foulberry was buried in his books most of the time. Her ladyship flirted with all of us, as if he was in his dotage. All Foulberry did was nod, and smile, and tell the servants to bring more wine. One night I saw him put his hand up a serving girl's skirt, but if she noticed her ladyship said nothing.'

Louise's face was whiter than any lady's powder, and Tom grasped her by the shoulders. 'Listen, Adam may have done nothing at all wrong. It's just that he won't talk to me. I've tried asking what he is up to, but he would say nothing except he knew what he was doing, and I should trust him. He said I should not question him again. Then he went silent. You know what he's like. I would never have dreamt he could do such a thing to you, and I still want to believe he has not, and will not. He adores you. Everyone knows that.'

'Thank you,' said Louise, slipping out of his reach and holding the brewhouse door open.

'I am a fool,' Tom said guiltily. 'I should have said nothing.'

'I'm fine,' she replied, and gave him a push. With a backward glance he left. His spurs scraped the cobbles as he crossed the yard, his stride so furious he almost struck sparks.

Closing the door, Louise sat beside the copper cauldron, hid her face in her hands and wept. For a few minutes the world went black, as if it had been emptied of everything that mattered. Then she wiped her eyes and got on with her work.

When she returned to the keep, carrying a pitcher of newly drawn ale, no one noticed her reddened eyes. Crozier was at the blacksmith's and Ella was quietening her youngest, whose first tooth made his cheeks flame and his cries reach a trumpeter's pitch. Unobserved, Louise pocketed a couple of apples, saddled her young gelding and left the keep, taking the uphill track that wound high into the valley. The wolf padded at the horse's side, close to his mistress's boots.

Once among the trees Louise loosened the reins and let the horse find his pace. Beneath the leafless beeches and oaks daylight was thin, a fragile February blue that promised a cold evening and frosty night. A breeze was gathering, and she closed her eyes, letting it wash over her face. A tear trickled onto her cloak, unnoticed, as she thought about her husband. Last night's assurance about Lady Foulberry had done nothing to allay her fears, which Tom's doubts had merely confirmed.

Most wives, she knew, would not dare ask such a question, nor be given an answer. Dalliances were common, not just in houses such as theirs, but in the village's hovels. No rank was above such things, but the wise hid their indiscretions, appearances mattering more than morals. A wife's role was to pretend she knew of nothing awry, and to welcome the straying husband with open arms when he had tired of his adventures.

Why should it be different for her? What made her think her marriage was unlike others? She and Crozier were close, but so no doubt were many couples who shared their affections beyond the marital bed.

The gelding picked its way into the forest, snorting in the tickling air, but Louise did not notice where they were headed. Before her eyes she saw not the track or the trees but Crozier's gaunt face and gentle, horseman's hands. If he had succumbed to the Lady Foulberry, could she wholly blame him? In ten years of marriage she had failed in her main duty. She would be thirty next year, but had yet to give him an heir. By some standards a childless wife did not merit the title. Since she had not earned the position better call her simply concubine, or housekeeper.

And yet she had tried. At the memory of the family they might have had, Louise lowered her head. Their lost child, in the early years of their marriage, was a grief she had never got over. Dead within days of delivery, as very nearly was Louise, baby Helene was buried in the woods within sight of their chamber window. Confined to bed as she recovered, Louise had stared for days at the trees beyond the shutters, unable to think, or sleep, or eat. Crozier had sat with her, his hand on hers, then would ride out alone, not returning till dark. Since then, there had been no quickening in her womb to raise hope or alarm, and the years turned and passed, bereft of children, but not empty.

Afternoon was fading fast, but Louise would have ridden on had the horse not come to a halt. The wolf padded in circles and whined, uncertain which way to go. They had reached a stream, usually no more than a ribbon, but now swollen with hill-snow and rain. The gelding tossed his head, eyeing the swirling waters. Louise dismounted and patted his neck, turning him back the way they had come. 'Good boy,' she said, stroking his nose, and giving him an apple. Leading him homewards, she called the wolf to heel, and walked for a time, her boots scuffing the crispened leaves that, this deep into the forest, had barely been touched by ice. Her eyes ached, as did her head, but a cold calm had settled on her. If Crozier had become enamoured of Isabella she would be desolate, but she had surely played a part. It was she who had urged him to join the ranks of people like the Foulberrys and act as if he was of their kind. It was her ill luck that in Lord Foulberry's home he had perhaps found the family he had always wanted, and the sort of woman he wished Louise could be. The thought sickened her, but a stony resolve was gathering. She would ask him to take her on their next trip to Foulberry's castle: not to spy on him, or show her mistrust, but to see what kind of woman this lady was, and to let her know that Crozier's wife wanted to meet her rival. These were times that called for courage, and she would not lose her husband without a fight.

In the great hall, where the clan was gathered at dinner, Crozier stood by the fire, reading a letter newly arrived by messenger. Seeming not to notice Louise's riding gear, or her late return, he drew her aside.

'Lord Foulberry has news of Dacre's deputy. He writes that Eure will be presiding over the Warden General's court in Dacre's absence early next month, and that he has agreed to stay a night with Foulberry, when his business has been dealt with.'

'Will you meet him?'

The borderer shook his head. 'Not yet. Although Foulberry has suggested I could eavesdrop on their discussions.' At Louise's bemused look he explained. 'He understands that I might fear they are hatching a plot against me unless I hear their deliberations for myself. His wife has suggested I could be privy to their discussion, but invisible too.'

'So you would sneak behind the arras and lurk like a thief?'

'Precisely.' There was a light in his eyes, and she knew an idea was forming. 'Or maybe it should not be me. Someone else could do it.' She raised an eyebrow. 'Tom, I was thinking,' said Crozier. 'Better perhaps that it is him.'

Louise put a hand on his arm. 'Whether it's Tom or you, can I come too?'

It took a moment for Crozier to register her meaning. When it did, his scorn was scalding. 'Have you lost your mind? Do you have the first idea of the danger, the risks you'd run? I would rather put my head in a hangman's noose than let you roam the borders while there is a war on, let alone allow you to set foot in Foulberry's place.' He stared at her as if he were stunned.

'I only thought . . .' Tears filled Louise's eyes, and she would have hurried from the hall before they could spill had Crozier not caught her arm.

'This is not like you.' He spoke roughly, but there was concern in his eyes. 'You should not even be out alone on our own lands this late. I was beginning to worry. What is wrong with you? What is the matter?'

The urge to tell him what Tom had said was overwhelming, but at the sight of his exasperation, the fatigue and worry on his face, she kept quiet. She could not bear to make him angry again, nor create trouble between him and his brother. Telling him would change nothing, except to make things worse. Instead she shook her head, and said she was sorry. 'Sorry?' he echoed, sounding surprised. 'What have you to be sorry about? It is I . . .' But she was already gone.

CHAPTER NINETEEN

March 1524

It was late afternoon, and a bay horse was galloping through the woods. The rider lay low on its neck, whipping it on until his lashes raised weals. An empty stirrup flailed, the man's left leg hanging useless, and he gripped the reins less like a horseman and more as if he were drowning.

The bay was toiling, eyes wide with strain, but the man in the saddle was unforgiving. On they raced, beneath a canopy of greening trees, across the border hills. Emerging onto empty moor, they picked up even more speed. Only when they found the cover of forest once more did the pace slacken. But when the turrets of Crozier's Keep came into view, the rider gave a moan and dug in his spurred boot, goading the horse forward. By the time they reached the walls, both animal and man were done.

Louise was in the kitchens when Hob called her to the gates. On the scrubbed pine table, baked trout sat in a row of jars while she heated butter over the fire to seal it for her larder. Crozier, Tom and Benoit were away, at Foulberry's bidding, and she was in charge of the keep. From Hob's voice, she knew at once that trouble had arrived. Clattering the butter pan off the fire, she grabbed a cloth and wiped her greasy hands as she hurried after him. At the gates, Wat the Wanderer was holding the horse's bridle, but there was no need. The creature was blown, running with sweat and barely able to catch its breath. The man in the saddle was swaying.

'Help me,' he said, when Louise appeared, 'please help me,' before he slumped onto his horse's neck, the reins falling from his hands. Wat and the guards dragged him out of the saddle, and laid him on the ground.

'Bring me water,' said Louise, kneeling to remove the man's helmet, and unbuckle the neck of his cloak. At the sight of long scarlet hair, drenched in sweat, she sat back. She knew this man.

'He's yin o the regent's retinue,' said Hob, raising him so Louise could trickle water into his mouth.

Gulping the water, the soldier opened his eyes to find himself propped up in Hob's arms. He looked around in confusion. 'You are safe here,' said Louise, as if to a child. 'Drink this. Then we will get you inside.'

'Will ye look at his leg,' said Hob, under his breath. The soldier's knee was twisted to the side, the leg lying askew like the limb of a puppet whose strings have been cut.

'It's broken,' she said.

Hob nodded. 'Aye, and badly.'

Gesturing to the guards, Louise followed as they carried the young man into the keep. 'Take him to the men's quarters,' she said, but as she spoke the soldier raised his head.

'No!' he wailed. 'They're after me. If they find me lying there, they'll kill me for sure!'

Louise's heart began to pound. 'Who is after you? What have you done?' But the effort of speaking had sent the soldier back into a swoon.

Hob took her elbow. 'Get him into the hall. We need to keep him conscious.'

Louise ran ahead of the guards to find a blanket. Old Crozier was dozing by the fire, the wolf warming his feet. He woke with a start as she brushed past him, and blinked at the sight of the stranger being carried in like a corpse. He put a hand on the wolf's head, to keep him quiet. The dog's hackles stirred, but he made no sound. When the soldier was stretched on the settle, and a rug folded under his head, Hob knelt beside him, and lit a bouquet of crows' feathers under his nose. At the foul smell, the young man awoke, twisting his head away from the stench, but though it made him want to retch it had cleared his senses. 'They'll be here any minute,' he said, his foreign accent sharpened with alarm.

'Who?' Louise repeated.

He looked at her, wide-eyed. 'The border guards, from Selkirk. They chased me out of the town. The town's people had cornered me and two were setting on me with clubs when the guard arrived . . .' He paused for breath, and wiped a cold sweat from his lip. 'They broke my leg, but with the good Lord's help I got onto my horse . . .'

'Where are the rest of the regent's men?' asked Hob, keeping the smouldering feathers near the soldier's chin.

His head sank back on the blanket. 'I have deserted,' he said. 'Albany will have me hanged if they find me.' At the sight of his listeners' shock, he gripped Louise's sleeve. 'It is a very long story. Please, madame, please hurry! They will almost be at the doors. You must hide me, or I am dead.'

The man was a deserter, and maybe worse, yet Louise had no hesitation. She turned to Hob. 'Take his horse out by the postern gate and down to the back field, so he's not in the stable when they get here.' He left, at a run. She looked at Wat and the guards, who stood by the fire. 'We shall hide him behind the walls. You know where I mean?' Wat nodded, and was bending to lift him when shouts came from the gates.

A guard ran out into the courtyard, and was back in a moment. 'They're here,' he yelled from the door.

'Keep them out,' cried Louise. 'They cannot be allowed to force their way in.' She turned to Wat, her voice rising with fear. 'It's too late to hide him. Go back to the walls. They have no right to gain entry without Crozier's authority.'

Swords in hand, the guards left. Louise looked at the soldier, who had closed his eyes in despair, knowing the end was near. 'What is your name?' she said.

'Antoine. Antoine d'Echelles.'

'From now on, say not a word in English. You are my French cousin, *comprenez-vous*?'

He gave a feeble nod.

There was the sound of feet from the stairwell, and Ella appeared in the hall, three of her children scampering around her skirts. The fourth was in her arms, sucking a rag, his eyes sleepy from crying.

Louise put a hand to her head, to calm herself, but even before Ella had taken in the scene, she had begun issuing orders.

It was only a matter of minutes before the courtyard filled with voices and the tread of boots. The Selkirk guards had barged their way into the keep.

Throwing the door back on its hinges, they entered the hall. Five men, in black leather and steel helmets, brandishing swords, stood at the top of the steps. At sight of the hall below, they were brought up short.

Around the table, a family dinner was being eaten. An old man, two women, and a young gentleman sat dandling spoons over pots of steaming fish. Ale mugs were half empty, the meal well under way. A scattering of wooden platters and crumbled bread told of children who had eaten their fill. Heedless of the adults, two boys and their sister raced around the room, human bees whose buzz would have driven the Selkirk men crazy in a smaller space. A large dog sat on his haunches between the old man and the young. His blue eyes followed the guards, but he did not move. A moment earlier, Louise had placed the wolf at the soldier's side, with the command to stand guard over him, and there he would stay until ordered otherwise. The children were also under instruction, urged to be as boisterous and rude as they liked. They could not believe their luck. Even the infant, in his mother's lap, found himself a role. Ella had given him an old horn, which he was banging against a tin plate as if to raise the dead.

Louise, seated at the head of the table, rose in outrage at their arrival. 'Guards! Guards!' she cried. 'See off these barbarians!'

Wat and his men appeared at the stairhead. 'Mistress,' said Wat, breathlessly, 'they would not be kept out.'

Crossing the hall, as the border guards descended the stairs, Louise stared up at them. 'By what right do you enter these premises?' she asked, her voice shaking. 'Who are you? What is your business?'

The leader of the posse would not allow himself to be thwarted by any woman, however outraged. 'We have reason to believe you are harbouring a fugitive from justice,' he said, removing his helmet in the hope that might dampen her fury.

She said not a word, merely raising her eyebrows in disbelief.

A man at the leader's back pushed forward. 'There is a heretic on the loose, and his trail has led us here. Unless he somehow turned himself into a bird and has flown off, he is in the keep, whether you know it or not. He was badly lamed. He cannot have gone any further.'

Emboldened by the deputy's confident tone, the officers moved towards Louise. 'We have the right to search the keep and its buildings,' said the leader, holding her stare. 'By statute of the warden of the middle march, we can demand entrance to any property we suspect of sheltering someone who threatens the country. If you were the regent himself, we would be within the law in crossing your threshold.'

'You do not have that right,' she replied with contempt, 'and well you know it. You cannot intimidate me with talk of laws. I may be a woman but I am not a fool. With my husband absent, and without my permission, you have no authority to be here. This is trespass. You are breaking the law.'

'Goodwife . . .' began the guard, but she cut him off.

'And why would we, of all people, be suspected of harbouring a heretic?' she asked, on a rising note of indignation.

'We don't . . .'

'We are all good Christians in this house. And like all good believers, here you find us, at our Sunday devotions. That you burst through our gates on the Lord's Day makes me question how devout you and your men can be.' She made the sign of the cross, warding off the presence of such ill-doers the way healers sniff herbs to protect them from the plague.

The children were running in whooping circles around the group, pretending they were corralling sheep, and Louise was obliged to raise her voice. 'You have disturbed a sacred family meal, officer, all the more precious as we approach the days of our Lord's Passion. Should you not also be at home examining your souls?' She fingered the rosary at her waist, examining the well-worn beads while she waited for an answer.

The guard coughed. 'Madam, we are obliged to work all days of the week. If a man commits an act of heresy on the Lord's day of rest, we cannot let it pass. For breaking this holy day his crime is thereby doubled, and his punishment with it.'

Louise smiled, the way a dog bares its teeth. 'Well, as you can see, we have nothing to hide.'

There was silence, each side weighing the other. If Louise had hoped the men would back down, she was to be disappointed. Planted before her, uncertain but still suspicious, they stood their ground. 'If you do not let us conduct our search,' said the leader, when it seemed Louise had no more to say, 'such obstruction would be viewed very seriously by the march warden, law or no law. In recent years he has had reason to doubt the loyalty of people in these ungoverned parts. You'd be wise to give him no further grounds for suspicion.'

Louise gave an irritated sigh. 'Very well,' she said, as if the last thing she wished was to displease the warden. 'My husband will no doubt chastise me severely when he hears about this, but you have my permission to examine the keep and its outbuildings. But be quick about it. He will be home soon.' She looked the officer in the eye, a nasty glint in hers. 'He is a reasonable man, but he does not like intruders. The last such, a miserable pack of thieves' – she turned to Old Crozier, who nodded at the imaginary memory – 'never left the keep. Their remains lie in the pit, behind the midden.'

With a harried air, the Selkirk guards set out through the keep, Wat and his men so close on their tails they might have been shackled. Only Hob remained in the hall, standing motionless in the gloom at the foot of the stairs. The French soldier's horse was grazing safely, his harness and saddle stowed at the back of the stables.

While two officers searched outdoors and two the keep itself, one remained posted in the great hall. Louise gripped her hands together, to hide their trembling. Seeing her expression, Ella's daughter Emily stopped playing and ran up to her. Before the child could speak, Louise crouched, smiling. 'On you go, poppet,' she said, and clapped her hands, sending the child back to her whirling games, though her cheeks were ruby and her legs growing tired.

Ella poured ale into a mug and held it out to Louise, who sipped it slowly in the hope of steadying her heartbeat. As she handed it back, the women shared a look.

The guard caught the silent exchange. He shifted, eyes narrowing and, after a second's hesitation, strolled towards the table, to get a better look at the languorous young man whose back was to the room, his face half hidden by the brim of his black felt hat.

Louise put a hand on the young soldier's shoulder. '*Antoine, mon ami, est-ce que tu veux un morceau de fromage?*' she asked him gaily. Turning to the guard, she explained. 'Our goat's cheese can rival even that from Antoine's homeland.' She repeated her words in French, and Antoine dutifully gave a gasp that might have passed for a laugh. Shaking his head, he replied at length. Louise translated. 'My cousin disagrees. He says he cannot bear cheese from Scotland, it is more sour than raw rhubarb. But our ale, he admits, is good.' She topped up his mug, and he drank it down in great gulping draughts that proved the truth of his remarks. Taking a cloth to his face, as if to wipe his lips, the young man contrived also to dry the sweat that was trickling down his neck.

Beneath the table, Antoine's leg was propped on a stool. On his lap lay a rug, to shield his canted limb from any casual eye. As the guard drew closer, Antoine looked over his shoulder. Removing his hat, he turned a curious gaze on the man, as if amused at his interest, and offered him a clear view of his face. At Antoine's side, the wolf's gaze was every bit as intent. A low growl tickled his throat. If the guard came a step closer he would leap.

'Where are ye from?' the guard asked the soldier, halting at the sight of the wolf.

Antoine's smile remained in place, though the pallor of his face was ghastly. The guard repeated the question, and Louise took a seat beside her new guest. 'He speaks no Scots,' she answered for him. 'He is one of our kin, but newly arrived. He is a soldier to trade, but has agreed to help my ailing cousin Benoit in his carpenter's shed for a time. I hope to have him fluent before the year is out.' She took his hand, and pumped it playfully on the table. Seeing the man's stare fixed still on Antoine, she continued: 'Antoine is my late mother's godson, the child of her dearest niece.'

'Ask him to stand up,' said the guard, as if she had not spoken.

The hall fell silent. The children had stopped their chase, the infant had tired of the horn and was sucking his thumb, and nobody at the table was able to breathe. Into this abyss charged Emily. With a squeal, she flung herself at the table, nearly toppling Old Crozier from the bench, and throwing her arms around the soldier, who came close to fainting once more as his leg fell off the stool. His face hidden in the child's embrace, he fought back the encroaching darkness, shook the ringing out of his ears and, with a look as grim as if carved from granite, made to get up. The girl loosened her grip, but before he could rise she held up a small leather-bound book. 'Look what I found!' Antoine's face went from white to grey, and Louise's eyes widened with horror. The book must have fallen from Antoine's cloak while he lay on the settle.

She leapt up, placing herself between child and guard, who advanced with outstretched hand. 'Give me that,' he commanded.

Escaping from behind her aunt, Emily danced off across the room, 'Catch me then, fat-face!' she crowed, leaping onto the settle, then across the fireplace, as if this was the best game she had ever played. Her skirts flapped as if she were an insect in flight, and her delighted laughter sent a rill of iced sweat down Louise's back.

At that moment, the chief officer returned from his hunt of the cellars, and his companion emerged empty-handed from the upper floors. Wat's curses on the warden's men flew around their heads as he and the keep's guards stationed themselves beside them. Moments later, the last Selkirk guard finished prodding the stable hayricks and the brewhouse vat, and joined them, plodding down the stairs with a disappointed tread.

The officers assembled, as if to confer, but sensing the altered mood in the hall they looked around with fresh interest. Louise was almost as ashen as Antoine. She no longer looked like the affronted mistress of a fortress, but a girl scared out of her wits. Ella was darting between table and hearth, trying to catch her daughter with one arm, a startled infant tucked under the other, and there was a sheen of excitement on the guard's face that told them he had found something.

'What's going on?' barked the leader, raising his hand to calm the hubbub. Emily, a stickler for doing as she was told, continued to jig and holler. Seeing the officers bearing down on the child with swords drawn, Louise screamed at her to be quiet. 'Bring me the book!' she cried. Frightened to hear her aunt so angry, Emily burst into a bawl and approached, sobbing. Louise took the book, and dropped a kiss on her head. 'You're a very good girl,' she whispered. 'Now, go sit by old Tom.' Old Crozier held out his hand and, hiccuping with tears, the girl climbed onto the bench beside him, pulling his arm around her.

Without a word, Louise held out the book. A sense of nightmarish unreality numbed her fear, and she no longer trembled, though she believed that whatever it contained would condemn her, and the soldier, to gaol, and probably far worse.

The leader of the Selkirk guards sheathed his sword and took the book. As he flipped through its pages the hall was hushed. In the shadows, Hob fingered his dagger. The wolf's growl thickened, haunches tensing as he readied himself to leap at the first sign of attack.

The officer frowned. Crabbit black print spread across the page. He saw scribblings in the margins, in a paler ink. 'Bible, is it?' He thought of the huge illuminated tome his priest read from in chapel. 'Seems small for a bible.' Turning it over he saw the embossed gold cross on the back cover, and the letters INRI. Even one who could not read understood what that meant.

The guard ran a finger over the leather binding, marvelling. No one he knew owned the holy book. Not even all priests had their own bible, sharing one between parishes, and copying out the parts they most often used. Many priests, he had heard, could not even read. They learned passages by heart, and spouted them at every chance, lest they forget them.

He handed it back to Louise. 'Read me some of it, then,' he said. Louise opened it. It was not in Latin, but in a language she did not recognise, though each letter was clear enough. Her eyes flew to Antoine, who was staring at the table with the air of a man on the scaffold.

She looked up at the guard with contempt. 'I cannot read. Does your wife?'

Sensing he was closing in on the mystery, the guard looked around. 'Someone here must be able to read it,' he said. 'A house such as this, there'll have been a bit of schooling. Otherwise what's it doing here?'

Louise went cold. Unsure what the book contained, she could not claim it was her husband's. Yet to say it belonged to her guest was to draw attention to him. That he had not already spoken up told its own story. She could not answer, and the longer she was quiet, the deeper the guard's suspicions would grow. Not knowing what words she would utter, she was about to speak when someone else did so first.

'I will read it,' said a hoarse voice, and a figure at the top of the stairs pushed back his hood and picked his way down to the hall. 'It is after all my book.'

'Father Walsh!' cried Louise.

'Apologies for my tardiness, madam,' said the priest, taking her hand, and bowing over it, 'but the confession hour overran. I am here now, though, for the family's weekly instruction.' He cast a look over Selkirk's officers. 'Lent is a serious business, my friends. No true Christian can reach the kingdom without first shriving his soul. But before we begin,' he continued, unclasping his cloak, and draping it over the settle, 'I see my little book has been amusing you.'

'Who is this?' the guard asked Louise, as the priest patted down his cassock and ran a finger under his collar.

'Father Michael Walsh,' she replied, 'the valley's priest and a friend of the family since my husband was a boy. And this man,' she went on, turning to the priest and biting back tears, 'is from the border guard, who accuse us of harbouring a heretic. They have searched the premises and found nothing, but still they persecute us.'

'Give me back my book,' said Father Walsh in his mild manner, 'I was vexed at leaving it here.' He turned the pages. 'Such handsome print,' he murmured, rubbing the page, 'and what an elegant typeface. A far richer paper too, compared to the copy in the church. Quality rags, that's the difference.'

'It does not look big enough to be a proper bible,' said the guard doggedly, standing at his shoulder.

'Indeed no, it is not,' said Father Walsh. 'It is my travelling bible.

This is merely the New Testament.' He smiled at the guard. 'So then, let me read you the first page, from the gospel of Matthew.' He put his finger under the line, and then looked up. 'No, I will spare you the endless genealogy.' He flipped further into the book, humming under his breath, until he found a passage some pages in. 'Now this,' he said, looking up with an innocent smile, 'this is a good text for the long days of Lent.'

He cleared his throat. 'Matthew chapter six, verse one.' He began to intone in Latin, his voice weak with advancing age, but growing stronger as the familiar, much loved words flowed. When he finished, he looked up. 'That was telling us to beware of doing good deeds simply so that we will be praised. As the gospel says, when you give alms, sound no trumpet before you, as the hypocrites do in the synagogues and in the streets, that they may be praised by men.' He turned to the Selkirk guard. 'You should know, sir, that the Croziers are a fine example of those who hide their light under a bushel. A more faithful, charitable, reverent family I could not wish to serve though they keep their good works quiet as the grave. Shall I read on?'

With a shake of his head, the officer admitted defeat. 'No, Father, I thank you. Our business here is done.' Clicking his boot heels, he bowed so low his fringe fell over his eyes. 'Goodwife, I beg your pardon. Please accept my apologies. It seems we have made a mistake.'

Not trusting herself to speak, Louise inclined her head. The guard turned to his men, to herd them out. One jerked his head in Antoine's direction but the officer pushed him towards the stairs. He could take no further humiliation. There was no apostate to be found here. As he and his posse emerged into the courtyard, the keep's guards nipping at their heels, he looked up at the darkling sky and the rooks posted on the battlements. Perhaps their quarry had indeed turned into a bird, to escape, cawing, over their heads.

CHAPTER TWENTY

Silence fell over the hall as the door banged shut. Father Walsh reached the settle, and sank onto it like an old man. The hands clutching the bible shook. Pouring him a goblet of wine, Louise joined him. He took a gulp, then set it aside.

'Holy Mother of Jesus,' he said, dropping the bible in his lap, 'where did you find this? It is heresy writ large. It's not in Greek or Hebrew or Latin, it is a plain translation, into Low German, the language of the common people. Possession of this is a death sentence. You must get rid of it at once, and whoever brought it.'

Hob appeared at the priest's side. He plucked the book from him, and threw it onto the fire. 'If only it was as simple to deal with its owner,' he said, casting a look over his shoulder at the table, where Antoine sat, head laid on his arms.

Louise rubbed the blood back into her hands before the sullen fire. Already the bible was curling in a snarl, and soon the pages would be ash. Had she or Antoine been found guilty of heresy, they too would have burned.

Leaving the priest to his wine, Louise gave the order for the soldier to be carried to the men's quarters and given the infirmary bed, set apart from the dorm. What followed was, for Antoine, almost as taxing as the hour that had just passed. When finally his leg was cleaned, salved, bound and splinted, his palms bore the stigmata of fingernails. Barely able to speak, he fell into a sleep deep as a swoon. Keeping guard beside his pallet the wolf licked the soldier's hand and lay down, refusing to abandon his new charge. Leaving Wat and the wolf to watch him through the night, Louise made her way back to the hall.

Her head throbbed. She was harbouring a fugitive, whose presence could bring them all before the executioner. A deserter was one thing, but to shelter a heretic was lunacy. A moment's pity for a man barely more than a boy had brought them all to the brink of disaster.

'I ken what you're thinking,' said Hob, finding her in the passageway. 'Me and all. Bleeding hearts we both are, and we nearly swung for it.' Yet there was no contrition in his tone, and his eyes brightened under the torchlight. 'That lad might be a dangerous fool, but there is no real harm in him. You can talk sense into him as soon as he is better.' He put a hand on her arm. 'You were as kind to me, remember. Without that soft heart of yours, I'd no be alive today.'

She covered his hand with her own. 'You were a child, Hob, and no one could have left an orphan alone out in the wilds. But this foreigner, who we know nothing about . . .' She looked at the groom who, in the years since she had rescued him, had become as dear as if he were a brother. 'We have problems enough without my adding to them.'

'You had no choice,' said Hob, as they stepped back into the hall.

'But what will Crozier say?'

'He will agree with me. Now, you maun eat, while I settle the horses.'

Early the following morning, Louise returned to the infirmary. The soldier had slept through the night, Wat told her, though he had thrashed and cried out in his sleep. At dawn Wat had changed his dressing and packed the torn flesh with moss, but though he had hissed with pain the boy had not woken.

'He looks feverish to me,' said Wat, examining the soldier's warm face. 'We need to watch him closely. The leg's turning yellow.'

'Go and get some rest,' Louise replied. 'I will send Hob to collect nettles and rue for a compress. Come back at noon.'

For a while she sat silently by the sleeping man. His features were fine-boned, delicate as a girl's. Though his hands were chapped and calloused with work they were sensitive, more like those of a troubadour or bard than a man of arms. Who could imagine trouble arriving in such gentle form?

Her thoughts turned to Crozier, and the dark days when she had sat vigil by his bed, not knowing if he would live or die. In those cruelly slow hours she had learned his face, every line and turn of it. Ten years on and nothing she had discerned then had changed. He was the same man in every respect. Only her love had altered, deepening with time, though in those early days, when she was drawn to him as to life itself, she would have laughed to think that was possible.

Her eyes went to the window, where morning was brightening behind the shutters. Opening them, she stood staring out at the treetops, fear of her husband's waning affection troubling her thoughts like the breeze among the pines.

When Hob returned with the herbs she mixed a compress, and together they applied it to the swollen, darkening leg. Wakening, their patient grew restless. Louise drew a cup of well water from the bucket, and held it to his lips. Not recognising her, Antoine put his hand over hers, to steady the cup. His fingers were hot, his eyes glittered, and he seemed eager to talk, but the jumble of words made no sense.

For several days Antoine lay in limbo, his mind wandering far from the keep. The task of nursing him was shared between Wat and Hob, the groom treating him as if he were an Arab steed; Wat, like an errant son. Under their care the infection began to ebb and the bone to knit. When at last the soldier regained full consciousness, he learned he would be spared Wat's long-toothed saw. A tear trickled down his face. 'You do not look much like an angel,' he whispered, 'but that is indeed what you are.' Wat gave a guffaw that made the invalid's head pound.

Louise was in the brewhouse when Hob told her the soldier had asked to see her.

'What does he want?'

'To confess all, I think,' he said. 'Should be interesting. Here, I'll finish the stir.'

She passed him the paddle she had been using to spread the barley and hurried out to the keep, the wolf at her heels.

Antoine was sitting on a stool by his bed. He was dressed in a long woollen tunic, the sort a monk would wear, and his splinted leg was stretched before him, as if it were not his. Louise cut short his effusion of thanks. 'What was it you wanted to say to me?' she asked, dusting her hands on her skirts, and taking a seat on a chest by the door.

'I owe you not just gratitude for saving my life, but an apology,' he replied, his words slow and clipped as if each had been dredged from a newly awakened memory. 'I have acted like a fool. In following my own conscience, I have risked your family's lives as well as my own. That is unforgivable.' He tapped a finger on his knee, in private reprimand. 'Lying here, this past week, I have had time to clear my thoughts. It has not been a pleasant experience.' He smiled, his eyes dreamy yet clear. 'Odd as it will sound, the fear of losing my leg was less terrible than facing my maker, and acknowledging my sins.'

'Sins?' Louise scuffed her boots on the floor. Of all the words she knew from the bible, sin was the one that made her most uneasy. It seemed to her a slippery notion, more often used to denounce those who had little to atone for than admitted to by people whose faults were plain.

'I have committed the sin of pride,' he continued, 'and I will make amends.'

'Enough of this,' said Louise. 'You need not confess to me, I am not your priest.'

She started to get up, but Antoine put out his hand. 'I am trying to explain, madame. I have made many mistakes. I need you to understand.'

Louise looked at the young man's earnest, anxious face, and sighed. 'I'll listen, then,' she said, and sat down once more.

His story took a long time to tell. By the time he had finished, Louise had set the tapers on the wall burning and the infirmary bedchamber glowed as if it had been lit by his words.

Antoine d'Echelles was from the north-east of France, a town on the tip of Germany's ear. The son of a merchant's clerk, he spoke French and German and English. For two years he had begun to train as a priest, but what he saw at the seminary changed his mind, and he entered a local militia, rather than become like the priests he had learned to despise.

He and a group of other townsmen had heard of a preacher who wanted to do away with the church. This man, who lived in Germany, believed that no one should come between God and his believers. The Catholic church, he said, was corrupt, and should be destroyed. After what he had seen, Antoine was quick to agree.

Passing themselves off as tradesmen, he and his friends went to Germany to hear this man preach. 'He was . . . was . . .' The soldier could not find the word he wanted, but his eyes brightened at the memory. 'Pure,' he said finally, 'and untainted, and true. It was this I was trying to tell the good people of Selkirk, when they turned on me.'

Louise shook her head in disbelief. The preacher, Martin Luther by name, sounded as if he had lost his senses. To condemn the Catholic church, and denounce the pope? He must enjoy a charmed existence still to be alive. So too Antoine, since he had escaped Selkirk's clutches with all but his bones intact.

With the hope of one day spreading Luther's ideas, Antoine had joined the French king's army. Before they went their ways, he and his friends had vowed to take the new gospel to every corner of the world. Stationed under the Duke of Albany's command, he soon heard they were to serve in Scotland. He knew at once that this was where he was called to witness to the new faith. Already, he said, there was a small group of true believers in the east of the country whom he could join, preaching as he made his way there. 'In order to share the message,' he said, with a childlike smile, 'we each carry a bible written for the people, buttoned into our shirts. It is not in Latin or Greek for priests to interpret, but in words everyone can understand.'

'We burned it,' Louise said. 'You must be out of your senses, to carry such a book. The guards could have locked you up and sent you to trial for that alone. And all of us with you,' she added.

'That is what I have been thinking on,' he said, quietly. 'And the sin for which I have begged the good Lord's forgiveness.'

Louise's voice was harsh. 'You expect us to house you, a heretic and a deserter? What have we done that you want to bring such trouble upon us?' She was as angry with herself for courting danger as with the man who had brought it.

'I know, I know,' he said so softly she guessed at the words rather than heard them. 'And as of this morning, I renounce the faith of the Lutherans. That, indeed, is the shape my penance must take. It is the worst punishment I could imagine, setting me once more at a distance from the Lord Jesus Christ, and I accept it gladly. Eagerly.' He looked up at her, his lashes wet with tears. 'I will return to the Catholic church, and submit to its teachings. If the good Father who saved my life will hear my confession, I will make it to him, and be on my way.'

Louise stood. 'My husband will be home soon. Once I have spoken to him, we can decide what is best for you to do. For the moment, though, you must rest.' She rose, clicking her fingers at the wolf, but he was curled at the soldier's feet, and had no intention of leaving.

From far down the valley, Crozier saw the plume of smoke from the keep's chimneys. He rode ahead of Tom and Benoit, anxious to be home. When he left, a week earlier, Louise had been quiet. She had said little when he told her he had been summoned to Lord Foulberry's, and even less on the morning he departed. She had raised her lips to his as they said goodbye, then turned and disappeared into the keep, without watching him ride off. He had not seen her at their window, keeping his horse in sight until the trees closed in and hid him, nor again at the parted shutters in the depths of the night, her tears flowing unchecked.

When the riders reached the walls, Wat and the watchmen raised their hands in salute, and the bugler blasted his horn. Crozier's eyes narrowed. The guards were tense. Something had happened while they were away. Before he could enquire, Wat had slipped off, like a vole into the waterbank. The borderer rode through the gates at a clip, but his first fears were allayed at the sight of Louise and Ella hurrying across the courtyard to meet them. In the confusion of children, chickens and stableboys he could do no more than cast a questioning glance at his wife as he dismounted. She smiled but her face, he thought, was drawn.

Not until the horses were unsaddled and their gear carried into the keep did he again find himself near his wife. He put an arm round her waist, and pulled her aside. 'I have missed you,' he said, bending to kiss the top of her head.

She raised her eyes to his. 'We have a visitor. And I have a confession. You will be angry, I know.'

When he heard her story, Crozier was too relieved for anger. Later, alone, the thought of what might have happened to her, and the others, made him dizzy. He had suddenly to sit, until the blood returned to his head. But as Louise first described Antoine's arrival, and that of the Selkirk guards, he merely listened in grim silence.

'He's nothing more than a boy,' she said. 'Too young to think straight. A week ago he was prepared to risk his life for his faith, and now he renounces it. He's like Ella's children, who scream for a toy, and then grow tired of it. And yet there is something innocent and likeable about him.'

'As soon as he can walk he will have to make his way back to Albany's army and face his punishment. Or return to France.'

'Of course,' she replied. 'But it might be weeks until then. For so long as he is here we're in danger, aren't we? The border guards could return any time.'

Crozier gave an odd smile. 'My love, we are always in danger. One more outlaw makes little difference.'

She nodded slowly, as if not fully understanding, or wishing to understand, the meaning of what he had said. 'Then,' she added, 'there's the problem of Barton.'

Crozier's smile faded. 'What about him?'

'Like the other men, he knows only that Antoine is one of Albany's army. None of the guards knows he is a heretic; they think he is merely a soldier on the run. But if Barton were to find out . . . I fear he would make trouble.'

'Has he done anything while I've been away?' Crozier's voice was sharp.

'No. He is the same as always. Creeping, quiet, and watchful. He gives me nothing to complain about, and yet I dislike everything about him. I cannot bear him near.'

'I will have him put to work on the fields, as far from here as possible. Let's hope he quickly tires of the country life.'

She smiled, and saw her husband's face soften. She put out her hand, and he lifted it to his lips before drawing her towards him and holding her close.

CHAPTER TWENTY-ONE

April 1524

Linlithgow Palace sat in a blaze of light, its gardens set afire by braziers, the courtyard and ramparts glowing orange under the torches on its walls. In the great hall, pipes, flutes and drums set a spirited pace for the dancers beneath them. At one end of the hall Margaret Tudor, the dowager queen, was enthroned on a dais, courtiers bending their legs before her or standing idly at her side, whispering gossip in her pearl-ringed ear while she sipped wine and tapped time on her knee. Occasionally one of her nobles would invite her to take the floor, and she would step with him into the sea of dancers, her wide skirts parting the crowd as if she were a warship carving waves beneath her prow.

Far from the great hall the palace lay dim and quiet, nothing disturbing the night but the clatter of a horse being led to the stables, or the shout of a servant rolling a barrel of beer across the back yard. All but the nightwatchmen and grooms were away from their posts. Even the serving girls and maids had been allowed the evening off, to watch the exalted throng from the gallery, where they would not themselves be seen.

Between one candle and the next, the passageways on this floor were dark. Only an owl would have observed the shape that darted into the queen's chambers. Thin and black as a noontime shadow, he wore a mask, cloak, and boots of the softest leather. Closing the door behind him, he opened the shutters and light from the gardens warmed the room.

He made for the high canopied bed, and knelt. Beneath it lay a carved wooden box which he drew towards him across the polished boards. It was locked, but he carried a ring of slender keys, one of which soon loosened its tongue. Rummaging among the contents, he pulled out two string-bound packages tied together by ribbon. These he took to the window, squinting to read the inscriptions, before ripping off the ribbon, unknotting the string and opening one of the letters. He needed no more than a scan to know he had what he was searching for. With a murmur of satisfaction he tucked the bundle into the pouch on his belt, returned the box to its place, and left. He slipped out of the palace like a slither of smoke, leaving nothing behind but a chamber bathed in light.

When Margaret returned, some time after dawn, she did not notice the opened shutters or the broken lock on her box. Tottering on her platform heels, which had grown more precarious with each glass of wine, she called for her lady-in-waiting, who hurried into the room to unfasten her gown and bodice and wipe off her powder and rouge. The dowager queen was asleep before the coverlet had been pulled over her, the stain of red wine on her lips the only adornment that could not be scrubbed or peeled off. Beneath her lay the box, its secrets flown.

In his ship's cabin, a few nights later, the regent looked at the letters, spilled across his table. The parchment of several was creased, the ink smudged, as if to alert the reader to what lay within. Tears had been shed over this torrent of words, some of sorrow, more of fury. The dowager queen's hand was neat, her turn of phrase elegant, but beneath this veneer Margaret's passions roiled. Written over the space of several years, the most recent little more than twelve months earlier, this was a record of a liaison that would have brought the Scottish court into disrepute, and Henry VIII with it.

It had been placed in Albany's hand at the dockside. Sailing that evening from the Gare Loch for France, Albany paid the burglar and boarded the ship, which was alive with crew preparing to cast off. He would be back in the country before autumn. If the letters proved as informative as he hoped, they could be put to use then. For now, his thoughts were already in Auvergne, from where his wife's physician had summoned him some weeks past. If he were honest – and he not always was – there was relief in abandoning Scotland. A more vexing, bitter, quarrelsome parliament he had never encountered. The lords of the realm were thirled to ancient ways and primitive fears, while the common man cared nothing for what his leaders did, or how the country fared, so long as he was left alone to squander his time in the tavern.

When he returned, he would find a way to enforce his rule. Some time at home to reflect on how that could be done would be more helpful than staying here, where his sleeve was perpetually tugged by whining advisers and cavilling courtiers, as if they were children and he a dog whose tail they loved to pull.

Shaking his head as if the tormented dog were ridding itself of fleas, he poured a goblet of Alicante wine, and pulled towards him a clutch of letters, written in a darker pen than those by the dowager queen.

Baron Dacre's writing was a hasty scrawl, the ink matching the man, but a few lines sufficed to show that the Warden General was canny. *Our business must be conducted soon, for the benefit of both our countries . . . I regret the anger I have provoked, and when next we meet will make ample amends . . . My memories of our long and most amicable acquaintance brighten my day, as must all thoughts of the most glorious Tudor line . . .*

Only in the last letter, a few lines written in evident haste, did the baron drop his guard. *For your majesty's safety, I press you most urgently to burn all correspondence you have received from me, if you have not already done so. To that purpose, I herewith return your letters, in good faith, that you might know I hold nothing in my possession that could ever bring you harm.*

There was a scratch on the regent's door, and the ship's captain appeared, his black cap askew from the wind. 'Wind freshening north-west, your grace.' He eyed the cluttered desk. 'Wise to lock up anything that might be spilled. It will be a turbulent night, but it will bring us into Boulogne all the swifter.'

Albany put a finger to his cap, and nodded. The captain bade him goodnight, and with a last lingering look the regent tied up the letters and put them in his trunk. There would be time to read them closely once he was home. Indeed, his wife would be the best judge of what they contained. If ever a woman could read between the lines it was she. A complicated smile settled on Albany's face as Anne appeared before him, pink-cheeked as the girl he married, not wan as the woman who had lately taken to her bed.

He was anxious, but hopeful. When he returned to her, so would her health. Again he cocked his finger to his cap before emptying the goblet in a silent salute and climbing, fully clothed, into his berth.

'I hear we have been graced with another of the baron's complaints,' said the cardinal, hurrying to keep pace with the king, as he strode across the palace lawns towards the archers' gallery.

'As his insolence grows,' snarled Henry, 'so our patience thins.'

Wolsey's skirts caught his slippers as he bustled in the king's wake. Fearful of tripping he lifted his robes, like a maid on her wedding day, revealing ankles clad in fine white hose. 'But your majesty,' he said breathlessly, 'to be scrupulously fair in this matter, he did concede to stay in post only until Easter. And as he rightly points out, Easter is now past.'

With a cry of exasperation, the king came to a halt. He looked the cardinal in the eye, his own inflamed as if with grit. Wolsey observed the bloodshot whites and reddened lids, and wondered if it was not the king's erratic health, rather than the waywardness of his courtiers, that wore his temper to shreds.

'Let us be very clear,' Henry said, each word of what followed pinned in place by a stab of his cane, until the grass was pitted with holes. There could be no bowls or croquet until they had been filled. 'Baron Dacre is precisely where we want and need him, and his own wishes mean as little to us as the maundering of . . . of . . .' – his cane turned up an earthworm, and he flicked it across the lawn – 'of a wriggling creature as lowly as that.' The comparison displeased him, sounding weak even to his own ears. He drew a deep breath, suddenly weary. 'Speak to Surrey. He has heard reports of further trouble from Dacre's people, who squirm under his command. It may be nothing more than tattle, but there is just the possibility that it is more serious than that. Until the matter is settled, he must remain in post. We fear that if we release him, he might slip his leash. And we want satisfaction in this matter.'

He drew close to Wolsey, who smelled the sourness of breath marinated overnight in claret. 'If the Baron Dacre has been feathering his nest at my expense; if he thinks the north is his bailiwick, rather than ours, we will put him right. Indeed we will. So put your head with Surrey's, and find out what is afoot. We wish to hear nothing more of the Warden General until you have clarified this matter.' The red eye wept, and with a shake of his head that sent tears flying the king stomped off to watch his bodyguard exercise their arrows.

At the barracks, Wolsey was ushered into Surrey's chambers. As befitted a soldier, the rooms were spartan, but the stools by the fire were soundly and amply made, and the cardinal eased himself onto one with a small groan, glad to rest his aching legs.

The earl stood before him, recognising the signs of discomfort, an expression not entirely untouched by pity warming his eyes since they reminded him of his ailing father. Rubbing his hands and their thickening joints, he pulled his stool up and sat knee to knee with the cardinal, the soldier's plain leather britches sombre beside the rich scarlet gown.

Surrey was holding a sheaf of papers. 'Our friend in the north is causing ructions. I expect you have had similar complaints to these.' He waved the papers, and without asking for their contents, Wolsey nodded.

'Almost weekly, though more from the eastern and middle marches than from the west.'

Surrey examined his knees. 'That might suggest our man is merely a scapegoat for his enemies' dislike. His heartland, in Cumberland, remains loyal.'

'He surely cannot be the marauder they claim if the west is easy beneath his rule,' said Wolsey, sounding aggrieved at the very suggestion.

'Or does he merely keep his thieving ways for the citizens furthest from home?'

Both men said nothing, contemplating Dacre, and what he was capable of. It was a long silence – the baron, as they well knew, refused to acknowledge any authority over him – and in that rare moment of accord, the suspicion and enmity between them was temporarily set aside.

Wolsey shook his head. 'The man is hardly an innocent, we all know that. Expediency is what matters most in these times, and in those parts. It's my belief he is a master of compromise.'

Surrey held a paper to the firelight at arm's length. 'Let me read you this latest. From the people of Bewcastle and Tynedale, who say that instead of punishing thieves and raiders, and making restitution to their victims' – here he squinted, to decipher the furious hand – ' "in default of correction the baron using them in his company familiarly emboldened them in the same misdemeanour, to the great hurt of the said good country".'

He picked up another letter. 'Here's a claim that Dacre's lack of action against criminals in the shires has resulted in 'the great increase and emboldening of all the said offenders'.'

Wolsey clicked his tongue in irritation. 'The same old story. A robber baron in their midst, hand in glove with criminals. But who are these people who are telling tales?'

Surrey's voice was filled with contempt. 'Needless to say, they remain nameless.' He tossed the papers to the floor. 'To my mind, only a signed complaint carries weight.'

The cardinal's face lightened. 'Very wise. None but a coward levels an accusation he dare not put his name to.'

'Or someone very frightened,' mused Surrey, sounding uncertain, despite himself. 'It could be said that their terror of being identified might equally suggest they are rightly fearful of Dacre's reprisals.'

'It is a confoundedly annoying situation,' said the cardinal, his colour rising. 'Would that Dacre were a more cautious man, and less high-handed. I have no doubt he does an excellent job, and no amount of evidence against him will ever persuade me otherwise.' He lowered his voice, though they were alone, and the door closed. 'The king talks of the north being his domain as much as Dacre's. Yet he has barely set foot north of York. He does not know of what he talks. Were Dacre to leave the wardenship, in times as fraught as these, who knows what would follow.'

Surrey's beaked face was stern. 'Again, we are in agreement. The real world is untidy in a manner no king can begin to imagine. Dacre is no fool. He may be unscrupulous – I have little doubt he is as much a master of deceit as of expediency – but he holds the reins of the north at high personal cost. His demand to be freed of this post sits ill with these complaints. A corrupt man would most surely retain his post until he had squeezed every last coin out of it for himself.'

'And yet,' said the cardinal, 'in light of his plea to be discharged, and these most clamorous complaints, we are obliged to institute some sort of investigation. If only,' he added, heavily, 'to appease his royal highness.'

'Indeed,' Surrey replied. He brushed a speck of mud from his britches. 'And I will see to it. It will not need, however, to be a lengthy process. I will visit Dacre myself, and see how the land sits. That should suffice to settle matters, for the moment at least.'

'I am obliged to you,' said Wolsey, rising with difficulty from his stool. He was unsteady, but Surrey knew better than to offer a hand, busying himself instead with collecting the papers strewn at his feet. With all in his clutch, he fed them one by one into the flames, which leapt at their dinner like ravenous waifs.

CHAPTER TWENTY-TWO

May 1524

Antoine hobbled into the great hall, crutches under his arms, bad leg trailing. In the time he had been at Crozier's Keep his soldier's frame had been replaced with a stooped, creaking figure whose halting gait was as painful to watch as Old Crozier's.

From his fireside seat the old man greeted his new companion. Antoine raised a crutch in reply. He and the white-haired clansman had become friends these past few weeks, Old Crozier regaling him with the history of the family, the valley, and the border. He was also schooling him in the complexity of local affairs, which, thought Antoine, made the wrangling between France, England, Scotland and Spain look half-hearted.

Already the soldier's English was accented with a border burr, and he understood, if did not use, some of the outlandish words peculiar to these parts. Between them Ella and Old Crozier had taught him the ballads. He could be heard singing to himself as he stumped his way around the courtyard, or disappeared into the woods, where he would sit all afternoon on a fallen tree, lost in silent thought, or carolling to the birds. One day he asked for paper, to set the ballads down. Old Crozier was startled to see that it was not only the words he was recording but the tunes themselves, marching across the page like rooks on a bare tree. Antoine was amused at his astonishment. 'It is simple, really,' he said. 'Bring me a recorder, and I will show you.'

Open-mouthed, Ella's brood sat at his feet as he picked out the melody on the instrument, each inky rook turning into a note that flew up to the rafters. Andra, Ella's eldest, could barely contain his excitement, flapping across the rush-strewn floor as the ballad filled the hall and singing louder than a church bell.

It was Andra who found Antoine, later that day, sitting in the woods. The boy approached him slowly, cradling something in his arms. 'What is it you bring me?' said Antoine, noting the child's bowed head.

'I found him, down by the burn,' Andra replied, his face streaked with tears.

'Put him down, boy. Careful now.'

Andra placed the creature at the soldier's feet. It was a hare, ears lying flat, eyes closed, body quivering with fear. It lay awkwardly, its hind leg useless, as Antoine's had been. 'It's hurt,' said the child. 'The crows were pecking it.'

Antoine ran a gentle finger over the hare's spine. The fur was matted with sweat.

'Boy,' he said, putting a hand on Andra's arm, 'the kindest thing would be to kill it.'

The child pulled away. 'No! You cannae do that. If your leg can be mended, so can its.'

Antoine sighed. 'It's not so easy with animals. They will not stay still, as I had to. Some die just being brought indoors. They are wild creatures, after all. And a dead hare will be a good dinner for a fox or the crows, who need to eat also.'

Andra shook his head, staring at the grass at Antoine's feet, holding back his tears. 'No,' he said again, kicking the fallen tree. 'We cannae just do it in.'

'Very well.' Antoine fumbled for his crutches and got to his feet. 'Carry it back to my room, and we will do what we can for it.'

Andra scooped up the hare, which lay limp in his arms, and followed the soldier back to the keep. There, under Antoine's instruction, he found a stick and, while the soldier nursed the hare in his lap, sanded it smooth of bark and knots. Antoine stroked the animal until its breathing calmed, then felt the damaged limb, fingering it so softly the creature did not move. It was a simple fracture. No bone was splintered, no skin broken. 'You may have a chance, little one,' he whispered, binding the hare's leg to the splint with strips of lint.

A nest of straw was made in a small wooden chest in Antoine's room, far away from the hounds. The wolf, who had followed them down the passage, put his nose into the box, sniffed the animal, and went back to his place by the great hall fire. From that moment, he added the hare to his duties, guarding him from intruders as he had done Antoine.

While the hare rested, Antoine despatched Andra with a list of plants he must find. 'I would come, but I will slow you down,' he said, 'and the most important is only found on north-facing slopes, so I could not climb there with this leg. Not yet.'

Memorising the list – poppies, shepherd's purse, sage and honeysuckle – Andra scurried off. When he returned with a pouchful of leaves and stems, Antoine picked through them. 'Well done, boy. You have found everything I asked for. If anything can save your hare, it will be these. Now, watch carefully.'

Pouring a flagon of water newly boiled over the kitchen fire into a bowl, he added the poppy heads and a handful of crushed leaves and left them to cool. Once the water was tepid, he removed the poppies, placed the bowl inside the hare's nest, and tucked a sprig of shepherd's purse under its ribs. 'And now we will leave him,' said the soldier, pulling the lid of the chest over the box until only a chink of light reached the hare. As the pair made for the great hall, the hare lay still as a dead thing. Later, when all was quiet, its nose twitched, and it lapped the bowl of water. Then it slept, for days.

Three weeks later, a party from the keep made its way deep into the woods. Antoine and Andra walked together, followed by Louise and Benoit, who was carrying the hare's box. When they reached the burn, they stopped. Benoit put the box down, removed the lid, and tilted it. The creature hopped out. For a second it crouched, nose quivering, ears at half-mast, before, with a leap, it was gone, darting left and right into the grasses, and out of sight.

Andra looked on, biting his lip, but at the sight of the smile on Antoine's face, his eyes lit up. 'We did the right thing,' he said to Benoit, who nodded, and placed a hand on his son's tousled head.

Oliver Barton was restless. He was being kept at work in the outer pastures, farthest from the keep, and felling trees on the fringes of

Crozier's land. It was hard labour, for a man of his age, and in springtime the hours were long. Some days his companions slept over in a stone hut, to save the walk. He resisted this until it became clear his days as lookout on the walls were over. Those long watches had offered the chance to slip away with little trouble. The men he reported to seemed not to care if he was gone a day or two. But out here, as part of the small gang of woodcutters and herders, his absence would be noticed at once.

He was itching to report to Dacre. At the arrival of Albany's red-haired soldier, he had known something strange was afoot. The Frenchman's presence disturbed him. Who was this young soldier, and what was his business, first an invalid, and now sitting in an outhouse grinding herbs and blending salves for villagers who brought him their lame mules and worm-eaten cows? Even before he had an answer, the Warden General must be informed.

As the weeks passed, and he found no opportunity to slip off to Harbottle, his impatience simmered, and with it his ill temper. Growing fractious, he was gaining a reputation as someone to be avoided, not only because he was a stranger they could not trust. Quickly angered, he was an alarming sight when carrying an axe. Nobody liked to work alongside him, but sometimes they had no choice. When the foreman broke up a fight between Barton and Wat the Wanderer's son, in which Barton had bitten Hewie's hand so hard his finger was nearly severed, the sailor was consigned to a solitary spell in the stone hut. Brooding as he sat on the narrow wooden shelf and watched the day crawl past between the moss-packed stone, he nevertheless laughed. It was the gang who were suffering, not him. They would have to walk the five miles home that night, and back again at dawn, while he could laze the hours away, staring at the stars through the ragged thatch.

Freed the next morning, he promised to reform. But a few days later he started another brawl and laid a woodcutter out cold. This time he was condemned to five days' confinement.

'Any more of this,' the foreman warned him, 'and it'll be Crozier himsel who sees to ye. Believe me, ye dinnae want that.'

Head low, Barton slunk off to serve his time in the stone cell. Only when the door had been locked on him did a slow grin spread into his beard. Shut in with a pitcher of water and a muslin-wrapped cheese to see him through, he was happy for the first time in weeks. The woodcutters' voices were still clear on the evening air when he took out the chisel concealed in his boot, and began to work at the loose stone walls.

The horse he stole from Hob's top field did its best to throw him, but a man who had sailed the German Sea and the Cornish coast in winter, pitched about deck like butter in a churn, would not be defeated by a border mare. Digging his fingers into her mane, and his boots into her belly, he clung on until she quietened, though he cursed her bony flanks. A few hours later, before sunrise, they trotted through a hamlet. Seeing a rope lying in the street, Barton tied the mare to a tree and slipped into the yard of the biggest house on the street. In a lean-to shack he found an old horse dozing. 'Easy, lad,' he said, as it shuffled, 'it's no you I'm after.' Lifting a saddle and bridle off the wall, he backed out.

Barton reached Harbottle the next evening. Weary and hungry after a night on the road, he did not argue when he was shown to the soldiers' quarters, and given a plate of lamb chops. Blackbird found him there some time later, lying on his pallet, chewing a wad of salt beef like a cow its cud.

'The Warden General is away,' the butler said, without ceremony.

Barton narrowed his eyes and looked at Blackbird as if he were blocking his view. 'When'll he be back?' He spat the beef onto the floor, and saw the butler's mouth tighten.

'Tomorrow, perhaps. No later than the day after.' Blackbird's reluctance to divulge his master's whereabouts was plain for both to hear. 'But you can leave a message with me.'

Barton lay back, and put his hands behind his head. 'I'll wait a day. There's no great hurry.'

'As you will,' said Blackbird, and left the bunkhouse, uneasy with Barton's eyes following him. In the sergeant's office, he took the troops' captain aside. 'Keep your eye on that man. He's the baron's informant, but a felon of the lowest rank. The sooner Dacre's done with him, the better.'

Warm and fed, Barton slept well. He rose, washed himself in a bucket of water from the well, and ran his fingers through his hair and beard. Thus freshened, he took his mess, slurping down porridge and bread as if he had no care in the world.

When the captain asked what he would do that day, Barton gave him a sweet smile. 'Take a ride to the coast, since I'm near. I'm a seafaring man, never right unless I can hear the waves. I will be back by nightfall to see the baron, *Deo volente*.'

Saddling up, he rode out of the castle and turned east. Harbottle was far below him, nestled in its springtime bowl of green, when he pulled the mare to a halt. Sheltered from the morning breeze by a lonely stand of elms, he watched the castle gates, so distant his eyes watered as he stared. The mare fidgeted, but he held her still, and after a few minutes she dropped her head to crop the grass. An hour later, he saw what he was waiting for. A figure in a long cloak rode out of the gates, followed by a helmeted guard, whose horse tailed hers at a few yards' distance.

It was just as he had hoped. An old guardsman had been grumbling over dinner the night before at this tedious duty. 'Waste of my time, and the baron's money,' he'd said, gnawing his chop. 'The girl won't come to any harm. She never goes far. More likely to meet trouble from the locals with me pointing my sword in their faces.' A murmur of agreement had run round the table.

'Still,' one of the group had said, pushing his plate aside, 'it's an easy posting, being nursemaid to a child. Better than chasing thieves and risking your life, like some of us do every day.' He'd leaned across the table towards the guardsman. 'Do you sit doing needlework with her of an evening, old man? Sing her lullabies at night, eh – or send her to sleep some other way? She's not the comeliest I've seen, but out here there's not much choice. Take whatever comes your way, says I. And at your age, be grateful for any port that'll have ye.'

The man had given a cackle as the guard threw his chop bone at him, and the group had broken up, in laughter and jeers.

When he saw the path they had taken, Barton set off across the hilltop. Some time later, he watched them pass below, and urged the mare down the hill in their wake.

Hearing approaching hooves, the guardsman turned his horse to face the rider.

'A good morning to you both,' said Barton, pleasantly, bringing the mare to a walk. He touched his helmet, and bowed to the girl, who was watching him with interest.

'It is your father's informant,' said the guardsman to his charge. 'We will let him pass.'

'I am merely ambling to kill the time,' said Barton, coming to a halt. 'I would not mind company. I was headed for the white sands at Alnmouth, to give my horse a run. Are ye going that way?'

'Not so far,' said the guardsman before Joan could answer. 'Her ladyship is merely taking the air for an hour or two.'

'But I would like to see the white sands,' she said. 'Is it a great distance?'

'Nothing a good rider would notice,' said Barton.

'A journey such as that would take the whole day,' said the guard. 'I cannot be away from my post so long.'

'Yet I am so tired of being cooped up, and it would be an adventure, would it not?' said Joan, holding Barton's eye, hers bright with mischief.

'Perhaps not that thrilling, my lady,' he said, lowering his gaze modestly. 'But a fine outing, on a fresh day such as this.'

The guard turned to Joan, and put a hand on her bridle. 'My lady, this is not a good idea. Your father would not like it. And he will be home soon. If you were gone, and no word of where you were, I would be punished on our return.'

Joan continued to look at Barton. 'Then let this man accompany me, and you can return to your post.' He began to argue, but she raised a hand. 'Do not be afraid. I will take the consequences on my own head.'

Keen as he was to hand her over, the guardsman would not be so easily usurped. The thought of the baron's wrath were he to relinquish his daughter to a stranger made him sweat. There was a small room in the castle cellars where miscreants were dealt with, and he had no wish ever to enter it.

'Very well, my lady,' he said, ignoring Barton, 'to the coast it is. I hope it will not tire you.' Slapping her horse's rump, he spurred his own mount onwards, leaving Barton to catch them up. But the sailor was not disheartened. There would be time enough to talk to Joan in the hours that lay ahead. A fresh plan for his future had filled his thoughts on the long ride to Harbottle, and after the success of this encounter he was beginning to believe it might work.

CHAPTER TWENTY-THREE

William Eure, Vice Warden of the English Marches, did not look like a man able to deal with the borderers. Tall but slight, his head drooping like a bluebell and his voice tremulous as a wren's, he had the appearance of a clerk or an apothecary. He wore his heavy leather riding gear like a boy who has borrowed his father's clothes, yet when Crozier shook his hand he felt the strength of the wrist, the swordsman's punishing grasp, and was reassured. No one reached a position like Eure's without a heart of iron, and a conscience to match. This man had both, well hidden though they were beneath a sweep of thinning fair hair and pale blue eyes that wept in brilliant sunlight.

Crozier had the advantage at this first meeting, though Eure could not know it. Some weeks earlier, he had eavesdropped outside Foulberry's private chamber while his lordship and the Vice Warden talked. Crozier had smarted at the mortification of behaving like a house-breaker, creeping beneath the window, huddling against the ivied wall, boots sunk in damp earth as he pressed his ear to the shutter left open, as promised, by their host. Tom was stationed at the postern door as lookout, but the only person who disturbed the night was Isabella Foulberry who, midway through the parlay, appeared with tankards of steaming spiced wine to keep the cold at bay.

At her approach a scolding blackbird had risen from its roost, and she froze by Crozier's side. Nothing else moved, and when the voices within the chamber continued without suspicion she gave him the mug, her hand covering his glove in a lingering touch almost as warm as the wine. Crozier met her eyes above the candle she carried. She did not smile but pressed a finger to his mouth, as if she feared he would speak. Crozier tasted primrose oil, and inclined his head for her to leave. With a backward glance she tiptoed off, her lamp fading until it was snuffed, and he was again alone in the dark.

Foulberry had placed Eure near the window, though his voice was so soft that some of his words were lost. The first half-hour was wasted in small talk, as the Vice Warden enquired about his lordship's land, and his affairs, and Foulberry politely asked about Eure's business at the baron's court. 'But I know you did not invite me here to learn how I dealt with this week's parcel of miscreants,' said Eure at last, after a detailed description of the unusually harsh punishments he had meted out – twelve hangings, sixteen gaol sentences, two deportations, and the lands of all convicts forfeited.

'No, my lord,' admitted Foulberry, 'fascinating though those matters are. But I certainly admire your zeal, and courage. You will not be popular tonight among the criminal class in this dale. Others, such as myself, will be toasting your name. But as you say, that is not why I need to see you. Or at least, only in part.'

Eure waited while Foulberry stared into his goblet, as if wondering where to begin. From his post, Crozier could see the crown of his lordship's cap. The Vice Warden was out of his view, but so close that a whistle from the borderer would have riffled his hair.

'S-s . . . so?' prompted the Vice Warden at last, unsettled by Foulberry's silence.

'You must understand that this conversation can go no further.' Eure must have nodded, for Foulberry coughed, took a slurp of wine, and leaned towards his guest. 'The governance of this border has for years concerned many of us. As long as Dacre kept order of sorts, we were prepared to tolerate infringements of our property and our rights. But the baron is now so wildly exceeding his authority, treating his loyal associates with such contempt and piling up riches for himself while allowing his cronies to steal from beneath our noses, that we must put a stop to it.'

'I have heard many such complaints, Foulberry, and not been able to doubt them all, though what I know of the man suggests he believes he acts for the common good. His methods may be rough, and even dubious, but he gets results. As to pocketing money that is not rightfully his – well, which of us has not done that at some time?'

Foulberry cleared his throat. 'Dacre might once have been an honourable man, or at least no worse than the rest of us, but as his years advance his tactics grow harsher and more careless. There is no denying he was once a fine leader of men. Few others could have held the border thugs in check. But now I believe he has lost control, and respect. The marches are in the hands of the Armstrongs, not the baron, and most certainly not the king's appointed men, such as yourself.'

As was his habit, Eure was quiet before he replied. 'So let me be clear,' he eventually said. 'What is it you are suggesting? That we somehow outwit or overpower the baron, and remove him from his post?'

Foulberry nodded.

'By any means?' Eure's pitch rivalled a castrato's.

There was another pause, and the sound of Foulberry sighing. 'No, my lord, not by any means. We are men of principle. Dacre may use his accomplices to kill and destroy on his orders, but we must be cleverer than that. If he is to lose his head, it will be by the king's command, not ours. If we were foolish enough to act like rebels and take the law into our own hands, our lives here would only get worse after Dacre is gone. Rightly or wrongly, Henry dislikes his barons being murdered.'

'And once he has gone?'

'Then, my lord, the position is surely yours.'

Again, the chamber was silent. A westerly wind was gathering around the castle, rain on its breath, and Crozier hugged the wall to hear the Vice Warden's reply. It took a long time. There was the sound of a bench scraping across the boards, and Eure's pate came into view. He seemed to be saying it was late, and he must retire. There was ill-disguised regret in Foulberry's voice. 'But of course. You must rest before your journey tomorrow. I will summon a footman to guide you to your room.'

A bell rang, but before the servant could appear Eure spoke. 'I must think on this, Foulberry, because I see the merit in what you say. Not for my personal advancement so much as for the marches. It is palpably wrong that Henry is unaware of what goes on here. To advise him would be an act not of treachery but of loyalty. I will sleep on it, and we will talk again in the morning.'

By the time Eure and his retinue set off back to the middle march, he and his host had reached an agreement. If Foulberry could produce written grievances signed by accusers from across the marches, then Eure would add his own testimony on oath, and present these damning documents to the king. Or to Cardinal Wolsey, more like, which amounted to the same thing.

'Did you bring my name into that conversation?' asked Crozier later that day, when he and Tom were seated on the bench occupied by Eure the previous night.

Foulberry shook his head. 'I thought it prudent not to do so. When you can present him in person with the accusers' sworn statements, all suspicion of you must surely fade. But to advise him in advance that he is to shake the hand of the enemy, and such an enemy as you, might kill our endeavour stillborn.'

Crozier looked at him. After a moment, he stood. 'I see you are not afraid of risk. That I like. For my part, I undertake to have the signed oaths by the end of the month. We must act swiftly after that.'

'Once you have assured me they are in your possession, I will summon Eure, and all three of us can sit down together.' Foulberry advanced on the borderer, both hands outstretched. He grasped Crozier by the arms, his face purpling with excitement. 'I can scarce believe we are already at this pass. It is beyond my most hopeful dreams.' He turned to his wife, who stood at the door, smiling on the group. 'Dearest, our fortunes are about to change, thanks to this man. This most stout-hearted man.' He pumped Crozier's hand, and Tom's, too choked with emotion for further speech.

Lady Foulberry had her hand in her husband's arm as, at the castle doors, the brothers mounted their horses. They bowed, as did their hosts. Unsmiling, Isabella held Crozier's eye. The borderer gathered the reins and turned away, and before he and Tom had reached the gates the studded doors had closed on the Foulberrys, who were once again sealed behind their thick walls.

A month and more later, when Crozier was brought into Eure's presence, the atmosphere in Foulberry's small chamber crackled as if the unlit fire was in full blaze. 'Sir William,' said Foulberry, flushing to match his robe, 'this is the man of whom I just spoke, in whose great debt we stand.' He pointed, as if Eure might not have seen the fully armed borderer filling the door. 'Adam Crozier, my lord, chief of the Teviotdale clan.'

Eure stood up at Crozier's entrance, but did not proffer a hand. Nor did Crozier, who looked into the Vice Warden's eyes, and met an expression of rank distrust. His own, he knew, mirrored it.

'Let us all be seated,' said Foulberry, fussing to find chairs and stools, as if that was his greatest concern. 'Isabella, dearest,' he cried, putting his head out of the door, 'fetch us wine, if you will.'

Eure raised a hand. 'No wine, please.' He moved to the centre of the room, obliging Foulberry to press himself against the empty fireplace. 'What is this, good sir?' The Vice Warden's voice was so low it might have been a hiss. 'Have you s-s-set me a trap? I thought we had an understanding. I do not deal with border scum, and well you know it.'

Foulberry paled. 'My lord, no!' he cried, as Eure's hand went to the hilt of his sword. Were it unsheathed in so small a room, everyone present would feel its blade. 'Stay your hand. This man is our friend. Would I betray you? Listen, I implore you, to what he has to say.'

Crozier, broadsword hilt in his hold, had the advantage. Standing by the door he could draw his sword with ease and bar Eure's exit. From the sheen on the Vice Warden's brow it was plain he knew he was cornered.

'Be assured, Foulberry intends no mischief,' said Crozier. 'And nor do I. Of course I am no more your friend than you are mine, but in the matter of Baron Dacre, and ending his rule, we are of one mind. I can be of use to you. And you, I hope, to me.' Eure stood unblinking. 'I bring with me signed testimony from the foremost families of the east, middle and western marches. Nine in all.'

As he put his hand into his jerkin, Eure drew his sword. Crozier did not look at him as he retrieved the papers from his pouch. 'You can put that thing away,' was all he said, the packet of letters in his hand.

'Now, we can either sit here and talk, or I can leave. If I go, I do not return, and these depositions go with me. Should that happen, your king will soon hear that his Vice Warden tried to obstruct justice in his lands, and I doubt the news will please him. A vengeful king, if what I hear is true. But then, we are all vengeful these days.'

Eure hesitated, looking from Crozier to Foulberry, his quickened breath loud in the cramped chamber. It was his host's face that finally reassured him; nothing in Crozier's offered comfort. Sheathing his sword, he spoke grudgingly. 'Talk, then. And show me the statements. Then I will decide what to do.'

It was far into the night when the three broke up their meeting. Seated outside the door, Tom rose and followed as his brother strode from the chamber and across the dim hall.

'We have him,' was all Crozier said, as they made for the stables.

'We leave now? At this hour?'

Crozier nodded, and quickened his pace. Buckling his cloak, Tom hastened after him. They left by a side door to the courtyard, and stepped into the blue darkness of night. The beeches and sycamores that circled the castle swayed like a river in spate. Casting a look of loathing at the high black walls, Crozier put a hand on his brother's shoulder. 'God forbid we should ever again—'

He did not finish. Before them, in the gloom, appeared a figure in white, shielding a tallow lamp with her palm. 'Gentlemen,' said Isabella Foulberry, wrapped in a fur-trimmed nightgown whose ribbons were loosely tied over her shift. 'Where do you go at this time of night? Your beds are ready, your horses asleep. Have we offended you in some way?'

Crozier halted. There was a pause, as if he were gathering his thoughts, but when he spoke there was a smile in his voice, a courtly tone Tom did not recognise. 'My lady, you and your husband could never offend me. Forgive our haste, but there is work to be done at home, and we have already been away too long.' He took the hand that was cupping the lamp, and bent over it. The unprotected flame went wild.

'We – I – will never forget what you have done for us. If Eure achieves what we believe he will, it may be that soon both sides of the border will be at peace, and we no longer enemies. Not,' he added, pressing her fingers, 'that we have ever been other than friends. And for what you and your husband have done for us, and our clan, I cannot thank you enough. I said as much to your husband, before taking our leave, but . . .' he paused, looking down at her, 'I am very glad of the chance to say it to you in person.'

'We will not see you again?'

Crozier let go her hand, which fell to her side, the lamp forgotten. 'Of course we will meet again, and soon,' he said, speaking low, as if his meaning was for her alone. 'And in more congenial conditions than these. But for now we must be gone.'

Minutes later they were on their way, riding fast out into the dark, as if the road north were lit by flares.

CHAPTER TWENTY-FOUR

June 1524

That summer the English marches began to simmer, rebels and reivers picking fights with the king's men and Dacre's guards, and even with themselves, as if to pass the time.

Across the border in Teviotdale, Crozier's lands were at peace. The calm made him uneasy, and with Benoit and Tom and his most trusted lieutenants he prowled the dale in search of the reason. It should not be this quiet.

Was it worry that made her husband so grim-faced when he was at home? Louise told herself it must be, but she was unconvinced. Since Crozier had returned from Foulberry's castle, he had lapsed into silence, his face hard as basalt, his words falling like stones. At night too, when they lay in bed, he barely spoke though he clasped her tightly, even in sleep. By day she would sometimes catch him gazing at her, a forlorn look in his eye, as if he were measuring the distance between them.

Antoine was now walking with a stick, ignoring the limp that pitched him to the side with every other step. Every morning he headed out to the woods with basket and bowl, collecting flowers and herbs and tapping trees for sap. Word had spread of his knowledge of bones, and the plants and seeds that mended them, and the parade of ailing animals brought to him for treatment was soon joined by villagers seeking help for themselves.

The Frenchman refused to charge for his services, saying it was mere guesswork and cost him nothing, but some dropped him a coin regardless. Such donations he gave to Louise, who put them in a jar. He would need money for his journey home, which was fast approaching.

'You will soon have to leave us,' she said one day, as Antoine pounded willowherb to a paste at the kitchen table, making her head thump like a barn door. 'Now your leg is almost healed you must think about what you are going to do next.'

Antoine stirred distilled water into the mush, and set pestle and mortar aside. 'I know,' he said, and the sadness in his voice startled her. She looked up from the fire, but he had gone, leaving behind the willowherb salve and its sharp scent of summer.

A few days later, Crozier took him aside. 'What are your plans, lad?' he asked, not unkindly. Antoine told him he had not yet made any. 'Then you must rejoin your army.'

'But they will throw me in gaol, as a deserter,' said Antoine, colour warming his cheeks. 'Maybe worse,' he added, seeing Crozier unmoved.

'No reason they need know you were running away,' the borderer replied. 'We can come up with a tale to explain why you were so far from camp when you broke your leg. Never fear, I will take the blame.' Crozier put a hand on the soldier's shoulder. 'A line from me, and Albany will be lenient. But you cannot hide out here much longer.'

Antoine shivered. 'I would rather join my brethren in the east of the country than go back to the army,' he said.

'I thought you'd given up that nonsense,' Crozier said, sharply. 'You promised my wife.'

'And I meant it. But if it is a choice between soldiering and doing what I first set out to do, I would rather stay here and take my chances as a preacher. I am likely to die in either case, am I not?'

Crozier frowned. 'Your life is entirely yours once you leave us. But so long as you are in my care, you are an injured soldier, planning to return to barracks as soon as you can walk without a stick. You understand? Breathe one word of your heresy while you live here, and I will have you whipped.'

Antoine bowed his head. 'I understand,' he said quietly.

'What will happen to him if he goes back to Albany's army?' asked Louise that night as she and Crozier sat beside the fire in their bedchamber. Her husband shrugged. 'If they believe us, then nothing, perhaps. But more likely he will be flogged.'

'But that might kill him!' Louise put a hand to her mouth.

'He will survive,' said Crozier roughly, bending to remove his boots. 'He's already been through far worse.' His face was flushed when he sat up and set his boots aside, but Louise did not notice, staring instead at the smouldering logs as if they were a problem she could not solve. She was still quiet when they climbed into bed. Long after she had fallen asleep, Crozier lay thinking about Antoine and his reluctance to leave, while the fire burned slowly to ash.

In the morning, Crozier was gone before Louise awoke, and his side of the bed was cold. She dressed and went down to the kitchens, where the maid had stoked the fire. 'Take Grandpa his bread,' said Louise, giving her Old Crozier's plate and cup, and laying out food for Ella and the children, who would be down shortly.

A minute later, the maid hurried back into the kitchen, the plate still in her hand. She opened her mouth, but could not speak, tears spilling instead of words. Louise picked up her skirts and ran across the great hall and down the passage to the men's quarters, where Old Crozier had a small room to himself.

Lying on his pallet, turned towards the wall, Crozier's grandfather was curled like a dried leaf, knees drawn up, head tucked down. Louise fell to her knees and put her hand on his shoulder. 'Grandpa,' she whispered, but he did not respond. His body was cold and stiff. She turned him towards her, and felt her heart kick at the sight of his face, eyes closed, mouth agape, the silvered cheeks hollow where his teeth had been knocked out many years before.

Putting her head on his chest, she held her breath. Eventually she felt his ribs rise and fall, though the lungs were weak as a fledgling's, and the air he sucked barely enough to sustain life.

'Fetch my husband,' said Louise to the maid at her side. 'Hurry, girl. Get him at once.'

Left alone, Louise put a hand on Old Crozier's brow. He did not move. Settling herself beside him she took his hand, talking to him softly all the while, until Crozier found her there. From the doorway he looked down at his once powerful grandfather, now so shrivelled that his blanket lay all but flat. 'Jesus and Mary,' he said hoarsely. He crouched beside Louise and took the hand she had been holding, rubbing it as if his touch could bring his grandfather back. But Old Crozier did not stir.

'What shall we do?' said Louise, leaning against her husband. 'He is scarcely breathing.'

Crozier shook his head. 'Make up his fire and keep him warm. Keep watch, and hope he awakes.'

There was a scrabbling from the passageway, and the wolf appeared in the door. Sniffing Old Crozier's hand, he licked his face. When there was no response, he sat on his haunches, whining.

Louise put a hand on Crozier's back. 'Antoine might be able to help,' she said.

'I'll find him,' he replied, and left the room, summoning the wolf to follow.

Antoine, when he came, was perplexed. After feeling for Old Crozier's pulse, and examining his chest and back, arms and legs and tongue, he sat back on his heels. 'I have never seen anything like this,' he said. 'He has no obvious signs of sickness. His skin is clear, and no limb is twisted or out of shape. Yet he is far, far away. It might be the prelude to . . .' His eyes flickered towards Crozier, who was staring at his grandfather's sleeping face. The word that hung heavy over the room remained unspoken. 'Or,' he continued, 'it may be a temporary oblivion, of a sort that he will wake from, refreshed.'

'For God's sake,' said Crozier, 'he is an old man. At his age, nothing can refresh him.'

'That I know, but . . .'

Crozier ignored him, and put a hand on Louise's arm. 'All we can do is take care of him, and see what happens.' She looked at him, unable to speak.

'I will nurse him,' said Antoine. 'With your permission, of course.'

With a glance at her husband, who nodded his assent, Louise agreed. 'We will take it in turns, then, you and I.'

Calling the maid to fetch ale and a sponge, she dragged a stool beside Old Crozier's bed. 'I will watch over him till nightfall.' She wetted the sponge and dabbed the old man's lips, but even at the taste of the honeyed beer he did not move.

A long week followed. It was as if a pall had fallen over the keep, everyone hushed and subdued as they waited for news from Old Crozier's room. The wolf took up post outside his door, leaving only for a few minutes at a time. Louise would call him to her as she sat by the bed, burying her hands in his fur, and laying her head on his. The wolf's warmth, his shining blue eyes and panting tongue, were a picture of life, while the husk of a man at her side seemed to grow flimsier each day.

A candle was set burning beneath a bowl of bay leaves, and the room was sweetly scented. Old Crozier could not be roused to eat, and the only liquid he drank was what trickled down his throat from the sponge pressed to his lips. His skin grew papery, and his face was becoming more skull than flesh.

On the third night, when Antoine relieved Louise from her post, he brought with him a jar of green unguent. 'What is this?' she asked.

'Foxgloves mixed with ground ivy and hemlock,' he replied. 'I can think of nothing else that might rouse his senses, or reduce his pain. If you allow it, I will rub it onto his chest.' He led her away from the pallet and lowered his voice. 'Your husband's grandfather is close to death, as you must know. Rather than cure him, this salve might hasten that process. Are you willing to take that risk?' He turned to look at the bed. Louise followed his gaze to where Old Crozier lay.

'I must speak to Adam,' she replied, a catch in her voice.

She found him in the great hall, seated by the fire, and took his hand as she repeated what Antoine had said. The line between Crozier's eyes deepened. 'I'm not sure it is our place to wager on Old Crozier's life.' Louise waited, knowing he had not finished. After a pause he raised his hands, as if for one of the few times in his life, he felt helpless. 'Yet though he makes no sound, he must be suffering, wasting away without food or drink. Another week like this, and he will be dead anyway. If the salve proves fatal, perhaps we will have eased his passing.' He gave a groan, and dropped his head. 'Jesus, Louise, I don't know. What do you say?'

'I do not know either,' she said, biting back tears. 'I want to trust Antoine. We know he means well. But to hasten his death? I don't know if I could carry that on my conscience. It would be a mortal sin.'

Crozier looked up, as if he were seeing through her to someone who stood at her back. He sighed, and took her hands in his. 'Then let it be on mine, Louise. Tell Antoine to do it.'

There was only one good bed in Harbottle. Blackbird's curtained recess by the fire in the castle's main hall was the envy of all, out of the reach of draughts and warm as a new-baked loaf. Yet for some months it had lain empty, the butler no longer retiring there at the end of the evening but to a truckle bed outside his master's door, where winds from all airts of the castle convened. Since autumn, the Warden General had been waking most nights, shouting, sometimes screaming, though not for Blackbird. Dressed in shift and buckskin slippers, the butler would tap on his door, giving him time to come to his senses before lifting the latch. The sight of a candle seemed to ease the baron's fear, chasing off the spectres that fouled his dreams, and he would wave his man away with an oath or a growl, as if it were Blackbird who had disturbed his sleep, and not the terrors he carried within.

The butler had hoped that light summer nights would ease Dacre's mind, but the nightmares came furious as ever. Blackbird should not have been surprised. Out here, on the lip of the civilised world, summer was but a name, and a short one at that. In June the wind was sharp as a winter squall, and the sun struggled to shine through clouds plump with rain, whose salt-laced columns scoured the hills and turned sweet meadows to mud.

Accompanying the night-time sweats was Dacre's daytime frown, a glower that clung to him like thickening fog as he set to work each morning. At night, over dinner, he drank his kegs and flagons dry, growing so testy that none but his brothers dared sit with him till the wicks guttered and the servants snored, and there was nothing for it but to make for bed.

A letter from court would cure all this, Blackbird felt sure. The baron was fretting, waiting for an answer to his last message, a querulous reminder he had despatched to the king in a skitter of dusted ink as Easter bells rang out across the shire, and his sentence had yet to be lifted.

But no reply had arrived, and now the butler's nerves were fraying at the sight of his master's unease. They were like a matching pair of guns, he thought, held in unsteady hands, and likely to blast fire from their mouths at the first sign of an enemy. He did not like his own, or his lordship's, volatile mood.

As Dacre's temper roughened, his hands began to shake. Of a morning he could not hold his reins steady until he had swigged from his flask, the mere scent of spirits as the bottle was unstoppered calming the tremor before he had taken a sip.

This was not the time to grow feeble. Rebel fires were flaring across the eastern and middle marches on the English side, and the west and eastern Scottish marches were turning ugly. Reluctant to withdraw from the east, where trouble brewed whenever the Warden General looked away, Dacre despatched his brother to deal with the Scots. Sir Christopher preferred chess to the chase, but when he caught the smell of the enemy he was, Dacre believed, a better soldier even than he, and crueller, more pitiless, for sure.

As children, Dacre and his brothers had fought the peasant boys on their Cumberland lands, hazel staffs against sapling sticks, crowbars against stones, but only Christopher had carried his games to the very end. There were several boys who rued their encounter, one so badly beaten he never spoke again, spending his few remaining years mumbling and sucking his fingers. And there was one who did not make it home, spitted on Christopher's first sword. Philip and Dacre had scrabbled at the earth and packed the body beneath it while their brother turned his face to the darkening sky, and told them to hurry.

In their neighbourhood, fear did the Dacres no harm. Yet now it was Tam who was afraid, something Blackbird would never have believed possible. As war with Scotland dragged on, Dacre grew more sullen. Summoned by Surrey, newly named Duke of Norfolk after his father's recent death, to broker yet another short-lived truce with the Scots, he would return hot-cheeked, cursing the duke for his deaf ear, which would not hear of his retirement. That humiliation was compounded by the duke's probing of his activities, the man's obvious suspicion of him settling like a black cloud over his head.

There were skirmishes and set battles across the border, the Scots taunting their enemy, and Dacre swift to reply. That year had seen some of the fiercest engagements Blackbird could recall, the Harbottle bugler working all hours as he called the alarm, or trumpeted the troops on their way as they poured out of the castle like ink spilled from a pot, before spreading over the dale. Yet even a bugle blast could not charge the Warden General with fire.

Previously, war had brightened his eye. Now he hesitated before setting out at the head of his men. Night-time forays were a memory, the baron taking instead to standing on the castle walls, watching darkness gather as if it, and not the northern tribes, was his enemy. 'I'll no venture out in that,' he would mutter. 'They'll never catch me that easy.' More than once Blackbird caught him speaking aloud when he thought he was alone, but whom he was addressing the butler did not know.

These should have been exhilarating days. News from over the border suggested the boy king James would soon be taking his throne, the factions around him and his mother finally reaching accord, and peace between their countries within reach. The regent's laughable last year had left the marches barely scathed, unlike Albany's reputation. Departing with undignified haste, yet still too late to reach his ailing wife, he would do well never to return. The garrison he had left at Dunbar Castle, in the east, kicked its heels, scanning the horizon for ships and news, but hearing nothing but the kittiwakes mewling over their heads. A catalogue of Albany's deeds was being compiled in Edinburgh Castle by the Lord High Treasurer, filling a book with the upstart's misdemeanours. Should he return, he would not be housed in Holyrood, or the dowager queen's bedchamber, but more likely the castle gaol.

Blackbird smirked. Two more dissimilar men could scarcely be imagined sharing Margaret's favours. Her alliance with the regent had been tactical: that he did not doubt, or condemn. The affection in which Dacre held her, however, suggested theirs had been a bond deeper than lust, little good though it had done them.

Was Margaret Tudor the root of his master's distress? He thought it unlikely. The death of Dacre's much-wronged wife Bess had chastened him, but only for a time. No woman could disturb him this powerfully, surely, except perhaps his mettlesome daughter. These days, though, Joan was docile, tamed – one prayed – at last. Content to wander Harbottle's grounds with her maid, or ride out with her pudding-faced guard, she was growing into a young lady. Not Blackbird's type, even had she been on offer, but he could see her charm: the heart-shaped face, the supple waist, the pert, intelligent eyes.

For the moment, Blackbird could do nothing but pace the castle walls at his master's heels. News was awaited from every quarter: the west, where Sir Christopher had been despatched to quell the debatable lands; the south, where Henry's court had turned its back on them; and the north, where the answer to their ancient quarrel might be found in the shape of a twelve-year-old boy, whose crown, if donned, would slip over his head and lie round his neck like a collar.

In the moorland wastes of Liddesdale, the Armstrongs had just received their orders. The day was bright, the wind boisterous, and in his whistling peel tower Sly Armstrong received Dacre's messenger, whose sodden shirt smelled sharp as vinegar. Sly listened, neither nodding nor shaking his head. When the list of commands had been delivered, Dacre trusting only to the spoken word in this cross-border alliance, Sly repeated them, like an altar boy reciting the catechism. The messenger interrupted, to amend a detail, and Sly tossed his head, not liking to be corrected, and began once more from the beginning. The orders were not complicated, but Sly was a man of action, not memory, and he was sluggish in this lesson as in nothing else. When finally he had it learned, he dismissed the messenger and summoned his men.

They were a large clan, not only in number, but built like men-of-war, with barrel chests and beefy arms, and legs so sturdy that when planted wide they could have anchored a bridge on the Tyne. As they filed into the room, weighed down with knives and clubs, cross-bows and quivers, the place shrank.

Sly stood among them, a silver-ringed hand stroking an unkempt black beard. Perhaps unwilling to expend energy he need not waste, he spoke with lips all but closed. His eyes too were slits, though the gleam that shone from under his lashes told his listeners that here was an expedition they would enjoy.

A few words were enough to send his outriders off to alert their Tynedale kin. The rest of them were informed they had three days to prepare and muster their men to Sir Christopher's side, at the gate that crossed from Bewcastle Waste into Liddesdale.

'We'll meet Black Ned and our Tynedale cousins there,' said Sly, into his beard. 'Dacre's our paymaster, as ye well ken, but he doesnae own us. This is a fight, nothing mair. Like all those afore, it is a paid deal. Our allegiance is tae none but oursels.'

His men frowned, and drew closer. 'Whit I'm saying, lads, is this,' said Sly, his eyes passing over each of their faces, the hangdog, the fat-jowled, the eager and cruel. 'Have nae fear if, in the ruck, ye spit yin o Dacre's boys. I'm no gonnae hand ye ower for justice. Accidents happen. Scots or English, it disnae matter whose throats we slice, so long as we're true to the clan. Ye with me?'

A growling assent ran round the room, accompanied by a scraping of spurs as the band dispersed to polish their steel and gather provisions for a week-long conflict, or more.

Across the border, in the northern reaches of Tynedale, Sly Armstrong's outriders picked their way with care. It was still light, though evening stars were pricking the lowering sky. Moorland stretched to infinity on one side, but on the other they saw a line of treetops over the next ridge of hills. On they rode, parched heather raising dust around their horses' hooves, setting the riders coughing beneath their scarves. Pulling to a halt when they reached the trees, the three men swigged from their flasks, wiped their faces, and knotted their kerchiefs around their necks. From here, they would be moving slowly.

What lay before them was deep, dishevelled forest. They entered and were met by toppled trunks, uprooted bushes and mounds of leaves, as if an angry hand had stretched down between the trees and knocked everything askew. As they followed the track, which was strewn with branches, twigs and stones, the wind quietened and the light faded like a lamp that was burning low. The tops of the trees shifted and moaned, but down here they were in a vault, the air as still as if it had not stirred in years. Fallen trees blocked their path at several points, obliging them to dismount and clamber their way around the obstruction. Unlike the unwary who strayed into these woods, the riders were not surprised to see that the trees had not fallen but been felled, the stumps where axes had swung lying like giant coins, clean-severed by Tynedale's foresters. Where the wiser of the unwary would have turned back, the posse drew their cloaks close, and continued. The track led them gently downwards, and after a couple of miles they heard water, at first a murmur, then a roar, and came to the edge of a gully, through which a river licked over a bed of sharp rocks.

The stone stumps of an old bridge stared up at them from the gloom, green with moss. Planks and rubble from the broken crossing had long since been overgrown or swept away. They could not pass here, yet they did not ride on. Instead their leader put his fingers to his mouth, and whistled. For a few minutes the messengers sat in silence, aware of the army of trees at their backs, and the slow-falling night that would soon trap them here. Upriver a fox barked; there was a slither from the riverbank as an otter slid unseen into the black waters and swam off down the stream; and there was a footfall, so quiet it might have been a bird, creeping up behind them. One of the horses tossed its head and whinnied, and they turned to see a figure in brown approaching, longbow in hand.

The Armstrongs got off their horses, and the leader approached the archer. 'I bring a summons from Sly, for Black Ned,' he said, grasping the archer's forearm in greeting. The man in brown jerked his head for them to follow. He led them upriver, through a thicket of holly and ash so low they had to duck their way through it. This was the Tynedale reivers' warren, a morass of woodland and marsh they had reshaped, and set with pitfalls, until only those versed in its maze could find their way unaided.

Where the river narrowed, the archer came to a halt and disappeared into a fall of rocks. He emerged carrying a fat rope over his shoulder, which he lashed to a tree on the bank and flung across the water, where a boy stood in the shadows to catch it. When it was tied, the archer sidled down the slippery mud embankment, walked into the water and, holding the rope tight, waded towards the other side. The current ran fast and deep, and he stepped in from thigh to chest in a few paces. Caught by the torrent, his body bent like a bow, as if he would have been swept away had he not been tethered by the rope.

When he had reached the other side, the messengers followed him down the bank and entered the water, bridles in one hand, rope in the other. Though the leader's mare reared in alarm as she slithered on the rocks, he kept her in line, tugging her in his wake as if she were weightless. In a shower of water she reached the far bank and scrambled to safety, and the others obediently followed.

Dripping, the three men squelched after their guide. They could smell logfires, but not until they were almost upon the settlement did they see the roof it came from. Covered in turf and earth so they could not be set alight, their cousins' houses were low and squat, walls deep as a castle's, and as thickly mortared, so they would not easily be smoked out. From the door of one house the next was invisible, hidden by banks of mossed earth and tightly packed trees, yet so close that a shout would bring people running.

This was the heart of Tynedale, the dread fold of the Armstrongs' cousins, outlaws all under their leader Black Ned. Few outsiders got as far as this; most were cut down, shot, or cudgelled in the forest's first mile, its hurdles slowing intruders to a crawl, when they could be picked off by ambush like dinner for the pot.

Black Ned sat by his fireside, a rosy-cheeked child on his knee. When the outriders appeared, he set the boy down and grunted a greeting, ignoring the child's girning. He did not get up, but his wife brought them ale, and they sat on the earthen floor, beneath Black Ned's gaze, feeling like children themselves.

'We're on the march again?' asked the outlaw, his scarlet beard brighter in the windowless room than his sluggish fire. Black was his father's name, and the son's temper, and no one was ever allowed to forget it. His wife kept her eyes low as she served their visitors, and fingered her skirts as she stood aside, awaiting further orders.

'Aye,' said the leader, 'and a guid raid it'll be, if all goes well. All ae us will be able to lie up for months, if we get what we're owed. Dacre's paying, but so will plenty of the houses and churches we pass on the way.' He rubbed his hands, palms slippery with greed.

'Been a while since we've had a good ride,' said Black Ned. 'I can bring something nice home for May, isn't that right?' he asked, without turning his head. 'Something to make ye look sweet and bonny.'

His wife murmured her appreciation. 'Can't hear ye,' said the outlaw. 'Jist the scrabble o' mice running over the dinner table. Leastwise, I don't know how else to explain the sour taste to most things ye're cooking these days.' He turned to his visitors, and raised his shoulders as if perplexed. 'And they wonder why sometimes we dinnae come hame, eh?'

With the message delivered, the Armstrongs stretched their legs before the sizzling logs, watching their britches steam while wildfowl roasted on the spit, and the daughters of the house poured them a fiery home-made brew. The wife disappeared to another corner, where she could be heard scrubbing the table, and her pots.

Before the guests rose the next morning, the Tynedalers were already up, sharpening their arrows with flint, and reshoeing their ponies for the raid that lay ahead. Two days later, with the Armstrong outriders barely keeping up, Black Ned led his men out of the forest and onto the moors, the thunder of their hooves more alarming to those who heard them passing than the worst of winter storms.

CHAPTER TWENTY-SIX

Louise touched Old Crozier's bristled face, and hung her head in sorrow. Like an effigy in the village church, he lay under his sheet with nose and feet pointed at the rafters. His hands had tightened to a dead bird's claws, and his mouth was sunken, as if to prevent his uttering a word, should he wake. But Louise doubted he ever would. His breath was no more than a whisper, his ribs lifting so little one might have thought him a corpse.

It was early evening, and Antoine's shift would soon begin. Several days had passed since the Frenchman had first applied his salve, and there had been no change that Louise could see. Every morning and nightfall, when she and Antoine washed the old man, his body seemed to grow lighter. Much longer like this and he would be ready for his shroud.

She trimmed the tallow lamps ahead of Antoine's arrival. Warmed by an afternoon's sun the room felt dusty as a coop, and she opened the shutters to let in a gasp of summer air. As she did so there was a flash at the window and in flew a swallow, whirling around the ceiling until it alighted on a beam, from where it looked down on Old Crozier with bobbing tail.

At that moment his eyes opened, drawn, it seemed, by the bird. Louise gave a cry, which set the swallow circling again, before settling this time above the fireplace. 'Grandpa,' she whispered, crouching by his side. 'Can you hear me? It's Louise.'

His eyes followed the bird and his lips parted, though only air escaped.

'Grandpa?' Louise touched his hand, which opened enough to clasp her finger. The old man dragged his gaze back to her face, and closed his eyes. A shuddering sigh left his body, but as Louise looked on in horror, thinking he had breathed his last, his lungs filled again and he began to breathe, slow but deep, his chest moving like a pair of rusty bellows. By the time she had summoned Crozier there was a hint of colour in the old man's cheeks. Though he was once more unconscious, a sere tongue licked his mouth as she wetted it with ale, and when she held the sponge to his lips, he sucked like a lamb at its mother's teat.

Arriving in time to see his grandfather turn his head aside and settle into sleep, Crozier gripped Louise's shoulder, not trusting himself to speak. Antoine was close behind him, standing breathless in the doorway.

'He is asleep now,' said Louise, 'but he was awake, properly, for the first time.'

Antoine knelt by the pallet and felt the old man's wrist. 'Stronger,' he murmured, as he picked up his stick and got to his feet. 'Do not be too hopeful yet,' he cautioned, but the look on his face said otherwise.

It was a week before Old Crozier could do more than sip from a tumbler and lie watching shadows cross the walls. When finally he could sit up and talk, he had no idea how ill he had been, nor for how long. 'Summer's passing gey fast,' he would say, bemused each morning by the time he had lost, not understanding where it had gone. The day he asked for a second serving of soup a shout went up in the courtyard, and the guards raised their tankards at dinner, in toast to their old friend.

With Old Crozier's recovery, the keep came back to life. It was as if an enchantment had been lifted, a household frozen in silence finding its voice once more. The old clatter and cries restored, only Adam remained quiet and withdrawn, going about his business with a preoccupied air, as if his mind were far away. Of what, or whom, he was thinking Louise could not tell, though she feared she knew the answer.

CHAPTER TWENTY-SEVEN

August 1524

Trouble kept the Vice Warden tied to the marches that summer. In a locked casket in his cellar lay the signed accusations against Dacre, and Eure thought on them often. By now he had hoped to have delivered them to his king, along with a detailed personal denunciation of the baron's criminal habits. But as if the fates were mocking him, he had been obliged to spend the past few months under Dacre's eye, as the English highlanders got out of control, and the Scots wreaked havoc on the middle and eastern marches and Henry, infuriated at the borderers' incessant roiling, sent the Duke of Norfolk north to handle affairs, and in so doing made things worse.

Arrogant and impatient, the hard-bitten soldier fanned the flames. Not literally, though he had tried. Eure heard that when the old campaigner begged the king's permission to use fire against the rebels, Henry's response had been chilling. 'They are our subjects, though evil men,' he had said, the quietness of his voice signalling the severity of his displeasure. As he picked a ragged fingernail, he lifted his eyes to the duke's. 'We do rather desire their reformation than their utter destruction.' Norfolk, as a result, was hamstrung, unable to turn the rebels' favourite weapon against them, and obliged to face them hand to hand, in so doing losing countless of his own men who, at the sight of the rebels bearing down upon them, blazing torches in hand, felt their bowels go slack, as well as their sword arms.

Now, with some of the king's finest servants murdered in raids or reprisals, the Scots in control of the middle border after carrying off and killing the Keeper of Tynedale, and the west as ungovernable as ever, tempers and fear were high.

These weeks, however, had been useful. If anything were needed to strengthen the Vice Warden's resolve in denouncing the baron, it was the unavoidable conclusion that Dacre was working as closely with Scottish outlaws as with himself. The Armstrongs were his bodyguard, human mastiffs who snarled and slavered at any who came close to the baron, and were sent out across the border on his command, like a swarm of hornets. Their name alone was enough to quell those who had thought to resist Dacre's rule, and the Warden General dropped it as a witch delivers a curse. Towns and properties a hundred miles south of the border thus lay in his palm, and few dared retaliate or whine when their houses were picked clean, or their fields and byres torched.

Summer drew to its height, and with the approach of harvest the borders fell quiet. As if mirroring their betters, the raiders' fury was dampened. With the news that the young King James was about to take control of his country, albeit with the help of his council, plans were being put in place for a peace treaty between the English and the Scots. The terms would include an assurance from the Scots that the Duke of Albany would never be allowed to rule there again, and that regular meetings between march officers on both sides of the border would be put in place, to ensure that those harmed by raids were properly compensated.

Sensing the mood, and the danger a formal peace would pose for them, raiders and rebels paused to remuster and rethink. Those relieved at the unexpected calm reminded themselves that it was probably no more than a lull before the raiding season began in earnest, when newly filled barns would be emptied or burned. In these parts it was said that those whose harvest was untouched by the end of Michaelmas were either able to afford well-armed guards or in Dacre's pay – or lay within reach of the Tynedale gangs, who would ride out regardless of moon or month.

Sir William Eure watched the wheat ripen. As green turned to yellow and then to gold, his face lightened. When the first teams of sicklers made their way through the fields, he knew the wait was over and he could leave. Dacre was being kept as close to Norfolk's side as if he were on leading reins. All summer the English court relayed messages to James V's guardians in Scotland, craving meetings and contracts and safe passes as the war came to an end. Negotiations dragged, and Dacre was distracted and tired. In a lull between active hostilities, and while the Warden General was stationed in Berwick, to await the Scottish court's contingent, Eure saddled up and with his manservant took the road to London.

August in the north had been fresh, kept cool with rain and wind. South of York they encountered a sun they had rarely seen, bearing down on them as if it were a warming pan held over their heads. With heat rising from the dust under their horses' hooves, they were roasted top to toe. When they reached London, ten days later, they were sunburned and parched, grit between their teeth, and their hose and boots sodden with sweat. Arriving at the city walls near nightfall, they took beds in an inn by the river, so close to the water they could hear ferrymen's oars sculling under their window and the whining wingbeat of swans coming in to land.

There was no time to enjoy the city. Rising early the next morning, Eure stood under the yard pump to wash off the journey with water drawn straight from the Thames, put on a clean shirt, and swallowed a plate of oysters and a pitcher of ale. A little later he presented himself at Westminster Palace, and learned that the king had left for the country. He and his retinue would not be back until the outbreak of plague had passed.

Dismayed, the Vice Warden clutched his leather bag to his chest. He had not anticipated this. In time of war, what king would abandon his court? And surely he was safe from disease in the seclusion of one of his city palaces?

As if in reply, the lackey fingered his silver buttons and, with a gratifyingly low bow, asked him to wait. A tray of wine and biscuits was brought to him as he sat under a window, and Eure took comfort from this, as he sipped and nibbled and watched the sun rise towards noon behind the leaded panes, warming the flagstones at his feet as if toasting a slice of bread.

There was a flash of scarlet at the edge of the hall, and a stout figure billowed towards him, slippers squeaking beneath his robes, his face as red as his garb. 'Your eminence,' said Eure, rising hurriedly and bending his knee as he recognised the cardinal.

'Sir William,' replied Wolsey, with a magisterial curl of his hand, 'if you will kindly follow me.'

The room Wolsey ushered him into was mercifully cool, shutters dimming the sun, stone walls exuding a perpetual chill. 'Take a seat, I beg you,' said his host, settling himself on a chest draped in a length of carpet and pointing Eure to a stool on the other side of the empty hearth.

The cardinal cocked his head, and waited for his guest to speak. Eure looked around the room, at the desk spread with papers, the ceiling painted with biblical scenes. He swallowed, suddenly aware of the act he was about to commit. He looked at the Lord Chancellor. Was that kindness or calculation in his watery eye?

Wolsey coughed, and adjusted his sleeve. When still the Vice Warden would not begin, he gave a low laugh. 'Forgive me, you must be thirsty on a day such as this. Would a glass of wine be agreeable?'

Eure nodded, and once it was in his hand drained it off and held it out for more. Wolsey masked his surprise at northern manners and refilled it. Disdain, however, was soon trumped by stronger emotions as, his tongue loosened, the Vice Warden poured out his story with barely a stammer before taking the incriminating evidence out of his bag, and laying it on the table. Silence filled the room as Wolsey turned over the letters, reading the accusations fast, but lingering on the signatures of men who would not dare lie. Drawing a deep breath, the cardinal poured a fresh glass of wine with an unsteady hand, and threw it back in one.

The Vice Warden had long since departed, assured of the cardinal's resolve to investigate the charges. Wolsey sat at his desk, staring at his knuckles. The summer evening refused to wane. He longed for night, and darkness. Eventually, with a sigh, he pulled open a drawer and laid upon his table a travel-worn letter bearing the Bishop of Carlisle's seal. The bishop repeated, as if it were a chant, the accusations Eure had dropped in his lap. His belligerent letter had lain untouched since

234

the previous month, Wolsey catching a whiff of score-settling. He had never trusted the bishop, with his mock piety and sanctimonious smile. Now, however, he would be obliged to address his claims, and put Dacre in the dock.

His lips thinned. As the Warden General's staunchest champion, more so even than Norfolk, his position was precarious. Following his denunciation he must dance across the hot coals of open justice, while yet saving face before a king who had no mercy on those he deemed incompetent or partial. If Dacre were proved guilty, Wolsey's judgement would be questioned.

That sweltering August night was short, dawn coming too soon for a city that yearned for coolth, but for the sleepless cardinal, who passed it at his desk, it seemed as if it would never end.

CHAPTER TWENTY-EIGHT

September 1524

The letter from the king had arrived at last. The court's messenger presented it with a flourish from his knapsack, as if a ride of three hundred miles into the wilderness was an everyday matter. The royal seal lay heavy in Blackbird's hand, glistening and imperious. The butler pressed the letter to his chest, and felt his heart grow large as he carried it to his lordship's room.

Blackbird was not a worshipful man, but he hoped this message might be the answer Dacre and he had prayed for. The past few weeks his master had been grey-faced with exhaustion, running diplomatic errands for Norfolk as if he were a pageboy, all the while manoeuvring his troops to curb the growing unrest across the dales. At night, the baron could barely climb the stairs, rubbing his thigh and knee as he went, and sinking onto his bed with a sigh of relief that was closer to a gasp.

Since the end of summer, Dacre's chamber had smelled of Blackbird's liniment, a rub he first devised for a lame horse but which worked for soldiers also. 'Next you know I'll be neighing,' grumbled Dacre the first time it was applied, stripping off his britches and lying face down on his pallet as his butler instructed. Blackbird did not reply, but rolled up his sleeves, spread butter on his hands, and set to pummelling his master's leg and haunches, like a cook tenderising beef. When the larded flesh had turned pink, he rubbed in the lotion, and waited for Dacre's response. After a few seconds it came, the baron hissing between his teeth as he clutched his leg, 'Jesus' sake, Blackbird, what in the name of God is in that stuff? It stings like the very devil.'

'It is meant to, your lordship,' replied Blackbird primly. 'As it soaks in, it dissolves the knots and tensions that pain you so sorely.'

'And the smell,' groaned Dacre, turning onto his back and sitting up.

'Ye'll get used to it,' said his butler. He turned to leave, but a grunt from the baron stopped him.

'My lord?'

'Thank you,' said Dacre. Blackbird's eyes smarted to see his master brought so low.

He would take the memory of the night Dacre returned to find the king's letter to his grave. It might, indeed, have brought it closer. When the baron had pulled off his riding boots and was making for the hall fire, Blackbird drew him aside.

'A letter from the court awaits you,' he said, careful to hide his excitement. 'I have put it in your chamber, but I can bring it down if you prefer to read it among company.'

Dacre pushed past him and hurried up the stairs, his bad leg forgotten in his haste. Hovering at the door behind him, Blackbird watched as the Warden General held a candle above the first page, and the next, peering as if he could not believe what the light revealed. Then he sank onto his bed, as if all breath had left him. The pages fell to the floor, and Blackbird moved swiftly to stop the candle following them. Taking the holder from his master's hand, he bent to retrieve the letter.

The baron's lips were sickly pale. 'To think . . .' he began hoarsely. The butler waited. Dacre shook his head and gave a laugh, like a cannon clearing its throat. 'Ye gods. All this . . .' He lifted his hand, though his meaning was unclear. 'All this, and they reward me thus.' He looked up at his butler. 'See for yourself.'

Blackbird opened the letter, though he had to read it twice for the sense to reach him. 'Star Chamber?' he said, stumbling on the dread words.

The letter came from the office of Cardinal Wolsey, in his role as chief inquisitor of Star Chamber, the king's most private and feared court. Feared, certainly, by Dacre, who had once sat there, in the heart of Westminster, a mouse caught in the king's claws, toyed with and left bleeding beneath its gold-spangled, celestial ceiling. Stories of the baron's days in the Fleet gaol had passed into family legend, an amusement for dinner guests that saw the table rock with laughter as

Dacre poked fun at himself as well as the old king. But Blackbird recalled very well the misery of Dacre's days in prison, and the vow the baron had made, when he was released, never again to find himself as trapped and helpless as that. The sight of his master in his cell each morning, white-faced after enduring the dark, had shocked the butler as a young man. Now, in advancing age, he felt abject fear at the prospect of Dacre's returning there. He read on, not daring to lift his eyes.

The letter was pompous and long-winded, Wolsey relishing his role. After a ponderous preamble, in which the cardinal laid out the duties and scope of Star Chamber – 'to reform enormities committed by the misuse of power in the king's realm' – he informed the baron that 'consequent upon information received of late by this court it is our duty to bring you before it, to answer the charges laid against you from several parties, each of whom has sworn on oath the probity of their testimony.'

> In order to discharge this difficult and regrettable duty, the chamber demands your appearance on the first Monday of October, in this the fifteenth year of King Henry's blessed reign. You will appear before a tribunal composed of myself as Lord Chancellor, the Lord High Treasurer, the Keeper of the Privy Seal, a member of the clerical estate – in this instance myself again – three justices of the court and two impartial witnesses, of your own estate. You will be allowed, and expected, to give a full account of your alleged misdeeds and crimes. Failure to do so, or being adjudged guilty of the indictments levelled against you, will result in imprisonment and further punishment, as decided by this court in accord with the king's wishes.

The Warden General had risen from his bed and was stooped, stoking the fire, when the butler put the letter aside. 'What do ye make of it, eh? Snakes not just at court, but beneath our very feet in the undergrowth here. Vipers, wherever we stand.' His tone was resigned, but the butler was cheered by his master's resolute look. Pale he might be, but Dacre was a soldier and surrender a word he would never understand.

The baron nodded, as if reading the servant's mind. 'I'll fight this, Blackbird. Damned if I care what the court thinks of me, so long as I do not spend the rest of my days in gaol.' He smiled at the poker in his hand. 'It would suit me well to be dismissed from this post. God rot my enemies, they might end up achieving what my begging letters never could.' He hung up the poker and stood, rubbing his back. 'If I am stripped of my station and sent home in disgrace, I will bless them, all of them, whoever they may be.'

But anonymous as his accusers were, Dacre was already compiling a list of likely candidates. The tabulation was in his head, otherwise a ream of paper would have been filled, there being so many who wished him ill.

A few days later the baron and Blackbird set off for London. The roads were dry, the weather was fine, and they made good speed. Neither spoke much as they cantered, knee to knee, down earthen tracks, or trotted smartly though pot-holed main streets, ignoring the beggars who clapped their bells and reached out their hands.

The middle counties slipped past under their hooves, accents growing nasal, words squeezed out of shape, and found themselves thinking of the soft-spoken, hard-living lands they had left behind. As London drew nearer, the countryside ripened, as did its people. Houses were higher, thatch thicker, waists and faces fatter. Even cattle and sheep had a prosperous air, while the sleek horses they hired at each posting house made the marches' nimble beasts seem stunted and clumsy as shelties. But these elegant creatures tired fast, and needed, said Dacre, as much rest and watering as a newly-wed wife.

The Warden General sniffed the air as they rode the last few miles into London on the old Roman road, and a lemony sneer settled on his face. 'Can ye blame me for no attending council as often as Henry would like? It is a foul place, always was. The putrid air turns my stomach,' he said, tugging a kerchief over his nose as fields disappeared beneath smithies, bakers, hovels and taverns. Blackbird nodded, as they trotted past a team of dray horses pulling a butcher's load of carcasses still running with blood.

The scent of freshly killed beasts was perfume compared to the smells that reached them when they passed through Bishop's Gate into the city, where river and street competed for stench. From the water came the yells and oaths of ferrymen, the calls and whistles of those hailing them, and the cries of merchants steering their barges between the nimbler rowing boats, whose jostling threatened to spill their towering cargo. Nevertheless, the cacophony was music beside the shouts from the street, as vendors of everything from 'Hot crab, hot!' to 'Ribs of beef!' and 'Fine writing ink!' bellowed their wares and pressed in upon passers-by. Blackbird's head was spinning as a taverner stood before his premises, reciting his best wines at the top of his lungs. Behind him, a weaver shrieked the quality of her silk stockings, her children lined up beside her, dangling the goods over their arms, where they trembled like ghostly legs.

'It is worse than I remember it,' said Dacre, as they rode through the crowds and past Old London Bridge. Blackbird was not listening, his attention caught by the tarred heads decorating the walls, spiked like black cherries on a stick. Dacre followed his gaze, and grunted. 'And they call us savages.' Blackbird noticed his master turned from the sight, though surely he could not fear that one day his own neck would be set on a pike for public display?

The lodgings Dacre led them to were upriver, where the water was clearer, and boats fewer. The Judge's Landing, a handsome, bow-fronted wooden house, had a small formal garden to the front, and backed onto the Thames and a private quay. It was where Dacre always stayed when attending court. 'Better taking a boat than trusting to the streets, with its thieving urchins and filth, my lord,' said the new landlady, curtseying in the presence of a peer of the realm, whose nobility and wealth were evident despite his plainly cut clothes and coating of dust.

She led them to a low-ceilinged room overlooking the river, hung with tapestries and appointed with enough candelabra and lamps to light a market town. 'Dinner will be brought to your room at five,' she said, leaving them with a smile, but not before a kick of her dark gown revealed a flash of rose-pink leg. Both men saw, as they had been meant to, but only Blackbird continued to stare at the door some time after it had closed.

Sunday passed slowly, church bells pealing in such a profusion of keys it was like listening to an ill-formed chapel choir being put through its paces. As the day wore on, Dacre sat by the window, growing quieter. That night at dinner he scarcely touched the steamed perch and three-bird roast, but he drank deep, and fell into bed as if he had been knocked unconscious. There were no shouts in the night, but his snoring kept Blackbird awake until his namesakes called the dawn chorus. Soon the river was loud with ferrymen, and the air with tolling bells, and there was nothing for it but to rise.

A green-painted boat pulled up to the quay at a servant's cry, and the men climbed into it. 'Westminster Palace,' said Dacre, sour-mouthed with wine. Dressed in black but for their linen shirts, they had a clerical air, though as much for their stony faces as their garb, and the sculler did not disturb their sombre mood but dipped the oars in silence.

Westminster soon came into view, and once the press of boats at the steps had eased, they alighted. The royal buildings soared into the clear sky, the living embodiment of stern, pitiless power. The Star Chamber was well known to them both, but the sight of it a few hundred yards down the river made Dacre's acid stomach turn. He belched, and turned aside to spit. The chamber was smaller than he had remembered. Narrow and high, with prominent bow windows reflecting the river, it was distinguished by a tall brick gable chimney that was incongruously homely. Flanked by halls where on fair days bear- and bull-baiting offered a grisly parody of what went on behind its doors, the Star Chamber looked onto the Thames as if disdaining the teeming palace grounds, where the populace scurried past.

The hour was still early, but already the place was thronged with pilgrims, packmen and pilferers. Ragged and barefoot, these thieves darted like shadows, out of sight as soon as spotted, hands filled, bags crammed, and their trail gone cold long before their victims discovered their purse-strings snipped.

Lowering his head, Blackbird crossed himself and took Dacre's arm to negotiate a path between the laden mules hurrying towards the quayside.

'Feel free to pray for yourself,' said Dacre, 'but don't do so on my behalf. I know the workings of this court too well. Not even the Virgin Mary could soften their hearts once they are made up. Whatever is to come, I shall carry it on my head alone. There'll be no need to blame the almighty if things go badly wrong.'

It was mid-morning when Dacre was brought to the chamber by an officer of the court. He paused at the door, ignoring the clerk's hand on his elbow. The blue ceiling with its heavy gold stars was startlingly bright, catching the river's reflection through the mullioned windows. Not for the first time he was taken aback at the mismatch between the chamber's heavenly appearance and its far from elevated function. This was where Wolsey held sway, a realm in which, they whispered, he wielded almost as much power as the king.

Until now the cardinal had been his ally, and that was what alarmed Dacre. The evidence against him must be serious for the Lord Chancellor to mount a trial. A man of his means, and methods, would more usually have dismissed inconvenient accusations out of court.

No matter; now the business must be seen through. Fingering the neck of his long black cape, the baron was led to a box chair facing a canopied dais at the far end of the room. There the members of the tribunal were arranged behind a silk-draped trestle, like guests at a wedding feast, Wolsey seated in the bridegroom's position, red-capped, in their midst. From an almost empty bench beneath the window Blackbird thought he could recall no bridegroom looking more eager for the day to unfold. He swallowed at the sight of his master, sitting alone before such a group, but the baron seemed composed, his head tilted, a sardonic twist to his mouth, as if waiting for an entertainment to begin.

The first hour was filled with paperwork, as Wolsey confirmed the tribunal's membership, and the identities of Dacre's accusers. Some the baron had never heard of, but most were foes of long standing. He nodded, grimly, as Lord Lethven was listed. A member by marriage of the Percy family, he was fiercer in protecting the Percy name than the old duke himself. As for his own Vice Warden betraying him like this – he who would willingly have given Eure anything he asked – had

242

the flagstones of the Star Chamber not been so newly swept, Dacre would have spat.

In chilling detail Wolsey then outlined the procedures and methods of the Star Chamber, which differed from every other court in the land. This was the only place where the titled and the powerful had no influence, their connections and money worth nothing. Instead, the Lord Chancellor's rule was absolute. His judgements were always upheld, and his prejudices too. That much was obvious even to Blackbird as the cardinal listed the court's manifold and complicated rules and regulations. By the end of the recital, Dacre's chin was propped on his shirt, and the butler's legs were twitching.

'Preliminaries hereby dealt with,' said Wolsey, raising his voice as if addressing a cathedral, 'we may now proceed. Since you are conducting your own defence, matters will be greatly simplified. We are all grateful for that, I am sure.' He stared at Dacre, and a wordless minute passed in which motes of dust spindled around the room, and the muffled sound of rivermen and peddlers reminded the assembly that in this chamber normal life was suspended.

'Baron Thomas Dacre,' Wolsey announced at last, 'I have before me ten most serious accusations against you, signed on oath, from some of the noblest and most honourable men of the realm, as you have heard. What say you to that?'

Dacre cleared his throat, but merely shook his head.

'You are not surprised?' asked Wolsey, archly amazed. 'Such accusations are a commonplace for one in your position?'

'They are no very unusual, if that's what ye mean,' replied Dacre, his northern brogue thickening in these surroundings, as if to counter the city's strangled vowels.

Wolsey looked down at a paper beneath his heavy-ringed fingers. 'I do believe you are already familiar with the workings of this court, my lord, having felt its authority when you were a far younger man.'

'Aye,' said Dacre, crossing his legs at the ankle, 'but that time it was the king himself who cross-examined me, and wrote out the deposition, and signed the verdict, and pocketed the fine. Very angry he was and all. But we made up, eventually.'

'Should this court find you as guilty on this occasion as the last,' said Wolsey, 'his son will be even more angry, I assure you.'

Dacre raised an eyebrow in reply.

'Then let me read you the litany of complaint I have before me,' continued the cardinal, adopting the sing-song tone of a man about to deliver a homily without fear of interruption. What followed would have unsettled most men, but as the denunciations rolled from the cardinal's tongue, Dacre's face betrayed nothing but boredom.

'This,' said Wolsey, brandishing a paper in the air, 'from Sir John Wetherington, a knight of the finest repute: 'Dacre does refuse to grant reparation to those whose lands and goods are destroyed by his henchmen, and not only will not bring such men to justice, but encourages them in their affairs, to the great detriment of the safety and wealth of the neighbourhood. Such is the lack of retribution that decent members of the community are now turning criminal themselves, for their own protection, or sustenance, so that the entire realm is like to become a den of thieves and murderers.' There was much more in like vein from the self-important sheep farmer, who had loathed Dacre since he refused him the vice warden's post.

Wolsey rattled on, like a skiff shooting the rapids, unable to stop even had he wished to. 'Or this from none other than the Bishop of Carlisle: 'My flock are too terrified by Scotch criminals to sleep at night, and must set guards on their walls and gates, to warn them of the raiders' approach. In this the Baron Dacre amply aids the afore-mentioned Scots and outlaws by offering them safe passage through his lands, and freeing them from gaol whenever they have been apprehended, which is not often.'

Still Dacre did not react, other than to unclasp his cloak, and drape it over the back of his chair. Beneath he wore black britches and a black woollen jerkin, the dress of a man whose mood is dark.

Wolsey continued. 'Or this, perhaps the worst we have yet heard, from Lord Foulberry, who claims that 'the Warden General holds a private court of law in the west march, at Ascarton, which makes an abject mockery of true justice. The victims, already suffering great loss and pain, endanger their lives by facing in court criminals who, if imprisoned, will be freed from gaol within days of committal, and can then take their revenge on their accusers. Few of the robbers or killers found guilty ever see gaol, most being let loose with only a fine – fines, I might add, which they pay by selling the stolen goods that landed them in court in the first instance.'

Wolsey laid down his papers, and, after conferring with the Lord High Treasurer, faced the baron. 'Not very edifying, I'm sure you will agree. These, and the many other depositions I have still to produce, paint a contemptible portrait of a man holding the king's law, and the king's reputation, in contempt. A man who all the while has, for personal benefit, incited the very mayhem and misrule he has been appointed – and well paid – to quash and dispel.'

Dacre raised his hand, to be allowed to speak, but the cardinal's back was now turned to address the tribunal, which had raised its face to his, as to a beneficent sun. They spent half an hour basking in its warmth, but eventually, amid much nodding and murmuring, Wolsey turned back to the chamber. He held his fingertips under his chin, as if thinking hard, but those who knew him could have seen from his bright eyes and glowing cheeks that he was enjoying himself, the Star Chamber his playground, and the tribunal, the accused, his marvellous playthings.

'It has been a long opening session, gentlemen, jury, and clerks of the court,' he said, speaking to the rest of the chamber as if it were packed, although beyond Dacre and Blackbird there were only a couple of junior clerks and the doorman, shifting from boot to boot to relieve his aching feet. The cardinal smiled. 'We will now adjourn for a break, and will recommence, to take the baron's defence of the charges so far levelled, at the hour of three.'

Wolsey's idea of time was not that of the clock tower, which had struck five before the tribunal reappeared. In the meantime, Dacre had been removed to a private cell on the ground floor, and given a plate of stew. Blackbird found a tavern offering hot pies, and returned at the appointed hour with gravy on his chin.

While waiting for the tribunal to return, Dacre asked for paper and pen. He sat scratching notes, seeming in no way discomfited by the delay.

When Wolsey and his men reappeared, the cardinal's strategy was plain. The lords at his heels walked gingerly, as if toeing a line. Some had their arms outstretched, to aid their balance. Ale was placed before them, but was soon augmented with wine, which swiftly followed what they had already supped. The cardinal, however, drank water. As the evening wore on, it became clear that his companions no longer required the long deliberations that had held up that morning's proceedings. When he turned to elaborate a point, or ask guidance, he was shooed back to business with a grandly waved hand, or a grave nod, whose seriousness was at times undermined by the hiccup that preceded it.

Blackbird settled back against the wall to watch. The trial, it seemed, would now be conducted between Wolsey and Dacre alone.

If it were a game, then the second round went to Dacre. Standing to deliver his defence, he put a hand on the back of his chair. His eyes roamed the room as he composed his thoughts, but when he began to speak he stared at a point above the tribunal's heads, as if he were addressing someone far above their station.

'Your eminence, my lords, let me begin with the accusation that lies beneath all the small individual complaints levelled against me by a gang – and I use the word deliberately – of collaborators, determined to bring me to my knees. Some have got it into their heads, it seems, that I am hand in glove with the criminals who roam my shires; that no only do I neglect to mete out justice to them as they deserve, but that I actively encourage them to persevere in it, presumably for my own financial gain.'

He gave a cough of laughter, but there was no humour in it. 'Allow me to remind the members of this exalted company that only last month I tried and hanged eight of the cruellest and most unforgiving Scots killers and thieves the borderlands have ever known. They were captured on a raid in Teviotdale, given a decent trial, and sent to the gallows. Half of Carlisle turned out to watch them swing, and the crowd roared and clapped them on their way to perdition.'

He passed a cloth over his forehead before continuing. 'Those lads were Armstrongs, to a man, yet that is the family I am supposed to hold dear, or so rumour has it. A clan I reputedly send out to do my bidding as if they were my own men. That particular charge has not been laid at my door, not in so many words, but it's in the very air we breathe in this fancy chamber. And I am here to tell you, it's a very strange notion, gentlemen, very strange indeed. One wonders quite where it was born. No out of truth, that is for sure. Though as this trial seems set to demonstrate, ye can never rely on truth prevailing, no even in a court of law.'

There was a flutter from Wolsey's chair, and the cardinal got to his feet. 'My lord, you can dispense with the philosophising. We are well capable of making our own deductions. Stick to the facts, and we will dress them as they require.'

The baron ignored this interruption and placed both hands on the back of his chair, which served as the prisoner's dock. 'And then there is Will Charlton. Even those who've never set foot beyond London town might well have heard of him, the most wily, ambitious, unscrupulous lout to be found outwith Carlisle's dungeons.'

A few heads at the table nodded.

'Well then, as ye likely know, he was bidding to turn the north into his own fiefdom, defying the king, defying me, and all his superiors and bringing ruin and death to those who tried to defend themselves. Did I let him roam free? Have I made a deal with him that has filled my coffers? What do you think?' Scowling, he looked at the heavenly stars above the tribunal's caps. 'I did none of those things, my lords. Instead I sent out a posse to find him, imprisoned him, and in due course of time, after a trial so punctilious and proper that even Saint Peter could no have found fault with it, brought him too to justice. This time by the axe.'

A thrill ran through the panel, part revulsion, part pleasure. The cardinal's head bobbed, as if in approbation, not that Dacre cared. 'Consequently,' he continued, 'Charlton's army of thugs is in disarray, the marches are breathing easier and, if I may be permitted no to philosophise but to speculate, there is no one of his stature who can take his place. Long before a successor can be found, the remains of the gang will have been picked off by my men.' He showed his teeth in a smile. 'That's a task I assure you they are already pursuing with a vengeance. So, as ye see, one of the worst cankers in the region has been cut out, by my own hand. Is this the act of the traitor these accusers would have ye believe me to be? The Duke of Norfolk, no less, personally congratulated me on this victory.' The baron paused, shifting the weight on his legs, and looked at his accusers. 'Aye. If only he was here to counter the torrent of bile and bilge being thrown in my direction. But I doubt even his word would prevail against the snakes hissing in the pit at my feet. As they say, venom is stronger than verity.'

He rubbed his thigh, and looked towards the guard by the door. 'Would there be a jug of water I could have? My throat is dry.' The cardinal waved the doorman off to fetch water, and while the room waited, there was silence. The baron cast a glance at Blackbird, whose face had settled in a frown. The butler gave a curt nod, enough to remind his master that he was not alone.

When water had been brought, Dacre drained the tankard, and placed it by the jug on the floor. He wiped his mouth on the back of his hand.

'What next?' He cast his eye down the list of charges, and shook his head. 'We'll be here for many an hour before I've dealt with all you have thrown at me.' He looked up. 'Well, I have nothing better to be doing. I trust your bench is padded.'

Wolsey tutted, and was about to rise from his seat once more when Dacre resumed.

'We come now, your eminence, my lords, to the matter of my private court at Ascarton. Against the accusation that it is run laxly and outwith the bounds of law, I refer you simply to the record books. A detailed account of each trial is kept by my notary, Rayner, a man even Beelzebub himself with all his wiles would find it hard to tempt off the path of righteousness. There's many a bishop could take lessons from him on rectitude, that's for sure. The man is a sore trial to me on many counts, but never in regard to his duties.'

He raised his voice. 'Anyone wishing to inspect the manner in which I run the court is most welcome to examine those books, and put Rayner on the stand, under oath. The catalogue of punishments handed down, and their severity, will make the keepers of the Tower of London look like bleeding hearts. I doubt you will find a better run establishment north of York. Nor,' he added with a dark smile, 'is it probable that any magistrate digs so deep into his own pocket to make reparation to the victims. In my time, I tell ye, I have doled out money to smallholders for their stolen flocks, tenants for their ruined barns, innkeeepers for loss of trade at the hands of reivers. Hundreds upon hundreds of pounds it has cost me, none of it repaid by the Exchequer or the king, though it is their business I have been conducting.' He gave a sigh. 'But it was ever thus, eh? Only a man made of flint could have done less. Those lands, and their people, are my own. I could not watch them suffer, and do naught about it.'

He turned to the windows, which were blackening as evening descended, as if they might offer a glimpse of home. Then he straightened, and faced the dais, his face grey and slack. He put a hand to his cheek, its warmth a reminder that he was not yet a dead man. Where blood was pumping, there was still hope.

'As for the neighbourhood turning to crime because it is their only option, I would laugh in your faces, if I did not risk being accused of contempt.' Taking a step towards his audience, he spread his arms, more like an actor on the boards than a man fighting to save his reputation. 'In the Lord's name, I ask are any of ye acquainted with my part of the country?'

Heads were shaken as he returned to grasp his chair. 'I thought not. Well, let me tell ye. Most of these people come out of the womb hungrier to commit a crime than for their mother's milk. They are natural liars and thieves and killers. Spend a month in their company, my lords, and you would dismiss each and every denunciation that lies before ye this day as the work of fantasy or malice. Then ye could send me back to do what I wager is one of the most difficult and least enviable jobs in the land.'

The cardinal was on his feet, sensing the baron was rousing his listeners to sympathy. 'Steady yourself, my lord. You must remain calm, otherwise I must call a halt to proceedings.'

'Calm?' The baron looked at Wolsey as if he were a midsummer fool. 'Would you be calm in the face of such provocation? When everything ye have ever done is cast into doubt by a parcel of ill-doers whose only desire is for mischief?'

'My lords,' said the cardinal, turning to the table, 'we will adjourn for the day.'

Dacre raised a hand. 'No,' he said wearily. 'I ask ye not to do that. I will continue, with your permission.'

There was a hush as Wolsey stared at the baron's flushed face, his awkward leg and evident exhaustion. 'Very well,' he said at last. 'But no more excitement. We have not judged you guilty, as you seem to believe. This is your time to rebut all the charges levelled against you. You have many friends and allies here, who wish only to see matters set straight. So, pray, continue. But gently.'

Dacre gave a grunt, which the cardinal chose to read as compliance, and settled his cloak around his shoulders. Reading the next item on his list, he snorted. 'Ha! We have reached the Bishop of Carlisle, and his sleeve of woes.'

The cardinal leaned across the table. 'Be careful, my friend. The Bishop is a man of God. His word cannot be cast aside as lightly as the others.'

'No,' replied the baron, with unexpected humility. 'I would agree with ye there. And in this instance, the bishop's grievances are, I am obliged to admit, not entirely unfounded. To be fair, he's absolutely right. He refers, I believe, to a most unfortunate incident in which – at first, at least – I consider myself blameless.'

The baron explained to his listeners that he had granted the Liddesdale Armstrongs a licence for Carlisle market day. It was a common enough concession to Scots from near the border, and greatly beneficial, he generally found, to the town's trade.

'But on one occasion, things got out of hand. A breakaway party, the younger riders, thought it would be a lark to raid a village near the border on their way home from the market. The place was near Lanercost, more of a hamlet than a village, and barely a soul in it. But they found cattle enough for their purposes, and drove off with them.

And then' – Dacre paused before continuing – 'and then they added the farmer's daughter to their spoils, and dragged her off as well. It was some days before they returned to Liddesdale, with the girl slung over a horse. She was alive, but only just.'

The baron's voice took on a different tone. 'Poor lass. None of us here who has a daughter can imagine what that was like for her father. And so – and this is where my testimony contradicts the bishop's, which he no doubt had second hand – and so . . .' Reluctant to finish his sentence, Dacre rubbed his chin. 'Aye, it was nasty. I will not dwell on the punishment – only to say it was bloody – but those five lads will never father children, nor ride in comfort again. The young woman was quickly found and returned to her family, and the clan paid them handsomely for the losses of goods, and the suffering of their girl. If money can make recompense for such an ordeal.'

The tribunal shifted, disturbed and fascinated by the story from a part of the country that seemed as far away and unimaginable as the moon.

'Such was the evil act, which I was swift to avenge, on which the bishop judges me. And he is right in regard to my not imprisoning the culprits, and letting them off – as you might say – unscathed. In a case of this nature, I find that mutilation acts as a deterrent far more powerful than gaol or even death.'

A murmur of assent could be heard from the table, but at a glance from Wolsey his associates fell silent.

Long into the evening, Dacre's denials continued. The tribunal was delighted to see such a man cut the ground from beneath the Lord Chancellor's slithery, slippered feet. Outwardly, its members avoided the cardinal's eye, and sipped their wine. Inwardly, they stamped their heels, as if on Wolsey's grave.

The tower clock was striking ten when Dacre drew to a close. Only Blackbird saw his unsteady hands and noted the stiffened leg, which could not now be bent. Night blanketed the windows, and the Star Chamber flickered under torchlight from the sconces on the walls and a candle on the tribunal's table. A low conversation began among members of the group, but ceased as Wolsey stood to face the baron.

'You have mounted a most admirable defence, my lord. I commend your fluency, and your memory. I trust tomorrow you can repeat the task, and the day after that.' He gave a thin smile. 'There are many further accusations to be dealt with, but we have time for only one more before we close for the day.' His drew his hands into his sleeves and faced Dacre like an emperor from the east, his eyes unreadable in the light of the candle before him. The baron sat forward, readying himself for what was to come.

'As you have already heard, my lord, it is alleged that you consort with Scots to a degree that throws your loyalty to the crown in doubt. You have answered those charges well, and I for one am ready to believe your innocence.' Wolsey's tone faltered, in a rare moment of uncertainty, and he half turned towards the tribunal as he continued, 'However, I am now obliged to break the tradition of this court, which relies most commonly on written evidence, because in this case the accuser cannot write, and does not trust any clerk to take his dictation.'

There was a shifting from the table behind him, as their lordships' wandering attention was caught. The cardinal make a gesture to the doorman, who left, returning shortly with a strapping, unkempt young man, who took off his hat at the sight of the chamber, letting a lock of lank red hair fall over his eyes.

'Your name, sir?' Wolsey asked.

'Andrew Robson, of Fa'side.'

'That being where, precisely?'

'Ten mile west of Harbottle, the baron's castle in the middle march.'

'And why do you come before us today?'

'To see justice done.' Robson fixed his eye on Dacre, and the baron felt his chest grow tight. He had never seen this man before, but there was a malevolence in his face that could not be feigned.

'Tell your story, please,' said the cardinal, resuming his seat.

'Aye, well, it is simple enough.' Robson spread his feet and put his hands on his hips, like a boy spoiling for a fight. 'This man here does not deserve to be called an Englishman. He may be a lord, but he has no right to the title.'

'Come to the point, sir,' said the cardinal, rapping the table.

'Right, I will then.' He glowered at Dacre.

'A year ago he let thirty filthy Scots murderers out of his prison, at Harbottle. Opened the doors, dropped gold in their hands, and all but kissed them goodbye.'

'How do you know this?'

'Because I wis one o' them. Or he thought I wis. I'd been banged up for theft and assault. Fair enough, I'd broken a guard's head the night afore – he'd caught me trapping rabbits – but when his lordship unlocked the gate, and ushered us out, was I going to complain?

'But here's what I don't like,' he continued, a grin smeared over his face like grease, 'Dacre here telt the Scots bastards he was in their debt. I heard him say that, loud and clear as a bell. What does that mean, eh? I'll tell ye. That the man is a traitor. It's plain as day. His head should be on a pike.'

There was a cry from one of the tribunal, a flutter of dismay. Then the Lord High Treasurer stood, gripping the table to keep himself steady.

'Boy,' he said, his voice wavery as his legs, 'have you been paid for this most damning testimony? Has gold been put in your hand?'

'Too right,' the young man replied. 'Would I come all the way down here for nowt? But that proves nothing. I know whit ye're thinking, I'm just a sneak, paid to lie. But I'm not. I could tell you a lot more about this baron, if you wis interested. So could any of us in Redesdale. Everything I have just told you is the truth, I swear to God.'

He looked around the room, knowing he held their eye. 'The men in Harbottle gaol were cousins, the lot of them. By the name of Armstrong. Black Ned was their leader. Ye'll have heard o' him, no doubt. Killed a Scottish warden and his gaolers at Jedburgh yin time, not to mention hundreds of us. There's been a warrant out on his head on both sides of the border the past few years.' He folded his arms, and looked at the baron. 'So what's the Warden General doing letting him go? That's what I want to know.'

CHAPTER TWENTY-NINE

October 1524

Dacre lay in the rushlit gloom, eyes upon the rafters. The Thames hurried past beyond the open window, but rather than lull him to sleep the sound carried him back to his youth, and a confinement far worse than this. It was the autumn of 1488, and he had been sent to the Fleet prison, where the river became his constant companion. As he listened to the water washing through the darkness and into the night, the baron was once more a young man, his vigour and arrogance no defence against the terrors that incarceration brought.

Nothing of that time was forgotten. He recalled how the river had seeped into his clothes, his food and his dreams. In the first few days after the key turned in the lock behind him and the bolts were thrown, the stench of oily water and tidal slime made his stomach roil. The cell's walls glistened, as if from the poisonous breath that crept under the iron door and through the shuttered bars. A hand put to the bare bricks came away damp and smelling of rot. Some nights he caught a whiff of putrid flesh, borne downstream at a doleful pace. Whether it was a corpse, a dead cat, or merely butchers' scraps, he did not care to know. He pulled his cloak over his nose and turned to the wall, hoping for a cleansing breeze to freshen the air. Weeks later, it had yet to appear.

After Christmas came the cold. London turned white and brittle under frost and snow, and though the prisoner's meagre ration of coal did no more than melt the icicles on the low ceiling, he did not complain. The chill had cleared the air. As he rubbed his knuckles and stamped his feet, he found his appetite. Wolfing the bread and broth his servant brought each evening, he longed for ale and lark pies, for roasted boar and hot-smoked eels, but such fare was not allowed in this place. Each day his ribs lost an ounce more fat, in time growing as taut to the touch as the bars at his needle-thin window.

Like all the Fleet's inmates, he was given only a single rushlight each day, and in the long, dim hours of a winter's afternoon he allowed himself no illumination other than from the open shutters, despite the freezing air. Not until the heart of the night, when the prisoners had settled and even the city had hushed, did he light the taper. Nursing it from draughts, in case it burned too fast, he lay on his pallet, staring into the flickering flame. In its smoky orange glow he caught glimpses of his home, so far from here it might have been another country. As the reed melted lower, his heartbeat quickened. When it guttered and sizzled into sightless silence, he screwed his eyes tight, as if to fool himself that the dark was only in his head. But the lack of light pressed in on him, enclosing as a velvet hood, and by the time dawn crept into the cell his nails had bitten into his palms, and his face was clammy with sweat.

Now, almost an old man, he was again lathered, heart thumping, throat thick with fear. With a great effort he turned his mind from the prison cell he was sure was once more awaiting him, but the thoughts that took its place were of no comfort. Instead of the Fleet, he was once more in the Star Chamber.

Who the devil had found and paid Robson for his story? Wolsey had refused to answer that. Dismissing the boy, who had spat at Dacre's feet as he left, the cardinal had insisted no questions could be answered since the day's business was now ended, and the court in recess for the night. But Dacre could not get the image of Robson's vengeful face out of his mind. He was damned if a cur like that would bring him to his knees.

Blackbird was whiffling softly in his sleep when the baron got out of bed and, fumbling for a flint, lit a fresh taper to replace the one smoking by his side. As the shadows faded, he got back under the blanket and continued his contemplation of the beams above their heads.

Robson's evidence must be fabricated. He had been careful, that night. None but Armstrongs had been in his gaol. The risk he had taken had been great, but he would have noticed a stranger, one different from the rest. Would he not?

The thought he might have made a slip gnawed at him. It was possible, he supposed, that this lout had been thrown into the cell shortly before the Armstrongs arrived. All but Dacre's most trusted guards were unaware of the baron's plans. When he freed the outlaws, it was on the pretence that they were being conveyed to Morpeth prison under cover of dark. That Harbottle's guard had fallen into an ambush on their way there, and the gang set free by their comrades, was a believable enough tale. After all, it happened all the time.

Dacre sighed, and closed his eyes. His duel with Wolsey would recommence in a few hours. He must rest, even if his mind would not. For a long while it seemed the rumpus in his head would never quieten, but soothed by the lamp, and the first chirping of birds, the baron finally slept.

The Star Chamber was in a different mood that morning, and Blackbird sensed it at once. Wolsey was tense, his expression rigid, and the tribunal fidgeted and fussed. Bringing Robson before them last night had been like tossing a hawk into a dovecot. Everyone's feathers had been ruffled, and this morning there would be blood on the floor, though whose it was too early to tell.

Dacre alone seemed unperturbed. There was a gleam in his eye that boded ill for Wolsey, but he leaned back in his chair as if he were weary, and age taking its toll.

'So then,' began the cardinal, 'we heard Andrew Robson's deposition last night. You have had twelve hours in which to prepare your defence, my lord. What do you have to say?'

Dacre got to his feet slowly. 'My lords, I say two things to ye.' He gripped the back of his chair, and lifted his chin. 'The first, that I utterly refute Robson's accusations, which are as mendacious as they are malicious. The man is a villain, as was plain to us all. If he has had the insolence to put his miserable cross on that statement we heard, he should be tried for perjury.' He coughed, and looked at the members on the dais, finding no hint of disagreement on any face but Wolsey's.

'But the second, perhaps more important, is that allowing Robson to give testimony in person is a blatant violation of the laws of this court. To entertain his verbal deposition would be to set a precedent which could ultimately overturn the Star Chamber's authority. I am shocked the Lord Chancellor would entertain such an idea, and wonder if, on closer consideration, he will see the difficulties this might cause him at a future date, long after my case, and I myself, are dead and buried. I beg him to be wise, and rethink his use of this vexatious and ultimately irrelevant piece of evidence.'

'Do not presume to tell me what I can and cannot do in my own court,' Wolsey said, spitting the words out like teeth. 'Be assured, Robson's statement falls within the rules. If you cannot or will not answer his accusation, you will suffer gravely.'

'Very well,' replied Dacre, unruffled, 'as you see fit.' He pointed to the chair. 'If you will permit me?' Wolsey gave an impatient nod, and the baron resumed his seat. 'I find I cannot stand as well as I once did, and my reply will not be swift. If one of ye could bring me water, please, before I begin.'

For the rest of the morning he had the chamber to himself. Relaxed as a fireside storyteller passing a winter's night, he painted a portrait of the English marches that sent shivers running up the spines of his listeners. Even the clerks who took down his statement would pause at his grisliest tales, pens aloft in disbelief.

'Get that down,' Wolsey would hiss, whenever the ink began to dry.

From the benches under the window, Blackbird watched as his master mesmerised his audience. He did not smile, but he allowed himself to lean back, with arms crossed, and enjoy the stories he heard.

With an old commander's vigour, Dacre continued. 'I was in the middle march, some years ago, when I realised just what these lands were like. Till then I had thought these people were ordinary thugs, criminals like any others. Not that day.' He rubbed his knee, and his expression tightened as the memories returned. 'Late afternoon, it was, and my brother Christopher and I were on the hunt for a man who'd killed a household – master, mistress, children and servants –

for a fish kettle full of coins. The scene he left behind can easily be imagined. What happened next is harder to credit.

'We followed the man's trail to his village, and found his hovel. Inside there was no one but three children, none of them older, I'd say, than ten. The youngest was crying, but the older two were crouched by the remains of a fire, which had gone out. The little girl, the middle one, ran towards me and threw her arms around my legs. I thought she was missing her father, and I put away my sword, and began to speak to her. Christopher sheathed his sword too, and the oldest child began telling us a story, about how his mother was ill and being looked after by a neighbour, and his father had gone to find help.

'He babbled on, and the girl clung to my legs, and I began to think something wasn't right. Before I realised what was up, the boy had run at me with a dagger, intending to stab me in the chest, and the girl had slipped from me to Christopher, a small knife in her hand, with the same idea.' He shook his head, still disbelieving. 'They weren't hard to fight off, but the shock of it nearly let them slide their knives between our ribs.'

His voice hardened. 'We found the father outside, in the bushes. He was made to pay, but the children were let loose. A few more years, and we knew they'd be coming for us again, that was for sure. But what could we do? Ye cannot gaol a girl of seven for doing what her father told her.' He paused. 'In parts of the north, they're all like that. I've seen withered old women on their deathbeds try to slit the throats of my men, and gangs of lads too young to shave whose only education is in blood. Boys like that think nothing of murdering their own kin, if they're well paid for it. And when it comes to the Scots, they see killing my men as sport, to brag of to their wenches. Better an Englishman's head to kick around a field than a sheep's bladder. No matter if he was just a ploughman doing his day's work, or a magistrate of the king. Any head will do.'

The tribunal registered disapproval and shock as his tales continued. Nor was Dacre merely spinning yarns. As his account of the trouble caused him by English northerners unfolded, the nature of the borderlands became clear. English highlanders had no more compunction about slaughtering or stealing from their neighbours than the Scots, and thieves from both sides of the border would join together and sweep the countryside like packs of wolves, loyal to none, not even their own.

'There are some Scots,' he went on, draining his tankard, 'who I would trust with my life; and men on Naworth's payroll who would cut me dead for a ha'penny. That is why, my lords, I do business with the other side. Sometimes it is required that I bargain with my enemies, and sometimes that I do deals, for the good of our country.

'Robson picked the wrong story to tweak my tail. If I really had let free the killer of Scottish wardens, why would any of us here be concerned? It does not damage our interests in any way. But if, as he has alleged, I am hand in glove with an outlaw band, it matters not if they are Scots or English, because it would be a serious crime either way.'

He spread his hands on his knees. 'Look at me, will ye? I have spent thirty years, and a small fortune, keeping the border under control. Our king here in London town has dealings with monarchs and emperors of countries that would destroy us, given the chance; my affairs are no different. But the idea that King Henry would open the gates of the Tower of London and set free those who should swing for their crimes is no more laughable than that I would do the same. I may be getting long in the tooth, but I am no a fool, no a knave, whatever the Bishop of Carlisle, or the Percys, or the rest of them would have ye believe.'

He ran a hand over his face. 'Bring out the rest of the accusations, and I will speak to them, best I can. But Robson's nasty little story should be dismissed from your minds. Only one who was tired of this world would deal such a treacherous hand as he claims I did. And I can assure ye I am no yet tired of life, though maybe' – he gave a wry smile – 'maybe of hard work. That I do confess.'

Noon passed, and afternoon crept in. There was no break as there had been the previous day, but food was brought into the chamber, and the tribunal feasted on chicken legs. Dacre waved away a plate, but accepted a tumbler of wine. Wolsey did not eat either but instead waded on through the allegations Sir William Eure had presented.

Four hundred miles away in his keep, Crozier could not know how the Star Chamber's business was proceeding, though he was anxious to learn its verdict. Until that time, mirthless though he could often be, he saw the humour in being the hand that shaped this most English and patriotic trial, a hand that everyone in the chamber would gladly have slapped in chains or, better still, severed from its wrist.

The days passed, autumn gathering outside the windows of the Star Chamber as Dacre defended himself, denial following denial. The Duke of Norfolk made an intervention, writing to the court to remind them of Dacre's crusade the previous year against Tynedale's verminous clans, a breed no one else had managed to scratch before, let alone exterminate. But Dacre did not fool himself that this would do him much good. Norfolk and Wolsey's enmity was set in stone, like one of the ten commandments.

By the second week the baron was wondering how much longer he could sustain this ordeal. Then an image of the Fleet would rise before him, and his determination deepen. It was scarcely less gruelling for Blackbird, though his fate was not held in Wolsey's hands. Only the snatched hours he caught with their landlady brought any colour into his days. And though she had hoped for an alliance with the baron, she found his servant satisfactory in ways she could not have anticipated.

It was the middle of October when Wolsey informed the court that their work was almost done. He peered at the baron over a sheaf of paper, biting his bottom lip, which had become chapped and raw during the course of this trial. Quiet fell over the Star Chamber, and those within froze, awaiting the cardinal's verdict.

'We have had quite a few weeks of it, have we not?' he said gently. 'Much evidence to sift, and an equally heavy weight of defence. One understands why the goddess Minerva looks so tired, balancing the scales of justice. It is not a light burden to take into one's hands, as this tribunal is all too aware.'

He left his place, squeezed past his associates, and stepped off the dais, approaching Dacre, where he sat. A skitter of leaves dashed at a window, louder than Wolsey's footsteps.

'We are finished here, I think,' he said, a note of regret in his voice. 'Your defence has been robust, my lord, but I speak for us all when I say I find it not entirely convincing. I wish I did, yet is it likely that all your accusers are motivated by malice or jealousy or ignorance of the facts? I think not.' Behind the cardinal, the tribunal nodded sad heads.

'Your eminence reaches that conclusion without knowing the north,' replied Dacre tonelessly. 'What might seem fantastical or improbable or downright impossible down here is commonplace in the borders. I intend no insult to this court when I say ye know not of what ye speak.'

Wolsey turned to look out of the window, eyes raised to a gunmetal sky. His lips moved, as if in prayer, and he raised the cross on his breast and kissed it before facing the room again.

'Very well,' he said. 'Tell me how that can be rectified. You are an old and valued servant of the king, even if it seems you have been misguided in recent times. I am loath to charge you with guilt unless I can be assured I have been fair. What, Dacre, would you have this court do?'

Dacre sighed. 'Set up a commission,' he replied. 'Send the king's investigators to the English marches, where they can speak to anyone they please, not only those who hold a grudge against me. Look into all my affairs, and those around me, and then make up your mind.'

Wolsey's face softened, and he seemed on the brink of tears. 'That I will, then, my lord, and I thank you for your counsel. But we shall meet here again in a few months, when their report is delivered. In happier circumstances, I pray.'

Dacre bowed his head, filled with a dizzying desire for sleep, and by the time he had raised it the tribunal had filed out of the chamber, and only he and Blackbird remained.

In his office, Wolsey opened his trunk, and took out a bottle of fine Spanish wine. He drank it from the neck, and as it slipped down his gullet and spread into his veins his eyes closed, and a smile lifted his cheeks. A blessed commission! Why had he not thought of it himself? Dacre's guilt – which he did not doubt – could now be confirmed, but at his instigation. He would tell Henry that he mistrusted the accusations lodged by Eure, and wished to conduct his own more rigorous inquiry. Which, he would make sure, would find the baron guilty. It would also demonstrate Wolsey's scrupulous sense of justice, during which his own reservations about the baron would nevertheless be in plain view, for the king to observe.

He finished the bottle and, taking out a large red handkerchief, wiped his chin. No longer did he need fear the king's wrath, which would be directed solely at the Warden General. Nor need he be alarmed at the prospect of the baron's imminent indictment. He could simply enjoy it, when the time came, as God intended.

CHAPTER THIRTY

Louise was seated on the mounting step in the courtyard, brushing the wolf's coat while he sat, tail sweeping from side to side like a birch broom. Beneath her filigree cap her hair matched the copper beeches that surrounded the keep, and watching her from the stable door, Crozier remembered the first time he had untied her ribbon and seen her hair fall to her shoulders.

His wife did not know he was there. She was smiling, listening to Antoine who was by her side on the step, grinding seeds beneath his pestle, which he seemed to carry on him at all times, as a hunter does his bow.

Leaning against the doorpost, Crozier observed them. Louise enjoyed the Frenchman's conversation. She might even, he feared, seek him out. In his company she smiled and chattered. With her husband she was reserved, not always meeting his eye, keeping her thoughts to herself where once she had told him everything, or so he had believed. Now, with a pang, he realised he could not recall when last she had thrown her head back with laughter at something he said. Yet there was a time when she had laughed all day long.

He kicked at the straw beneath his boot, troubled by a feeling he could not name. It was one thing having to deal with Isabella Foulberry, and keep the image of her and how he had behaved out of his head when he was with his wife; quite another to watch Louise sitting so close to Antoine. Were it any other man, Crozier would have punched him in the face for his presumption. It might not have improved matters, but it would have made him feel better. But Antoine had saved his grandfather's life, and was still their guest. So Crozier's fists itched, and he grew curter than ever, even with his wife, who had done nothing wrong except doubt his love for her.

Had he not cured Old Crozier, the soldier should have left the keep weeks before. He no longer walked with a stick, though his leg had set crooked, and when he was tired his limp was pronounced. Even so, Crozier knew he was fit for the army once more, and back he should go. Louise had once begged him not to pack Antoine off to the French garrison at Dunbar, but now he was resolved. The time was coming when he must order him to leave.

Benoit crossed the courtyard, and raised a hand. 'It's no like you tae be doing nothing,' he said. His eye followed Crozier's, and his smile disappeared. He nodded. 'Ah, Our foreign friend. He's gey friendly, is he no?'

'We owe him Old Crozier's life.'

'And he owes Louise, and you, for his,' said Benoit. 'I'd call that quits. In fact,' he put a hand on Crozier's arm, 'he remains mair in your debt. His lunacy nearly cost us all our lives. Ye could boot him out the morn and still feel pleased with yersel.'

Crozier said nothing, but scuffed the cobbles. Frowning, Benoit pulled him back into the stable. 'What's wrong?' he demanded. Unversed as he was in affairs of the heart, his own marriage being easy-going and uncomplicated, Benoit was neither blind nor unfeeling. He had seen his sister's wan looks these past few months, and felt the chill of Crozier's wintry mood himself. For a wife, that temper could not have been comfortable.

Like Tom, he was not entirely easy about the borderer's relationship with Isabella Foulberry, though unlike Tom he would never have spoken of that to Crozier, or to Louise. It was his view that a man could break his marriage vows and still be a good husband. He had seen it often enough. Lust was fleeting, perhaps even healthy, and it did not destroy a lifelong bond. True, he would not have thought it Crozier's style, and he could not imagine being unfaithful to Ella – the idea made him queasy as well as nervous – but he had met Lady Foulberry, and recognised her kind. When such a woman wanted a man, he would have to be strong indeed to resist her. He knew Crozier had a will of iron, but he also knew he was playing a deep game. Quite how far he was prepared to go in its pursuit, Benoit could not tell.

When Adam still would not speak, Benoit sighed. 'For Christ's sake, Crozier, jist tell him to go. Ye cannae be worrying about your wife and another man like this. I'd wager Louise hasnae thought of him as anything but a friend, but the way you've been carrying on of late, perhaps ye shouldnae take the chance.'

He waited for Crozier to shout in anger, but the borderer did nothing but pick a straw off his cloak. 'Has she said anything to Ella?' he asked. 'Has she spoken of me, or us?'

Benoit was shocked. 'Dinnae be daft. She's like a clam on that front. Always has been. It drives Ella demented.' He grinned. 'She'd spill the beans about anything to anyone, my girl.'

Crozier's expression changed, as if he had not been listening. 'You and I may have a long journey ahead, brother. Let Louise have company she enjoys until we are back. It is innocent enough, I am sure.'

'Where are we going?'

'France. Unless Albany replies to my messages in the next week, we must go to him.'

'For evidence to incriminate Dacre?'

Crozier nodded. 'He promised me those letters before he left. I know he has them because his servant sent word the day they sailed. But now he ignores my pleas. The man is not to be trusted, that I always knew. One day he may return to Scotland, but I doubt it; certainly no time soon. No one here wants him or needs him. Only me, it seems.'

He banged his fist against a stall, startling the horses, who shifted uneasily. Benoit was alarmed. He had rarely seen Crozier so over-wrought. 'And there's more, I heard last night. It's as though we are cursed.' Benoit drew closer as Crozier dropped his voice. 'Baron Dacre has been freed from the Star Chamber. They are bringing no charges.'

Benoit's eyes widened in horror.

'All those oaths we gathered – as good as useless.' Crozier laid his forehead on the stall, as if weary beyond words. 'I heard in a letter from Lord Foulberry, who sounds weak-kneed with fear. We might have guessed how it would be. The king's men look after their own. They say there's to be a palace commission to investigate Dacre properly, but what will come of that? Nothing, you can be sure. And already Dacre will be back in the marches, raring for revenge. A word about me from any of those we persuaded to inform on him, and we are in trouble.'

'They wouldnae . . . surely . . . ?' Benoit began, but Crozier's laugh cut him short.

'No? You think we can trust any of them, people of that sort? If they need a scapegoat they won't hesitate. And knowing Dacre, they will be made to squeal all right. Squeal and then beg for mercy. Not that he will give them any.'

Benoit was silent. Outside, the wolf barked.

'So you see,' Crozier went on, looking towards the sunlit yard, 'the cooling of my wife's love is not the worst of my problems. I will learn to live with that if I have to, so long as she survives what lies ahead. She, and all the rest of us.'

'And the letters are our only hope?'

'I believe so,' he replied. 'And even then, a slim one.'

Dacre's journey home from London was slow and winding. He had insisted they saddle up and leave the day Wolsey dismissed the case, though it was noon before they left the Star Chamber. 'But should we not stay the night, my lord, and make an early start tomorrow?' said Blackbird, concerned at the baron's pallor, his lips a shade of milk.

'I have to get out of this place,' Dacre replied. 'I cannot bear the noise, or the stench. I will sleep better knowing I am already on the road home.'

Blackbird bowed, packed their few things, and within the hour they were riding out of Bishop's Gate, along the old Roman road. Neither looked back, but the sound of London followed them into the dusk, and they knew it had not finished with them.

As they headed north Dacre seemed like a man in a dream, swaying in his saddle, mumbling to himself, and sipping wine from his old tin flask, which he refilled at every stop. Blackbird said nothing, but found them the best inns, so that even should the baron lie awake, as most nights he did, he would do so in comfort.

'I must see my older daughters,' Dacre announced the morning they left Nottingham, his face as slack and sickly as tripe. 'I miss them. In that terrible chamber, under all those gold-painted stars, I found myself thinking, your heart could burst, Tam, and ye could go to the next world any day now and not remember what the pair of them look like, it's so long since ye set eyes on them.'

He put a hand to his breast. 'This blasted wardenship, Blackbird, this poxy war. They are hellbent on destroying my life. That is what they would like. But I will not let them. I will not.' He clenched his teeth, and on they rode, heading towards the Yorkshire dales, to visit the lady Anne and her ruddy-faced baron, and thereafter turn west towards the Pennines where Mabel, his eldest daughter, lived with her wealthy husband and young children. From there, he told Blackbird, they would continue to Naworth. A visit to his own lands was long overdue.

October was almost gone when at last they reached Cumberland. Rain and sleet had driven into their faces the last few miles on the crest of the wind-bitten moors, but the baron's horse picked up speed under his heels as they came off the hills and drew near the castle. Beneath his mud-spattered helmet, Dacre's face held the hint of a smile as Naworth came into sight, its glowering walls and well-tended fields promising a haven.

Servants and hounds ran out at the sound of their approach, but Blackbird looked beyond them, and gave a gratified nod. His message to Harbottle had reached her. At the door of the castle's high-vaulted entrance, Joan was there to welcome them, pressing herself into the baron's soaked cloak with no thought of her velvet gown.

Dacre's eyes watered, perhaps with fatigue, as he pushed her gently away. 'Steady, girl,' he said. 'Ye'll knock me off my feet.' Laughing, Joan took her father's hand and led him to the fire, where hot wine and a bearskin rug were laid out for his comfort.

The Warden General did not talk much over dinner that night, but Blackbird watched his pasty colour melt away, as if he were thawing. Over the next few days, the baron of old began to return, his voice louder, his laugh rich, and his sleep more like that of the just. Nights were no longer to be dreaded, Dacre so exhausted that not even ghouls could disturb his rest, though a lighted candle was still put by his head when he retired, to keep the dark at bay.

For the baron's recovered spirits Blackbird thanked the old gods of Naworth. The place was part of him, as if he, like the castle and its lands, had sprung from the earth beneath, and to be uprooted and replanted anywhere else was to weaken and wither.

The respite could not last. Early in November, a messenger arrived from the Duke of Norfolk. Dacre's presence was required at Berwick to negotiate the detail of a peace settlement between the English and Scottish courts. 'They think I'm an assassin and a thief, but still they can't do without me.' Dacre shook his head in disgust, but instructed Blackbird to pack his saddlebags.

Rising from the fireside, Joan turned to leave the hall and tell her maid to gather her things, but Dacre called her back. 'What are ye thinking, miss? Ye're staying here for the time. Winter in Harbottle is cruel, and if the snow sets in it could be weeks before we can come back to Naworth.'

The young woman looked at him, thoughtfully, and shook her head. 'No, Father. I am coming with you.' Her odd expression caught Dacre's attention.

'What now?' he huffed. 'Worried about me, are ye? There's no need. I'm good for a few more years, never ye worry.'

'I want to,' said Joan, touching his arm. 'Please. I find I like it there.'

When Dacre could not dissuade her, he sighed. 'Is this because I said Mabel wants you to stay with her? Ye can't put that off forever. I've told her she will soon have to find you a husband.'

Joan hung her head. 'I know. And I will do that, and go to court, whenever you say I must. But for now . . .' she raised her head, her green eyes pleading, 'for now, I am coming with you. When you are gone, Naworth is as cold and empty as Harbottle, and the weather worse, I swear. Who knows,' she added, with a smiling grimace, 'if I am to be married off, this might be our last winter together.'

Dacre frowned at the prospect of losing her, and allowed himself to agree. Watching from the doorway, Blackbird silently saluted the girl. Her devotion to Dacre was touching. 'Ach, you're getting old and soft,' the butler muttered, sniffing as he hurried up the stairs. But the memory of Joan's tender insistence stayed with him, sparking a glimmer of regret that he had no daughter to take care of him.

CHAPTER THIRTY-TWO

November 1524

The night before he and Benoit left for France, Crozier spoke to his wife as he had not done for weeks. Alone in their bedchamber, as Louise filled his pack for the journey, they each felt the unspoken hurt that lay between them.

At times in the past few months Louise had thought she must be dreaming, since nothing on this earth could diminish the love they had for each other, and she must soon wake from this misery. But the plodding beat of her heart, the dragging days when Crozier seemed barely to see her, the distance that descended in bed as soon as their gasps faded – even this conducted as if they hoped to deceive themselves that nothing had changed – all this told her that she was deluded. As she was slowly coming to see, disbelief might for a while provide some comfort, but it was no defence against the truth that she must one day steel herself to face: that their marriage had been tarnished, and was now dull.

'Why, if you are going to France, do you need first visit the Foulberrys?' she asked as she folded his shirts, unable to keep the edge from her voice. 'Could you not take a boat from this side of the border, and get away sooner?'

Crozier put down the boots he was waxing. 'I need Foulberry's help. He has a boat and a skipper who can take us to Cherbourg, and his wife's family have livery stables in the town where we can hire horses. Foulberry will come with us – he knows the road to Paris – but this is the last time, I hope, that I will need his help.' He put a hand on Louise's wrist. 'Believe me, Lou, after this visit I wish never to see him or his wretched wife again.'

Louise stopped packing. Tears filled her eyes, but she would not let him see them. If Isabella had meant something to him, even for a night, she would remain between them for the rest of their lives. Crozier might regret whatever he had done, he might even tell himself it had been nothing, but these stony few months told her that in this, if nothing else, he was not being wholly honest.

She turned to the window, to close the shutters, and stood listening to the rising wind. 'It's a bad time to sail. I won't be easy until you are home.'

Crozier joined her, and pulled her round to face him. 'Nor will I. But you must know I will be thinking of you every mile. Pray God when I come home we can begin to live normally once more.'

Lady Foulberry rose from her fireside when the borderers arrived, and spread her arms so wide her furs slid from her shoulders.

'Gentlemen,' she trilled, 'I am overjoyed to see you. His lordship has been talking of nothing else these past few days.' Drawing her arm through Benoit's, she led them to the bench by the hearth.

Lord Foulberry joined them shortly, and the evening began with a heated, anxious discussion of what Dacre might be planning in retaliation for their attack. Foulberry's face had grown more purple since last they met, though from strain or drink, Crozier could not tell. Yet, though the Warden General now knew Foulberry was his adversary, as were so many others, his lordship was remarkably sanguine. Since writing to Crozier with the bad news, he appeared to have regained his courage.

'My men are well armed,' he said, 'and this castle is a fortress. But in any case, it is my belief that the baron will not be so unsubtle as to launch war against his denouncers. After all, the court is now watching him, even though it has cleared his name.'

'For the time being,' Isabella chipped in.

Her husband nodded. 'Indeed. Dacre would be ill-advised to pick us off before the Commission has reported. We have until then to bring things to their proper conclusion, or so I trust.'

Crozier was terse, which did not go unnoticed.

'You are fretting I believe,' said Isabella, as she directed the servant to refill his glass.

'Not fretting, my lady, but concerned, as we all should be, and keen to bring this business to its end.' He tipped his glass in her direction, trying to lighten his tone. 'But when his lordship and I have got the letters we need from Albany, things should move fast.'

'Ah,' said Foulberry, swallowing the last of his clams, and wiping his lips with a cloth, 'you are under a misapprehension. I am afraid I cannot accompany you to France as I had hoped.'

Crozier looked at him, and Foulberry's colour deepened. He dug into his belt, and produced a letter from the Duke of Norfolk, who required his presence at a northern council in York.

'A last-minute affair,' said Foulberry, uncomfortable under Crozier's eye. 'Unavoidable, I regret. In the present circumstances, with Dacre on the prowl, it behoves me to stay on the best of terms with Norfolk and the court. But,' he continued, more heartily, 'this does not impede your journey. You shall sail with Henryson at first tide, and be at Cherbourg some time the next day. It is only a few miles from port. There you can present a note from Isabella at the stables, and be assured of thoroughbreds for the Paris road. Also of hospitality at her family's coaching inn, which is one of the best appointed in the district.'

Isabella gave a girlish smile. 'The Villenuit family own the finest stables in Normandy, gentlemen. The inn is comfortable too. I only wish I could go with you. I spent happy hours there as a child, when my nursemaids were not watching. The smell of those creatures, their glossy flanks—' There was a catch in her voice. 'Oh, how I miss the freedom to ride I once had. Sometimes this place is like a prison.'

Lord Foulberry placed his hand over hers. 'These days, none of us has the liberty we once enjoyed, my love. That is a sad truth of our times, is it not, gentlemen?'

They raised their glasses in a silent toast, each thinking of what they most desired. Isabella's eyes found Crozier's, and she looked away, blushing.

Sobered by the thought of everything they stood to lose, the party broke up early. The next morning, long before dawn, Foulberry was in the courtyard, clutching a cloak over his nightshirt, to bid goodbye to his guests. There was no sign of his wife.

He handed a letter to Crozier, for the head ostler at Cherbourg. 'That should secure you good horses at all posting inns, and in both directions.' Along with the letter was a fat pouch of French coins. He waved away Crozier's protest. 'They will speed your journey, and that's what matters, sir. The French do not trust our money.'

Crozier leaned down from the saddle to shake his hand. 'I am grateful,' he said, before nudging his horse into a trot behind the servant who was to take them to the boat.

Henryson was bow-legged and stout, a human echo of his deep-bellied boat, the *River Pearl*'s elegant name more than a little misleading. Bobbing by the wharf in Foulberry's lonely creek, the squat ship sat low in the water, laden with a cargo of coal which, if anyone asked, was to be offloaded in Brest.

'Your quarters are cramped and basic, sirs,' he said as they crossed the plank. 'I doubt ye'll be comfortable. And if the wind stays sluggish in this quarter, it will be a slow passage. We cast off at high tide. Ye can stay above board till then. After that, I'd prefer ye remain below deck, out of our way.'

They obeyed his orders, and he was correct on all points. By the time the borderers disembarked in France three days later, they were so coated in coal dust a stray spark would have turned them into torches, and their legs were jack-knifed like a grasshopper's.

Paying a farmer at the dockside to let them sit on his dray among his turnips until he reached Cherbourg, they breathed the country air with relief, and felt their legs regain their strength. By the time they reached the Villenuit coaching inn they were ready to ride, and took off in a swirl of dust higher than any wave they had seen since they set sail.

Crozier and Benoit had left at first light, and the keep was in Tom's charge. Unable to work for thinking of her husband, Louise whistled the wolf to her heels and set off for the woods, heading down the valley. The day was mild but a gale was gathering, and her cloak flapped around her. Overhead the trees swayed, loud as breaking waves. The wolf's thickening winter coat riffled in the wind, rising around his neck like a ruff.

Down near the stream, where the hare had been set free, Louise sat on a fallen oak and stared at the sparkling water. Masked by the sound of the lashing trees, Antoine's appearance took her by surprise, and she pressed a hand to her heart.

Smiling, he apologised, and sat beside her, showing her the plants he had gathered that morning. Louise feigned interest, but she wished to be alone, and her replies were clipped. Antoine, perhaps sensing her mood, also fell quiet. For a few minutes they both stared ahead, but just as she thought he was about to leave he took her hand gently in his, and began to speak. Jumping to her feet she pulled away, her cheeks flushed with anger. 'What do you think you are doing?'

Antoine too was on his feet, his blush matching hers. 'It was . . . I only meant . . . I believed that . . .' Under her furious gaze, he could not get the words out.

Louise pulled her cloak around her. 'How dare you?' she said, more quietly. 'If my husband were here . . .'

The Frenchman got down on one knee among the litter of leaves, and bowed. 'Madame,' he said, 'you misunderstand. It was an act of friendship. Nothing more. I would never insult you, or your husband, who have been so kind to me. Indeed,' he added, raising his head, 'I did it because I knew you were thinking of Crozier.'

'Get up, please,' said Louise, turning away. 'You look ridiculous.'

Antoine rose, brushing down his britches with a lop-sided smile. 'Fortunately, that has never worried me.'

Louise looked at him, frowning. 'I don't understand. What has this to do with Adam?'

'You have been sad about your marriage, I think, for a long time. I have observed you, and him. You are both of you unsettled, and perturbed. Perhaps I can help.'

Louise's eyes narrowed. 'Be very careful.'

His composure regained, the Frenchman was undaunted by her tone. He put out a hand, and touched her arm. 'Come, sit down. I will explain.'

'I will stand, thank you,' she replied, while he took his seat.

'As you wish.' Not looking at her, he dug into his bag, and pulled out a pinkish sprig of flowers, earth still clinging to their roots. 'Mallow,' he said. Another followed, with tiny leaves and a sprinkling of small blue flowers. 'This one, as you will know, is speedwell.' The last he produced was a stem of juicy catnip leaves. He laid them on the tree, and looked up. 'All can cure the barren, madame, given time. Used well they can bring new life, where nothing before would grow.'

Louise put a hand to her throat. She could not speak. This was impertinence beyond anything she had ever met. She had spoken to no one but her husband about their longing for another child, and even then they had said little, the subject too sore.

Antoine had broken off a catnip leaf, and was holding it out to her. 'Taste it,' he said. 'It is not bitter. If nothing else, it is an excellent aid to sleep, and all of us need help with that in these difficult times.'

Louise put it to her tongue, and felt its peppery rasp. Still unsure, she took a step towards the stream. 'How would it work?' she asked, over her shoulder.

Antoine spoke to her back. 'An infusion, twice a day, for several weeks.'

'My husband will be gone for some time,' she said, twisting her hands at discussing something like this. 'Two weeks, a month, maybe more.'

'Once it has set things right, time makes no difference. I do not promise it will change anything,' he said, 'but I have seen it work before, on those older and less healthy than you. Sometimes the problem is in the womb, and sometimes in the mind. In each case, these plants can help.'

Louise took a long breath, and pulled her cloak close. After a pause she spoke. 'You have been a good friend to our family. I will trust you, and do as you suggest, but you must speak of this to no one. Adam and I have suffered enough without raising anyone else's hopes, let alone our own.'

Antoine looked grave. 'One day I will have to leave. It would make some atonement for the terrible danger I brought your family into if, by the time I go, there is good news.'

The wind rushed hard at the treetops, and the woods moved around them, wild as the sea. Louise put out her hand, and after a brief hesitation Antoine took it, and bowed his head. 'I am in your service,' he said.

They made their way slowly back to the keep, neither speaking. Louise did not know what to think, or hope. Some would say she had lost her wits, to put herself in the care of a heretic. She had heard him, reciting his bible, in the harsh language she did not know. He might say he had changed his ways and gone back to the true faith, but she doubted that was the case. And yet, she thought him a good man. He was a healer, not a preacher. There was a gentleness about him that she had never seen in anyone before. He seemed to look beyond people, as if they were but a speck in his eye that blotted them from his sight, but he was unfailingly sweet, and kind, almost childlike in his eagerness to help, or cure, or care. How he would survive when he left the keep, she did not like to imagine. She quickened her step. That was a problem for another day.

From the far bank of the stream, behind the low branches of a yew, Oliver Barton watched Louise and Antoine head back up the path. He sucked his teeth. Something was brewing between that pair that went far beyond cousinly love. But while it would be useful to see where their liaison led, it was the Frenchman who held his attention. Barton no longer doubted there was something suspicious about him. He wondered what he was up to. That it was nothing good, he already could tell. Those herbs and potions, his miraculous cures – Barton pulled up his hood, making the sign of the cross, and turned towards the fields. Was the man a simple healer, as everyone said? He shivered. It seemed to him there were more sinister forces at work.

CHAPTER THIRTY-THREE

December 1524

The weather was turning, birds making for the safety of tree and hedge, sheep and goats gathering in hollows, facing into the wind. It was only midday but already the road before them was disappearing into gloom as a steel-grey sky lowered itself over the Normandy plains and a thin rain began to fall. Keeping their heads down as they rode into the squall, the borderers hoped the roofs and spires of Cherbourg would soon come into sight.

Saddlesore and filthy, they had been on the road for six days and nights since leaving Fontainebleau. Changing horses twice a day, merciful on their beasts but not themselves, Crozier and Benoit had ridden as if chased by an incoming tide, pausing only for a few hours' rest, and something to eat.

Tied to Crozier's belt were the letters they had come for, a fat pouch that could bring down Dacre, and others besides; but no one would have guessed that their journey had been a success. The borderer's expression was hard as ice, his thoughts far from the country passing beneath their hooves. He had been a month away from home and before his eyes he saw not Normandy's loamy fields and its wide, empty roads, but smoke and fire-licked stone as Crozier's Keep burned. He smelled not the sweat of his horse, or his well-worn shirt, but the pitch torches of Dacre's secret army; heard the screams of those trapped in the keep as they toppled from the walls. Not until he was back and saw his people safe would his face soften. The letters might secure the Croziers' future, but he was uneasy, afraid that such a future would not arrive before the Warden General sent his men their way.

Benoit gave a shout, and Crozier raised his head to see the pale city walls loom into view across the valley below. Raising his hand in reply, he dug in his knees and sent the post horse flying, the road disappearing in a froth of sodden earth.

Unwanted days had been added to the borderers' journey when they learned that Albany was not in residence with his king in Paris, as he had promised before he left Scotland, but at Francis's hunting lodge, deep in the forest of Fontainebleau. Turning south-east, they followed the road through the forest, narrow, pot-holed, and slow. Crozier had arrived at the old lodge in a barely contained rage. Not only had Albany ignored his letters, but it was beginning to look as if he had wilfully misled him.

After tying their horses in the trees, the borderers had been left to wait in the hallway, where a log fire crackled, and the sunken eyes of the deer and bears that adorned the walls shifted under the shadows, as if they were watching. The duke, they were informed, was out on the chase, and would not be back for hours. If they preferred to find accommodation in the village nearby, they could return the next day?

Benoit told the footman they would wait. His French was rough but clear, as was his impatience. The lackey clicked his heels and returned to the servants' quarters, where he described the Scots who were muddying his floors, his audience of cooks and maids clapping their hands in mirth.

The king's arrival brought no duke. Shortly before dusk the borderers heard the huntsmen return, at the back of the house, but no one appeared in the hall. When it became clear their presence was being ignored, they made their way to the courtyard, where stableboys were leading away the hunters, whose flanks and bits were foaming. The king's party was already gone, leaving behind a cart piled with gralloched deer whose stomachs gaped like open mouths.

When Benoit asked where Albany could be found, a stable hand pointed across the yard to a back door. The borderers went in, and up a set of stairs to a low, torchlit corridor lined with doors.

They got no further. An armed guard was on duty, and his face lit up at the sight of strangers. Hunting animals was no fun. It was people he enjoyed catching. Eyeing the sword pointed at his breast, Benoit once more explained their business, fearing he too was about to be disembowelled.

They were led downstairs to wait, this time in a poky room off the entrance, but it was another hour before Albany appeared, sweet-scented in an emerald green jerkin and jewelled cap, a silver pomander around his neck. He gave a shallow bow. 'You have had a long journey,' he said. 'I hope you have not had an equally tiresome wait.'

Crozier was curt. 'Did you get my messages? I sent three, these past few weeks.'

'I did. They were sent on from Paris, but I have been busy.' Albany fingered the pomander, as if the Scots brought with them a smell he did not like.

'In that case,' Crozier continued, 'you will understand our urgency. We need those letters you spoke of. They are our only hope now of bringing Baron Dacre to justice before he hunts down his enemies.'

Albany turned his attention to the hearth, fluffing the lace at his wrist. 'It all seems so far away now, all so unimportant,' he murmured.

Crozier took a step towards him. 'You will not think that when you return to your country and find Dacre's hand directing Holyrood's business from behind the scenes, and turning the court against you.'

The duke turned slowly. 'Ah,' he said. 'You have not heard, then.' He smiled, without warmth. 'Dacre cannot harm me now. I am no longer regent. In my absence, your parliament has deposed me. I received notice of this only a few days ago. Quaintly worded it was. Very – shall we say Scotch? – in its coarse brutality.'

'I did not know,' said Crozier impatiently, 'but it makes no difference. You promised me those letters, and I am here to get them.'

The duke moved away from the fire, and took a seat on a deep oaken chest, which had once held a queen's trousseau. 'It is not as simple as that,' he said. 'I find myself in a position where those letters might one day be useful to me. You and I are no longer associates. We may have served each other's purpose in the past, but that is now at an end. I will never see Scotland again and,' he examined his fingernails, 'I cannot say I am sorry.'

He got no further. Crozier had him by the collar, dragging him onto his feet and slamming him against the wall, where he held him in a choking grip, a knife pointed at his throat.

'Give me the letters.' He spoke through his teeth. 'If you do not do as you promised, or if you call the guards and have us murdered, it is not you our clan will destroy but your children, your mistresses, and your new young wife, whoever she will be. You will live to be an old man, knowing you allowed them to be butchered because you were too dishonourable to keep your side of a deal.'

Sweat trickled down Albany's temple, but his voice did not shake. 'Let me go, and we can talk like civilised men. You're nothing but a dirty thug, Crozier. I always knew that.'

'As if I cared.' Crozier's hold tightened. 'Remember, if you shout for help, you will be dead before it arrives, and the rest of your family will follow, one by one, in the months ahead.'

Albany nodded, unable to speak, and the borderer let him go. The duke dropped onto the chest and ran his hand under his collar, his throat working hard to swallow. He cast a malevolent look at the Scots, as if wondering how he could outwit them, but when he had caught his breath he stood up.

'You can have them. Maundering stuff; they turned my stomach. I'll be glad to be rid of them. I will fetch them now, and bless the day you disappear out of my sight, and all thought of Scotland with you.' Turning to the grate he spat on the logs, which sizzled as if with loathing. 'Do not follow,' he barked, as the Borderers started after him. 'Despite what you think, I am a man of my word. You are safe. For now.'

Neither spoke while they waited for Albany to return. The bustle of the kitchens preparing dinner reached them, as did the aroma of roasting meats. Benoit's stomach growled, the only sound in the room. When finally the door opened, Crozier's knife was in one hand, the hilt of his sword under the other.

'Here they are,' said Albany, tossing the package to him. 'Now, be gone.' He might have been dismissing a beggar.

Unhurried, Crozier put away his knife and opened the package. He spread the letters on the chest, read quickly, and was satisfied. Tucking them into his belt, he turned to the duke.

His eye ran over the puffed sleeves and earringed lobe, the opal nestling in his cap. No words were needed to convey his contempt. Already a bruise was darkening on the duke's neck. It would serve as reminder of the borderer for many days to come. So too would the knowledge that a couple of brigands had bested him, as had their country. Sneer though he would for the rest of his life about the viper's nest that was Scotland, Albany would never have the courage to return, and everyone in that room knew it.

L'Auberge de Villenuit was blanketed in rain. A long, low wooden house, wreathed in yellowing vines, it sent smoke from a jumble of chimneys into the misted air, but still the place was cold. Crozier and Benoit took a room, had their horses stabled, and, rubbing their hands, made for the taproom, where food and drink were served. The place was quiet, few travellers out at this time of year, fewer still in the gathering storm.

Crozier had sent a message to Foulberry's skipper, who was awaiting them at the port. 'He'll be kicking his heels, wondering where we've been,' he grumbled, as they tucked into a plate of mutton stew, swimming in succulent fat. 'We're already a week late.'

Benoit spoke through his food. 'Doubt he'll care much. Wi' the wind rising like this, he'll be relieved to be in harbour and no blown onto the Cornish rocks.'

Crozier growled. 'This storm'll pass by tomorrow. We have to get back.'

'Aye, I ken,' Benoit replied, draining his tankard, and beckoning for more, 'but it looks as if it's settling in. Be patient, man. There's nothing you can do about it if we have to wait another day or two.'

Wind buffeted the inn, setting doors banging and shutters rattling. It howled down the taproom chimney like bloodhounds on the scent. Crozier lapsed into a brooding silence as the pair watched the haywire flames, waiting for word from Henryson. When it arrived, long after dark, it was as Benoit had feared. There would be no sailing tomorrow, or the day after that. The skipper would send word as soon as the storm had abated, but it might be several more days.

With the aid of ale and a pair of dice, the borderers had begun the tedious task of passing the time when heels were heard in the hallway, and an imperious French voice called for help. There was a babble of obsequious conversation as orders were given and servants despatched, before a well-dressed young woman entered the taproom, pushing back her hood, and cast a swift glance round before disappearing again.

The men played on, but were soon disturbed by the innkeeper, who approached them with a servile stoop. He had, he said, offered them the best room in the inn, not knowing the company he was about to receive. He now begged their indulgence, and asked if they would be prepared to take another, smaller room at the front of the house, so that a lady and her maid could sleep in comfort and peace. Their things would be moved to a nice warm chamber, overlooking the road.

From the hallway came the scuff of servants carrying bags up the stairs, and the click of impatient boots on flagstones as the newly arrived guests awaited the innkeeper's return. Benoit told the man to do as he pleased. Straightening to his normal height, the landlord was all smiles. 'It is her ladyship,' he explained. 'She always demands the best room.'

Moments later, the young woman returned, peeling off her gloves. Behind her came her mistress, a fur-tipped hood hiding her face. The maid helped her out of her cloak, and the woman stood looking round the dimly lit room until she found the borderers, whose backs were turned to the door.

'Well, well, well,' she said softly, walking towards them in her nailed boots. Startled, Benoit turned, and saw Isabella Foulberry. Her face was in shadow, but as she laid a hand on Crozier's shoulder, and he looked up, his expression was plain to read.

'I did not expect to find you in these parts,' said Isabella. 'I had thought you'd be long since home.'

'What are you doing here?' Crozier asked.

'Visiting my family – their seat is only a day's journey from the city. Henryson brought me, when he returned from your own passage. I had hoped to embark on the *River Pearl* tonight, but find I have to spend the night here – perhaps longer. Such a bore. But less so now I find such good company, here and, of course, for the passage home.' She smiled, and pulled up a stool to sit beside them.

Crozier looked at Benoit, and drained his tankard. He rolled the dice on their table. 'You will be disappointed, I think, my lady. This is all we can do to pass the time,' he said.

'Really, do you think so?' she replied, her hand again settling on his shoulder.

Crozier removed the hand, and looked at her levelly. 'If I have ever led you to expect or hope otherwise, my lady, I ask your forgiveness. It was uncivil of me to use you in that way. But now all pretence can be at an end.' He turned back to the dice and glanced at Benoit. 'Your cast, brother.'

The men ought to have been back long before now, and Louise and Ella were anxious. Tom, however, was untroubled. 'They must have met with some delay on the road to Paris,' he said, whistling his way about his business as he always did. They nodded, but remained as worried as before.

When another week had passed, Louise took Hob aside. 'You and I are going to the Solway port, to find out what has happened,' she told him. 'Have the horses ready before light.'

He would have protested, knowing the risks such a journey involved, but the thought of Crozier's anger if he led his wife into possible danger was as nothing to the sight of her thin, drawn face. 'Will do,' he replied.

The next morning they set out, telling none but Ella where they were going. The storms of the past month had eased, leaving only a scudding wind to keep them company, but the tracks were thick with mud and loosened stones, and uprooted trees marked the passage of the gales as clearly as flags.

Now the war was almost at an end, crossing the border was less perilous. The greater danger was the miles they must ride through the Elliots' and Armstrongs' lands in Liddesdale, which lay between them and the firth. Skirting the dale on its westward edge, they rode fast, stopping only to rest the horses. But it was as if the place had been emptied, its people blown away. They met no one on those lonely roads, and when on their second day they slipped across the border, Louise threw back her hood and laughed. It was years since she had ridden this far, and though it was fear that propelled her, the thrill of the ride set her pulse racing, and she felt her anxiety lift.

Reaching Rockcliffe, they rode a few miles farther to where a sandy track led to Foulberry's private harbour. Coming off the clifftop, where the breeze snatched their breath, they reached the sheltered cove where the deep stone haven was built. A pair of fishermen were on the harbourside, caulking a boat. Beyond the walls, a choppy sea moved like an army of steel bonnets, flashing in the noonday sun. Shielding his eyes, Hob asked for Foulberry's skipper, and was told he had not yet returned. The younger of the fishermen squinted at him. 'How's it your business, lad, where he is or isn't?'

'I'll tell you, one day,' Hob replied. 'For now, is there somewhere we can stay, until the boat comes in?'

A long look passed between them, and the older man shrugged. 'My cousin runs a small place, no far from here, halfway up the hill. Not grand, but the rooms are cheap. You'd be welcome enough there, so long as it's not for long. Scots are bad for business, he says.'

The tavern was built end-on to the sea, which surged onto the shingle beach below its hillside berth, as if to eat the cliff away and watch the inn collapse. It would soon crumble without any such help, Louise thought. The place was grimy, cold and damp, and the landlord looked her over as if she were a pie, hot and tasty from the oven. Mean as it was, it had one thing in its favour: from its door, and their upstairs window, they could see the harbour mouth. And so they set up watch.

The days passed as if time had stopped. Louise dared not think what she would do if the boat arrived without Crozier, or news of him. Playing chess with Hob at the taproom window, or prowling the cove on foot, she could not allow herself to contemplate what might have happened to keep him in France.

As each day faded without the boat's return, darkness brought a strange comfort. The lamp at the harbour entrance burned like a beacon, keeping her company as the night drew on with no sign of life but a passing gull's cry, or the bark of the harbour dogs. A rowing boat's lantern would raise her hopes, soon to fade as its size was revealed. But at last, one morning, as dawn drew back the dark, a light could be seen far out at sea, bright as the morning star. Hob was on watch, and he shook Louise awake. Soon they were at the harbourside, hearts hammering as the ship bore steadily towards the cove. Only lobstermen were awake at this hour. They grunted a greeting as they jumped into their boats and rowed off down the coast, to empty their creels while the creatures and their claws were still half asleep.

Light had broken when at last the *River Pearl* slipped into harbour. Ropes were flung onto the stanchion, and a sailor jumped ashore as soon as the quayside was close to wrap them tight.

Louise clutched Hob's arm. They stood far back, under the cliffs, watching the plank being lowered. A sailor ran onto the quay, a crate across his shoulders. Then came another young fellow, stooped and coughing under a metal trunk that he carried like a lumberman's sack. He staggered, unsteady on the quivering plank, and dropped his load on the stone quay before returning for another, smaller trunk, which he again deposited on the quay. That done, he went back once more, and this time reappeared holding the hand of a small figure in a dark cloak who tiptoed over the water.

Louise put a hand over her eyes, to see more clearly. A cry escaped her as she recognised Benoit disembarking, followed by Crozier. 'Thank God,' she breathed, turning to see Hob's reaction, but he kept his eyes on the boat.

'Who's that?' he asked, and Louise watched in dismay as a lady in red boots and a fur-trimmed cape reached for Crozier's hand. There could be no doubt who she was.

Louise's legs felt weak, and her head was light, as though she might faint. 'We must go,' she said. 'I cannot watch this.'

'Wait,' said Hob, in a voice she did not recognise. He held her arm tight.

Only the skipper was still on board, moving about on the deck. He raised a hand to the borderers, who saluted him in reply. His passengers made their way slowly down the quay, Lady Foulberry's maid and servant shouldering her trunks, Crozier with a hand on Isabella's elbow. As they approached the place where Louise and Hob were standing, her ladyship's face came into view. She was scowling, her frown dusted with soot. Her servants' faces were almost as grey, and their cloaks were filthied with coal from two days in the grimy quarters below deck. The borderers, meanwhile, were clean enough, having stayed above board, where the waves and mist had doused them.

The menace in Crozier's face made him look like a stranger. By now he had dropped his hold on Isabella, and she rubbed her arm angrily. She had begun berating him, her words carried away on the breeze, when she caught sight of Louise. Arrested mid-sentence, she came to a halt. 'What have we here?' she tittered. 'Your little wifie come to see what you've been up to?'

She moved towards Louise and put a hand on her cheek. 'I pity you, my dear,' she said, 'with a man as gutless as that. No wonder you have no children.'

Louise turned crimson, but the woman passed on, her servants trailing in her wake. They had a long climb up to the road and the coaching inn where the castle's mules awaited.

Crozier looked at his wife. 'You have seen for yourself,' he said. 'You cannot doubt me now?'

'Aye,' said Benoit. 'The besom got something of a shock when Crozier told her what was what, back in that miserable inn.' He shook his head. 'But I reckon the skipper will lose his job for letting you lock her below deck.'

'He had no choice,' Crozier replied, 'with two swords pointed at him.'

'Aye, but the way he grinned as you tied up the latch . . .'

Crozier had hoped to use Foulberry's seal when he sent the letters from Dacre and Margaret Tudor to the English court, but Isabella's humiliation had severed that connection. Even had she not told her husband what had happened – though Crozier suspected that theirs was a marriage where the seduction of others was known to both – he dared not waste the time, or risk the danger, of returning to Foulberry's castle. Instead, he wrapped up two of the letters, one from the dowager queen, professing her love, the other from Dacre begging their correspondence be destroyed, and set out along the border to Berwick Castle, where the Duke of Norfolk was posted over Christmas as the tedious business of sealing a peace treaty dragged on.

It was late at night when a servant tapped at Norfolk's door. 'A parcel, your grace, left on the doorstep. Whoever brought it had gone before I answered his knock.'

Rising from his bed, Norfolk lit a candle, pulled a nightgown over his shirt, and opened the letters. They crackled in his arthritic hand. An accompanying note, which was not signed, promised many more from the same source. Norfolk called his guards to find the messenger, but he was long gone, as he had feared. The next morning, he despatched a courier with a note for the cardinal in London.

Quoting the most damaging lines from Margaret's letter, Norfolk went on to inform Wolsey that, given irrefutable evidence of collusion with the enemy, Dacre's reputation had been irreparably damaged.

I for many years have stood by him, as did my dear departed father, respecting his military guile. My regard for his firm hand overruled my scruples about his unorthodox methods, but such leniency can no longer be extended. When your Commission reports, it must find him guilty. I need say no more on this, knowing you to be most sharp in matters of expediency. Naturally, these letters need never be mentioned.

It remains only for me to tell you that I shall hold on to this most incriminating correspondence against the day when, in your role as Lord Chancellor and Master of Star Chamber, you might require me to appear before it. I need not tell you how ill the king would view such evidence, and the suspicion it casts upon you, given your repeated avowal – during the very years Dacre was dallying with the royal widow – that he was loyal to his backbone. That we discover he was sneaking behind all our backs, bringing the country into danger and disrepute, must strengthen your resolve when the Commission returns, and you are obliged do your duty.

The Duke sniffed, and rubbed warmth into his fingers before continuing with a gallows smile.

There remains also the matter of how the king would respond to the knowledge that his own sister had been so treacherous. Such behaviour sullies the Tudor name, and you are a more confident and brave man than I if you believe Henry would not be enraged at such an association. In that eventuality, heads might roll.

Understand, please, my dear and most trusted friend, that I hold on to these letters as a precaution, not as a threat. So long as I remain safe in our king's favour, so shall you.

The Duke signed his name, then paused, dustbox in hand, and added a scribbled rider.

How these letters were found, and by whom, I do not yet know, though I have my suspicions, and will do my best to confirm them.

Part Three

1525

The Earth's Cold Face

CHAPTER THIRTY-FIVE

January 1525

Cardinal Wolsey's morning eggs curdled on his tongue when Norfolk's letter arrived. His stomach churned like a laundry maid's tub, and he pressed a finger to his mouth, as if alarmed at what would issue if it were allowed to open.

When his fury could no longer be contained, it was a stream of oaths that flowed from his lips, so fast and thick it might have been the Fleet itself, running with filth. Where a man of God had learned to curse so vividly his servants could only guess. Unversed in the ways of seminaries and the corridors of ecclesiastical power, they could not know that the pope's chosen ones were fluent not only in Latin and Greek, but also in invective. It was an essential weapon of self-defence, and they wielded it with pride.

Today, Wolsey felt not pride but fury. Norfolk's name was kicked around his chambers like a dirty shoe, bringing servants running to his door to listen, wide-eyed. None dared lift the latch or offer help. 'Crazy as a rabid dog,' whispered one, with a grin. 'Could turn and bite us if we get too close.'

When the first storm of rage had subsided, Wolsey sat breathing hard, mashing a fist in his palm. There was nothing before his eyes but Henry's face when he heard of Dacre's liaison. That the Warden General might swing did not upset him, but his picture showed two sets of legs dangling on the gibbet, and one was wearing embroidered slippers.

In those minutes, Dacre's work for the crown came to an end. The Commission's report lay on the cardinal's desk, delivered the week before. As they had been charged to do, the Star Chamber's officers had found the baron sadly wanting. Testimony from across the marches confirmed his favouritism towards criminal associates, and barely an approving word was said of him. At such an obviously partisan report, Wolsey had at first been worried. Dacre would know, and protest, that he had been dealt with unfairly.

Now, with news of his treason, Wolsey's scruples faded. If Dacre bleated a word of discontent at his treatment, the unfair bias of the Commission and its conclusions, Wolsey would let him know that his life hung on a thread. But that was a conversation for the cells, not the courtroom.

Calling for his bearskin cloak, the cardinal left Westminster by boat for Greenwich Palace where the king was in residence for this most tedious month of the year.

Henry received him in his private rooms, not only glad of distraction, but sensing victory. He nodded at intervals as Wolsey explained the Commission's findings, but his attention was as much on the cardinal's face as on his words.

'You seem troubled, your eminence,' he said at last, when Wolsey's speech had ended. The cardinal sighed.

'I do not deny it, your highness. It grieves me to find such a high-standing and respected servant of the court capable of such grave misdemeanours.'

'You persist in thinking him innocent?' Henry sounded surprised. 'The last time we spoke, you seemed to have reached our own view, that he was lying through his teeth.'

'I have not changed in that opinion, your highness, but the obligation to charge him lies heavy upon my conscience.' He took a deep breath, and looked the king in the eye. 'It will be like arraigning a friend. He and I have been long associates. We are not close, nor are we fond, but until lately we have enjoyed mutual respect.'

Henry scoffed, and tickled the head of the hound that sat at his side. 'Qualms are not what we expect of our Lord Chancellor. Rather, we would have him stalwart, resolute, and stout-hearted in defence of our realm.'

Wolsey blanched. He had gone too far. Twisting his hands in his lap, he forced a smile onto his face. 'Your highness, you misunderstand me. Mine is the ambivalence of a priest, all too aware of the flaws in the common man's heart, his own included.' He uttered a laugh, though feared it sounded more like a yelp. Recognising a fellow sound, the hound's tail began to brush the flagstones. Henry stroked its back, his hand knuckled with gold.

The cardinal pressed on. 'I fear for the baron's immortal soul, and would wish, once he has been charged, to act as his confessor. With your permission, of course.'

Henry's eyes were unblinking as he held Wolsey's glance. He noted the tremble at the edge of the Lord Chancellor's mouth, the fidgeting fingers that would not be still. 'We will have him imprisoned,' he said at last, 'and let him know our severe displeasure. Command him in my name to appear in the Star Chamber the first session of next month.' The king's hand gripped the hound's neck, and it whimpered. 'We might attend his arraignment ourselves, your eminence, and see how you handle your fears.'

So it was that some days later, Blackbird placed another letter in Dacre's hand. Harbottle lay in its frozen hollow, buttressed in snow, and the courier's cloak was crusted with hoar as he handed over the missive. The baron broke the royal seal, read its summons, and tossed it onto the fire. 'Back we go,' he said to Blackbird, 'as soon as the roads are clear.'

That night, and from then until he departed, the devils returned to Dacre's dreams.

CHAPTER THIRTY-SIX

February 1525

In an outhouse near the stables, the Frenchman stood hunched over a deep copper pot, stirring a steaming brew. Snow and ice clung to the keep, and Antoine's breath clouded the air, but he worked on, whistling. From the rafters overhead hung rows of herbs and plants, neatly tied. A shelf near the fire held rows of jars with labels round their necks. This was his dispensary, where the villagers came for help, but at this hour of the evening, when all was quiet, Antoine had the place to himself.

Hidden behind the outhouse, Barton shivered. The Frenchman worked by firelight, and the hole the sailor had poked in the wall the night before offered only a keyhole view. Even so, what the man was doing was obvious enough. Barton stifled a cough. Lately his chest had been hot and sore, and he had been allowed back from the woods to lie in the warmth of the men's quarters until he was well. Stifling his spluttering by holding a rag to his mouth, he worried the hole with a finger, and pressed his cheek once more to the wall.

Antoine worked on, oblivious of the bloodshot eye upon him. The potion was simmering nicely. He disappeared from Barton's sight, but soon returned with a small black bottle in his hand. Pushing back his hood, he stood by the pot, eyes closed, his right hand raised. The hairs on Barton's neck prickled as the Frenchman began to intone. The words were low and indistinct, but their meaning was clear. The man was casting a spell.

Antoine began to sway, as if transported by his incantation. His voice rose and fell, the sound more like harsh music than ordinary speech. When at last he fell silent he opened his eyes and blinked, as if surprised to find himself still in the shed. The sailor watched him add a few drops from the black bottle to the pot before lifting it off the fire and ladling the steaming, dark mixture into jars.

Barton had seen enough. He crept off across the courtyard and back to the keep. Despite his fever, he felt cold. Could it be that this man was a sorcerer, and using his powers to help Crozier? Fearful that the Frenchman might discover that he had been spying, and send his evil spirits after him, he lay trembling under his blanket, pressing his crucifix to his lips. The next day he returned to the woods. When the foreman, hearing his cough, tried to send him back, he begged to be allowed to stay. Suspicious, though of what he could not say, the woodcutter agreed. A look crossed Barton's face that was as close to gratitude as it ever came. Shaking his head, the woodsman picked up his axe, and told Barton to join his old gang.

CHAPTER THIRTY-SEVEN

The cell door scraped shut, a key turned, and the bolts were thrown, one, two, three. As the iron bars slid home and he was again confined, Dacre raised his head, like one determined not to be bowed. His hands were fists, his eyes tight shut, yet it was not the prison he feared but his own mind, which had sprung a trap more secure than any cell.

That morning he had been granted a visit from the cardinal. Dacre had been in the Fleet for just a few days, but the prospect of walking farther than three feet before meeting a wall, of seeing something beyond the filthied stone of his cage, made this encounter welcome, whatever its outcome. His keys rattling on his belt like a courtesan's bracelets, the gaoler had led him up the stairs to a room containing a single stool. The cardinal occupied it. When Dacre came in, Wolsey remained as he was, knees spread, his scarlet lap so bright against the Fleet's unlit murk that the baron blinked. As they looked at each other, the gaoler posted himself at the door, staring ahead with the expression of one who is sightless and deaf.

'It will do you no good,' Wolsey began, 'pestering the court like this.' He sounded peevish. 'The king wants you to know his wrath. He is exceedingly angry.'

The baron began to speak, but Wolsey waved a hand to silence him. 'I have worked hard, Dacre, protecting you from his displeasure. I – like Norfolk – have for many years been your bulwark, against the fate you should have suffered long ago. Neither of us would have believed you guilty of the charges brought against you last week.'

'And yet I confessed them all.' Dacre's voice was hard.

The cardinal whinnied. 'It was astounding! Much as I have seen in that chamber in my time, I have never been so surprised. The courtroom gasped, as did I.'

'I heard.'

Wolsey looked at him for an explanation, but the baron shrugged. 'I have had enough. Enough of being the butt of suspicion. Enough of spending my own money in the king's service, without his respect or his thanks. Enough, eventually, of everything. I begged to be released, but this is my reward: humiliation, stripped of my post, left to rot in this place with debtors and frauds, perhaps until I die. Which I doubt in this cold will be far off.'

'Yet last year you defended yourself superlatively. I believed every word.'

'And every word was true. Or close to the truth. But the Commission ye so cleverly devised undid all that good work, as it was meant to do. So what, I reasoned, was the point of arguing? I have not always been scrupulous in my affairs. Few men in my position could afford to be. But what would ye all have?' His voice rose. 'How in God's name can the border be kept tidy and safe, neat and bonny, when the place is at war with itself? Find me an answer, if ye will, and I'll maybe rest easier in here.'

'Calm yourself,' said the cardinal. 'You are growing heated, and there is no need. Henry does respect you, in his fashion. Otherwise, you would be awaiting execution. He wishes only to make you see sense, to atone for your misdeeds. The biggest of which' – he lowered his voice – 'is to have believed yourself more powerful than he. Setting yourself up as monarch of the north, that is your most serious crime.' He spread his hands, as if the matter had nothing to do with him. 'One day, trust me, you will get home.'

A silence fell, in which Dacre bent to peer out of the tiny window, which looked onto a dank brick wall. The cardinal cast him a sidelong glance. 'So having confessed, you do not question your sentence or wish to lodge a complaint? I had thought that the reason why you called me here.'

'I asked to see ye to be allowed more candles, and some paper and ink, that was all. But never ye fear,' Dacre replied, in a voice that was far from reassuring. 'I can read the runes. I know nothing I say will change my fate. But you, I can tell, are nervous. My indictment is proving troublesome for ye, though in what way I am unable to imagine. Perhaps I will find out.' His eyes bored into the cardinal, who turned his face away. 'Indeed, I am pretty sure,' he continued softly, 'that I *can* find out.'

Wolsey stood, brushing out his skirts. 'You are growing fanciful, my lord. I am not nervous, merely concerned for your welfare. But our business today is finished. I shall see that you are allowed the attentions of your manservant while you are here, and have access to fresh air once a week. That should surely ease your discomfort. Candles will be more difficult to secure, and paper is allowed only on condition of excellent behaviour, and after a long time of confinement. Yours having only just begun, I cannot oblige you there.'

Dacre did not reply, but drew himself up, his bulk filling the room, as did his mood.

'Very well then,' said Wolsey, when he remained silent, and signalled the gaoler to open the door.

Back in his cell, when the turnkey's steps had faded, Dacre's shoulders drooped. There would be no swift end to this sentence, that much he could tell. He stood, willing the pounding in his head to ease, the sweat on his shirt back to dry. When the tongs in his chest let go his heart and he could breathe rather than rasp, he lowered himself onto the stool by his pallet with an elderly groan.

His hand rubbed his knee, his gaze fixed on the stone wall, though he did not see the obscene drawings, nor the bloodstains where prisoners had picked at the mortar, or walloped their heads. Instead, he was far from here, crossing the Cumberland moors, and catching the first sight of Naworth, its torches beckoning him off the hills at dusk. He was beguiled for a minute into forgetting where he was, but the image began to fade. He stretched out a hand to call it back, but it was gone, in its place the wall and a window so narrow the noonday sun barely reached the cell, washing its walls a watery grey. Lowering his head he clenched his hands, determined to hold his nerve. Wolsey and Henry would not destroy him. He had fought and beaten men more dangerous and sly. Were he not locked up, it would be they who were frightened, not he.

He snorted, and wiped his mouth with the back of his hand. He'd smelled Wolsey's fear, that he had. There was something the cardinal did not want Henry to know. Something to do with him, perhaps.

Worrying at that thought got him through the night, with no unwanted guests. In the morning he felt weak. The grate in his door slid open, and he heard voices in the passage. Then the bolts were pulled back, the key scraped, and Blackbird appeared, bearing food and ale, and a badger skin cloak so newly made it reeked still of the beast.

When he had eaten, he waved Blackbird away and lay down, turning to the wall. Though the room remained dim, it was no longer dark. Safely through the hours he dreaded, now he could perhaps sleep.

In this manner, Dacre survived the Fleet, turning day into night. When his lamp died, in the hours before dawn, he schooled himself not to panic. Closing his eyes, he would travel around his lands. Roaming the western march was his delight, the horse beneath him, the trees overhead, the smell of the rain-sodden dale. But he thought often, too, of his dead wife, and their early years together. When he first found her on his mind, he shied away, fearing the distress it would bring. But Bess's presence was kind and the memory did not hurt. She smiled, her elegant hauteur softened by a wide, warm mouth, and a tongue that was quick to mock. She'd made him laugh, that she had, and none of the ladies he had since thought to marry could ever boast of that.

He would lie these nights hearing the dark stirring around him, like air down a well. Rather than open his eyes, he turned them inward, to his earlier life. There were foul images as well as comfort, and he would shift uneasily at the things he had done or condoned, though he still believed them necessary. Faces of the murdered and slain kept him company on the blackest nights. They did not frighten him, but a sadness descended that would not lift. It was not right, it could not be right, that life had to be this cruel.

Valiant though he was in his fight against sleep, there were times when he succumbed. Within minutes of drifting off, his tormentors would appear, crowding the cell, their red eyes alight, poking their fingers in his chest, swivelling their hips like a sodomite's dream. For

Dacre these apparitions were beyond nightmare. They were not figments of his imagination, he knew, but as real as he. He knew also that they would one day devour him. Waking, clutching his sodden shirt, he would bang on his door and scream for a light. But the request was never granted, and he would curl up on the floor behind the door, guessing the hour by the sounds from the street, and thanking God when the first birds awoke, and then the clocks, and he was no longer alone.

Since Dacre's trial, Blackbird had lodged in a tavern overhanging the river. His room was no larger than his master's, and being so close to the Fleet there were days when it smelled almost as bad, but he barely noticed, so concerned was he about the baron.

Twice a day he visited, after dawn, and last thing at night, when Dacre's vigil against the dark was just beginning. He was not allowed to stay long, but the short conversations he had were troubling. Sometimes Dacre barely noticed him, at others he would clutch his sleeve as he left, his eyes brimming with tears. These were not of regret or remorse, but something closer to terror. Blackbird was not an imaginative man, but he began to think the baron was in fear for his soul, and thought the devils who visited him at night had come to claim him as theirs.

After a month of this, when Dacre would often neither eat nor speak, the butler left the gaol and hurried along the banks of the Fleet until he reached a church. He returned with a priest and the guard wearily waved the churchman through. If the prisoner made his confession and quietened down, they would all feel better.

The priest was with Dacre all that day and the next. Blackbird left the baron's food with the guard, not liking to interrupt the voice he heard droning behind the door. When next he saw his master, he could not believe the change. The baron raised his head when he entered, and looked him in the face. His voice was stronger, and his colour had returned. 'I have slept, Blackbird,' he said, like one who has witnessed a miracle, 'all through the past two nights. That man of God has cleared the room, and my spirit, of those devils.'

Blackbird blinked. 'An exorcism?'

'He did not use that word. It was more an act of protection, to shield me from the malevolent forces that have tried to destroy my mind. He said the powers of darkness were so strongly pressing upon me, he could almost see them himself.' The baron shuddered, as if the mere mention of the devils might conjure them again. Reaching for a vial that lay by his pallet, he pulled the stopper and dabbed a drop of liquid onto his finger, and rubbed it on his forehead. 'Holy water, Blackbird.' He shook his head. 'Ye saints, to think I've come to this, as pious as a nun. I'm even saying my confession, though I take care what I say, lest I give the man a seizure. It would be comical, if I felt like laughing. But better all this, wouldn't ye say, than how I was before?'

Dacre never disclosed what else the priest and he had discussed, but though the weeks in prison dragged into months, and it seemed he had been forgotten, he kept his spirits up. The devils, it seemed, had been banished. Once a week, the priest returned to conduct mass, take confession, or sit in prayer. The lip service Dacre had paid to God these many years now was heartfelt, and by permission of the cardinal he was allowed a bible. Blackbird was thankful to see his master passing his time reading the gospels, his grammar school Latin brought out for a polish and shine, like an ancient suit of armour. The butler, however, felt no need to join him in his devotions. Assignations with the landlady from the Judge's Landing offered all the sustenance he required.

The months passed, and Dacre began to reminisce, dipping into the past like a waterwheel, forever taking another plunge. Blackbird would listen, full of sorrow. His master had never been one for this. Perhaps he sensed there was little ahead, or maybe captivity turned everyone's mind back to where it had come from.

'Remember all this, do ye?' Dacre asked one evening. 'I begin to think I've never been away, and the time we've had and the things we've done over the last thirty years is nothing more than a dream.' He tugged his beard, and sighed. 'I could've been locked in here a century, it feels so cursed long. D'ye recall, though, how Henry would tiptoe down the stairs and perch on a stool, his mouth tight as a shrivelled prune as he tried not to breathe?'

Blackbird nodded. 'He liked to make sure you were suffering.'

Dacre shook his head. 'No, it wasn't that, I don't think. He was just plain angry. He could not keep away. He was like my own father, telling me again and again how much I had disappointed him. And now, at this age, I can see what he meant.' He cackled, his face brightening. 'I damn well nearly brought the country to war, or so he said. It was the arrogance of youth. There I was, my army at my back, trumpets blaring, ready to deal with Moresby. His army was larger than mine, but my men were tougher, that I knew. But of all Moresby's men, I have to take on the scoundrel Parkes, slice off his ear, and cause an unholy row.

'How was I to know he was a friend of the Scottish king? For all his airs and armour, he looked like a peasant, a trumped-up nobody. And for that lapse of judgement Henry would never forgive me. Not for years did he soften. He'd ignore me at council, as if I was the black sheep of the room, and even when I was safely back home, out of his reach, I felt his eyes on me, following whatever I did.'

His laugh filled the room. 'As Bess's guardian, he made my life hell. He wrangled over each pound of her inheritance, every mile of land I wanted to claim as my own. All to punish me for riding off with her under his nose. As if any red-blooded man could have resisted!' He paused, and gave a sigh. 'Yet I could not dislike him. Not at all. He was a man of the old stamp, a hawk whose eye was on everything. Tough on wayward boys like me – and right to be – but trusting us, too, in an odd sort of way. He knew we were loyal and would turn out fine. We just had to burn off our youth, that was all, without causing too much damage.'

He fell quiet, and for a minute both men inspected the floor. The distance that lay between now and those far-off days was too painful to contemplate. Since the trial Dacre's hair had turned silver, and he shuffled around the cell, his limp grown worse with confinement. Blackbird's legs were slower too, and like an old man he now woke before dawn, and could not get back to sleep. Nor did all his visits to the landlady end in bed. Sometimes, he just liked to talk.

CHAPTER THIRTY-EIGHT

March 1525

News of Dacre's downfall reached the north, and word spread fast through the dales. There was celebration in some quarters, in villages still in ruins after an Armstrong raid, or in the castles of lords who had felt the baron's greedy hand or baleful eye upon them. Sir William Eure, Vice Warden, no longer slept with a sword by his side. Lord and Lady Foulberry threw a banquet, and danced through the night. The Bishop of Carlisle spent an hour on his knees in thanks before the altar, then called his priests to help him enjoy a crate of fine Spanish wine that had been lying for months in his cellars.

When the information finally reached Crozier's Keep, sent up from the village by Father Walsh, Crozier felt only fatigue. He went about his business that day as if nothing had changed, but by night-time, when the clan was gathered in the great hall, the talk was of nothing else. Unable to join in the revelry, he left long before the merriment had ended. While the hall rang to the sound of singing and pipes, Crozier and Louise sat side by side before the fire in their chamber. They said little, but listened to the snapping of pine cones in the flames and breathed their soothing scent. That night Crozier slept so deeply he hardly seemed to be breathing. When he did not wake at dawn, Louise crept out of the room. Crozier did not appear until noon, but where Tom and Benoit seemed to have grown younger overnight, their faces cleared of strain, his mouth was still set hard. These were volatile times, with Dacre gone, the marches unwatched, and the baron's allies vengeful and afraid.

'So we can stand down the double watch?' asked Tom, gulping down ale to clear his wine-thickened head.

'We do no such thing,' his brother replied, and gathered his men in the courtyard. Until order was established, and a Warden General in place, they were not out of danger, he told them. 'Could be things will be worse than ever. The double guard stays on duty, and the watch in the valley, and none of us goes beyond these walls without my say-so.'

Standing near the back, out of Crozier's view, Barton chewed his black wad of beef, and spat. He eyed the Frenchman, listening doe-eyed to the borderer as if he were an innocent, and not a henchman of Beelzebub himself. The sailor crossed his breast, and fingered the crude crucifix he now wore round his neck.

Mayhem was unloosed, as Crozier had predicted. Sluggishly at first, riots broke out in the west, where Dacre had held firm sway. Sir Christopher stamped on these, and for a time they appeared to have died, but as soon as his troops returned to their barracks, the uprising licked farther along the border. Sir Philip, in residence at Harbottle, was nervous. There was bad blood in the air, everyone sensed it. Joan should not be out here, where forces from all corners might meet. Yet with the border riders out in strength, did he dare send her south for safety?

She settled the matter for him, refusing to move until her father came home. Since Dacre's imprisonment, Joan had been moody and restless, given to tears and outbursts, and spending long hours alone in her father's chamber, which she now used as her own. Philip had neither time nor patience for such matters. Only his brother's affection for the girl prevented him from losing his temper. Agreeing testily that she could stay, he dismissed her from his mind. Already Tynedale was beginning to buck beneath their feet, as if an earthquake were on its way.

And an earthquake it almost was. In the following weeks, the border clans seemed to put aside their grievances and join as one to show the English king that with the Warden General gone, the land, and the power, was theirs. There had never been such turmoil in Dacre's yard. Cumberland seethed, Naworth on high alert, and the barracks at Carlisle were never at rest, soldiers despatched in relays, day and night. But it was in the east that the worst unrest was bubbling.

A courier sent to the king from the Bishop of Durham informed him that the city was almost under siege, and assistance urgently needed. Newcastle, meanwhile, was in the Tynedale highlanders' sights. Village by village, the outlaw Armstrongs and their gang advanced upon it. There was no doubting their intention. There was panic within the city, and the raiders had reached alarmingly close to its walls with barely a check before the king's men brought them to a halt. At that point, the conflict did not end, but grew more murderous.

Those who had no thought of taking town or city took instead to the roads. The riders' secret ways over the Northumberland hills into Scotland were flattened as raiders rode as if into battle, scavenging and scathing until the north of their own country was all but barren, and the Scots fearful their lands would soon be picked clean as well.

The ferment raged all spring. While Dacre languished in his cell, his border sizzled and roared under fire. Days after flames had been doused, black ash still drifted on the wind, a diabolical snow. Footsteps crackled, and the smell of cinders and burnt wood clung to everything, an invisible shroud that sent cattle mad and made peasants shiver, as if this acrid scent were a harbinger of the end.

Cardinal Wolsey hurried to York, where he met the Duke of Norfolk. His first greeting was to inform the Duke that the bishops of Durham and Carlisle had sent word they dared not leave their charges in case the unrest deepened.

'More likely frightened to set foot outside their gates in case they get lynched,' muttered Norfolk, taking a seat in Wolsey's apartments, and casting a jaundiced eye over the comforts an archbishop could command. Wolsey raised his eyebrows, not disagreeing, and waited until his rich white wine had sweetened the soldier's tongue. 'If this continues,' Norfolk said, putting down his glass and waving away the servant who would have filled it again, 'or if the situation grows any more grave, as I fear it will, Henry must come north, and be seen at the head of his army.'

Wolsey looked shocked. 'Surely it is no more than a brief flaring?' When Norfolk said nothing, the cardinal began to wring his hands in his lap. 'You think this is serious rebellion?'

'Most certainly,' Norfolk replied, not unpleased to see the cardinal's anxiety. The man who played monarch in the Star Chamber was a mere commoner, and a cowardly one at that, in the face of armed revolt. Norfolk wondered when Wolsey had last drawn a sword. With a cough, he continued. 'The insurrection stretches from west to east. The Cumberland rioters are making a point, enraged, one presumes, at Dacre's fate. But from the middle to the eastern marches, each outburst is connected in some way to the next. For once in their benighted existence,' he said, with something close to venom, 'these brigands are forgetting their differences, and forging a united front. It is a front, I must advise you, that could see the north splinter from the south. That, as we all know, would be disastrous. The king is close to making peace with France as well as Scotland, yet if it becomes known his own people are in open revolt and rebellion it would weaken his position in negotiations, and – perhaps worse – make him a figure of fun far beyond France.'

'It would seem the bishops were not exaggerating,' said the cardinal, so quietly he might have been talking to himself, 'and I have underestimated the risks they face.' He raised his head, and looked into the duke's cold eyes. 'You have a plan for dealing with this, I presume? A hardened campaigner such as yourself generally prefers to give orders than to take them.'

Norfolk ignored the insolent tone, recognising that only when threatened did Wolsey grow uncivil. 'Indeed I do. It is a last resort, and one the king's lawyers are queasy about, but in the north it works.' Now he beckoned the servant to fill his glass. 'Usually, anyhow,' he added.

Wolsey too drank another glass. He nodded, his expression grave. 'I believe I know what you are about to suggest.' His tongue searched for the last traces of wine, and his lips glistened. 'We must take pledges as security for good behaviour?'

'Pledges, and many of them. Across all three marches.' Norfolk's voice was that of a commander, instructing his men. Suddenly he appeared to be looking beyond the room, seeing not the rich blue tapestries that hung from the walls but the forests and hills and hidden villages of the borders, whose ceaseless unquiet would follow him, he feared, until the day his mouth was plugged with earth.

'The most powerful families and the most pernicious clans must be forced to hand over one of their high-ranking men, or several of those less important, who will be held in custody until peace is restored. If trouble erupts and their promises are broken, the pledges will be killed. The borderers hold to a code of honour incomprehensible to those of us who live in the south, but a reminder of the primitive manners and cast of mind they live by. For some reason, it proves effective. Clan loyalty matters to these people in a way none like us can begin to comprehend. For all their barbarous ways, the prospect of one of theirs being killed to atone for their misdeeds seems to keep them in check.'

'Then why do the king's legal advisers so dislike this tactic?'

Norfolk gave a bark of laughter. 'Poor, sheltered souls, they are uncomfortable at the idea of an innocent man being made to pay for someone else's crime. Yet these pledges are innocent only, I should add, in the sense that for so long as he – or she – is in custody, they cannot be said to have taken part in whatever outrage then leads to their execution. In all other respects, these pledges are as guilty and culpable as the rest of their brethren, and their deaths disturb neither my sleep nor my conscience.'

Wolsey rose, and took a turn around his chamber. 'We must settle this without dragging Henry out of London. That will do nothing to improve his temper, which of late has grown ragged.'

'I had not noticed,' replied Norfolk, merely to provoke. Wolsey ignored him, and paced on. At last, when it seemed he would have worn out his buckskin soles, he came to a halt.

'Can you undertake to have pledges taken, and swiftly?'

The soldier nodded. 'The bishops can instruct their men to begin the process at Durham, Carlisle, and all points between. I shall personally oversee pledges in the middle march, where the worst offenders live.' He smiled. 'The border gaols will be full within the week. A pleasant thought, is it not?'

Wolsey looked at him as if nothing to do with the north would ever be other than objectionable.

'I suppose,' said Norfolk, to break the silence, 'our good man Dacre has no advice to offer for the extirpation of the border thugs, and the restoration of peace?'

'I had not thought to ask,' Wolsey replied, taken off guard. 'Surely he would see that as weakness on our parts, and confirmation that he alone can keep the north under control.'

'Even so, we both know Henry will release him one day. Dacre could surely be persuaded that helping us in this matter might bring that day closer?'

'I wish to have as little to do with him as possible.' Wolsey gestured dismissively with one hand as if the baron's plight in no way mattered to him.

'Has the king visited him in the Fleet? I am merely curious,' said Norfolk, watching the cardinal's face.

'I have advised him against it. Not only is the place verminous, but Dacre must be made to feel he has been cut off, and is in a state of utter banishment. Henry would not wish him pampered.'

Norfolk let the subject drop, and even during dinner – a stilted, stuttering evening which both longed to get through so they could retire to bed – he did not raise it again. He did note, however, that the cardinal was drinking hard. Covering his own glass as the bottle was carried round the table, he knew that the man was afraid.

CHAPTER THIRTY-NINE

Barton's last visit to Harbottle had been disturbing. Still troubled by his cough, he had led his mare to the stables, her hooves skittering on the glazed cobbles. It was not Blackbird who spoke to him at the door, but a servant he had never seen, who told him his visit was fruitless. The baron was gone to London a few days before, and nobody knew when he would return. 'I will see her ladyship, then,' said Barton, trying to enter, but the doorman blocked his way.

'With her father away, her ladyship cannot receive visitors.'

At that moment Barton heard Joan coming down the stairs, chattering to her maid. He began loudly to protest, but Joan's descent took forever, and the servant was eyeing Barton's boot, which was rammed against the door, with a look that suggested he would very soon stamp upon it before at last the young woman heard their voices, and recognised her father's friend. 'What brings you here?' she asked, the maid at her elbow like a brown velvet shadow.

'I have business with your father,' Barton said, bowing low, cap in hand. 'But this good gentleman informs me he is away.'

The life disappeared from Joan's eyes, and she waved a petulant hand at the doorman. 'I will see Barton,' she said. 'Please bring ale to the hall for our guest.' Answering the disapproval in the man's face, she added: 'Fret not, Walker. My maid will remain with me at all times. There's no need to be concerned.'

Rolling her eyes, she led Barton to the hall, where Mary chased off the dogs, who were hogging the hearth, and stoked the fire with fresh logs.

In the warmth, Barton was for the moment racked by coughing. Ale helped douse his bark, and he was soon under the ministrations of two young women who had too little to do and nobody to care for. A blanket was found for his shoulders, and a mug of mulled wine followed the ale. Soon the party was cheerful, Mary as intrigued as Joan by Barton's tales of border life on the far, and darker, side.

'I cannae tell ye my business with your father,' he said eventually, with regret. 'But I wish him home speedily. There's trouble brewing at Crozier's Keep, that's for sure.'

'We've had our own difficulties here too,' said Joan, looking at Mary for confirmation, and the girl nodded dolefully.

'Like what?'

Joan hesitated. 'Devils,' she said.

'Eh?' Barton's leg jumped.

Joan nodded. 'He was being visited by horned devils, every night. They were making him ill. And now he has been taken to the Star Chamber, and we may never see him . . . we may never see him again.' Tears coursed down her cheeks, and Mary put a solicitous arm around her shoulders, which she shrugged off as if she'd been scalded. Barton's face was all consternation. 'How long has this been going on?'.

'Months now,' Joan said, wiping her cheeks with her sleeve. There was a look in Barton's eyes she could not decipher. 'What, do you think you can help?'

He shook his head. 'I'm not sure, m'lady. Something about this is very odd, that's all I'm saying.' He stood up, the blanket falling from his shoulders as he thought of Antoine and his incantations. 'It is possible I know the source of his troubles. But I must get back, and fast.'

'Already?'

'I will return soon,' he promised, bowing again, 'if only to find out if your father has returned. But I would hope to offer something more, my lady.' He took her hand, as if it were a natural thing for a man of his rank to do. 'I pray I can bring an answer, and a solution to his problems.'

Joan returned his grip before turning away as if she had been found out in a crime. She said nothing as he left, but the memory of her tender clasp remained with him for many weeks to come.

The night after Crozier ordered his men not to leave the keep without his permission, Barton left, with his blessing. The borderer had found the sailor, pack on his shoulder, crossing the courtyard from the workers' quarters and heading for the gates. Asked where he was going, Barton had not answered, but kept walking. Crozier caught up with him, and barred his way. 'What do you think you're doing?'

'I'm getting out of here.'

'I told all the men to stay within the keep. You cannot obey a simple command?'

Barton hoisted his pack higher on his shoulder. 'I've had enough, you could say. Farming's no to my liking,' he replied, spitting onto the cobbles.

Crozier took a step closer, until they stood chest to chest. Barton avoided his gaze, and shifted sideways to get past him, but the borderer's hand grabbed him by the neck, his knuckles pressing on the windpipe. 'No you don't,' he said softly. 'Not without an explanation. I don't like men slipping off behind my back without a word. It makes me suspicious and when I get suspicious, I won't stop till I get answers. You understand?'

Barton laughed as if he were truly amused. 'Very intimidating you are, cap'n. A real warrior. No, no, mate,' he raised his hands in appeasement, 'I sincerely believe you are a first-rate fighter. Everybody says so. But a man who cannae keep his own wife under control? Now, that kind of man doesnae scare me.' He shook his head, a contemptuous grin revealing his snaggled teeth.

Crozier's grip tightened as he dragged the sailor towards a wall. Still Barton refused to look frightened. He chewed, and spat again.

The borderer's first fist caught his chin, and the second jerked his head backwards against the stones, with a loud and sickening crack. Barton slid slowly down the wall until he was sitting, head on his chest, blood dripping from his nose.

Crozier walked off, returning to throw a bucket of well water over him. The sailor grunted, and lifted his head to see the borderer standing over him. 'Lost ye there for a minute,' he mumbled, trying to get to his feet. Crozier gave him all the help he needed, dragging him towards the walls, where the night watch stood, gates thrown wide.

'You piece of miserable scum,' Adam said. 'I don't know what your game is, but you stink of trouble. I should never have taken you in.'

'The Frenchie's another one you should have thought about twice an' all,' Barton replied, through swollen lips. 'Sweet-talking your wife whenever you're gone and slipping off to the woods with her. The things I could tell you, cap'n, if you wanted to know. But what I'll tell you for nothing is, if she was soon to find herself with child at last, I wouldnae be surprised. It'd be mighty strange, wouldn't it, after all the years you've been married?'

Fearing he would kill him if he lifted his fist again, Crozier hurled him out of the gates, where he sprawled. 'See him out of the valley,' Crozier shouted at a watchman, who nodded and drew his sword. Prodded to his feet, the sailor rose and set off shakily down the woodland path, from where the whistling refrain of a shanty song drifted up the track and followed Crozier into the keep.

The warden of the Scottish middle march did not like the look of Barton. Bruised and bloodied, the sailor stood in his guardroom, more like one he should throw in his cells than trust for information. Yet he could not ignore the man's story. 'Only doing my duty, sir,' said Barton. 'A rogue like that should not be at large.'

The warden eyed his informant with distaste, but after a brief hesitation he sighed. 'We will send out a party today. If we catch him, you will be rewarded in the usual way.' He lifted a finger to his lieutenant, and the sailor was taken away to be given a berth for a night. The informant's broken face and dragging limp seemed not to trouble him. If anything, the warden thought, he looked strangely content. Gleeful, that was the word.

Jedburgh Castle, the warden's stronghold, was a morning's ride from Crozier's keep. Helmets gleaming, the posse cantered across the hills and into the valley, reaching the walls before noon. The sun was brilliant upon the battlements, the trees washed in new-budded green, and the warden held his gloved hand over his eyes as he called the guard to bring Crozier to the gate.

They did not have long to wait. Crozier stepped out and looked up at the warden sitting over him on his horse. 'What's your business?' he asked.

The man leaned towards him. 'We have been informed you are sheltering a sorcerer.'

The borderer almost laughed. 'A sorcerer? What sort of nonsense is this?'

'Deadly serious, I assure you,' the warden replied. 'We are informed you have a guest, a Frenchman by the name of Antoine d'Echelles, who casts spells and consorts with the devil. We have a witness to his deeds. I need not tell you what fate awaits those who deal in the occult, or aid such malefactors in their fiendish work.'

Crozier jerked his head at Wat the Wanderer, and the gates were drawn wide. 'You may enter,' he said to the warden. 'If you can find a sorcerer, you'll be as good as a magician yourself.'

The warden and his men rode into the courtyard and dismounted. Crozier, no longer looking amused, stood before them, Tom and Benoit at his side. 'The sorcerer, as you call him, is a soldier. He is also a healer. You can examine his potions and herbs yourself, over there.' He pointed at Antoine's shed. 'Speak to any of the villagers who've been cured by him, and they'll tell you he is as holy and good a man as any of the pope's elect.'

The warden sucked in his breath. 'Careful, now,' he said. 'That's heretical language.'

'I think not,' Crozier replied. 'Antoine is a simple man of God, as our priest will confirm.'

The warden waved his hand. 'Bring him to me.'

'He is not here. He has returned to the French army.'

'Mighty convenient, isn't it?' The warden looked interested. 'Gone just as we come to catch him. How d'you explain that?'

Crozier shrugged. 'Go seek him yourself and ask. He will be with the garrison at Dunbar Castle by now, and sailing home to France from there at the earliest opportunity.'

Antoine was, at that moment, galloping in the other direction, across the western march towards the Galloway hills and the Solway coast, where he could take a boat to the continent. Barton had been scarcely a mile along the road to Jedburgh, the evening before, when Crozier told Antoine he must leave. There was no doubting the malice the sailor intended towards the Croziers and, as a deserter, Antoine must not be found with them.

As Crozier saddled the horses, and the soldier packed his belongings, farewells were hurried, though the embrace between the soldier and Old Crozier was like that of father and son. He came to Louise last, with a tender smile. 'You will have good news soon to share, is that not so?' She blushed, and nodded, before hugging him tight.

'Nobody knows yet,' she whispered.

Antoine left without another word, following Crozier into the night, and onto the westward road. It was first light when the borderer returned, the Frenchman safely beyond the middle march, and the sea so close he could smell it.

'Who is your informant?' Crozier asked the warden, who threw his reins to one of his men.

'He gave no name, but he had a sailor's gait, and the bound hair. And a brand on his neck you couldn't miss . . .'

Adam shook his head as if with pity. 'Oliver Barton, that's who he is. The man bears a grudge. I kicked him out of here yesterday. This is nothing more than petty revenge, and a waste of your time. I am surprised you believed the word of someone like him.'

'Nobody better at catching a felon than another just as bad,' said the warden resentfully.

Crozier stepped back. 'Well, you can search the premises, but I would prefer you took me at my word. I have no reason to lie.'

The warden looked unimpressed. 'A clansman's word is as slippery as his sword. I will never trust you, or your kind.' He came closer to the borderer, his voice falling. 'You have had trouble of this kind before, have you not? You were thought to be harbouring a heretic, that time. And now it is a sorcerer.' He cast his eyes around the yard, at the keep's glowering battlements and the wall of trees that encircled them all, and shuddered. 'A den of thieves and murderers this place always was, but now, it seems, it is worse than that.' He screwed his eyes tight against the sun. 'Common vermin I understand. Devil worshippers are something else again. They are not natural, and nor

316

are those who consort with them. If there is any truth in the accusation, I will be back. There is no punishment too cruel for those who do Satan's work. In the name of all that is sacred, I will make sure you suffer.'

He got back on his horse, and his men lined up behind him, bridles and spurs jingling. In silence, the clan watched them go. Bright though the day was, it felt to Crozier that the sun was suddenly cold.

CHAPTER FORTY

April 1525

The longer he spent in prison, the clearer was Dacre's mind. Although the devils had been banished he still stayed awake at night and slept by day, his main torment now the dark itself, not what it held or hid.

Calm restored, he could think more lucidly than he had in years. Heartened by the old testament and its doctrines of vengeance and destruction, one day he startled Blackbird by picking up his bible and beginning to read.

'Hold on there now,' the butler began, 'I'd rather you didn't preach . . .' But Dacre ignored him and ploughed on. The Latin was incomprehensible to Blackbird, but he recognised the expression on Dacre's face. Now he understood. With a grudging smile he leaned back against the wall, and waited for the words to end.

When they did, the baron turned to him, his eyes wide. 'Roughly put, the psalmist is asking, 'Can wicked rulers be allied with God, who frame mischief by statute? They band together against the life of the righteous, and condemn the innocent to death. But the Lord has become my stronghold, and my God the rock of my refuge. He will bring back on them their iniquity and wipe them out for their wickedness . . .' The baron tapped the book. 'Wipe them out, Blackbird, did ye hear? Wipe them out, he says.'

'Keep your voice down,' the butler whispered. 'This is seditious talk.'

Dacre put a finger to his lips, as if he were a child playing a game, but there was nothing juvenile in his look. 'There's something else,' he said softly. He felt under his pallet and drew out a letter, the paper stained, the writing so crooked it was as if a bird had walked through ink and then onto the page.

He looked at Blackbird, and raised his eyebrows. 'See this? It all begins to make sense now.' He handed it to the butler, who deciphered the erratic line. *It was Crozer killed the horses, and set the devils on you. Of this you can be sure. I am now gone from there. B*

'Who'd have thought he could write?' he murmured.

Dacre scoffed. 'I doubt he can. He will have paid someone to compose this, but that's not the point. He has left Crozier's Keep, because he has proof it was Crozier who was acting against me. Of all the names that came out in court, his was never once mentioned. And yet, I can picture it: he had them all under his whip, dancing to his tune. Behind every accusation, his hand was at work. Wastrel and thug that he is, he thought he could bring me to my knees. Hah! No man's managed that yet.'

The look on the baron's face was hungry, eager for revenge. 'I need you to go north, Blackbird. Set the Tynedale men onto Crozier. Make him suffer, however it is done.' Blackbird nodded. 'But I need more than that.' Dacre rubbed a hand over his matted beard. 'Crozier has been plotting for months to ruin me, of that I'm certain, but there's something else afoot, something the cardinal wants hidden, though what it is I haven't an inkling. Whatever is keeping Wolsey awake at night will have nothing to do with Crozier. You must do some digging for me, Blackbird. Ought to have set you to this weeks ago, so I should. Damn me and my wavering mind.'

The butler looked puzzled, but as Dacre told him of Wolsey's visit, and the suspicions it had raised, Blackbird's smile slid into something less warm. 'I may be absent some weeks, it seems,' he said, when Dacre had finished, but the baron seemed unconcerned.

'Be gone, then,' he said, flapping his hand, whose rings now slid down to his knuckles.

Blackbird left the prison, a frown on his face. Whistling for a ferry, he watched the dim lamp swing towards him through the dark, and a hand reached up to help him into the boat. Sally would be surprised to see him tonight, but this was no social visit. If she would arrange to take the baron his meals, he would head north and find whatever it was that had made Wolsey avoid the Fleet since the day he and Dacre had talked. As the river washed under his trailing hand, Blackbird felt the first stirring of hope since the cardinal had struck the table in the Star Chamber with his hammer and told the guard to tie Dacre's hands, and he had watched his master being led away, like a bull to slaughter.

CHAPTER FORTY-ONE

June 1525

The servant bobbed a curtsey and informed Lady Foulberry that there was a man at the gate. 'Indeed?' she asked, looking up from her needlework. She sat by an open window, the summer day warming her back.

'He says the name is Blackbird, my lady. He is Lord Dacre's man.'

Needlework was thrown aside as Isabella picked up her skirts and ran to her husband's office. 'We cannot see him!' she cried.

'Quite the contrary, my love,' her husband replied. 'Of course we shall admit him. I have been expecting a visit of the kind. To send him away would be to confirm our complicity.'

'But we are complicit, and he knows it! Our deposition was read out in the Star Chamber!' Isabella clasped her hands, which would otherwise have flapped around the tiny room.

Lord Foulberry stepped out from behind his desk, and pressed her hands between his. 'For pity's sake, be calm. Follow my lead. We shall survive this, I promise. Do not forget that Dacre lies in prison. He poses no immediate threat.'

Blackbird was shown into the great hall, to be met by the stone-faced Foulberrys. Her ladyship's arm was through her husband's, though what appeared to be a display of affection was more a support in case her legs buckled.

'My lord. My lady,' said Blackbird. 'I doubt this visit will come as a surprise.'

The Foulberrys did not speak, and the three remained standing, as if a formal dance was about to begin. Blackbird moved closer, stripping off his riding gloves. His hosts could not know that they were the first of the many detractors on whom he had called who had allowed him over the threshold. The other accusers, the length of the border, had sent their guards and dogs to see him off. At Sir John Wetherington's gates he had been obliged to draw his sword to quell a mastif's zeal. It would not bark again. Yet here was Lord Foulberry, one of the most powerful of Dacre's enemies, willing to see him.

'I have not come to alarm you,' Blackbird continued. 'The part you have played in my master's destruction is for your confessor to judge, not me. But you should know that Baron Dacre will not be forever in prison. The Lord Chancellor himself has assured him of that. When he returns, the baron might be more willing to live in peace with those who turned against him if they try to help him now.'

'Why should—' Isabella began. Her husband pinched her arm, and she fell quiet.

'My lady intends to ask, sir, in what way we can help him?' The oil in Lord Foulberry's voice was like balm to Blackbird. After a month of hard riding and humiliation, here at last was a man prepared to do business.

'Please,' Foulberry said, 'be seated.'

Blackbird perched on a stool, the couple took their settle, and for a moment no word was spoken. The chittering of finches in the courtyard wafted into the hall, and tension eased. The butler watched as her ladyship's face relaxed, her hand on Foulberry's arm less like a claw. His eyes travelled over her painted face, the low-cut bodice, the silken, embroidered shoes. The wealth this pair enjoyed could not match Dacre's, but no wonder they had fought him off, intent on keeping what was rightfully theirs. The baron's neighbours, they were also among his worst foes. What Foulberry had to say about that would be interesting.

'Sir,' his lordship began, unhitching himself from Isabella, and clasping his hands together as if in prayer, 'sir, we owe your master a great apology. I did indeed put my name to testimony against him, but it was not done willingly. I was the victim of coercion of the most evil kind, by one whom I dared not offend. My wife here . . .' Foulberry's voice broke, and he pressed his fingers briefly to his lips. 'My dearest wife was taken hostage, and not returned until I had agreed to do his bidding.'

Blackbird's eyebrows lifted.

'The man of whom I speak – beast would be a better word – is one of the wolves of the border. Adam Crozier, head of that clan, and the most vile, noxious and pernicious robber in Teviotdale. It was he who betrayed your master.'

'In what way?'

At some length, Foulberry described the collecting of depositions. 'Many were given willingly, I am sure, though it grieves me to tell you that. But Crozier needed my name to persuade the others to take part, and that is where he would not take no for an answer. He forced his way inside here, and at swordpoint he took my oath.' Lord Foulberry turned his face aside, as if the memory were still bitter. 'I cannot bear to recall it. Lest I be tempted to inform Dacre of what he was doing, he . . . he abducted my wife, and . . . and . . .'

Isabella touched his arm, and he closed his eyes, as though willing the terrible images to depart. 'It is all right, my sweet,' she whispered. 'I am home and safe; it is all over now.'

Her husband raised wet eyes to the butler, who was watching the pair intently, but if Foulberry had hoped for sympathy, none was forthcoming.

'I believe there is more you can tell me, is there not?' Blackbird prompted. 'Something else beyond the accusations heard in the Star Chamber. Something damaging not just to Dacre but to certain members of the court?'

There was a glint in Foulberry's eye as he looked up, quickly concealed. 'So that is what you are after?' he murmured. 'I can help you there, then, my man. Most certainly.'

Isabella looked at her husband fondly, then turned to the butler. 'But before he says more,' she said quickly, 'what can you offer in return?'

Blackbird held her gaze. 'Ma'am, you will have the certainty that if this information helps Dacre secure a speedier release, your slate will be wiped clean, and Dacre not only forgive you but perhaps acknowledge he is in your debt. You can then sleep well at night. I very much doubt you get much rest at the moment, knowing his men could arrive any day.'

He stared round the hall, with its high black beams from which hung coronets of candles, cold wax curling down their necks like druids' beards. 'It cannot be pleasant, sitting on Dacre's doorstep, after denouncing him as you have.'

'It has been like living in hell,' spluttered Foulberry. 'Utter torment. I cannot express to you how this chance to put things right with the baron liberates my soul. I am like a new man . . .'

'Tell me first what you know,' said Blackbird, 'and then you can feel shriven.'

'Very well, then. Very well.' Foulberry fussed with his sleeves, while he chose his words. 'By devious and no doubt violent means, Crozier obtained letters between the dowager queen and Lord Dacre. Most incriminating their contents were. If they had landed in the wrong hands, your master would already be dead.'

'And who did he send them to? Cardinal Wolsey?'

Foulberry shook his head. 'The Duke of Norfolk, I believe. But one can be fairly certain that the duke has informed Wolsey of their contents.' He sat back, with the beginnings of a smile. 'Is that likely to prove useful to Dacre? I think it surely must.'

Blackbird got to his feet. 'If what you say is true then it might well be what the baron was looking for. You will be informed if so.' He clicked his heels, the Foulberrys bowed, and he was gone, so fast that they could almost have believed they had conjured him merely from their fears.

Blackbird rode slowly over the Cumberland fields, enjoying the sights of home. As Dacre had instructed, he had one more duty to fulfil before returning to London, but first he would spend a night or two at Naworth.

The castle welcomed him with its smell of polished wood and scented rushes. In his absence, the housekeeper and her army of servants had not grown slovenly, and he looked round with approval as he walked through the great hall and down the corridors, glimpsing the orderly rooms beyond. Joan was now home, awaiting her father's release, since Harbottle was no longer in his command. When his punishment ended, it was here he would return. She rushed to hear word of him, clasping her hands as she plied the butler with questions, though the news he brought of the baron's good spirits and high hopes did little to soften the anxiety on her whitewashed face.

He patted her cheek. 'Fret not, little one. He will be home very shortly, and all will be well. It'll be just like old times.'

Tears filled her eyes. 'You cannot know that,' she said, angrily. 'Until he is free, nothing is certain. Nothing at all.'

The next morning, Blackbird was leading his horse out of the stables when he saw a slovenly figure cross the yard towards the well. It was Oliver Barton, shucking off his shirt before plunging his head into a bucket.

'Hey there!' Blackbird called him over. 'What brings you here?'

Barton approached slowly, shrugging himself back into the shirt. 'Like everyone else, I'm waiting for Dacre's return.'

When he was within reach, the butler grabbed him by the scruff of his shirt, and pushed his face into his. 'Useless informer you proved to be. Crozier was planning Dacre's ruin right under your nose, and you saw and heard nothing until it was too late. You send a note, as if that's of any use now, and save your own skin by getting out before Crozier knew what you were up to. Now I suppose you're hanging around for your fee, and eating your head off while you wait. But you'd best get out of here before the master gets back. Dacre owes you nothing more than a boot up the arse for wasting everyone's time.'

Barton's eyes registered nothing. He sniffed, and hawked on the cobblestones, and the butler quickly stepped back.

'Aye,' the sailor said, 'I found out it was Crozier and his cronies. I had news of that for his lordship, but by the time I reached Harbottle he had gone, and you with him. That is what I was "hanging around" to tell him, in case the letter didnae reach him, or the scribe had got it down wrong. But thank you for the permission to be gone. I might well. Pay me what I'm owed, and I'll be off.' He sniffed again, and pulled off his shirt, wiping himself under his arms. 'Not much round here to keep me amused, that's for sure.'

He sauntered back to the well, his ribboned hair hanging in a curl down his naked back like a large, wandering slug.

The following day Blackbird reached the Tynedale forest. He reined in his horse, and stared at the forest edge, brooding and dark as a curtain wall. Summer seemed to shrivel in its face, light sucked in by the profusion of ivy that snaked up every tree. He drew his knife and laid it across the pommel before putting his fingers into his mouth and whistling. A mimic replied from nearby, and another, a mile or more hence. Staying on his horse, Blackbird did not move. Behind him the hills were bright and warm, but he was glad of his jerkin and cap.

Soon he heard the sound of feet, and a boy emerged from the trees. With a flick of his head, he instructed Blackbird to follow. Some time later, the butler crossed the river and came to Black Ned's village. Children flapped and squawked between the hidden houses like the chickens beneath their feet, and their mothers looked on, unmoved, as they pinned clothes onto the trees to dry, or coaxed goats off their low thatched roofs to be milked.

Legs spread, hat tipped back on his head, Black Ned was seated outside his house, sharpening a quiver of arrows. The butler did not talk for long, and the outlaw scarcely at all. Blackbird gave orders, and handed over a pouch of silver. More, he intimated, would follow on completion of the task. The outlaw's beard nodded, and the money disappeared somewhere beneath his cloak. There was nothing more to say, but for a moment the men looked at each other, the glitter in one set of eyes matched by the glint in the other.

CHAPTER FORTY-TWO

July 1525

At the foot of the valley below Crozier's Keep, where the stream broadened into a river, Louise picked her way across the birch-lined meadow. The silvered barks were almost blinding in the afternoon's glare. She was stooped, finding plants and herbs for Antoine's store, to replenish the shelves now he was gone. The soldier had left receipts, but some of his remedies she remembered without help. High summer was when many plants were in flower, and she plucked and pulled, stuffing her bag with willowherb, comfrey and viper's bugloss. Later, once the plants and their seeds had dried in the sun, she would make the potions and salves Antoine had shown her, ready for winter, when the keep and the village came out in rashes and sores, and people shivered with ague.

The wolf rustled through the grasses behind her, then sank panting by her side, his ribs heaving in the heat. She sat beside him and put a hand on his head and together they listened to meadow pipits chirruping from the cloudless sky. A pollen haze lay over the meadow, heavy as fog in the still air. Bees droned, broom seeds popped, and a dragonfly hovered, brighter than a rainbow. The wolf put his head on his paws, and dozed. Louise lifted her eyes to the valley and the towering banks of trees, patient under the sun. Her hand rested on her stomach, and the small bump beneath, where her child was sleeping.

Antoine had been the first to guess her condition, and she still was not sure how he could have been certain. She told Crozier the following evening, when they were alone in their chamber. The expression on his face would be with her for the rest of her life: first disbelief, then a flush of colour that made him look as young and vulnerable as a boy. Unable to speak, he took her hands. 'It is true,' she said shyly. 'All thanks to Antoine and his potions. I did not like to tell you, in case they did not work. I dared not allow myself to believe they would.'

Crozier shook his head, a smile dispelling his shock. 'What trouble that man was, but may God preserve him now.'

He put an arm round Louise's waist, and she placed his hand on her stomach, covering it with her own. She spoke softly, as if not to disturb the new life she carried. 'We must be careful not to hope for too much. It is very early still. And with Helene . . .'

'Hush,' he said. 'It will be different this time.'

'But it might go wrong again. You know it could.'

Crozier held her close. 'Be calm. That will not happen. But even if it did, Lou, we will endure, you and I, whatever comes.'

Sitting by the fire late into the night, they spoke little, contemplating the revelation and the fresh prospects and fears it brought them. The borderer's face was serious as he eyed the flames. He might have spoken with confidence to reassure his wife, but he was no less anxious.

For some weeks they kept the news to themselves, until it was impossible to hide, but it was noticeable that, amidst the backslapping and cheers, their joy was subdued. Not even in her most private self could Louise look ahead to the baby's birth and what lay beyond. Her hopes were so high they frightened her. The child was to be born the month before Christmas, but she dared not indulge herself by picturing its arrival, or imagining how she and Crozier would feel. Until she had conceived this child, she believed she had buried part of her heart with Helene. Now she knew that it was as fully alive as it had ever been, and was yearning to love. Frightened of the pain another loss would bring, she tried to temper her excitement, and so the early days of summer were passed in a see-saw struggle between soaring happiness and dampening common sense.

On an afternoon such as this, however, it was hard not to let one's mind drift to the possibilities ahead. Louise smiled, and for a moment closed her eyes, like the wolf, to soak up the sunlight and the benign promise of a contented future its warmth seemed to hold.

Suddenly her eyes opened, and she sat up straight. She smelled smoke. The wolf yawned as Louise scrambled to her feet, looking up the valley towards the keep. It felt uncomfortably far away from this, its lowest field. Only the tip of the towers was visible among the trees, but no cloud rose from there. Turning in the direction of the valley mouth, she stared, eyes screwed tight against the brightness. She could not be sure, but she thought she saw a thickening of the air above the slopes that hid the village. On a windless day, no ordinary fire's scent would reach this far.

Untethering the gelding from its tree, Louise set off at a canter along the riverside. The wolf loped ahead, tongue lolling. The smell grew stronger, and before she came to the road that led into the village fragments of ash began to float past, hanging like moths on the still, hot air.

It was then the noise reached her: men's shouts and children's shrieks and a dismal wailing that made her stomach turn. The gelding snorted, and as they came round the bend to the village it shied at the sight of flames leaping into the sky. The whole place was alight, as if it were a bowl of fire. Cottages burned like braziers, and screams from those trapped within could be heard all too clearly above the savage roar of the blaze.

Struggling to keep the gelding under control, Louise did not see the horsemen stationed around the village, nor Black Ned, circling his mount among the mill of terrified villagers, and scything heads with his sword. Smoke rolled towards her and her eyes stung as she peered ahead, trying to make sense of what was happening. She could not see those who broke free from their funeral pyres and raced into the street, onto the ends of their tormentors' swords, but she did hear their choking cries and the raiders' laughs and jeers.

The wolf's demented barking brought her to her senses, but not soon enough. By the time she understood that the village was under siege, one of the horsemen was bearing down upon her, his dim outline thickening as he barrelled through the smoke.

With a cry, Louise wheeled the gelding, but its terrified skittering was no match for the raider's warhorse. Axe raised above his head to bring down on hers, the man was about to strike when, as if out of nowhere, the wolf leapt with a snarl and sank his teeth into his shoulder. With a bellow, the rider fell off his horse, weapon thrown aside. Louise dug her heels into the gelding's flanks, but as the horse careered off and finally found its speed, she looked back and saw the rider stagger to his feet. Teeth bared, the wolf held him at bay, crouched for another attack, but the man's axe was in his hand again and as the dog flew at his throat he buried it in his chest. There was a terrible twisting of limbs in the air, Saint George and the dragon cruelly reversed, before the dog landed, spread-eagled, its pale coat turning scarlet. The wolf's dying howl rose over the village and was locked in Louise's head as she galloped for home.

The alarm had been raised before she reached the keep, and Crozier and his men were already on the road by the time she reached the forest. They pulled to a halt at the sight of her, and she told them, breathlessly, what was happening. 'Get home, and close the gates!' Crozier roared, leading his men on. In a tornado of dust they disappeared down the track, but Louise did not linger to watch. At the keep she set the guards to work, then with Ella gathered the children, Old Crozier and the servants into the great hall. She barred the door, stoked the fire, and finally paused to catch her breath. It was then the pains began.

At the sound of the Croziers' horses, the raiders tried to escape. Abandoning the burning village they set off across the fields, but where the smothering smoke ended and clear air began they found the clan, lined up to meet them. The keep's horses were stamping, and their riders' swords were fresh.

Black Ned's outlaw band were not cowards. They were reckless, undisciplined, but strong, and when the fight was on they did not care what it cost them to win. Benoit and Tom fought side by side, ferocious in their fury, but the battle was hard. Both were sliced by the raiders's swords, and both saw off their attackers, ending their insolence there, on the hillside, now their last place of rest.

At the other end of the village, Crozier and his archers were picking off those who, driven back to the village, were trying to slip off through the smoke. The arrows found their home, the raiders were brought down, and gradually the sound of shouts and oaths began to quieten. When it seemed the place had been almost emptied of the enemy, Crozier's men began pulling people from their homes. Some were still alive, though barely, but many were not, and when they broke down doors and found smoking corpses and charred bones, there was no clansman who did not retch.

There were only two stone houses in the village, the blacksmith's and the priest's. Both had been banked high with lit straw, the raiders liking to cook people alive in their homes, as if they were rooks in a pie. A lick of red was creeping across Father Walsh's roof, but before Crozier reached his door he caught sight of Black Ned, skulking behind the blacksmith's forge until he could slip off unseen. Quietly, he rode into the yard, behind the smoke-stack of a house. Black Ned gave a snarl when he found himself cornered between outhouse and wall, the only escape blocked by the borderer, whose advancing figure trembled and shimmered in the heat.

Too close to the burning house, the outlaw's stallion was frothing at the bit, its eyes reflecting the flames. Crozier's mare was calm under his hand, and the borderer urged her forward until he could lunge, his sword finding Black Ned's chest as the raider's frightened horse bucked and pranced, fighting its rider's steel grip on the reins. Armstrong's sword flailed as he tried to hold his beast steady, and a second strike knocked it out of his hand. Before Crozier could draw closer, Black Ned was off his horse, an axe held before him. He began to circle the mare, swinging his blade in an arc that made her snort and shy. A sneer had begun to spread over his face when his stallion, seeing its chance, charged past him, out of the yard. Its back hooves clipped him, pitching him against the smiddy walls, where the straw bonfire had become a furnace, melting the house beneath.

For a moment, caught in the fire's embrace, Black Ned could not move. Then, as the flames crawled over him, he staggered, shouting, out of their clutch, and found Crozier's sword at his neck. The borderer pressed him back into the blaze, step by step, and held him there as if on a spit. Fire clawed at the outlaw like a bear, and his flesh quivered as if he were made of wax. His face was misshapen with terror, his mouth slack, and his eyes clung to Crozier's. Then he began to scream. As his body started to twist and curl, engulfed in an orange tide, the borderer sank his blade home, and the screams were no more.

Crozier and the men returned to the keep that evening, grey-faced with ash. Several were brought home slumped over the backs of their horses, to be laid out under sheets in an outhouse, and buried early the next day. When Benoit, Tom and Adam dismounted they were giddy with fatigue. Once the last of the raiders had been dealt with, they had joined the rescue. Many cottages were nothing but a slump of burnt wood, the bodies that lay under them destroyed beyond recognition, and the smell of roasted flesh the only sign anyone had once lived there. The blacksmith's cremation was well under way when Tom and the others kicked the door in, found the family, and dragged them out, coughing as if they would never breathe easy again.

The priest's house, one of the first to be fired, was engulfed in flames. The clansmen stood back, smoke-blackened sweat pouring down their faces. If Father Walsh had been at home when the raiders arrived, he was now in the arms of Saint Peter. They crossed their breasts at the sight, and turned their backs to the inferno, to help those who were still alive. It was a week before they learned that the priest had been far away when the raid took place, visiting a monastery in the next dale. His reappearance amid the ruins was first taken as an angelic apparition, and then as proof that God had not utterly forsaken the village. In the keep, there was as much joy at the news as if he were their own kin.

By the time Crozier's men left, the village was a charred wasteland. That night, and for many to come, people would be sleeping in stables and barns. The dead were dragged to the square, arms folded over their chests. Dozens lay there, old and very young, as twilight mingled with the drifting smoke and a haze fell over the village, softening the sight of its desolation in a brief act of mercy.

At the keep, Crozier strode across the courtyard, Tom and Benoit at his heels. A deep cut on Benoit's face was oozing black blood, or so it looked in the fading light. 'Why the village?' he asked, wiping his cheek with a rag. 'They've done nobody any harm.'

'It was me they wanted revenge on,' said Crozier. 'Looked like they were Dacre's outlaw army – some of the bastards I caught had brands on their necks. Word must have got back to the baron that I helped bring about his disgrace, but without him at their side his men would never dare attack me here, in the keep.'

'Will they be back?' Benoit asked, fear undisguised.

Crozier shrugged. 'Their leader is dead, and the village ruined. What's left for them now?'

Tom coughed, smoke still burning his lungs. 'That sort's loyal to no one and nothing but money,' he wheezed. 'If Dacre's been dismissed, as they say, he won't be able to afford them much longer.' He glanced at his brother with a glimmer of awe. 'And it looks as if he's not coming back – or not as the man he was, thanks to you.' He slapped Crozier's shoulder and, arms round each other's necks, the three made their way into the keep.

Louise was sitting by the fire in the hall, hunched like an old woman. With Ella she had begun to tend the wounded, but the pains had grown so severe she could now do nothing but rock herself back and forth, arms wrapped around her stomach.

Crozier was at her side, and before she could speak, he had lifted her and carried her to their room. He reeked of smoke, his clothes were spattered with blood, but she clung to him as if she would never let go.

Laying her on their bed, he loosened her bodice, tugged off her boots and pulled a coverlet over her legs. Louise did not move, doing her best not to cry. What she had heard and glimpsed in the village that afternoon made her fears seem very small. When Crozier placed a concerned hand on her forehead a few tears fell, but they both pretended not to notice.

Ella fussed around as if Louise were her youngest child. She brought hot water, and rags, and pressed a bitter infusion of wintergreen into her hands. Crozier lit the fire, and its pine crackle kept them company through the unsleeping night, when waves of pain convulsed her, and she could barely breathe, able only to clutch her husband's hand.

'What if we lose this baby?' she whispered. 'I could not bear it. Nor could you.'

Crozier stroked the damp hair off her face. 'Hush yourself. We'll bear whatever we have to. We're strong, and we have each other.'

'I am a bad wife,' she sobbed. 'I have given you no child. If this little one should . . .'

Crozier's voice was unsteady. 'I did not marry you for children, but for yourself. And thank God I still have you.' He looked at her, frowning. 'I am not one for words, you know that. I expect you to read my thoughts. But you must also know I would never betray you. The way I behaved with Lady Foulberry was cruel, but not in the way you perhaps imagined. I have not dared to tell you everything, in case you would think of me with shame, or worse.'

Louise stared, frightened of what she was about to learn. Crozier turned away, unable to meet her eyes. 'I led her to believe I might be interested in her.' He stopped, as if that was explanation enough, but after a long pause he continued. 'With a treacherous pair like them I thought it necessary. I knew they would think nothing of betraying me if and when it suited them. Hinting at what could happen, I thought, was a way of inveigling myself and entrapping her. And maybe I was right. In fact, I'm sure of it. But what mortifies me is that I began to enjoy it. A woman like that, who thinks she can have whoever she likes at a flick of her fingers – she was not only easy but a pleasure to trick.' He looked at his wife, his face clouded with regret. 'Lou, she would have destroyed our happiness – anyone's – without a thought. I hoped I might inflict some damage on her marriage. Instead, I almost ruined ours.'

He gave a low, unhappy laugh. 'You wanted to meet her, but the very thought made me sick. You should not be in the same room as someone that conniving. And so I told her, at the end.' He shook his head, remembering the shrieks and hysterics, the pounding of fists on his chest in the French inn, where it had taken three servants and a tub of dishwater to dampen Isabella Foulberry's fury.

'I did not like the kind of man I had become – calculating and callous as the very people I despised. That was the worst of all. I felt unworthy of you.'

'So you and she – you were never tempted . . . You never, not even once . . .'

He closed his eyes for a moment. 'God forgive me, Lou, that you could even think such a thing. The lady Foulberry might make fools of most of the men she meets, but she could not make one of me. She is not an evil woman, perhaps, but she is vain, and wilful, and dangerous. Her manner is designed to capture hearts. Whereas you are lovely beyond anything she could dream of, and you do not even realise it.'

Louise covered her face to hide her tears. 'I thought you had grown to love me less,' she said, when eventually she could speak. 'I was so miserable.'

Crozier bent closer, speaking low and stern. 'I love you with all the love there is. You must never again doubt it.'

Putting a hand up to his face, Louise would have spoken, but the pains began once more, and this time they were followed by blood.

Dawn was breaking when at last the convulsions eased, the bleeding stopped, and Louise fell asleep. Crozier's arm was around her, his hand resting lightly on her skirt's swell, willing the restless life within to stay. Light seeped through the shutters, and the first birds began to stir. Holding his wife as if she were as fragile as the baby she carried, the borderer closed his eyes, but his mind filled with the image and sound of Black Ned dissolving into the flames and he quickly opened them again.

The taste of ash on his tongue suited his wretched thoughts. For the crimes he had committed over the years, the lies he had told, the men he had killed, he deserved to wear sackcloth for the rest of his life. Yet he did not believe he had been allowed any choice. A groan escaped him, as if he were wrangling with his conscience. There was an afterlife, he knew, but the comfort of knowing a better place awaited them did nothing to diminish the distress people had to suffer before reaching it. The Church preached patience and pity, but those words had no place in the borderlands, where safety lay in power alone.

His hand circled, as if to soothe his child, and he looked up at the beams above the bed. If it lived, please God this infant was a girl. A boy would not only fall heir to the misery of these lands, but would add to it, as had he. A life of suspicion, fear and violence was not what he would have chosen, nor the inheritance any father should pass on to a son. But what other way of existing was there if one wanted to survive, save for running away? And if this barely alive scrap of humanity was tenacious enough to be born, who was he to give up or fall into despair? Boy or girl, it would carry the family name, and bear some or all of its burden. Crozier could not promise a peaceful future, for he believed no such thing existed in this world. But he could raise his child to strive for better as, from now, would he.

London was dry as a withered leaf, and the dust his horse kicked up as he entered the city made Blackbird's throat tighten. He plodded through the filthy streets, head held high as if by raising his nose it might not be offended by the stench that rose from the gutters, the river, the dark-eyed urchins who clutched at his boots, whimpering for a coin.

Westminster broiled, its pallid stone and new-laid roofs reflecting the light as if to turn summer's glare back upon the sun. The yards and alleys around the abbey teemed, though with only the lower sort, the court and its hangers-on having decamped some weeks earlier to the countryside. Blackbird's horse clipped over the cobbles, weaving between packmen and beggars, merchants and whores, their clothes clinging to them in the heat, their cries half-hearted and dry. Despite the warmth, a shiver crawled up the butler's spine. This place unsettled him.

The Star Chamber did no business at the height of the summer. At this season, the cardinal would often be found in his Yorkshire diocese, keeping cool under northern skies, but pressing affairs of state had called him back to the capital, and Blackbird had learned he was to be found at Westminster Palace, its long corridors and tapestried rooms entirely at his disposal while his king was out of town.

Wolsey received the butler with ill grace. His face was hot with summer and the disagreeable diplomatic crisis he was obliged to avert on Henry's behalf. The king's reckless liaisons and desires were proving more troublesome than a monarch's usual dalliances, which harmed no one but the queen, and often not even her.

'Well?' he snapped, greeting Blackbird in the palace's entrance, and expecting him to talk as they walked through the grand hallway and down a narrow passage to the small, picture-lined room he had commandeered as his own. Blackbird made no comment until they were closeted alone. 'Well?' the cardinal asked again, before noticing the grime on Blackbird's jacket and grudgingly pouring him a mug of warm ale. The butler drank greedily, and slapped the tankard down.

'As I informed you in my message,' he said, his voice deepened by dust, 'the baron and I have come by information we think relevant to his captivity, and the undue length of time you've been holding him.'

'So you indicated,' said Wolsey testily. He closed his eyes for a moment, appearing to will himself into a state of patience. Casting a thin smile on the butler, he refilled the northerner's tankard before settling himself on a small stool that was completely lost under his skirts, so that it appeared it had been ingested, and he was merely squatting. 'I am agog to know what it is you have to say to me.'

'Ah, now, your eminence,' said Blackbird, after the second pint pot was emptied, 'it is not as simple as that.' He flashed the cardinal a glimpse of stained, flagstone teeth, but there was nothing friendly about his smile. 'It has come to the baron's notice that certain affairs of state have been conducted beneath the king's nose, which he feels his majesty should learn about. I could not divulge these affairs to you without first being sure that you will present them to his highness or, at the very least, use them to order the baron's immediate release and reinstatement.'

'Indeed?' Wolsey seemed in no way put out by this disclosure. 'I will not ask what this sensitive information consists of. Not yet, anyway.'

Blackbird pulled out a cloth and mopped his forehead and neck. 'Devil of a journey, these past few days,' he said conversationally. 'Sun almost stewed me in my own juices.'

Wolsey glanced at the butler's stained hose and limp shirt sleeves, but said nothing. Untroubled, Blackbird continued. 'I have just this minute come from the Fleet, which, I might tell you, stinks worse than the Thames itself. I speak with his lordship's authority when I tell you that he wants you to attend upon him this very day, to settle the matter. Should you fail to do so, he will have no alternative but to instruct me to take this information and lay it before Henry himself.'

'But, my dear man, until I find out what this is all about, I am working in the dark. My jumping at the baron's command might prove a waste of all our time. Perhaps he is entirely right to want whatever news he possesses placed before Henry, rather than me. I might myself advise that, if I were clear what this relates to. Otherwise, as it stands, at the moment . . .' He spread his hands and shrugged, indicating helplessness.

Blackbird's genial air faded. He walked to the window and looked out upon the river, its lazy waters dimmed by the thick bottle glass, yet bright enough still to set spangles dancing on the chamber's walls. He spoke as if to the ferrymen. 'Believe me, your eminence, that is not a course you want to take. It would be most injurious to your health. It is of little concern to Dacre which of you he informs. His life is already ruined, and he does not believe he has long to live. But in only one scenario do you continue to retain King Henry's regard. I think you must by now have an inkling of what I am referring to.'

The cardinal put his hands on his knees and examined his rings. He sounded weary. 'Very well, though the cloak of mystery you and your master relish throwing over everything is tiresome. But since I owe Dacre a visit in any case, I will pass by the prison this evening.'

'You will be heartily glad you have done so,' replied Blackbird, facing him once more. 'Your neglect of him has been shameful, and you a man of God. If this is the justice meted out to peers of the realm, heaven help the little man. No wonder so many of them take the law into their own hands.'

'Do not push me too far,' said the cardinal, rising from his stool to plant himself before the butler. His voice shook with fury. 'You are nothing more than a peasant with puffed-up airs, but you fool nobody. Like your master, you have low manners and even lower morals. I will not be given orders by the likes of you. Whatever it is you think you can threaten me with, it is as nothing – trust me – to what I could level against you in retaliation, were I of a vindictive disposition. Happily for you, I am neither cruel nor unjust. It would be beneath my dignity to stamp on a worm like you, simple – and amusing – though it would be.'

Blackbird laughed as he turned to leave. 'Worms, your eminence, are all part of God's good creation. They have their rightful place. My master knows only too well that it is as necessary to deal with low-life as with the high-born. He tells me that at the end, it is impossible to tell them apart. They all beg for mercy. They all bleed. They all disappear from the face of the earth like—' He slapped dust from his gloves, and left the room, the motes of traveller's grime dancing on the sunlit air, as if his words had taken shape.

For a second time, Dacre was led up to the small chamber in the prison where Wolsey was waiting. The baron shuffled into the room, his chained wrists were freed, and the guard took up his poker stance by the wall. 'Be gone, man,' said the cardinal, waving the guard off. 'Close the door and wait outside.'

He indicated that Dacre should take a seat and, lowering himself, unsteadily, the baron did so. Wolsey examined him from beneath hooded lids, shocked at the change in him. The broad, commanding figure was now slack and bent. The pulp of a paunch still rolled under his belt but the baron's shanks were bony, his face sunken, his hair, beneath its black woollen cap, now a wintry white.

'So you found time to see me, eh?' said Dacre softly.

'You bade me present myself,' replied Wolsey. 'And, as befits a good friend, here I am.'

'Friend?' The word fell between them and lay, broken, on the earthen floor. Dacre shook his head, and looked out of the window, for a second seeming to forget why he was here. The sky was darkening, but he lingered on the sight, the view of ivied wall his first glimpse of the outdoors in a month. He began to rise for a closer look, then remembered the fatigue that any exertion brought on and sat back down. He swivelled his head towards the cardinal. 'Blackbird did his work well, to get you here so fast. Scared the life out of ye, I expect.'

Wolsey leaned forward, and spoke in a tone whose anger was

molten. 'Enough of this posturing. Tell me what you think you know, and then we can talk.'

'I do not think it,' said Dacre. 'I have proof that you have been told of my negotiations and association with the king's sister. That you had the means to send me to the gallows, and yet kept silent. Friendship the reason for that?' he scoffed. 'I think not, eh? You leave me to languish here for a six-month, without a word, yet you save my skin by keeping these letters to yourself. Why would that be, I wondered. Why, of course!' He slapped his knee. 'They would alert Henry to the fact that you do not have control of the country and his council, as you assure him you do. That, on the contrary, your authority is not just incomplete, but blind. You have been caught out. Because of you, England was for a spell a more dangerous place.'

He cackled, and wiped spittle from the corner of his mouth with a shaking hand. 'Not something he would wish to learn about his Lord Chancellor, I would have thought.'

Wolsey was motionless, his face rigid.

'So then,' Dacre continued, 'I began to consider what I have to lose by telling Henry all about your negligence. Me, I am already as good as a dead man. And at least I have a purseful of memories to keep my old bones warm. Margaret Tudor is but one of them. Whether I go to meet my maker in this noxious prison, or on the scaffold, or at home in the north, I doubt I have long to live. I might as well leave this world safe in the knowledge that I have caused your utter ruin, as you have brought about mine.' Again he laughed, like an old wheezing bellows, his mirth turning into a rich, hacking cough.

The cardinal, knowing the worst, leaned back against the wall. He too looked to the window. A sigh parted his lips, before he gathered his thoughts. 'Your incarceration has led to feverish thoughts, my lord. Your head is addled, you are not thinking straight. I would never withhold information his majesty should know, not to benefit you, nor myself, nor anyone else in the kingdom. I do not think like that. I believe in transparency, in the prevailing power of the truth, as you should be well aware by now.'

He eyed the baron. 'But what you tell me is troubling. You have been a fool, and perhaps something worse than that.' Turning his gaze to the window, as if he could not bear the sight of him, he shook his head. 'Whatever the truth of this business, Thomas, I find your apathy about your own mortality a cause for pity. You seem almost to wish yourself upon the gallows. Is that truly because of the treachery you claim to have committed with the old queen? Or is it, I wonder, guilt over a lifetime's dirty work?'

Dacre said nothing, but rubbed his leg while he waited for Wolsey to finish.

The cardinal was silent for a minute, contemplating the sliver of sky visible from the room. When he turned to face the baron, he sounded brisker. 'Had your case been brought before the Star Chamber when you were a younger man, you would have been outlawed, or dead, many years ago. I have been your great supporter, your mainstay at court, yet you think to repay me by attempting, in the most underhand manner, to destroy me.' He silenced Dacre's reply with a stern finger. 'Enough. You can believe whatever it is you choose. I know the truth, and it pains me. My conscience is completely clear. Even so, I understand your tactics. I almost, I confess, admire them. You think you have outflanked me, and maybe you have. Be that as it may, whatever the facts, and regardless of your venom towards me, I will bring your situation before Henry, and urge clemency, with the greatest possible haste.'

His voice dropped, and he leaned forward. 'Truth to tell, Thomas, I have been uneasy about the term of your incarceration. You may not consider me a friend, but that is what I have been to you. As you yourself indicate, you are an ailing man. To look at you is to know you are right. Your time is measured, no matter who holds the clock.' He cast the baron a glance that held a morsel of charity. 'I do not wish you to die here. Nobody should, and most certainly not a loyal servant of the crown who has given many years of excellent service, regardless of his indiscretions.'

Getting to his feet, he put a hand on the baron's shoulder. 'When the business I am attending to this week has been dealt with, I shall make it my duty to see the king, and press for your release. It should not be difficult to secure. His majesty has been hinting of late that your penitential period is drawing to a close.'

'And have my title as Keeper of Carlisle restored?'

'I shall see what I can do. It's most likely, I should think, since Henry has appointed his son as Warden General. But if he cavils, that surely is of no great concern? What you most desire is a peaceful life, is it not?'

Dacre nodded. 'I would keep that title, if I could, so my return is not one of absolute disgrace. But no, if I go back as the plain baron I am, so be it. I will at least be home.'

Wolsey rose at dawn the next morning to complete his diplomatic correspondence, hoping his assurances would dampen the rage that was beginning to gather over the continent like thickening clouds over England's clear skies. That delicate task completed, he retired to his chamber, shutters drawn and a cold cloth on his brow. The following day, calling a ferry to the crumbling pier, he set out for Greenwich Palace. Beneath the rising sun and his velvet cloak, he sweltered, but his physical discomfort was as nothing to the lather of panic created by Dacre's discovery.

His fear was well hidden when he found the king, knocking a ball with a mallet in the walled garden, his queen and her maids cooing and clapping as if he were leading a joust. Henry's face glistened in the late morning sun as he acknowledged the Lord Chancellor with a wave, before continuing to tap the ball between the hoops, bowing extravagantly as his entourage applauded and cheered.

When he had chased the ball to the end of the lawn, he handed his mallet to a footman and sauntered over to Wolsey, who smiled as if he had come all this way merely to witness a scene of summer games. The cardinal bent his knee. 'Your majesty.'

'Walk with me,' Henry replied. They left the walled garden by a narrow door and entered another, prettily laid with flowerbeds and box hedges, sweet with the scent of espaliered pears. Their shoes crunched on gravel. 'So you have sent those letters?' The cardinal affirmed that he had. 'Very good.' Henry wiped his damp hands on his silken britches. 'Yet was there a problem with them that you are here to discuss?'

Wolsey looked grave. 'No, your highness. It is an altogether less important matter that brings me here, but one I feel we should settle sooner rather than not.'

Around the path they walked, as Wolsey told him of his fear that Dacre would soon die, and that if he did so in their custody it might prove awkward.

'So this is a mercy call?'

'Indeed,' the cardinal replied, steepling his hands as a reminder that his first position, his main obligation, was to his holy superior in Rome.

'How long have we been holding him?'

'Six months or more. The gaoler says he has suffered two fits in that time, one where they feared they had lost him.'

Henry rubbed his beard, releasing the scent of sandalwood. He did not speak as twice more they patrolled the garden. Eventually he stopped and faced the cardinal, his chest puffed out like a pigeon's. 'We will agree to this,' he said, 'but not for reasons of pity, nor because Dacre has any claim on our good nature. He lost that right when we found him guilty of corruption and collusion. Were we less lenient, he would now be dead.

'But we will release him, for the simple reason that it seems his presence keeps the border quiet. Or less unquiet. With his return, our young Henry's position as Warden General will be made less irksome, and I will not have to worry constantly about the state of the marches. Whereas at the moment—' He clicked his tongue in vexation. 'As it stands, every day seems to bring bad news from that quarter. Would that we could set our army loose on it, and knock sense into people's heads.'

The cardinal smiled. 'A nice thought, your majesty, but likely only to aggravate matters in the long run.'

Henry sighed. 'You may be right. For a man of scripture and codices, you are most worldly and sage.'

Wolsey bowed.

'So, then,' the king continued, 'you can tell perfidious Dacre he will be set free, but only on certain conditions.' His eyes grew small as he counted out his terms on his fingers. 'One: he is stripped of all office, not only as warden of the west but as Keeper of Carlisle. Two: we will fine him handsomely for his misdemeanours, in the form of a tithe, to be taken each year at Michaelmas. Three: he will repay with his own money those whose compensation at his courts remains outstanding. And four: if we hear of a single instance of retribution or malice against those who testified against him, he will be dragged back to the Fleet in chains.'

He paused, eyelashes fluttering as he searched his mind for more. 'Ah, yes, of course.' He smiled. 'Please inform him he must also return to Berwick to lend his aid in the negotiations for the final settlement of peace with Scotland, under Norfolk's command. His presence will speed matters.'

When he was sure there was nothing more to be added, the cardinal repeated the orders. Hearing the depths of the baron's disgrace recited back to him, Henry beamed with satisfaction.

'Come,' he said, taking the cardinal's sleeve, and guiding him towards the lawn. 'Join our game, and stay for the night. Your usual room will be made ready.'

'With pleasure,' Wolsey replied, sounding as if he meant it.

Dacre left the Fleet on Blackbird's arm. He barely seemed to notice when the prison doors closed behind him, and London took him in its hold. Head hanging, his feet all but dragging, he shuffled down the street. 'We're just round the next corner,' Blackbird said, as if to encourage him onwards.

When the sign for his inn came into view, Dacre raised his eyes, and his step grew firmer. 'What sort of midden is this ye've been living in?' he asked.

'The kind I could afford,' the butler replied. 'I have had a room set aside for you, for as long as you like. Perfectly clean, it is.'

'One night only,' Dacre growled, gripping his arm. 'Soon as I'm on the road north, I'll be back to my old self.'

It took longer than that, but as they plodded out of London on a pair of wind-broken old horses, some colour returned to the baron's cheeks. He let the reins lie slack, and raised his face to the sun, tears running off his chin. Whether they were of weakness, relief, or misery at what he had endured, Blackbird could not tell. Nor, perhaps, could his master, who did not wipe them away, but let them flow unchecked. The butler watched him anxiously, keeping their pace as slow as if they were in a state procession. That Dacre did not complain at the dolorous speed was itself disturbing. It almost seemed as if he noticed nothing except what was in his head. Sleeping where Blackbird told him, eating a little of what was placed before him, saying barely a word except to mutter to himself, he was like a man in a trance, under a spell that refused to loosen its hold.

Not until they reached the high west country did his strength begin to return. His appetite grew with the fresher September air and the scent of open hills. His seat in the saddle straightened and by the time they reached Cumberland he was riding as he always had, hand steady, grip firm, urging his horse on at a soldier's clip. As the miles were eaten up, he brightened at the sight of woodland and wide skies, and the sound of the birdsong he had so badly missed.

A day or two later, he rediscovered his voice, and with his new-found words the last lingering touch of the Fleet was sloughed off. 'By God, Blackbird,' he said one night, as they sat in a tavern over their beer, 'I thought that cell would be my crypt. They had forgotten about me, hadn't they?' His butler's look was blank, though in his heart he agreed. 'I could have mouldered there till I was bones for all they cared. Wolsey pretended the king was considering my release, but that was a lie. Fear made him charm the king into changing his mind, of that I have no doubt. But it was you, my good man, who saved my life, you and your bloodhound search.'

The baron shook his head as he sipped his drink. 'Never expected to be set loose, but here I am, feeling alive for the first time in months, and raring to get back to Naworth and set my lands in order. By God, I will make the most of it now. No more politicking. No more bargaining. Just simple good living, in God's own good country.'

Blackbird smiled, the sight of his master's pleasure as enjoyable as feeling it himself.

'Never thought I'd say it,' Dacre continued, 'but that priest made me think. I'm no candidate for a saint – it's far too late for that – but I know now where my allegiance lies, and where honour's due. Old dog that I am, I can still give that much. And I'll tell you this for nothing.' He lowered his voice, the tankard trembling in his hand. 'I'll never again bend my knee to our king, not if I'm at swordpoint. God willing I will not set eyes on him or the pox-faced Wolsey this side of the pearly gates.'

He raised his tankard, Blackbird lifted his, and they swallowed down the last of their pint, their cheap beer tasting, that night, as sweet as nectar.

As they neared Naworth the following day, the baron's tears returned. Elms hung over the road, dripping in the rain, and the baron's wet face went unnoticed as they trotted the last few miles through a gusty squall. Head down against the weather, Dacre breathed deep, the scent of wet earth and harvested fields setting his pulse kicking like a young man's.

At the castle gates, the guardsmen sounded their horns and the place burst open, servants hurrying to usher them home. Joan stood at the doors, almost hopping with excitement. Her tears matched her father's as she clung to him, and neither had the power to speak.

'Welcome home, brother,' said Sir Christopher, stepping forward when it seemed their embrace would last forever. Sir Philip was at his shoulder, bowing low.

Dacre clasped Christopher's arm, and nodded, but his mouth was slack, and his hand shaking. Christopher slapped an arm round his back and, exchanging a look with Philip, hurried him into the hall. 'We can talk over dinner,' he said. 'Plenty of time for that. But first you must rest.'

Blackbird led the baron to his room and settled his master, who was already dozing, fully clothed, before he had unpacked his bag. The room was airless and stale, warmed by a roaring fire, and Blackbird opened the window. A Cumberland draught tickled the canopy over the baron's bed, and he thought he saw a smile on Dacre's lips as the air reached him, and he turned on his side, sinking into a gentle, dreamless sleep.

His brothers stationed themselves at Naworth for the autumn. Nothing was said, but it was understood that they would stay until the baron had fully regained his health. Joan fussed over her father, but Christopher and Philip were equally solicitous. Were he a less impatient man, Dacre would have smiled to see their mothering. Instead, he growled and barked and challenged them to cosset him, if they dared. That office was granted only to Joan and to Blackbird, and even the butler was occasionally nipped on the ankle as he went about this risky business.

The baron was, however, recovering. His gait was still that of a man who had been confined so long that his back was stooped like a willow, but his figure was gaining strength, his face once more ruddy, and his step full of vigour. 'You are stronger, even now, than most men the age of your sons,' Joan said one evening, as they sat alone in the hall by the fireside.

'We come from a good line,' Dacre replied, leaving his goblet half drunk. Wine did not agree with him so well now, nor did he need it to fall into sleep. The devils had taken flight, and for that alone he ought to be grateful for his days in the Fleet. He missed the dockside priest, but the wisdom he had offered had been committed to memory, never to be forgotten. Back at Naworth, Dacre summoned the local priest for a twice-weekly mass, to the surprise of all at the castle. In no other regard did he appear devout, but his daughter could not miss the cross he wore round his neck and kissed before he headed up the stairs to bed.

'Have we always been noble?' Joan asked. 'Doesn't each family start from humble beginnings? Were we not once commoners, peasants, or worse?'

Dacre surprised her by laughing. 'Worse we've been, that's for sure. And peasants too. Of course. Name the Englishman whose ancestors did not at one time doff their caps and pull a plough. That's why our stock is so strong. There has not been time for us to weaken the blood with the effete or sickly rich. But, my girl,' he said, suddenly serious, 'since you are so interested in the family, it is time to talk of you. I have promised Mabel that come Candlemas you will stay with her, and learn the ways of court. It is my dearest wish that you be happily and safely settled before next year is out.'

Joan looked at him, pale even in the firelight, her eyes filling with tears.

Her father frowned. 'What makes you cry? Do you not wish to be married, and have your own house, and children? You know you cannot stay forever by my side, living more like a boy than a maid.'

Joan attempted a smile. 'It is that I dislike hearing you talk this way. It sounds as if you are settling all your affairs before leaving this life. I cannot bear that thought.'

Dacre tutted. 'Don't be ridiculous. I am not planning to die before my time. But I would be foolish if I did not secure your future while I can, so I would. If I were many years younger and in the best of health I would still think ye must soon find a husband. You are no longer a child but a young woman, and now that our country is at peace, with France as well as Scotland, the court will be in a mood for matches. How long such tranquillity will continue, God only knows. With Henry at the helm, I doubt it will last long.'

Joan wiped her cheeks, and bent to stroke the hound at her feet. 'I am quite willing and ready to marry,' she said, then gave a sob, and fled the room. Dacre looked after her, concern hardening his face. The girl's volatility was all his fault, for spoiling her and letting her have her own way, an indulgence her sisters had never enjoyed – and how settled and happy they both now were. After long contemplation of the fire, he decided he would send her to Mabel before Christmas, rather than after.

The next morning he informed her of his decision. Joan turned linen white and sat suddenly, as if she had been chopped behind the knees. Losing patience, Dacre grew angry, berating her for being selfish, childish and foolish. She nodded, head lowered, the colour slowly returning to her cheeks. By the time he had finished, her face was flushed. 'I am sorry for being such a disappointment to you,' she whispered. 'I will marry, I assure you. And I will rejoice to do so. Just do not shout at me, I beg.' And again she ran from the room, weeping into her hands.

CHAPTER FORTY-FOUR

October 1525

Benoit rode fast up the track to the keep, urging his horse on. The village was slowly being rebuilt, and by the end of each day he and his assistants were exhausted. At dusk he returned to the keep sore-armed and coated in sawdust. Normally he plodded home, letting the aches settle, and planning the next day's work as he went. Today, though, he was in a hurry. His saddlebag clattered with tools, and as his horse cantered the pack dug into its flanks like a goad. Snorting, it quickened to a gallop, nearly throwing the carpenter off. 'Whoa!' cried Benoit, hunched over its neck, but it was too late. The keep's walls were within sight, and so was the stable, and his mount wanted only to be rid of its burden.

Clattering into the yard, the beast came to a stamping halt. Throwing the reins to Hob, Benoit ran into the keep. Louise looked up from the table, where she sat with Old Crozier. 'Where's Crozier?' Benoit panted. Disturbed by his haste, Louise began to get up. 'Naw,' he said, gesturing to her to stay seated. 'It's nothing bad. Just some news he ought to hear.'

'He is up the hill,' said Old Crozier. 'You'll find him at the northern watchtower.'

'What sort of news?' asked Louise, sinking heavily back onto the bench. Though there was more than a month before her baby was due, she was already weighed down. Seen from behind, she was the slender girl she had always been. Viewed sideways, she was a keg. 'Another like Benoit in there?' Ella would tease, though by now her husband was almost as lean as he had been as a youth.

'I've heard news of Oliver Barton,' said Benoit, 'our snake of a cousin.'

Louise's mouth tightened. Barton had brought trouble, as they had feared, and even with him gone his presence could still be felt, as if he were wishing them ill from afar – but not far enough.

Crozier's face took on the same tense expression when he returned. As the hall filled for dinner, and the table was laid with food, he and Benoit stood by the fire. 'It was yin o' the pledges that saw him, or so he says,' the carpenter said quietly. Crozier listened, head bent as if the rushes on the floor needed his attention.

With the peace with England at last arranged, the pledges on both sides of the border had been released. Those who had been held prisoner in castles and houses said goodbye to their polite keepers and their families, more as if they had been on a sociable visit than under threat of execution; those locked in gaols and towers spat their farewells, and had no gracious word for their guards. In the more remote gaols, however, where rules had been relaxed, the pledges had been allowed to roam by day, returning to be incarcerated at night, like sheep to the pen before dark. At such prisons, there were handshakes at parting, and promises of enduring goodwill.

Whatever the conditions in which they had been kept that summer, all the pledges made their way home unscathed, the ties between them and the enemy strangely strengthened by their ordeal. It was one such, held in the Bishop of Carlisle's outhouse, who brought news of Barton.

'Jardine remembered him well,' Benoit told Crozier. The young lord from Kelso, whose father Samuel was one of Crozier's allies, was an occasional visitor at the keep. Exchanged for one of the Percy heirs, he had been allowed his liberty once a week, if accompanied by a brace of guards. From his prison windows he had seen Barton among Dacre's soldiers in the bishop's yard. On one of his outings into the town, he swore he had seen the sailor leaving a tavern in the high street. The man was half blind with drink, but when Jardine shouted his name he had looked round before scuttling into the next tavern, like a rat with a terrier on its tail.

'Jardine wis on his way here to tell you himsel,' said Benoit. 'He didnae ken Barton had left us, but he kent fine what had happened to the village. A'body across the marches had heard. It wis his belief that Barton must've been involved in that.'

'Mine too,' said Crozier. 'I always suspected it. Now it's clear the man was Dacre's agent, sent here as a spy. And not just a tale-teller. He was plotting with Dacre to bring us down.' He looked at Benoit with an air of lassitude that meant he was about to act. 'How long ago was this sighting?'

'A couple of weeks, just afore Jardine's release. They also say he has been making himsel at hame at Naworth while Dacre's been gone. A bit too cosy wi the baron's daughter for some folks's comfort, by all accounts.'

A glimmer of hate crossed the borderer's face. 'I will find the felon, and I will kill him. It can't undo what happened to the village, but we will be avenged. And we'll all be safer for it.'

'I'll come with ye,' said Benoit, putting a hand to his sword.

Crozier shook his head. 'No. I must go alone. The keep will be in your and Tom's care. As will Louise. Her time is not yet near, but I must not have her unprotected.'

Benoit nodded. 'We'll take guid care of her, I swear.'

From the table, Louise had watched their conversation. 'What is it?' she asked as Crozier led her aside.

As he explained what he intended to do, she grew distressed, but Adam's decision had been made, and Louise knew she could not – perhaps should not – try to change his mind.

'But what if the baby arrives . . .' she asked pitifully.

'Lou, you still have some time to go, and I will not be away long. Two weeks, possibly less. If I cannot find him in that time, I will return, I promise. But I need to do this. Who knows how else he will try to destroy us if I don't deal with him now? He may soon leave the country, and my chance of finding him will be gone.'

'And what if . . .'

'What?' Crozier almost smiled. 'What if he kills me? It's not likely, is it?' He took her hands in his. 'Come, love. You have nothing to fear. I will be back, and the baby will be born safely after that. And with Barton dead, the world will be a little less dangerous.'

She looked at him, and eventually she sighed. 'I know you have to do this. But I am not as brave as I used to be. There's too much to lose. If anything happened to you . . .'

'It won't.'

'You can't promise me that,' she said. 'Nobody can know what will happen.'

'No,' he replied, taking her into his arms, 'but we both know it is probably true. And that has to be good enough.'

She held him tight, her cheek pressed against his chest, where his heart beat slow and strong. Unheard, the echoing beat that lay between them squeezed quick and quiet.

CHAPTER FORTY-FIVE

10 October 1525

To the roar of the German Sea beyond the windows, a truce was arranged with Scotland. Seated in Berwick Castle, speaking loud so all around the table could hear above the screaming wind, the emissaries of Henry VIII and James V agreed to a three-year settlement. The treaty was signed, the Scottish nobles watching tight-lipped as their erstwhile enemy set their names alongside their own. When the ink was dry, the grey-cloaked Scots stepped forward to shake the Duke of Norfolk's and Baron Dacre's hands.

There was a grudging few minutes of talk. 'Peace for our countries, and less turbulent times at the palace of Holyrood too, or so we pray,' said the Duke of Argyll, a chapped smile warming his weather-beaten face as he pulled on his gauntlets. 'The young king's guardians are no longer at each other's throats. They've agreed to share his supervision, taking it in turns. So we can hope the squabbling between the dowager queen and her former husband will now be a thing of the past. After all, if two nations such as ours can arrange peaceful terms, surely she and Angus, who once shared a bed, can do likewise?'

Norfolk cackled. 'There's no worse foe than a former love, didn't you know? I wish you and your parliament safe passage until James comes to the throne.' He did not add that, from what he had seen of the Earl of Angus, every sea he crossed grew as turbulent as his temper. He cast a glance at the baron, who remained impassive. One would have thought the name of Margaret, and reminder of her amours, meant nothing to him.

There was more desultory conversation before the Scots cast anxious glances at the storm-blown windows, and after a flurry of unctuous bows the room emptied.

In his room in the west wing of the castle, Norfolk threw off his cloak. Dacre pulled his closer and rubbed his hands, taking a seat by a parsimonious fire. For a moment neither spoke. The past week had been gruelling, messages relayed from the courts on both sides of the border, delays, doubts and last-minute conditions whirling over the negotiators' heads as loud and furious as the gulls above Berwick beach.

'Well,' said Norfolk eventually, 'we did it.'

'Aye,' replied Dacre heavily. 'It's been a good day's work.' He lifted his head, and looked at the duke. 'Of course, we shouldn't have been at war in the first place. It was all a parade, a waste of everybody's time, and too many lives.'

Norfolk raised his eyebrows. 'You sound disaffected, my lord. Still smarting from your time in the Fleet?'

'Ye might say,' said Dacre. 'But tired also of the tricks at court – the Scots being every bit as bad as we are, and maybe worse. But we are all cuckoos when it comes to the keys of power. All feathering our nests at the expense of others, getting rid of our rivals. Even friends are stamped on as we make our way higher, richer, nearer not to God but to the golden apple, which none of us ever reaches.'

Norfolk frowned, and turned away, to hide his consternation. 'Are you referring to the lord the king has appointed to the wardenship of the west march? He is a good man, from what I have heard. He will do the job well enough.'

A snort from the fireside confirmed his guess.

'And what about the keepership of Carlisle?' Norfolk persisted. 'I hear you have refused to hand over the keys of the city, though your post has been removed.'

Dacre's growl was almost a purr. 'They can come and get those keys off me, if they dare. Hah! Whelps, the lot of them. Frightened by an old man, are they? Then they don't deserve to have them.'

His eyes met the duke's, red-rimmed and rheumy. 'The people of Carlisle do not want Henry Clifford. Earl of Cumberland he may be, and a decent soldier, but he knows not the first thing about the city. Whereas I know everything there is to tell about it. It is my home town, my heartland.'

Hearing the rising note in his own voice, he raised a hand to stem his mounting anger, and sighed. 'To give back the keys would be like hanging up my boots. That's about the size of it. It's a question of pride. Not that I have much of that left. My name is in tatters, my fortune too.' He stared into the sluggish flames. 'Not that I care for that any longer. I have enough to settle on my youngest daughter to make a good marriage, and old, widowered chiel that I am, that is all that matters.'

'Come, my man,' said the duke. 'What sort of talk is this? You have just helped secure peace for our kingdom. Henry will richly reward both of us. And there is much life left for you beyond being Warden General and Keeper of Carlisle. In your position, and at your age, many men would rejoice to be given their liberty at last.'

'For many years I have been doing the work of many men, your grace, which has been my undoing.'

'Nonsense. You are speaking like a man who needs his dinner. We will eat, and then things will look brighter. You and your servants can set out early tomorrow, and you'll be back in your lands, with your family, before the week is out. The melancholia of your time in the Fleet has not yet left you, I can see, but it will, I promise you.'

Dacre looked unconvinced, but he summoned a livelier expression, and took the tumbler of wine the Duke held out to him. 'To better days,' he said, as they drank, 'however few there may be.'

By morning the storm had washed itself out, and the eastern march lay docile, the sky a weary grey, the land resting and bruised after its whipping. Dacre and his guards made good time as they headed west, and the baron's mood began to lift. There was truth in what Norfolk had said. Why was he fuming at his dismissal, when for years he had been begging to be released from his yoke? Aye, said another voice, that's as may be, but ye wanted to remain as Keeper of Carlisle. But ye are not fit for that, argued the first voice. You're a spent force, a wind-broken horse. Let a younger man do the task. Give up with good grace, and be glad of what ye have. Dacre muttered in reply, but after a few miles the argument petered out, and he allowed himself to enjoy the journey, and the beguiling sight of the trees and hills, their gold and orange fading to chestnut as winter beckoned.

Two nights later, they reached Naworth. Dacre pulled up as they crested the moorland hills and looked down across the dale, where, far in the distance, the castle nestled. Even from here its magnificence was plain. The best-fortified castle in the region, it was also the best maintained. Fields and woods and villages spread out under its shadow, a small country of which he was king. It was enough, surely?

The baron turned to his guards. 'Ye can go ahead, back to the castle,' he said. 'Since I am here I will make an inspection of the eastern boundary. Tell Blackbird I will be home before nightfall.' The guards saluted and rode off, soon out of sight in the thickets below. Alone, the baron looked to the clouds. A damp wind tossed his horse's mane and freshened his cheek. He turned his face into its breath, and closed his eyes, the westerly's buffeting firm and friendly as his nurse's hand when he was a child, and she was soaping him under the pump. Opening his eyes, the baron shook off sentimental thoughts, spurred his horse into a trot, and made his way off the hills.

CHAPTER FORTY-SIX

Little was made of Crozier's departure. Louise and he said goodbye in their chamber, where she stayed as he saddled his horse and left. Ella found she needed Louise's help in the kitchens, and the rest of the day passed in chores. Only at night, as she lay in their room, the bed half cold, did she think of what might happen. Crozier was the stronger, but Barton had a cunning her husband could not match, and he might not be alone when they met. Eyes wide in the peaceful night, Louise wished the wind would blow and the rain lash, to match her troubled mood. But the woods were quiet, and the skies clear, and the only sound that kept her company was a fox's bark, far up the hill.

Many miles over the border, Crozier lay by his horse, wrapped in a blanket, sleeping lightly. As soon as day began to chase off the dark, he was on his way, he and his mare a dark arrow flying across the moors.

By nightfall he had reached Naworth. The mare needed rest, as did he, and leading her quietly through the woodland that circled the castle he found a hiding place, on a small rise, where he could settle until dawn. Leaning against a tree, hat over his eyes, he dozed. The mare cocked her fetlock, and her breathing grew slow and deep. A badger snuffled past, giving them a wide berth, but they heard nothing. Overhead, a murmur of leaves soothed them in their slumber, and when voices woke them it was already morning. Soldiers were rising, shouting orders, and scurrying across the castle courtyard to their tasks.

Creeping through the trees for a better view, Crozier saw there was no way he could get through the gates without being seen. The place was like a fortress, the entrance under guard, the walls ten feet thick. The rest of the morning he spent watching the castle going about its business, servants criss-crossing the yard, soldiers riding out in a posse, a stern-faced captain at their head. It would appear that Dacre was not at home. Nor was there any sign of Barton, though who could tell how many of Dacre's pack were hiding out in their quarters.

With the soldiers' departure, the place fell quiet. By late afternoon, none but house servants was around. Crozier bit his lip. Should he bluster his way into the castle, or find a way to creep in at night? Slipping off back through the woods, he made his way to the village. It was dusk when he entered the tavern, a richly appointed wooden-beamed inn whose prosperous air suggested it was patronised by those who had regular pay. Dacre's soldiers would come here, he guessed, and the baron himself, no doubt.

At this hour the place was busy, but the landlord noted his arrival, and watched him approach the counter. 'From over the border, are ye?' he enquired, as Crozier asked for beer.

The borderer nodded. 'Business will be picking up again, now we're almost at peace again,' he said.

The landlord looked sour. 'Will any truce last? I doubt it.' He put down the brimming tankard and took Crozier's Scottish coin, holding it up against the torchlight. Crozier raised an eyebrow, but said nothing. Propped against the counter, he took a long draught, then, looking around him as if hoping none would hear, leaned forward. 'I'm looking for work,' he said. 'Maybe you can help.' Continuing, though the landlord had begun to protest he could be of no assistance, he lowered his voice. 'I think a cousin of mine is up at the castle. Name of Barton. Hank of tied hair, and a brand on his neck . . .'

'Oh aye,' replied the landlord, his lips compressing. 'You're another of that sort, are ye? You have the look right enough. Well, you might be out of luck. That's his post there.' He pointed to the end of the bar. 'Used to come in every night of the week. But I haven't seen him for a while. Unless he's dead, or in prison – and both are likely, if you ask me – he has gone.'

Crozier drank, to hide his disappointment. 'Any idea where?'

'How would I know?' The landlord wiped the counter, and turned to another customer. When he had served him, he came back. 'I suppose you could ask that man over there.'

He indicated a tall, lank soldier, who had just entered and was hanging his tan leather cloak on a peg by the door, To this he added his wide-brimmed hat, so it looked as if there had been an execution, the body suspended as a warning to all. When the man reached the counter his drink was already waiting, and Crozier recognised one who was used to command. This was no foot soldier, but no doubt the captain of Dacre's patrol.

The borderer edged closer, ordered another beer, and from beneath his hat looked the soldier over. The face was ungiving, plain features distinguished only by a purpling nose and red-veined cheeks. He drank as if his throat were a sluice. When the first pangs of thirst appeared to have been assuaged, Crozier struck up conversation, if the man's one-word answers qualified as that. As his mug was refilled, so fast it might have sprung a leak, Crozier mentioned Barton's name. The man paused, his drink halfway to his lips. 'Barton, ye say? What's yer interest in him?'

'He's my wife's cousin,' Crozier replied. 'I was hoping he could help me find work.'

'God knows what Dacre's thinking, employing scum like him. But he's left, praise the saints. Disappeared last week, along with one of the scullery maids. Poor girl.'

Crozier appeared disheartened, and lapsed into silence.

'What sort of work?' the soldier asked, when another tankard had been dealt with. 'You another one hiding from the law?'

Crozier looked affronted. 'Cattle's my line. So many herds have been stolen and killed in my part of the world, I was looking to start again, somewhere better.'

The soldier nodded, gravely. 'Well, good luck to ye. I don't know of anything going round here, but—'

'Forget it,' said Crozier, draining his mug. 'It was a bad idea.' He nodded a farewell and left, squeezing his way through the crowded room. At the door he lifted the soldier's cloak and hat from its peg, and was gone before anyone noticed.

'Ye're back soon, captain,' said the sentry at the castle gates. Crozier swayed in the saddle, as if he had been long enough at the bar, and raised an impatient hand. Face hidden by the soldier's hat, wrapped in his buff-coloured cloak, he rode into the yard. The place was quiet, the walls high and smooth, the gates that had just been closed behind him as heavy as a portcullis.

The stables were on his left, and as he dismounted he threw the cloak behind the horses' dung-heap before finding a stable boy and, without a word, giving him the mare's reins.

He strode towards the castle, making for the rear. At this hour of the evening the servants were busy making fires and preparing dinner. Watching the back door, Crozier waited until a kitchen maid was stooped over the courtyard well before slipping into the passageway, past servants carrying trays laden with platters. He made his way to the heart of the castle by the servants' stairs. No shout stopped him; nobody even gave him a glance. Sir Christopher and Sir Philip were in residence and serving their dinner made the kitchen servants blind to anyone but the cooks. Had they been questioned later that night, they would have confessed complete innocence. They had indeed seen a dark figure pass between them, but they did not notice it.

The bustle of the kitchens faded, and when he stepped into the castle's hallway the only sound came from the fireside, where a pair of greyhounds lay, tails thumping at the sight of company. He bent, tickling their ears, and they whined with pleasure. 'Come on then,' he said, clicking his fingers, and the dogs unfolded their legs and followed him, tails held high.

Another flight of stairs brought him to the castle's private quarters. Before he could think where to find the baron's daughter, a young woman in a linen apron stepped into the hallway, carrying a ewer. She looked up, and would have dropped the pewter jug in fright, had he not caught it. Water splashed over the flagstones, but he laughed, and she joined him. The dogs lapped at the soapy spill, and the girl was distracted, and confused, answering Crozier without thinking when he asked, 'Is there anyone in that room?' At her reply, he put his hand over her mouth, and dragged her into the chamber she had just left. This time the ewer fell, its crash dulled by a rug. Above Crozier's hand her eyes rolled in terror.

'Don't be afraid,' he whispered, 'I won't hurt you if you help me. When I take my hand away, you must not shout, or else I will be obliged to use my knife. You understand?'

She nodded, trembling like a rabbit in a sack.

'So then,' said Crozier softly, pushing her onto the bed, and sitting close, his hand around her arm. The greyhounds prowled the walls, as if sniffing out its secrets for him. 'Is this the young mistress's room?'

She shook her head. 'Sir Philip's,' she said, so quietly he could barely catch the words.

'Where is she then?'

The girl gave a moan. 'I don't know,' she said. 'She's left.'

'Along with the scullery maid?' Crozier sensed something worse than he had expected. But again the girl shook her head. She began to cry.

'It is Oliver Barton I am looking for,' said Crozier. 'I'm interested in no one but him. Do you or your mistress know where he's gone?'

The girl's eyes were wide with fear, and he realised it was not him she was scared of. 'I promised not to tell,' she stammered. 'The mistress and Barton said they would have me whipped and dismissed if I breathed a word.'

'Where have they gone? If you do not tell me . . .' Crozier pulled out his knife.

The maid whimpered, making the dogs' ears prick up. She spoke in a gabble. 'Mistress Joan told everyone she was going to stay with her sister near Bolton, and had made arrangements with the Bishop of Carlisle to travel that far with his entourage, on his way to London. She got her father's guards to chaperon her to the bishop's palace, and made the scullery maid tell the cook that *she* was running off with Barton, to give them time to get away together.'

'So where have they gone, Mistress Joan and Barton?'

'They were going to make for the Scottish border, to get married there.'

'Married? To a man like that?' The disbelief in Crozier's voice made the maid blush.

'Mistress Joan loves him. She says he looks rough, and acts rough, but he is just like her father, firm, and brave, and kind. He makes her feel safe. And yet she left in tears. Terrible, it was. Barton had to throw her onto their horse, and they rode off together. She kept looking back . . .' The girl wiped her eyes on her apron. 'Will I get into trouble?' she whispered.

'Only if you don't tell me exactly where they were going.' Crozier eyed the door, but the passageway was quiet. He fingered the tip of his knife, as if testing its sharpness.

'She said there is a family place near the border where they could stay once they were married, until her father got over his rage.'

'Its name?'

'I don't know. A tower house, near Liddesdale, where there's always feuding.'

'Your mistress is a fool,' said Crozier, pulling the girl off the bed. 'That man will never marry her, or stay with her if he does.'

'So I told her. But she slapped me and told me to shut up.' She began to sob.

'Be quiet!' he hissed. 'I need you to get me out of the castle, and then you will be safe. If you call out or set the guards on me, I will kill your mistress as well as Barton. But if you help, then I will see she gets safely home.'

'H . . . h . . . how do I get you out of here?' she asked, her eyes liquid with tears. 'I am not allowed out after dark, without permission.'

'I give you mine,' said Crozier grimly, and looked round the room for paper and pen.

A little later, the maid rode up to the castle gates, on Crozier's mare. She was dressed for the road, in riding cape and boots, the greyhounds trotting behind her. 'Let me pass,' she called up to the sentry, waving the paper on which Blackbird's permission was indecipherably written, as was his style. 'I am on my mistress's business,' she said, 'with her dogs for protection.'

'Late night out for you, pet,' the guard replied, releasing the bars and drawing back the gates, without a glance at the paper. 'You sure you're not off to meet yer swain?' He chortled. 'Lucky man, he is. If I didn't have a goodwife of my own . . .'

The maid responded indignantly, with a flirtatious lift of her chin, hoping to keep the man's eyes on her alone. As the gates swung open, Crozier sidled along the dimly lit wall, and under the arch. He was beyond the gate when the guard caught sight of him and gave a cry, but by then the maid had ridden beyond the walls. Grabbing the saddle, Crozier leapt up behind her and took the reins. Before the guard could summon help, the horse had bolted, and the pair were almost out of sight, the greyhounds racing far ahead, elated at their freedom.

'Let me down!' the maid cried, struggling against him as Crozier rode headlong, the castle now far behind, but not until they reached the village did he pull up the reins, and let her slide off.

'Your mistress will be safe home one day soon,' he said, as she stood staring around her in dismay at being such a distance from the castle. 'Don't look so alarmed. The dogs will keep you company, and you'll find help in the tavern.' He laughed. 'You can tell the captain he'll find his cloak in the midden.' Touching the brim of his hat, he turned the mare towards the fields, and was quickly swallowed by the night.

The baron was growing weary. He had criss-crossed the eastern boundary of his lands, and found much to perturb him. Unlike the western reaches, the dales and hamlets in these parts were in poor repair, ragged from constant raids, the people almost as unkempt as their ravaged hovels, the hilltops blackened by recent fire, and the valley pasturelands all but empty of cattle and sheep.

He had just left the last settlement he would see that day, and was frowning. The villagers had crowded around his horse with tales of the Liddesdale reivers and their scathing of the land. The baron had listened, and assured them of his help, but this barely mollified them, and it was with some difficulty that he rode beyond their clutches, and found himself once more alone on the moorland track. Unsettled at so much destruction, he rode briskly, contemplating the rising tide of vengeance across the marches in his absence, and wondering what role he had played in fomenting such trouble.

The afternoon was advancing, and he was many miles from Naworth. The sun hung heavy in the west, disappearing behind misty banks of cloud. Woodsmoke filled the air, and despite what he had seen that day he felt content. He was home now, and could begin to take care of his territory and his people, as he had always intended. Wrongs would be righted, he would make sure of that.

On he rode, the hazy light softening the horizon. His thoughts had turned to the dinner that awaited him when he saw a figure flitting across a distant hill. Raising a hand against the sun's dying glimmer, he made out a rider cantering along the ridge. A single horseman was nothing to alarm him, yet something stirred in his gut. He rode on, eyes fixed on the rider, who having spotted him had cut off the hill and appeared to be heading his way.

The letter had lain in Dacre's room, upon his bed, for several days. Joan had written it the night before she left for Bolton, telling Blackbird it was to be passed to her father as soon as he returned from Berwick. The butler had given it no thought, until he heard of the maid's ordeal the night before. The girl had been brought back to the castle by the captain of the guard, sobbing like a child. Little sense could be got out of her or the captain, who was soused as a barrel of brine. All that Blackbird and the housekeeper could make out was that the maid had been set upon by a Scottish thug, and forced at knifepoint to tell him where her mistress was. 'I told him she was with her sister in Bolton,' she wailed, hiding her face in her hands. 'I had no choice. What could he want with her?' A groan escaped her, and she began to rock herself back and forth, the night's excitement too much for her nerves. The housekeeper looked at Blackbird, who shook his head. Given a warm infusion of camomile, the girl was sent to bed.

By morning, she was calmer. Once more questioned about her attacker, she chattered on about his knife and his sword one minute, and the next avoided Blackbird's eye and stumbled over her words, as if she were hiding something. Nothing more was learned from her.

When Dacre's guards returned a few hours later, to say the baron was on his way home, but would not be back till nightfall, Blackbird ran upstairs to his master's room, and found Joan's letter. The ink was smudged, he now saw, as if droplets had spilled on the paper.

Snatching it up, he called for a messenger, gave him the letter, and told him to find his master out on the eastern dales. The note, at first so innocuous, now reeked of trouble. He should have opened it the day she left and braved Dacre's wrath for his impudence.

The messenger's horse stamped and snorted as it reached Dacre's side. The baron reined in, recognising the soldier, who reached into his saddlebag. The baron's heart began to hammer. He held out his hand, took the letter, and opened it, squinting to make out its message.

Dearest Father, it began, the writing starting out neat, but turning into a scrawl by the end of the page.

> By the time you are returned from Berwick I will be married. I have left with Oliver Barton, and we are to be wed, and I love him, so you cannot be angry, but happy, indeed I trust you will be for you have long wanted me settled and I shall be, and most joyfully, though not if you are angry. You must not be. Your most loving and respectful daughter, Joan.

The messenger watched the baron. The only sound was his horse's laboured breath. 'Is there a reply?' he asked, when it seemed Dacre had forgotten he was there.

'Mmm?' Dacre looked up, and shook his head. 'Nothing urgent. Tell Blackbird I will be home in time for a late dinner. You go ahead, boy, you will ride faster than me, but I won't be far behind.'

With a salute, the messenger left, he and his horse dwindling to a speck on the hillside before disappearing. Dacre watched, unblinking, as if he had been struck by lightning, and could neither move nor think. He crumpled the letter in his fist, a taste on his tongue so bitter it might have been gall. The murderer and thief he had sent to spy on Crozier had betrayed his paymaster instead. He had been a fool of the most witless kind to think he could bring a man of that sort into his house and not suffer in some way. Barton, meant to be the agent of his revenge, had brought ruin to his house.

Seeing in the baron's daughter an opportunity of untold wealth, the sailor had grabbed it, as men like him will always do. Such a brute could have no idea of her real value. Dacre could admit now that he loved her more than he had ever loved before. She was a treasure, compared to which silver was worthless. And now her future was blighted. No lord or gentleman would marry her after this. She was fit only for the nunnery.

Tears rolled unchecked down his face. Staring at the dusk-lit hills, he felt the power ebbing from his limbs and a pain begin to drill behind his eyes. He shook his head, to sharpen his thoughts. This would not do. Kicking his horse onwards, he wrapped the reins around his numbed hand. Ruin be damned. He would bring Joan back, and get rid of Barton, and all might still be well. He need only reach her before the news got out. No one need ever know about this, marriage or no, and with Blackbird's help he would avert disaster. A few days hence, with Joan safe at home once more, he and the butler would be laughing to think of this moment of despair. He tried to smile at the prospect, but his mouth refused to oblige.

The horse's canter soon slowed to a walk. Dacre's hand was slack on the reins, his legs leaden and almost lifeless. He did not have the strength to urge the stallion on, and after ambling for a mile or two it dropped its head to crop the grass. A short time later a roar of rage and misery rose from the valley, sending crows circling above the trees. It was the baron's last sound, his cry of defeat. Staring in horror at the narrowing sky, Joan's letter clasped in his glove, he recognised that the darkness beginning to wrap itself around him was not the approaching night, but the end of all things.

CHAPTER FORTY-SEVEN

After a few hours' sleep on a frosted hillside beyond reach of Naworth's guards, Crozier made good speed as he headed north. The maid had not known the name of Dacre's peel tower, but he had a fair idea where it would be. The baron had several outposts, kept in the hands of loyal retainers, and even on the Scottish side there were some in thrall to him, or his purse.

Across the borders countless peel towers rose, as if growing out of the bedrock. Stumps of featureless stone where clansmen could fight off attack and locals seek safety, they had no windows on the lower floors, and those on the upper levels were wide enough only for an archer to take aim. Stone-slated and smooth as ice, they were almost impregnable. Nothing but hunger or pestilence could overcome their inmates and bring them to the door.

Dacre's alliance with the Armstrongs was well known, and Crozier headed for one of the narrow passes into Liddesdale, where the clan made their home. The baron would not be brazen enough to have a property on Armstrong land, but it was very possible he had a redoubt in the wastelands that lay between the devil's own dale and Cumberland. It would be a tedious business finding it, but Crozier had faith in his persuasive tongue, and even more in his sword.

Neither let him down. On the edge of the woods by a hamlet north of Bewcastle he came upon a mother penning a flock of sheep which were more biddable than the three children who skirled around her heels. The woman's face was warm with annoyance. 'I'll skelp youse good and hard if ye dinnae behave!' she cried to the boys, who were tugging her apron, and goading the sheep. She looked up at the sound of Crozier's horse, and the sight of the armed rider brought the boys to order. Fingers in their mouths, they huddled behind their mother, and a whimper was heard coming from the smallest.

Crozier smiled. 'I didn't mean to frighten them, goodwife,' he said. She looked at him, suspicion sewing her mouth tight. The borderer edged his horse closer, until he loomed over them, and explained what he was looking for. 'A peel tower used by Baron Dacre, the man who was Warden General of the English marches.'

Disdain crossed the mother's face. 'I ken him well,' she said. 'A killer like a' the rest.'

She turned to point east, beyond the hamlet, towards the Scottish border. 'I couldnae say for sure, but I've seen him and his men skeltering down that road often enough. Could be the place you're speiring after is out that way.'

Crozier thanked her and turned his horse back onto the track. A misty drizzle set in and he lowered his head against its clammy touch. Behind him lay rich oak and sycamore valleys, but now he was climbing onto barren, scoured hills, the march's northernmost border scarred as an old soldier's face by weather and raiders' hooves. The wind quickened. The sound of whipped grasses and the forlorn cry of a curlew, tossed above the moors like a leaf, made a melancholy music that he had loved since a boy.

The first peel tower he came upon emerged out of the rain like the bole of a giant oak, dark and menacing against the sky. It looked deserted, and so it proved, after he had prowled around its weeded base, no prints of horse or man near its door.

The next tower on his path, a few miles on the English side of the border, lay in ruins, wood pigeons resting in the gaping roof, its door an empty mouth. From the knoll where it stood, Crozier could see across grey-lagged hills to the line of spartan heath that marked the boundary of Liddesdale. As he gazed, a curl of smoke met the clouded air from a hidden fireside down the valley, and he caught the smell of its oaky scent, sweet as roasting chestnuts.

Clicking his tongue, he nudged his horse on, soon coming off the moorland top and into the valley. The wisp of smoke disappeared, then was visible once more, though whether this was a trick of the rain, or of a careless hand stoking the hearth, he could not tell.

The rain turned from drizzle to downpour, and by the time he reached the slope behind which the smoke issued, the afternoon light was a bruise that would soon darken to dusk.

The fading day was in his favour. As he rounded the side of the hill, the peel tower faced him. There was no knowing if this was where Barton and Joan were hiding. Retreating and taking cover further up the valley, where trees protected him from the rain, Crozier waited for dark.

When at last he could approach the keep, he made for the stone hut some yards from the tower. In times of war, all horses would be taken into the keep, but he was in luck. The hut was housing a threadbare mule and a dappled stallion, whose pedigree went back farther, and more nobly, than that of the Dacres. Few in these parts would own such a horse. Crozier noted the expensive bridle, the rich blanket over its back, and knew he had found his quarry.

That night he slept soundly, under the pattering trees. At dawn, he rubbed down his horse, led her to the stream, and fed her oats. After lashing her reins to a tree, he made his way to the peel tower, where he crouched behind an outcrop of rock, waiting to see what daylight would bring.

Another dreary day awoke, the sky an ashen shawl. A fug of mist clung to the valley floor, and wrapped itself around the moors. Though the cold and damp were numbing Crozier did not move. Fresh smoke puffed from the tower chimney, and at last the door opened. A tall, crooked figure stepped out, an empty pack over his shoulder. Leaning on a stick, the man made for the hut, and a few minutes later he left, leading the mule towards the track at the bottom of the hill.

Late that morning he returned, the filled pack strapped across the mule's back. He dropped the sack at the door before taking the animal into the hut. When he got there, he was unsaddling the mule when a shape stepped out from behind the straw bales stacked by the door and punched him on the side of the head. He fell, face forward, and Crozier had bound the man's hands behind his back before he realised what was happening. 'Keep it shut,' the borderer said, as the man twisted his head to see his assailant. Crozier tied a rag around his mouth and dragged him to the back of the hut, where he bound his ankles. The man tried to speak through his gag, but only squawks emerged. When he felt the grip of the ropes that held him he slumped, his eyes an oily glitter that boded ill for the borderer should he ever get free.

At the keep's door, Crozier hoisted the pack into his arms like a child, and knocked hard. After a long wait, he heard steps. The door opened a crack. 'I'm back,' he said gruffly, and holding the pack in front of his face, he pushed in, groaning as if with the weight of his burden.

For a second, perhaps two, he had the advantage, before Barton saw who he was. It was enough. Over the threshold, he was up the steps and into the tower. Hurling the pack behind him, knocking Barton back against the door, he ran into the hallway, saw stairs to the next floor, and took them three at a time. Barton was on his feet, and chasing, but Crozier reached the upper hall, where Joan was seated by a fire that hissed and spat. She shrieked, but Crozier was upon her before she could do more than get to her feet. Arm around her chest, he dragged her to the wall, his knife pointed at her neck.

Barton came to a halt at the entrance, panting.

'Do something!' cried Joan, struggling against Crozier's hold, until the tip of his knife sliced her skin, and with a moan she felt her legs go weak, and a trickle of wet run down her leg to match the blood on her throat.

Louise was wandering through the woods, lonely without the wolf. She did not go far these days, missing his company and protection. By the stream she leaned against a fallen tree, too weighed down to hoist herself onto it. Her palm rested on her belly, and she felt a kick, one of many that had kept her awake that night. Had Crozier been there, his arm around her shoulder would have sent her back to sleep, but the empty sheet where he should have been stole slumber more surely than the unborn infant.

A wood pigeon cooed overhead, and a sharp pain shot through her stomach, making her eyes water. When it had passed, she felt sweat break out on her back. She stood, and was beginning to walk back to the keep when another stab made her gasp. She would have fallen to her knees but for knowing that once down, she might not be able to get up. Pressing a hand to her side, she stumbled through the trees. The pains should not have started so soon. There were four or five weeks before this child was meant to come into the world. Biting her lip, she pressed on.

She had reached the keep and crossed the courtyard before the next spasm. As it swept over her, she called out and leaned against the wall. Running from the stables, Hob was soon at her side, and once the pains had passed he helped her indoors. Ella, coming up from the kitchens, saw at once what was happening. Anxiety spread over her face, but as she hurried to Louise she smiled. 'Dinnae be feart,' she said, putting an arm around her. 'Everything will be fine.'

Crozier smelled Joan's fear, and saw the hand creep to her round belly, to protect what lay within. Barton took a step into the hall, knife in his hand. Ignoring Joan, he addressed himself to the borderer.

'Let her go, Crozier. She's just a girl. Let's you and me settle this.' He swiped the knife before him, as if to exercise it.

'Married, are you?' said Crozier. 'What godforsaken place is this to bring your bride? You'd think you were ashamed of her.'

Joan lifted her chin. 'We have made our vows before God. We're married in the eyes of the church, and the law. I am of age, and we did not need a priest.' She spoke like a noblewoman putting a peasant in his place.

'That's right,' said Barton, in a tone of sarcastic triumph, 'we're man and wife, and nothing can part us now but death. Her father will get used to the idea. And since she's his favourite, he'll no cut her out of his will, now will he?' His eyes glinted, perhaps at the prospect of the wealth that would one day be his, but more likely in anticipation of sending Crozier to his maker. He laughed. 'Come on, what kind of man would kill me, when there's a bairn on the way? You know yoursel, my friend, how precious the wee yins are.'

The borderer let Joan go, pushing her aside. Drawing his sword, he advanced on Barton. 'You will be dining with your forebears tonight. You have ruined this poor lass, but that's nothing to what you tried to do to me.' He looked the sailor in the eye, but the man could not hold his gaze. Crozier's voice was soft. 'Your sweet cousin gives you a roof over your head, I find you work, yet you betray us to Dacre, slithering back to him with news of what we're doing, like the reptile you are.' He carved a slice in the air, sending Barton dancing backwards. 'This is for the village, which Dacre's men destroyed.' Another flashing arc sent Barton staggering down the stairs, an arm against the wall to steady himself. 'That is for the wardens you brought to our door. And now this, and all that follows, for frightening my wife near to death . . .' The blade scythed through the silence.

'Whoa!' cried the sailor. 'My wee knife against that muckle sword, it's no a fair fight.'

'It isn't meant to be,' Crozier said, forcing him down the stairs, the blade drawing closer to his windpipe with every swipe.

Barton's eyes darted from side to side, and a slick of hair clung to his forehead, plastered on with sweat. Crozier pressed him back, step by step. The shining steel in his hand held Barton mesmerised. Too late Crozier heard the rustle of skirts behind him, and Joan's cry as she brought a pair of bellows down on his head. There was a sparkle of brilliant light, a whirl of empty air in which his sword flailed and fell from his grip, and he tumbled down the stairs, landing in an awkward sprawl at the bottom of the steps.

Before the sailor was upon him, Crozier kicked himself backwards, till his back met the wall. He was dazed, but not hurt. His sword was out of reach, but as Barton scurried for it he lurched to his feet and threw himself on his enemy with a roar. He knocked Barton flying, the sailor's knife skittering across the stone floor. Joan's screams told him she was coming down the stairs, but as yet she was no threat. As Barton began to turn, the borderer thwacked him hard on the back of the head, pounding him again and again until his knuckles bled. But the sailor would not be stilled. With a groan, Barton wrenched himself from Crozier's hold, and swung a punch that cracked his jaw. Panting, the pair closed with each other, wrestling across the floor like crabs. Joan hovered at the foot of the stairs, unable to get near to the sword or the knife.

Barton tried to get his fingers around Crozier's throat, but the borderer's reach was longer. His hands circled Barton's neck. Though the sailor clawed at his wrists, Crozier's hold on his thrapple tightened. Barton's sinews were thick and taut as he strained against his noose, his flesh mottling purple and grey like a turkey-cock's craw. His eyes were turning bloodshot, the whites marbling with red, and it seemed they must soon burst out of their sockets. With a guttering growl, he gave a last fierce kick, just as Crozier raised the sailor's head, and, with a powerful twist, broke his neck.

There was a howl from the stairs, and Joan flung herself on Crozier, fists battering his head. Breathless, he staggered to his feet, and grabbed her arm. A loud slap rendered her for a moment silent; then she began to sob, a girning so abandoned it was as if she had turned feral.

Hob caught Ella's arm as she left Louise's room with a basin of water. 'How's she doing?' he asked.

Ella shook her head. 'It's no goin to be easy. The pains are comin every few minutes, but the baby's no budging.' She wiped her face with a forearm. 'Ye can go and sit wi her, if ye like, while I get mair hot water.'

'Would I no do better to get the midwife from the village?'

Ella thought of the wifie's ale-sour breath, the filth on her apron and under her nails. 'No, lad, she's safer with us.'

In the bedchamber Louise lay in her shift, which was moulded to her with sweat. She turned when Hob entered, and gave a weak smile. He was shocked at her pallor, the puffiness of her face, and of the hand she held out to him. This he took, and held between his as if it was something precious.

'It wasn't as hard with Helene,' she whispered. 'I didn't expect this.'

Hob rubbed her hand. 'I've seen it with the horses. They strain and strain, and you think it's never comin, and then it does, and when it's over they forget as soon as they see their foal, healthy and well.'

Louise turned her head on the pillow and looked at the window, where mid-afternoon was leaching the light. The room was growing darker, but the tapers had not yet been lit.

'Two days it's been now,' she said softly. 'I'm holding on till Crozier gets back.' Her eyes were glassy, as if she could see something beyond the shutters that was hidden to everyone else.

There was no knowing when the master would return, but Hob's tongue had a mind of its own. 'He'll be here soon,' he said, 'I ken he will. Just you keep going. You mustn't give up.' A lump thickened his throat, and he got up. 'I'm off to get something that might help.'

He found Ella in the kitchens. 'I've seen mares in her condition,' he said, 'when the foal's twisted the wrong way round.'

'For Christ's sake, she's not a horse,' said Ella, fear making her fierce.

Hob put a hand on her arm. 'If you can give her an infusion of dog mercury and juniper, it might help.'

'Oh yes?' asked Ella, sounding suspicious. 'How on God's earth is that going to help our wee lassie?'

Her shrillness brought Benoit to the door, and Hob explained. The drink would loosen her pelvis, and give the baby more room to move. And, if he mixed it with poppyseed, she would feel less pain.

Benoit nodded. 'It cannae harm her, surely. Off you go, lad, and get whatever you think she needs.'

When he had left, Benoit put his arm around Ella. They did not speak, but both were remembering how different it had been for her. Their children had been born in haste, a splash of broken waters, an hour of wailing, and out they slid, slick and easy as lambs. Wiping away a tear, Ella sniffed, and got back to the stove, where the water was bubbling.

Upstairs, Louise curled. Her voice was hoarse from moaning, her lips bitten raw. She felt herself growing weaker and so, she knew, was the baby. As darkness fell, the room glowed softly in the light of the log fire and rush lamps. Tears slid down her cheeks. It was like being in a trap, with only one way out, and the doorway growing narrower with every hour.

That night was a torment, Louise racked with rolling breakers of pain, but the baby unable to move. A dishwater light was seeping through the shutters when Louise pulled Ella close. 'Get me paper,' she whispered. 'I can't last much longer. I must write to Crozier. He won't get back in time.'

'Hen, he'll be here. I promise ye, he'll get here,' said Ella, but her tears belied her words and she left, as fast as she could after two days without sleep.

Hob was in the passageway, propped against the wall. He slipped into the room while Ella was gone, and took a cloth to wipe Louise's forehead. 'Have ye drunk the brew?' he asked, 'the juniper draught I brought you?' Louise nodded, though she did not open her eyes.

Ella returned and, helping Louise to sit up, put paper and pen in her hand. She and Hob watched, bitter-faced, as the crow's feather scratched over the page. Louise's cheeks were flushed, but a tear-stained smile lifted her mouth as she pictured her husband, her clumsy pen and ill-spelled words sending him a farewell that he would only read when she was cold and gone. When she was done, she sank back and closed her eyes.

Benoit was at the door. Ella's stricken look answered the unspoken question, and he set off at a run to fetch Father Walsh.

The fire crackled, and from the trees outside a robin scolded the breaking day. Hob looked at Ella, and knew she was defeated. Drawing her to the window, he lowered his voice. 'No,' he said. 'We cannae leave it like this. Ye have to trust me, Ella. I ken what to do.'

'It's no right, you helpin, wi a woman who's no your wife.'

Hob passed a hand over his face and looked at Ella, who was grey with misery. 'If I don't, we'll lose the bairn as well as her.'

Shaking her head, but too tired to argue, Ella fetched hot water and cloths, as he instructed. The boy washed his hands, and spoke to Louise, who had passed almost into unconsciousness. 'Lou,' he said, 'I'm going to try to turn your bairn. If the infusion's done its trick, I'll be able to reach him. Can you bear any more?' She gave a moan, and what might have been a nod.

Lifting her shift, Hob felt gently around her abdomen, and then set to work. What he was doing might save the child, or the mother, but though he did not allow himself to put the thought into words, he did not believe it possible that both would live.

The messenger returned to Naworth, informing Blackbird, Sir Philip and Sir Christopher that Dacre was close behind. It was already dark, evening closing in around the castle and the dale. Unable to settle, Blackbird paced the hallway. At the least noise he went into the yard, hoping to see the baron's horse. His master would surely have ridden home fast, to avoid the dark. What was taking him so long?

Dacre's place lay empty while the brothers ate their dinner, but when the table was cleared the servants left the baron's mug and platter untouched. Later, the hour of ten having passed, the cook ventured out to ask Blackbird if he could go to his bed. Ignoring him, the butler threw on his cloak, and called for his horse.

He rode out into the night, knowing he would find nothing good. His master's health was poor, and he might have been taken ill, stranded on a hillside, waiting for help. How would he feel if he had not gone to his aid?

Beneath the trees the blackness was smothering, but out on the road a rind of moon appeared fitfully from behind the clouds. He took the eastward path, soon reaching the hills and the boundary of Dacre's lands, which he followed like a seamstress stitching a seam.

In the darkness, his horse could go no faster than a trot. Midnight had long passed when he reached the hamlet that lay in a hollow beneath the hills, beyond which the messenger said he had met his lordship.

The eerie quiet of the early hours breathed on the back of his neck. Blackbird's heart was beating hard as he rose onto the hilltops and felt the freshness of the moorland air, and the empty miles beyond them. The clink of his bridle was the only sound as he rode, other than the cries and scuffles of creatures his horse flushed from the grassland. A startled grouse flapped into the sky, making the stallion rear in fright; a rabbit got under his hooves; and a moth-eaten fox cast them a sullen backward glance as it slunk into a coppice of beech, a rat's tail dangling from its mouth. Blackbird had never felt so strongly that he was an intruder in the wilds.

The wind eased as he began to descend from the hills, to the path on which Dacre had last been seen. He reached the village beyond the hills, where the baron had been besieged by villagers, and still there was no sign of him. Perplexed, Blackbird turned, and looked down the track, back the way he had come. He could smell a baker's oven, and in a few cottages fires were already lit. At the trough in the market square, he dropped the reins to let his horse drink, taking a gulp from his flask of ale as he did so.

Day was on its way, darkness easing like a thinning fog. Slowly now, he walked back along the path between the trees towards the open hills. He began to call, shouting for his master, but his voice soon grew tired. Pulling up at the edge of the sycamore woods, he scanned the road ahead. Already it was growing visible as morning crept on, and the moon and stars retreated. In an hour it would be daylight, and he would be able to retrace his journey, searching as he went.

He dismounted, patting his horse, and leaned his head on its neck. The stallion was lipping his sleeve when its ears pricked. Lifting its head, it gave a whinnying neigh. Startled, Blackbird heard an answering call from deep inside the woods. Getting onto his horse, he guided it between the trees, and they picked their way through the shadows. Beneath the canopy, night clung on, the black pressing upon him like a blindfold. He shook his head, as if that would clear his vision, but nothing emerged beyond the outline of tree trunks, a shade darker than the sky.

He called Dacre's name, and the distant horse neighed once more. As he made for the sound, out of the murk a pale glimmer beckoned. When he reached it, he found himself on the edge of a clearing, where daylight was creeping at last. Stumps of felled trees were scattered in the grass, looking, in the half-born light, like an army of men cut off at the knee. A saddled horse was making its way towards them, whickering as it skirted the stumps, its tail held high. Blackbird recognised Dacre's stallion, and his master's round-backed saddle. It was then he saw the shape trailing along the ground behind it, as if a deformed shadow clung to its side.

In an instant he was off his horse and lashing the stallion's reins to a tree. Dacre's body dangled, his boot caught in the stirrup. He hung face down, and when Blackbird turned him over it was clear the horse had bolted in panic through briars and thorns with his master dragging behind.

A sob was caught in Blackbird's chest, making it hard to breathe. The horse stamped, desperate to be freed from its burden. Yelling at it to be still, Blackbird wrenched the baron's boot from its vice, and the leg fell to earth with a thud. Pushing the horse aside, Blackbird sank to his knees beside his master. He touched the scratched and dirtied face, but it was cold as iron. The eyes stared, and the blue lips were parted, as if he had a last message to impart. Taking the gloved hand in his, Blackbird found it clenched. A scrap of paper was curled in its palm, crushed as the baron's heart.

CHAPTER FORTY-EIGHT

November 1525

Crozier stood swaying a little, light-headed after the fight. Joan was weeping over Barton's body, and did not look up when he told her she would one day be grateful to him for ridding her of a man who would only bring her grief.

'Rape you, did he?' he asked, wearily picking up his sword, and sheathing it. 'Made you believe you had to run off with him to save your honour?'

The girl's sobs were arrested. She turned to him, eyes wide with surprise. 'It was not rape,' she said slowly. 'Not really . . .' Then she covered her face with her hands, and her cries resumed, louder and more despairing than ever.

'Get yourself home, lass,' said Crozier, making for the door. 'The keeper is in the stable. He'll take you back to Naworth, where you belong.'

Out on the moors, he rode fast. After the rains, the skies were emptied of colour, matching his woebegone mood. His jaw throbbed, his knuckles ached, and his stomach turned queasy at the memory of Barton's flesh under his hands. Thoughts crossed his mind, but found no hold, his head reeling as much from the brutal encounter as from being cracked on the stone floor.

It was two days' ride to the keep, but as darkness drew on the mare's pace slowed. She moved with the suspicion of a limp, and Crozier made camp for the night. Checking for loose nails or stones under her shoes, he rubbed her hock with liniment, praying the swelling under his fingers would not get worse.

The next day he rode with care, though he wanted to gallop headlong. It was ten days since he had left the keep. The danger Barton posed had been dealt with, but in these times, leaving home was always to unlock a door that trouble could creep through.

Liddesdale's pitiless moors rolled on, harsh on the eye and the spirits. This was a deadened land, well suited to its masters, whose souls were as barren as its soil. He saw a pack of riders disappearing over a far-off hill, Armstrongs out on the hunt. They had not seen him, and he met no one else, the miles passing easily beneath him. Not until dusk did he cross into Teviotdale, its soft peaks and loamy earth welcoming him back. He slept sounder for being near his own lands, the smell of the oakwood around him the memory of childhood, and home.

The following morning the mare started fresh and fast, but after a few miles her pace slowed, her gait uneven and sore. Crozier dismounted, thinking the limp was worsening, and that she might be suffering a sprain. Sunlight danced on the grasslands, burnishing beeches in the woods below. With a sigh, he lifted her hoof, and found a stone lodged under her shoe. It was a minute's work to free it with his knife. Running his hand over her hock, he found the swelling that had worried him had gone down. 'Good girl,' he said, as he got into the saddle, and urged her into a trot.

The mare was as keen to be home as he. Crozier's mood began to lift as the cool autumn air cleared his head and the dale spread out beneath him, a tapestry of browns and gold and fading green, melting in the distance into a sky so blue it was like a newborn's eye. Three years and more he had lived with fear worse than he had ever known. Even now that Dacre had been disgraced he dared not believe he had been vanquished. His power, however, had been severely curtailed and that, Adam hoped, was enough. Slowly the truth was beginning to feel real: with the Warden General deposed, and Barton dead, and Scotland and England making peace, the Croziers were safer than they had been since he was a boy.

The beat of the mare's hooves kept time with his quickening thoughts, his growing assurance that all would be well. He began to make plans. In the next few months he must strengthen the alliance of clans that safeguarded the shire. The better protected it was known to be, the less danger they would face. Benoit had earned himself a place as his second lieutenant, as fit as Tom to run the clan's affairs. Both would now be given a more prominent position, under his watchful eye.

Reaching the woods that marked the boundary of his land, Crozier did not spy the buzzard on the boughs above, watching beneath half-closed lids. Rather, he was thinking of his wife. By the time he reached his western lookout there was an unaccustomed gentleness in his face. Reining in beneath the tower, he hailed the guard. 'All well?' he shouted, raising a hand. The watchman looked down, and in that second Crozier's heart contracted. 'What?' he cried, at the guard's hesitation. 'What's wrong?'

'Your wife . . .' the watchman began. 'I'm no sure, ken, but they say . . .'

Crozier did not wait to hear what they said. He was gone, the mare kicked into a canter through the woods, her hooves setting the leaves in a flurry, as if the north wind had passed. Crouched low on her neck, he saw nothing but the path ahead. The dread that threatened to overtake him if he slackened was kept at bay by his whip.

At his approach, a bugle sounded and the keep gates opened. Crozier reached the courtyard and leapt off the mare. The stableboy who ran out to meet him looked anxious, as did those servants who saw their master's return, but Crozier had no eyes for them. He was inside the keep, and calling for Louise, before anyone could speak to him. The great hall was empty save for Old Crozier, asleep by the fire.

Crozier took in the scene. The fire was dead, and there was no sound of kitchen or children. Striding across the hall, he made for the passageway, and still there was no one about. He raced up the stairs and reached the door of his chamber, where he found a scarlet sheet, cast out of the room on the flagstones. Beside it lay his wife's bloodied shift, so red and wet it could have been dipped in dye. With a groan, he opened the door, his pulse hammering in his ears.

Though it was day, the room was shuttered, lit by candles on the wall that cast a church-like glow. By the fireside, on the settle, Hob was asleep, chin slumped on his chest. On the bed lay Louise, pale as the fresh sheet that had been pulled up to her throat. She was barely recognisable, face swollen and mouth bruised, her skin the colour of rain. Her eyes were closed, her hair had been combed tidily over her shoulders, and she had a look of peace, as if she were finally at rest.

With a cry, Crozier was at her side, grasping her by the shoulders. Only then did he feel her warmth. Louise gave a sigh, and her eyelids flickered, but they did not open. A sob escaped him, and he sank his head to the sheet, trembling with relief. 'Thank God,' he mumbled, 'thank God.'

Reaching for Louise's hand, he pressed it to his lips. He put his cheek to hers, and spoke in her ear, his tears darkening the sheet. Murmuring his name, she slid back into the deep sleep he had disturbed.

Wakened, Hob stood by the bed. 'We gave her something to make her sleep,' he said. 'She had a terrible time of it.' Crozier saw the blood daubed on his shirt, but before he could ask what part he had played there was a scratch on the door and Ella came in. She too looked haggard. In her arms she carried a bundle, swaddled tight in a shawl. Crozier felt giddy.

'Our child lives?' he asked hoarsely, reaching out.

'They both do,' Ella replied, and placed in his arms two berry-red babes, nestled close to each other. The borderer stared at them, putting a finger to their hot faces, love licking through him like fire. Brushing a kiss on their foreheads, he passed them back.

All that day, and into the night, Crozier sat by Louise. He watched as his wife breathed softly. Unable to rest until he knew she would live, he laid his head on the bed, a hand on her wrist. Sometime after midnight, the first of the winter gales began to whistle around the keep, battering like a wayward traveller asking to be admitted. In the hour after dawn, as the shutters rattled and the chimney moaned, Louise woke at last. Feeling her stir, Crozier lifted his head. With a look as sweet and unfocused as that of their twins, Louise stretched out to him, and he held her close, the wind-blown forest outside the window muffling their broken words.

In a room down the passage a wet nurse suckled the infants, the girl as hungry as her brother. Warm and fed, they stared milkily at the rafters before descending into sleep. The nurse clucked, and pulled the shawl over the boy, whose head bore the marks of the pincers Hob had used to draw him forth. In his first minutes of life, Crozier's heir had felt the touch of iron, and come into this world less innocent, and more knowing, than most.